THE
ASHENBORN

MATTHEW W. FENN

ISBN: 978-1-7339945-5-2

Fenn. Matthew W.
The Ashenborn

Edited by: Elizabeth Russell

Published by Warren Publishing
Charlotte, NC
www.warrenpublishing.net
Printed in the United States

Thank you everyone that has encouraged me to do this. I'm blessed beyond measure. I especially want to thank my wife Keri for all she has done to push me to pursue my dream of writing.

PROLOGUE

The man's body shook as he held the enchanted weapon in front of him. He was sweating, and the veins in his forehead protruded. He gritted his teeth and tightened his grasp on the ancient weapon.

"Once more," he said, his chest heaving.

The cloaked figure across from him hesitated, then opened the crimson-colored book and flipped through the yellowed and torn pages.

"If you insist," he responded as he lifted a hand toward the twilight sky.

Bolts of golden flames poured from his palms—a shower of golds and yellows. They fell onto the ground like rain and soaked into the dry sand. The dirt sparked and shook as a tentacle-like light rose from it. The tentacles wove themselves around the cloaked man, interlocking and solidifying into a dome of pearlescent gold. The cloaked man was outlined in blinding electricity.

"Do not hold back your strike!" the cloaked man shouted, his amplified voice reverberating from inside the dome.

The man clenched his teeth as the ruby and obsidian stones within the pommel of the weapon began to glow.

He yelled as he charged. The sword whistled beside him as he ran. He cleared the distance and raised the sword high above him. He used all his strength as the blade arced downward, slamming into the magical barrier. The aura vibrated but stopped the blade and held it rattling in place.

The man breathed heavily and lowered himself to one knee as the blade sank into the dirt, leaning on the hilt to steady himself.

The cloaked man lowered his hand and looked at the barrier with interest.

"You managed to scratch it this time," he said, pointing at a cut in the aura.

As he spoke, a cracking noise ripped through the air, catching the man's attention. The cloaked man's eyes widened as the aura cracked and splintered into smaller pieces of glass and light.

The man wiped away the sweat from his brow with a fierce look on his face.

"Are you satisfied now?" the cloaked man said. "You have finally reached your goal."

The man rose, a glint in his eye.

"Not yet," the man said. "Not yet."

He sheathed the weapon behind him and sighed.

"What now?" the cloaked man asked.

"You take me to him. As you promised."

The cloaked man nodded. "But first what we agreed upon."

The man reached into his pocket and tossed a bag of coins to him.

Without looking, the cloaked man snatched it from the air and eyed its contents.

"I will take you to him." The cloaked man smiled, a poisonous look in his eyes. "What do you intend to do?"

The man narrowed his eyes.

"I plan to kill him," he answered.

The cloaked man looked at him with surprise. "Kill him?"

The man wielding the sword cleared his throat. "Yes. It is time to release those who are bound in chains."

The crackle of magic filled the air.

"Even if it means taking from one to give to another."

CHAPTER 1

LIFESVEIL

———✳———

Elder Derrick hurried toward the glass chest; although the chest was clear, the contents were hidden. With a wave of his dark crimson sleeve, the chest opened with a solid thud that resonated throughout the ornate, yet empty, temple. Reaching within the chest, his dark, wrinkled hands pulled out several glowing fragments of stone.

The stones appeared to be gems of the common variety at first glance, but they glowed as he touched them, indicating their significance. Colors of various shades illuminated Elder Derrick's weathered face, making his grayish-brown hair look multicolored in the gleam of the stones' light. His eyes widened as the fragments began to shake gently in his hand. Bolts of color burned from them as the stones warmed. He let out a grimace. Furrowing his brow, he placed the opposite hand over them, extinguishing their light. He closed his eyes and muttered something indistinguishable. In a moment, his eyes snapped open.

...he a parchment and seal," the old voice spoke.

...endant standing nearby bowed, grabbed the items, and returned hastily.

"Is something wrong?" the young man asked.

"Surely," the elder answered. "But nothing that cannot be solved."

The attendant handed him the parchment, which was decorated with strokes of gold and silver. He also produced a fine gold dragon-claw seal that was intended to address the scroll.

"Bring a candle as well," Elder Derrick requested, rubbing his temples. "My eyes are not quite what they used to be."

The flame of the candle added additional light to that of the already flickering torches. Elder Derrick wrote a simple message with a quick stroke of the feathered quill and wrapped the parchment carefully, pressing the red ink into the cup and upon the letter. He grabbed a sword beautifully decorated with rubies and sapphires from the wall. He dipped the dragon-inscribed hilt into the ink and carefully pressed it onto the parchment beside the dragon claw. The symbol depicted a mountain with a dragon flying around it. That was his specific signature among the order. Each symbol, depending upon rank, was different from the other. Derrick himself was one of the higher ranking members of his order.

I'm not sure what good that will do, he thought, *when things need to be righted among them.* He shook his head and rubbed his temples again.

"Have a bird deliver this immediately," he said as he wiped ink off the hilt with a cloth and tied the sword to his belt.

The attendant bowed and left through the large, ornately decorated door, the main entrance of the temple. Derrick looked around the immense open space before him. Stones decorated the floors, with illustrations depicting battles of the past. Dragons and knights were interspersed with spirals of ancient symbols whose meanings were long forgotten. The flickering torch light caused the markings to appear to ripple with regal flashes of wine red and shimmering gold. In the expanse were fine linens and an altar separated by dense cloth and rope.

A place of calm and learning, Elder Derrick thought as he looked around. *A place of peace.*

With a sudden burst of light, the door creaked open.

"My apologies, Elder," said a familiar voice, "but the king wishes your company."

"Tritus," Derrick replied with a hint of amusement in his voice. "It seems coincidental us meeting like this."

Tritus looked at him questioningly, one eyebrow raised. The man standing before Derrick was a newly enlisted soldier of the King's Guard. He was no more than twenty years, and already he had a hint of a black moustache and beard forming on his smooth skin. Derrick was fond of him because he always sought new knowledge to better himself and always had so many questions.

"I was headed that way myself," Derrick said, shaking his head. "I am surprised you don't have any more questions to ask."

Tritus stepped aside, bowing as he did so.

"I am on my way to guard duty," Tritus said. "I have no questions yet, but the day is young. My apologies, Elder, but the king wanted me to inform you that this matter is best attended to with haste."

Derrick nodded. "Then I must waste no time in responding to his summons."

Tritus bowed again and excused himself.

"How the young grow, and the old remain old," Derrick chuckled to himself. His thoughts turned to the king's summons. For the king to require haste meant the matter was of extreme importance. Derrick was thoughtful as he walked the marble path past a few houses leading up to the castle. The grandiose marble stronghold shone brightly in the morning light. The castle stood on the furthermost edge of the mountain, and from it stretched thick, fortified walls that surrounded the kingdom of Lifesveil. These barriers, despite having seen battle in the past, gleamed as white as if they had never seen a day of conflict.

Derrick smiled with pride at the sight of the many houses of straw and stone scattered throughout the inner safety of the walls. The incandescence of something so massive made him feel small, despite the importance that he carried among the people. He passed the blacksmith's shop, blackened from the continual use of fire for the benefit of the kingdom. The flags of Lifesveil could be seen fixed upon the many watch towers built into the walls. The stone path, worn from use, led him straight to the large doorway that opened into the castle of Alanias, the king of Lifesveil. Two flags swayed in the wind; the highest was a white flag bearing the image of a white dragon outlined in black, roaring and spewing gold flames. Below it was the flag of Lifesveil, which possessed the same decoration as the seal on Derrick's sword—a dragon circling a mountain. The highest flag represented

High King Archkyris, who ruled over the entire realm of Yadir.

The Ashenborn temple was relatively close to the castle, not only for convenience but to symbolize its importance. Elder Derrick approached the entrance and found it guarded by four men dressed in copper chain mail. Hanging from their necks were chains strung with single silver claws representing their rank among the Guard. The claw that Derrick wore was golden, signifying his authority. Only royalty or the highest of the guard of Lifesveil or generals could wear a golden talon. By his count, there were six other than himself who possessed the golden symbol.

The guards nodded and parted as the chains were cranked, opening the gateway to the passage of the king. The massive columns of stone moved, and fragments of mirrored stone shone as they tilted in sunshine. Several nobles greeted Derrick along the way, and though he acknowledged them, his attention was preoccupied with his own thoughts. He snapped back to his surroundings to find that he was outside the war room. The king could often be found in the war room, a meeting place of great importance.

The servant leading Derrick bowed graciously as he entered, and with a gesture from the king, he announced the arrival of the graying and prudent elder. Derrick was impressed by the regal look of the king's golden crown, inlaid with white opals and sparkling rubies. It was not often that the king chose to wear his crown.

King Alanias was adorned in pale blue garb with the emblem of Lifesveil stitched upon it, a dragon like that of many who served under the greater rule of the High King. Standing next to the king was General Zarx, who was significantly younger than both the king and the elder. Zarx was middle-aged but had the complexion of one who was no more than twenty. His hair was jet black and stood in stark contrast to the white of Alanias' head. The general boasted a reddish beard, and beneath it, a golden talon hung from his neck. Zarx was the first to acknowledge Derrick. Zarx respected Elder Derrick but did not approve of the magic that he and other members of his order, the Ashenborn, possessed.

"Elder Derrick Ashen-Elder," he said, putting a hand to his chest and bowing slightly.

Elder Derrick returned the motion, surprised at the show of respect from the general, and turning to Alanias, bowed longer and lower.

"Your Highness, and General," Elder Derrick said, nodding to each of them.

Alanias smiled "You have no need to call me 'Your Highness;' you are my equal and more than I could ever hope to define. But if you must continue to call me so, then that is your choice."

Elder Derrick blinked. "My king, you honor me." Bowing again for good measure, he added, "Besides, I would show honor to my king."

Zarx turned back to the large scroll sprawled out on the wooden table in front of him. The table was large enough to seat a war counsel of thirty if circumstances so required.

Elder Derrick joined the two men and examined the scroll, noting that it was a scale map of Yadir, including a limited portion of five islands to the south called the Minos Isles, a region outside of the High King's realm. Of the kingdoms under the reign of Archkyris there were seven, one being Lifesveil, where they resided. The closest to them were the kingdoms of Malfait to the north and Mavet to the south.

"We have received word of a disturbing situation. One that should alarm the ears of all who hear it," Zarx said hoarsely.

"What is it?" Derrick asked, untying his sword and placing it beside Zarx's sword, which lay against the far wall. This was out of respect and often symbolic of equal footing within this specific room. The king's royal sword rested upon the same wall.

Alanias watched him with interest.

"Hroth, of Mavet, has sent word that a small battalion stands at his gates," Alanias said. "He seems unable to deal with it at this time."

"What makes this any more unusual than usual?" Derrick asked. "It's not like Hroth makes friends with everyone. Barbarians dwell in the mountains in the south; he has done nothing other than kill and route them. I imagine I would respond in kind."

Zarx snorted in amusement.

"This is correct, Elder, but the description and circumstances say otherwise," Zarx said. "These are not giant men of the mountains." He pointed to the kingdom of Mavet on the map, a hand's length away from Lifesveil. His finger made a dull thump as he tapped the map.

"Hroth sent word that after examining the combatants, he saw the mark of the reaper's hammer upon their cloaks, which oddly enough, covered all their faces."

"The symbol of Mavet? Are the people of Mavet going to attack themselves?" Derrick said. "It is simple to conclude the barbarians merely stole these garments from Mavet and want to cause trouble."

Alanias nodded. "That's what Zarx and I were discussing before you arrived. However, when Hroth sent men to meet the battalion, they provided a more curious report."

Alanias opened a scroll he had in his hand and began to read aloud. "They burned our men with what we believe to be magical flame, and when archers fired arrows, they pierced them, but none succumbed to mortal wounds."

Zarx rolled his eyes. "Hearing it a second time makes me wonder how Hroth rules his kingdom, too often calling us to aid for something that he could easily handle himself. A few juveniles with swords could easily deal with this supposed problem."

Derrick cast him an amused look.

Alanias' gaze was fixed upon Zarx for a moment before he slowly turned to Elder Derrick.

"I asked you here because magical fire is cause for concern, and I would think it would be wise to have your opinion on a response. You alone are the most qualified in dealings such as these."

"Let them figure it out," Zarx growled. "Whoever it is threatens war. If we become involved it may cause further conflict."

"We could remain aloof, but Mavet is a key merchant trader. They are an ally, so any war or battle would result in us assisting them. Even if it may be foolish," Alanias said flatly, remaining focused on Derrick's face.

"There is that issue …" Zarx said with a smirk.

Elder Derrick ran his fingers through his own beard.

"A reaper's hammer," he said, speaking of a weapon specific to royalty that resided in Mavet. A scythe and battle hammer forged together. A weapon such as that would cause immense damage to any who crossed its path in hostility.

"Is there any detail as to what made the fire?" Derrick said thoughtfully, his gaze elsewhere.

"None has been specified," Zarx replied. "My opinion is it is nothing but smoke."

"What do you think, Elder?" Alanias asked again.

"This is speculation, but I believe it could be linked to something that alarmed me earlier in the temple," Derrick said.

Zarx gave him an inquisitive look.

"The dragon eyes have begun to pulsate and shine hues of color, unlike the usual dull color that they possess," Derrick said.

Alanias' eyes gleamed with excitement.

"They are kindling, as the Ashenborn put it?"

Derrick nodded. "Their power can be felt from within the temple. I have sent word to the Ashenborn."

Zarx scratched his hand.

"What would this signify?" he asked, turing to Alanias. "Forgive me; I do not have much experience in dealing with magic stones."

Elder Derrick put his right wrist outward. Bright shards of light pulsated under his skin.

"My Ashenstone's natural hue is a reddish brown, signifying the power that I carry. With it, it enhances my already natural magic. Its power to bond with another is at its fullest when it begins to glow. The oldest of us can feel them.

When the stones glow, called the kindling, the Ashenborn then are able to bestow the right to use its power."

"When this occurs, it means that new Ashenborn will enter the world," Alanias finished Derrick's words.

Derrick nodded, "Precisely."

Zarx shook his head. "So, the implication is great in that case. I had always wondered where your abilities truly came from. I had guessed it was from books or incantations."

"Books are for knowledge. Spells are for darker beings than you or I," Derrick replied.

Zarx tilted his head, considering what that meant.

"There, however, is an issue. When the Ashenstones kindle, there are those who often follow like moths to flame," Derrick said.

"Who are those that follow?" Zarx asked.

Derrick shook his head, unsure of himself.

"Again, there is not enough proof just yet to give an answer. I am an old man, bound by old wives' tales and ancient stories." He laughed.

Alanias approached the window overlooking the kingdom and looked out.

"I do not want to take Hroth's claim lightly, nor do I foresee it to be too troublesome or something that cannot be dealt with. It is still worth my time to discover for myself," Derrick said.

"Better to see it for ourselves than to be bothered by more of Hroth's scrolls," Zarx confirmed.

Alanias pursed his lips, then spoke.

"Derrick, I would like you to appease Hroth by going and satisfying whatever question you have about how the stones may be connected to this incident," Alanias said. "At least it would be a good step forward, even if there is nothing to be concerned about."

Derrick agreed. "It could very well be nothing. But if it is something, we have more to lose by not going."

"Indeed," Alanias said. "I will send you with twenty men to investigate." Alanias paused. "You do need men, correct?"

Elder Derrick let a short chuckle escape him.

"You flatter me, King. You think me a god, do you?"

Alanias laughed vigorously. "Humbleness, my friend, your best attribute. Ten men I will provide; any more and you might appear that you need it."

Zarx grinned.

"I will prepare men for the journey. What would you have me do, my king?" Zarx said, enjoying the exchange and looking forward to the excitement of a journey.

"I would like you to focus on guarding the Ashentemple while Derrick is away. And continue securing the kingdom for the coming Ashenborn Festivities."

Zarx looked disappointed as he dutifully bowed and left the room, after strapping on his sword, with a customary salutation. With the sound of retreating footsteps, they knew he was gone.

"Peacetime is boring to a general, I hear." Alanias sighed and shrugged, his gaze following the direction Zarx had taken.

Elder Derrick shifted uncomfortably.

"I have a question for you as well, King," Derrick said hesitantly.

Alanias raised a brow. "Oh? You wished to wait until Zarx left?"

"Yes," Derrick said. "It has come to my attention your sons have come of age. Will they participate in the Ashen?"

Alanias smiled. You don't have to worry about discussing things with me. Why the interest?"

"If the fragments are active, and the Ashenborn give me the rite of Bright Flame, your sons would be the most qualified to become Ashenborn," Derrick said.

Alanias smiled with pride. "They would most certainly be honored to, but let's watch them in the tournament and decide from their moral choices. I want the best for them always."

"I apologize for not bringing it up around Zarx, but I know he has distaste for magic. He would surely argue such things."

Alanias sobered for a moment.

"He hates magic because of what happened to many in past battles. All could hate swords for the very same reason. He means well. I can relate to his reasoning."

Derrick accepted this reasoning and bowed. "The loss of the queen will never be forgotten."

Alanias looked somber for a moment, his eyes gleaming with unshed tears.

Then he smiled, dismissing his sadness. "She will never be forgotten. We will speak more on this soon. Send word to me when you have come to a conclusion."

Derrick bowed. "Yes, Your Highness."

"And Derrick …"

"Yes?"

"Be careful."

Elder Derrick bowed and left the room. Looking back, he saw Alanias move back to the window with a look Derrick took as sorrowful.

———————❈———————

The splendor of the mountain astounded Selaphiel. The kingdom below looked like a white blur, barely visible even if he tried to squint or strain his vision. Selaphiel was the middle brother and tallest of the three. He had been adopted as an infant by Alanias, the king of Lifesveil. His tawny eyes scanned the dense foliage of the forest. His brothers, Jakobin and Cordoc, had traveled ahead of him, but he had detoured to the clearing.

He wanted to kick himself for always sightseeing instead of sticking to the path. He shrugged and pushed back his brown hair, which was stuck to his forehead with sweat. He wore leather hunting armor, with a blade of steel strapped to his side and a small bow on his shoulder. Selaphiel looked at the great mountain ahead of him and caught a glimpse of platforms made of what seemed to be starlight. These platforms wrapped around the top plateau of the mountain. *The Light Prison,* he thought. The result of a war before his time, the structure still served as a prison for war criminals and the most deranged atrocities of society.

It also held unspeakable power and a glow that Selaphiel often noticed from his chambers in the castle. Selaphiel rubbed the familiar golden claw hanging from a chain around his neck. Being a prince had its privileges, though he felt unworthy of them. Alanias often assured him otherwise, something he was thankful for. With a huff he ran back toward the forest, trying to catch his brothers. Within moments he was back in company with his eldest brother.

"Sightseeing again, Brother?" Cordoc said, half-amused. Cordoc was the most agile of the three brothers. His blinding blonde hair matched his bright blue eyes. His jaw was strong and set, and he was considered by most to have a serious aspect to him, but Selaphiel knew otherwise. Cordoc was strong like Selaphiel, but humorously the shortest brother, often a topic of joking between the three. *A birthright is not measured in two or three inches,"* was a frequent saying from the heir to the others.

"Yeah," Selaphiel said elongating the word. "Seeing sights," he said.

Cordoc flashed a smile.

"Where is Jakobin?" Selaphiel said as they passed into the shadow of a group of trees.

Cordoc rolled his eyes. "Sightseeing maybe?"

Selaphiel fake-laughed, "Funny."

"He went ahead, so I've been enjoying the sounds of the forest," Cordoc continued.

Selaphiel stooped mid-step and grabbed an object from the ground, which was old and rusted, revealing age. Upon further analysis, he realized it was the rusted metal head of an arrow.

"Perhaps remnants of a battle fought here?" he said.

"Or someone hunting," Cordoc suggested, adding, "Be careful not to let that cut you."

Selaphiel shrugged and tossed the arrowhead into the brush, uninterested.

"I saw the Light Prison on the overhang. We are close."

The sun had begun to slant through the forest. A reddish-gold hue painted the trees, surrounded by splashes of dark purples and blues.

"It's getting late," Selaphiel noticed. Cordoc nodded. The prison's keep came into view. It stood starkly against the sun, a looming giant overlooking the kingdom, which lay beneath its shadow.

"We are here … finally," Cordoc said with a sigh.

The keep stood at an enormous height on the mountain face. The glow of the prison made the formidable walls look dull, as though the glowing prison were sucking the life from it. A guard patrolling the walls called down to them. They held up their crests, which glistened with flecks of gold, and in response the door opened with a muffled thud. Side by side they entered the door and as quickly as it had opened, it closed behind them with a loud thump. After passing through a second gate, the brothers could see the path to the prison winding upward on a staircase of old worn steps.

"Here we go again; we will have legs of steel," Cordoc complained.

Selaphiel smirked. "We should reach the top by the time the sun sets," he said, pointing to the lowering sun.

"No doubt Jakobin is already on this mountain," Cordoc said bitterly. "Always impatient …"

"You sound like Father," Selaphiel said.

"I know the both of you enjoy beating me in a footrace, but I will have my day soon enough," Cordoc said as a cold breeze cut through their clothes.

"Shivering in fear, Brother," Selaphiel jested. The sun began to sink, the sky's wispy clouds reflecting the orange and red of sunset.

"Father was kind to let us venture from the castle to give us a break from studies," Selaphiel said, grateful to be outside.

"And for such an honor as this," Cordoc said, also happy to not be cooped up in the royal dwellings.

They reached the top to find their brother Jakobin already there, looking quite pleased with himself. Jakobin had blue eyes and blond hair identical to Cordoc's, but he had a narrower jaw. He was tall, with broad shoulders, and was stronger than both of his brothers. The only similarity shared between Jakobin and Selaphiel was their height. Jakobin sat in his crimson tunic, a regal designation he favored.

"A myth moves faster than you two," he snorted, standing up dramatically, as if he had been there for hours. The spot where he had chosen to sit was beside the third gate, which entered the ledge of the prison. This was the only entrance that could be reached on foot, for the prison hung off the side of the mountain.

"Have you ever thought that the Light Prison needed more gates?" Jakobin quipped.

Daemos, the guard of the watch, appeared on the other side of the gate. He was muscular, with thick shoulders. His brown hair was tinged with gray.

"Princes of Lifesveil," he said in a northern accent. He bowed, his eyes remaining downcast until permitted to rise. "I have requested that more gates be built at the king's convenience," he said, having heard Jakobin's comment.

Cordoc motioned for him to stand.

Daemos' face brightened, and he flashed an overly white set of teeth and opened the gate. "Welcome," he said. "We are honored by your presence."

"The pleasure is ours, old friend," Cordoc said kindly.

"Old?" Daemos said. "Well, maybe," he laughed.

The four men turned and gazed at the structure before them.

The greenish-golden glow of the prison encompassed the whole ridge. There were six platforms total. The prisoners were held in orbs on a platform, each of which was large enough to fit multiple inhabitants. Chains of light held the platforms in place on the side of the mountain.

"It is always an amazing sight," Jakobin said.

Cordoc agreed. "The last remnants of the great war," he said in awe.

Selaphiel gazed at the dark shadows of the prisoners in the orbs. The shadows moved to and fro, but gradually Selaphiel became aware of the inhabitants turning to watch him, sending a shiver through him. Their features were hidden in the cloak of darkness within the cells.

Daemos looked at the prisons with less awe and more familiarity. He turned and locked the gate behind him. There were two guards assigned to each gate. The night had finally arrived, and now they could clearly see constellations shining above the prison.

"To what do I owe the pleasure of being visited by my princes and my friends?" Daemos said.

"We have something to give you. We thought it would be better to come in person for such a degree of recognition," Cordoc said.

"Captain Daemos," Cordoc said, gesturing to Selaphiel, who removed a cloth-covered object from his cloak.

"We are here to present you with this. An honor that is to be cherished, since you have been nothing but family to my brothers and me."

"Father agreed with our decision. He knows you are not a fan of flashy honors, and so he allowed us to be the ones to present you with this," Selaphiel said.

He removed the cloth, revealing a dragon-inscribed, pearl-handled dagger. The details were masterfully carved, each line delicate but also stark enough to see the overall design.

"Alanias, our father, has taken note of who you are, and he wishes you to serve him directly, second only to General Zarx of his armies," Cordoc continued.

Captain Daemos reached out with trembling fingers to grasp the dagger. "King Alanias blesses me with more than I deserve," Daemos stuttered.

"It is only fitting that our father wishes you to serve under General Zarx. You are like no one else. You are truly worthy of this," Jakobin said.

"This is only an invitation, but once you accept you will be initiated into the King's Guard, third in command," Selaphiel said, smiling.

Tears swelled in Daemos' eyes.

"Captain Daemos, former captain of the Light Prison, and White Dragon of King Alanias," he said in awe, tying the dagger to his side and bowing. The designation of White Dragon was only given to the strongest and most courageous of Lifesveils' men and women. The White Dragons specifically guarded the king, and to be leader over them was a high honor.

"Thank you, my princes."

Selaphiel hugged him. "You are family."

"To be a White Dragon is the highest honor any could receive from Alanias. It is what I have worked for," Daemos said, wiping his eyes.

"It is well-deserved," Cordoc paused, adding, "You have shown nothing but respect and honor to our father, and to us as well."

Daemos looked at the dagger with pride.

"Thank you."

The wind began to swirl around them, a sudden gust sending dust and debris whirling in front of them.

"Attention, men," Daemos said, composing himself. "Elder Derrick is approaching."

A gray-brown form began to descend toward the prison. The form was massive, with giant topaz colored wings. The large mass appeared as living mineral, large and angular. It had boulder-sized scales, which glistened as if wet. Its massive yellow eyes glowed eerily in the darkened sky. The men of the prison stood at attention, swords raised.

Cordoc and his brothers smiled. The dragon landed heavily on the platform, folding its membraned wings as the prison shuddered under his weight. The sleek and serrated neck turned, and the dragon laughed with a deep rumbling sound.

"I did not expect to find you here," the dragon thundered, its face aged and wise, with a frightening array of teeth that could easily snap a tree like a small twig. It folded its wings and stretched its long claws.

"We were presenting Daemos with a white dagger," Selaphiel said, stepping forward. "Father wishes him to be a member of his personal guard."

The dragon raised a curious brow, and a mirthful look came upon his face.

"Daemos is most worthy of this honor. I am pleased to hear it." The dragon bowed its head, and despite its bowing came nowhere close to their eye level.

Daemos smiled and looked pleased to have received congratulations from a dragon.

The dragon looked around, snorting with pleasure at seeing the men at attention.

"The honor is great, Daemos, but your men need not be bothered. I am here simply to check the fortification of the prison."

With a burst of light, the massive outline of the dragon began to shrink and finally folded into the familiar shape of an old man.

Daemos waved the men away, and they returned to their duties.

"Elder Derrick, you are a sight to behold."

"One never truly gets tired of flying," he smiled, stretching his shoulders.

"It is good that I have found you three as your father wishes to speak with you. I imagine he has sent word to you of returning to the kingdom for his advisement."

Jakobin rolled his eyes. "Father and his advisements," he said sarcastically.

Derrick narrowed his eyes before turning to the others.

"He has important words to discuss with you; I am sure the content is secret."

Derrick turned from the brothers, then placed his hands on the prison walls and closed his eyes, repeating the motion several times as he walked along the platforms.

"Forgive me if I am being nosey," Selaphiel paused, then asked, "But what do you do when you do that?"

Derrick snapped his eyes open after a moment.

"Your curious nature never bothers me, Selaphiel. This may not make sense to you, but I can feel the power of the prison. It is a constant feeling, much like placing your hands into a flowing river. You feel the current and the power of the water pushing downstream. That's how the power of this prison feels to me. It has never failed, but there are recent rumors that make me especially cautious. I am being sure of the prison's security because I will be leaving on an errand soon."

He walked over to a nearby wall and ran his fingers along it, his touch making the prison spark.

"The defenses are sufficient," he pronounced.

Derrick turned to Daemos.

"Be ever vigilant. My absence will not go unnoticed. You should not have to worry, though."

Daemos bowed with his fist to his chest, replying, "As always, Ashen-Elder. It will remain secure."

Derrick turned back to the three princes.

"I shall return soon. Within a day or so. I apologize for my quickness to leave, but there is much to do. May each of your flames burn bright, and may they warm all who see them."

The brothers bowed in return.

"As well to you," Selaphiel said, echoing the elder's sentiment.

"Good journey to you," Cordoc said.

They each covered their eyes, in preparation for the change from man to dragon.

Elder Derrick raised his vambrace-covered arm in front of him. His body began to emit shards of brilliantly colored light. There was a flash of light that would have blinded them temporarily, if not for them being prepared, and the large form of the dragon stood in front of them again. With a burst of strength, the dragon's claws sparked on the light, and it shot into the sky, the prison again seeming to tremble. Selaphiel turned and noticed the dark figures in the pods were watching Derrick fly away.

"I almost forgot," Derrick called down in deep tones.

"Daemos, I look forward to seeing you in the king's court! May the blessings of Archkyris be upon all of you." Turning, he launched into the denseness of the sky. The remnant wisps of clouds dispersed in the wake of the massive wings. What hung before them was now pure starlight. It was oddly quiet once the dragon was out of sight.

Selaphiel smiled. "I still cannot fathom the Dragon-Ashen. I have seen it thousands of times, yet I never grow tired of it."

Jakobin and Cordoc nodded in agreement.

"Daemos, we must go see Father. We will proceed with your recently appointed status soon. But, as Elder said, we are needed elsewhere," Cordoc said.

"As you wish, Princes," Daemos said, still in awe of the night's events.

They were escorted out of the hold, and the gates locked behind them. The path they had chosen wound through the forest for some time, but eventually the thickness of briars and foliage began to thin, and they traveled with more ease.

"What do you think Father wants?" Selaphiel asked Cordoc, as leaves crunched under their feet.

"Derrick is the strongest of us. He possesses great power, even outside of the Dragon-Ashen. So for Father to choose him for a mission is very peculiar."

Jakobin snorted. "He said it was an errand; besides, why would Father send off our second-best warrior?"

Selaphiel looked at Jakobin, aware of where he was going with this question, but decided to play along.

"But Brother, whatever do you mean?" Cordoc asked sarcastically.

"I am the first," Jakobin snickered.

Selaphiel sighed. "Perhaps at double-bladed combat, but against Derrick, you might as well be wielding a fish."

Cordoc smiled, amused at the thought of Jakobin attempting to stab someone with a trout.

Jakobin side-stepped a tree, as he appeared to have not been paying attention to his surroundings.

"To have such power ...." He trailed off, his thought unfinished.

"The trial of Bright Flame has not been performed since the end of Dothros, however cruel a ruler he was," Cordoc said.

They had begun to approach a large clearing within the forest.

"Complacent old men," Jakobin said flatly.

"That is for them to choose, not us. Though it is not easy to ignore Derrick's criticism of their inability to get off their chairs," Cordoc said.

Selaphiel's eyes suddenly flickered a metallic bronze color as he drew upon his magic, his hands encompassed in golden orbs of bright light. The sudden burst made Jakobin and

Cordoc jump. The glow was brilliant against the darkness and gave everything a richer appearance.

Cordoc turned to him, alarmed.

"What is it, Brother?" Cordoc said.

Selaphiel's pupils shined brighter.

"I do not know."

Jakobin paced, kicking up leaves.

"Let go of your magic! You are a beacon! Anyone who would want to cause us harm could easily see us," Jakobin said, knowing Selaphiel only responded this way when danger was near. "Why else travel in the safety of darkness?"

A growl reached them, making all three freeze. Leaves moved in the darkness.

Jakobin eyed the location the noise came from and slowly began to move his hand toward the sword on his hip.

"Someone is coming," Selaphiel said quietly.

The noise continued for a moment and then stopped altogether. Each of them strained to hear.

Through the brush came the wide-eyed messenger known as Gerriff, who stumbled after a moment of trying to balance himself.

He looked at them, confused.

"Gerriff ..." Cordoc sighed. Selaphiel's eyes dimmed and he lowered his hands.

"You do realize it is not wise to sneak up on someone?" Jakobin asked. "Princes, even worse."

Gerriff shook his head. "Yes, and I do apologize, but I fell over some briar bushes trying to follow you. Thus the noise you just heard. Sorry my lords, but I have come to summon you to the king."

"We have heard from Elder Derrick. We are on our way there now," Cordoc said.

"Oh," Gerriff said. "Then I suppose I shall head home to confirm you received the message." He bowed and ran off into the void of the night.

"That new messenger is strange," Jakobin said, his face scrunched up.

"His disregard for royal etiquette is confusing," Cordoc agreed.

"I am losing my touch." Selaphiel looked down at his hands, embarrassed by his overreaction.

"It happens, Brother," Cordoc said, patting Selaphiel on the shoulder.

"But you would not let anyone sneak up on us," Cordoc finished.

Jakobin snorted. "Yes, Geriff, sneak up on us," he said, his voice oozing sarcasm.

Selaphiel stared off into the distance, stopping behind the rest of them.

"What?" Jakobin called back, turning his head to look at his brother.

"I … I do not know." Selaphiel said, his gaze still fixed on the path leading back to the prison.

"Perhaps you still hear Geriff?" Cordoc suggested.

Selaphiel paused.

"No, it's not that. Someone is headed to the prison," Selaphiel said with a quizzical look on his face.

"Probably a change of guard or something. Selaphiel, let's go; Father summoned us and you know we shouldn't keep a king waiting." Cordoc hesitated. "Or at least I think that's how the saying goes."

Jakobin shrugged and turned to continue walking down the mountain.

"Okay," Selaphiel said, abandoning his search and trudging to catch up to his brothers.

"Do you both realize the Ashen is within a few days?" Cordoc said, changing the subject.

Jakobin beamed. "Yes, years of preparation and the ten years of waiting and finally the Ashen has come upon us once again."

"Do you remember the last one we had?" Cordoc asked. "Zarx won that one. It feels like so long ago."

"It was," Jakobin said. "We were ten years of age then, hardly able to carry a sword."

"Is Zarx competing this time?" Selaphiel said, a worried look on his face.

"No," Cordoc laughed. "Generals do not compete in Ashens. That would be like putting a tortoise up against a horse in a race."

"Says you," Jakobin snickered. "I fancy myself the horse."

Selaphiel neighed, mocking Jakobin.

"Seph, you may be decently good at swordsmanship, but this is my time," Jakobin said seriously.

"Mmmm, I do not think so," Selaphiel replied.

"In the end, Seph's kindness will lose it for him," Cordoc said. Selaphiel turned to look at him as they continued walking.

"You know," Cordoc paused. "You struggle to kill game while hunting, much less striking down an opponent without hesitation. I've seen you let children beat you in spars."

"Taking life is different. Beating you two would be easy," Selaphiel said, fighting laughter. "Besides, children aren't used to winning, just like you two."

Cordoc pushed him before almost nearly running into a tree.

"Both of you have nearly run into trees that do not move. Yet, you can beat me?" Selaphiel mockingly challenged.

"There are more trees than I remember." Cordoc coughed, pushing back his hair. Jakobin held his ribs, crying from laughter, and nearly slid on some leaves.

"Laugh while you can; I am more formidable than trees and leaves," Selaphiel said, making his voice as tough and hard as he could.

Jakobin gathered his composure, wiping his eyes.

Cordoc quickened his pace, pretending he hadn't almost run into a tree. He cleared his throat.

"The walls should be coming into view soon. We better act like princes, or else the people will not respect us," Cordoc said seriously, though still not able to remove his smile.

"Normal princes would not be going outside without armed guards,"

Selaphiel said.

Cordoc shrugged. "We are anything but normal."

———————✤———————

"Rumors of monsters have reached my ears and continue to spread throughout all of Lifesveil."

"How many have you told, Captain?" Zarx questioned the man.

The man shook his head. "Only you."

"Who told you this?" Zarx asked as he strapped on his sword and opened the large door to the armory.

"Anath, of the house of Grimolith."

Zarx's face darkened. "Those of that house should be trusted sparingly."

"Dilwyn, we cannot afford this information to spread; please bring me Anath. Tell no one else; the last thing we need is people believing there are monsters creeping into their pantries and under their beds."

Captain Dilwyn looked at him, perplexed. "You do not believe him?"

Zarx shrugged. "I am a born skeptic it seems; just fetch Anath, and we will hopefully find no truth to this rumor."

Dilwyn ran away clumsily, dodging attendants and servants at their work.

Zarx scratched his chin. Twice this rumor has reached me, he thought.

He grabbed the golden talon on his neck. This would require the strength of the Silver Talons if the leads were true. Zarx grabbed his gleaming silver armor and threw it on, tying on the loose-fitting pieces. He twisted the gauntlets on and worked the chainmail around his muscular shoulders. The last to be put on was the sharp layered boots of strong metal. They went on easily enough but Zarx often found them uncomfortable. With a clank, he traversed the shining marble floor. The door opened and the armored guards on either side of the door bowed to him.

The long hallway was decorated with banners of white and gold and the different colors of the houses of Lifesveil. Other colors signified those houses under the rule of Archkyris.

Zarx traced his fingers on a few of them, stopping at the black and purple emblem.

"The house of Mavet," he muttered.

The scene when he approached the outside was that of men and women performing daily tasks. Some children ran along the stone roads, obviously in some form of game or play. A young boy ran after a little girl who seemed to be in an argument with him over whether to play soldier or house wife. The boy, however, seemed intent on her being a dragon and himself a knight.

Zarx smiled with pride, blinking his eyes at the change of light.

"General Zarx," came a voice. He turned.

"The princes of Lifesveil returned last night and are currently in counsel with the king," a short brown-haired servant said. "Your presence is also requested."

Zarx turned and trudged up the stone staircase. *The work of a general is never done. I wonder what it would be like not to be needed as much.* He shook off the thought, knowing very well he loved the position he held. As he passed, there was the occasional bow, which he curtly acknowledged but only for a moment considering his presence was needed by the king. Zarx approached his destination and moved to open the door before the attendant could utter his titles, making the servant gargle his words and finally simply say, "General Zarx."

He walked into the golden throne room and saw Alanias dressed in purple garb, wearing not the royal crown but instead a smaller, simpler crown of silver.

"Zarx," Alanias motioned him forward to where he sat on the golden throne with the three princes standing around him.

"What is the status of Elder Derrick?" Cordoc asked.

"No word yet on his return. It has only been a day, and I know Derrick is accurate in his investigations. I imagine that he will arrive before the small garrison I supplied will," Alanias said.

Jakobin tapped his foot, his gaze searching, as if he had a lot on his mind.

"I mean to ask to enact the rite of Bright Flame," Alanias said bluntly.

Everyone stopped breathing and looked at Alanias with wide eyes.

"You mean to ask permission from Elder Derrick?" Cordoc inquired.

"Yes. He believes that the time for new Ashenborn is now."

"My king," Zarx said. "Such an act has not been done since the War of Stones. Besides, who knows if the Ashenborn would even do it?"

"Is it that bad?" Selaphiel asked softly.

Alanias stood, which would have been a commanding gesture, if not for him having to hold the arms of the throne.

"I believe monsters have returned to Lifesveil, from what information Derrick has already sent. He believes strongly that we are not dealing with hollow stories. We could be dealing with the Taneemian once again."

Zarx gave him a disbelieving look.

"I have heard rumors of these creatures, even within our city walls, but I do not believe them. Surely it is some misconstrued understanding. To claim something such as that would suggest they are back in this world again. I thought them to be gone with the death of Dothros, their master in the past war."

"How credible is Derrick's claim?" Cordoc asked. "Could it be possible he is wrong?"

"He did not wish to send details, as he believes there could be someone interfering among the kingdoms, and therefore wishes to speak to us in person." Alanias paused. "But as you all know, Derrick does not play into falsehoods. It is fact if he believes it."

"There are two sources that say there are Taneems. They are not fairy tales that were told to us when we were children," Jakobin said, disagreeing with Zarx.

"Yes, they do exist," Alanias said. "I trust Derrick, and I do not take this news lightly. Especially when he is the one giving it."

"My king, with the respect of your servant, I would like to see for myself. Rumors have circulated from the south side of the kingdom, along with word of villages sending similar tales," Zarx responded.

"Derrick has confirmed through magic that the Taneemian are now in this realm," Alanias said.

Zarx tilted his chin back and crossed his arms.

"I understand your skepticism, but this report can be trusted. We must begin to assume that their numbers will grow," Alanias said.

"Let us hope for your people's sake it is not," Zarx said.

"I believe Derrick, but if they are here, I would wish to check the villages to the south. Based on the accounts, the southern village would be the most vulnerable to any attacks," Jakobin said, alarmed by the idea of something so sinister being true.

Alanias eyed Jakobin with pride, aware that his sons were becoming men.

"I remember when each of you played soldier, even pretending to go on dangerous journeys to the unknown. Those are days long past, I am afraid," Alanias smiled fondly. "I accept your idea of further investigation. Jakobin, you will check the villages. Zarx, I wish for you to investigate within our walls to be sure there are none among us. Find this proof you are unconvinced of."

Alanias turned to Jakobin.

"I will assign you ten of our Silver Talons, in case the rumors are true. As strong as Lifesveil is, we cannot afford to underestimate this situation. We will proceed more with this once Elder Derrick has returned. He will give us more clarity as to how to better proceed."

"What of Selaphiel and myself?" Cordoc asked. "Would you wish us to accompany Zarx and Jakobin?"

Zarx waved his hand.

"I will bring my best men with us, but I believe you two would be best served within the kingdom. You both are strong, and we need no weakness inside the city as well. Instead of Jakobin going outside the walls, would it not be wiser to send me?" Zarx asked.

"What do you think, Jakobin?" Alanias asked.

"I have no issue with searching the villages, Father. I believe this is a chance for me to prove my worth," Jakobin said, irritated by Zarx's words.

"Very well, then it is decided." Alanias spoke firmly.

"Thank you for the compliment, Zarx," Cordoc added. "We will make sure our people are taken care of, especially so close to the Ashen."

Alanias turned to Selaphiel, whose mind seemed to be somewhere else.

"You have been very quiet, my son," Alanias said to Selaphiel.

"Father, may I make a request?" Selaphiel ventured.

"You may; what is on your mind?" Alanias smiled warmly.

"May I go with Elder Derrick to check the Light Prison when he returns? I have inquiries regarding it myself."

Zarx turned to him, a look of concern on his face.

"Why the Light Prison?"

Jakobin squinted his eyes.

Selaphiel paused, a little unsure of himself.

"If anything should be concerning, it would be that prison. We all have knowledge of who is within its confines. I do not think we should ignore it. The Taneemian served those who are imprisoned, so it could be their first ambition."

"The Light Prison is well guarded, but to add more guards would be a good idea, as well as looking at areas that might require better attention there," Zarx said.

"It is something to be discussed with Derrick, considering he provides part of the power that upholds it," Cordoc said.

Zarx nodded. "I will speak with him. If his magic can do one thing, it is to hold those monstrosities."

"Good," Alanias said as he stood. "I have words to speak with him as well."

Zarx's gaze followed Alanias as he walked across the room.

"You mean the Rite?" Jakobin said bluntly.

Alanias winked. "All the better time to bring up the subject."

"And you think," Zarx paused and scratched his chin, "that the Ashenborn will cooperate?"

"Their purpose is to fight the Taneemian and those who threaten the life of all," Alanias said. "Or so they say."

The brothers made their respective and proper good-byes and left to prepare for their upcoming assignments.

Jakobin smiled broadly as they closed the war room door behind them, leaving Zarx and King Alanias in the room.

"What?" Selaphiel said, looking at Jakobin as if something strange had happened.

"You heard Father," Jakobin beamed. "He has entrusted me with carrying out the investigation and defense of the south village."

"It seems Father trusts you more each day, Brother. You have gained his respect as you have grown," Cordoc said.

"Plus you made a very good point and spoke wisely," Selaphiel added.

Jakobin walked down the hall as if he were a hundred feet tall.

"Do not let it go to your head, however," Cordoc said, watching him.

"I was not amused by Zarx attempting to take me away from it," Jakobin said.

"He just cares for you," Selaphiel said. "Besides, you know how Zarx is skeptical of magic. We and Derrick are the only ones who wield it with whom he seems to get along."

"It explains his not really acknowledging the evidence that Father said Derrick provided," Cordoc said.

"Maybe that makes sense," Jakobin said as he came to a stop. "Zarx has better cause to hate magic than any of us do. He fought in the War of Stones and saw the majority of his family killed in it. No wonder he is hesitant to believe the Taneemian have returned."

"Or too afraid to acknowledge it," Cordoc said.

———— ✸ ————

The man stood in the darkness of the shadows. He wore silver armor that covered the gleam of magic in his eyes. He crouched on the mountainside, viewing the large expanse of the prison with hungry eyes. He looked down at the vambrace on his arm and the silver fragment that was wrapped around his wrist. He watched as the guard changed, and the new men began to crank the chains of the prison, causing it to lift into the air, giving the appearance it was floating. The prison sat at an angle until chains pulling it from the opposite side straightened it. Its height, after several minutes of watching, was breathtaking. The man placed his opposite hand over the fragment but stopped as he saw another man in silver armor walk into the prison.

"Zarx," he whispered, annoyed. He stooped on the ledge, listening to the conversation below him.

"Make sure to be ever watchful. The king wishes for us to be more cautious than ever," the man heard Zarx say.

"What is all the fuss about? This prison is never bothered."

Zarx looked at the guard, agitated.

"Do not ask me why, but follow my order. An order of the king should not be questioned. Next time you ask a question like that, I will have you striped for insolence."

The guard went red in the face and gave a curt "Yes, sir" before heading back to his post.

Zarx walked around the prison, looking disgusted.

Daemos approached the red-faced guard and whispered a few words to the man, who nodded in return.

"Why the look?" Daemos asked Zarx, after having chastised the guard.

"These walls are not made by an ordinary person. I am not a fan of Ashenborn magic," Zarx spat.

Daemos chuckled. "You hate what you do not understand. If the Ashenborn are all like Derrick, then they are a fine people."

Zarx looked amused at Daemos' statement.

"May I ask what you are looking for, General?"

Zarx ran his hand across the wall of glowing light.

"Before leaving for the king's errand, I wanted to check the prison, though what I expect to find I am not so sure myself." He put his hand up to his face, as if he expected to find the light smeared upon his fingers, as if it were slime.

"Derrick has said there is no need to supply more guards, though I have been arguing the opposite. His belief is the prison will hold against anything."

Zarx looked around sternly. "Daemos, what are your thoughts?"

"I trust Elder Derrick; there has never been a reason to be concerned, and all here remain vigilant, despite the fact that this place is all but impervious to attack from the ground."

Zarx snorted, "So attacks from the air could be problematic."

"Well, what could reach up this high?" Daemos said, unconcerned.

"Dragons," Zarx said.

Daemos raised an eyebrow.

"It is nothing. The prison seems fine; no worries of an enemy dropping from the sky," Zarx said only half in jest as his gaze landed on the shadow of the man standing on the mountainside.

"What about there?" he pointed upward.

The man in the shadow held his breath, not daring to move, unsure as to whether Zarx saw him.

Daemos followed his finger and saw the large overhang high above the prison.

"If anyone attempted to enter the prison that way, the fall would kill them," he answered.

Zarx nodded and squinted up at the ledge. His eyes held on that point for what felt like minutes to the man, but finally Zarx shook his head and brought his eyes back down to Daemos.

The man in the shadows breathed out and clenched his fists.

"Another perfect opportunity ..." the man said sarcastically to himself. "Just leave," the man whispered, following the two men with his gaze, knowing full well that they could not hear him.

Zarx paced back and forth, his cloak swaying behind him.

"Daemos, congratulations on becoming a White Dragon. I look forward to serving with you in the castle," Zarx said, changing the subject abruptly.

Daemos bowed. "Thank you, General; it has been my dream to serve the king directly."

"The highest honor indeed; I can now refer to you as one of the elites," Zarx grinned.

"Thank you. I serve at the king's pleasure," Daemos answered.

"Will you miss it?" Zarx asked.

"The prison?" Daemos replied, regarding the walls of light. "Only a little. I imagine my vision will improve from not having to look at these lights constantly."

"Indeed whom have you selected to replace you?"

"Sephor, as he has proven himself to me."

"An excellent choice."

Zarx began to pace, seemingly bothered by something.

"Is something wrong?" Daemos asked, becoming aware of the continual movement.

"I am not sure," Zarx said. "I feel … displaced?"

"Displaced?"

"Like I should be doing something else, or there is something I am missing."

The man in the shadows clenched his teeth.

Just leave, the hidden man thought again.

Finally, Zarx shook his head, as if clearing his thoughts.

"Well, Daemos, I expect to see you in a few days, actually the day after the Ashen," Zarx said, preparing to leave.

"Thank you, sir." Daemos bowed, and with a turn of his cloak, Zarx headed for the gate, his men behind him. At the gate, he turned.

"I almost forgot. When he returns, Derrick will come with Selaphiel to visit the prison again. It is no cause for concern, just making you aware." With that last word, he departed.

Daemos stood where he was, turning his eyes to the ledge where the man hid. Daemos squinted and cupped his hands over his eyes.

"Dragons?" Daemos whispered, confused by what Zarx had meant. After a moment, Daemos disregarded the area and left as well. Sephor, second-in-command to Daemos, took his spot.

"Too late now, and who knows when there will be none watching so persistently," the man whispered. He looked at the vambrace on his arm, and back at the prison.

There is more planning to be done. Fewer mistakes to be made this time. He slowly walked to the edge of the mountain and looked down at the treacherous landscape below him. He felt heat radiate through him as he prepared to jump. He left the cliff with a clack of rocks hitting the mountain side. He let the cold wind race around him, embracing the feeling of exhilaration. He opened his eyes just before he hit the jagged rocks and flew away into the night.

———————�֎———————

Selaphiel concentrated, his eyes bright with magic. He formed orbs of bright light, making them spin around him in the stable. The royal stables where were the best horses of Lifesveil were kept. With effort, he willed larger orbs of light to form, making several dozen around him in total. With a wave of his other hand, he formed them into various patterns, straight lines, even zig zags. Sweat formed on his face as he willed them individually to move.

The princes' inborn ability to use magic took effort to control. He and his brothers practiced regularly to maintain that control by doing exercises such as this one. Their power, he knew, was a gift, but there were those who called it magic. This was not the most appropriate word for it, though it was often referred to as such. Selaphiel even referred to it as magic and did not mind the use of the word to describe their power. True magic, however, was actually power gained by spells from books, not something that could be used by blood.

Cordoc had his nose buried in a scroll next to him. Selaphiel glanced at Cordoc, who was paying him no attention. He noted that Cordoc was squinting in the dim light. One of the larger orbs drifted above Cordoc, illuminating what he was reading.

"Thank you, Seph," Cordoc said, not looking up.

Selaphiel let out a puff of relief, releasing his power except the one orb hovering over Cordoc.

"Elder Derrick sure fooled me into believing that doing this is easy. Though each time I feel like I am making more progress," Selaphiel sighed.

"What are you reading?" he asked, looking over his brother's shoulder.

"Just information regarding your and my estates."

Selaphiel looked at him as though this were the most boring thing ever.

Cordoc rolled up the parchment, and simultaneously the light flickered and dissipated.

"We will both maintain estates soon. Father has said we will gain our own holds after the tournament."

"I just want a place to fish, with lots of woods."

Cordoc shook his head.

"You and your common lifestyle."

"I enjoy time to myself; when you fish you …"

"… Always enjoy it even if you don't catch anything," Cordoc interrupted, adding, "But I wonder if you ever come away empty-handed when you fish."

"You never will let that large trout I caught go will you?" Selaphiel said, winking.

"How could I? You were the only one who caught something, and a massive fish at that. I sat there for hours and still had nothing to show for it," Cordoc said bitterly.

"You will catch something one day," Selaphiel said encouragingly. "You are just not following the techniques I showed you."

Cordoc scowled, for he was not one to like being beaten at anything, and if he was, he worked hard to make sure he was not outdone again. However, fishing seemed to elude him no matter how hard he tried. He laughed, knowing that his brother's technique was to chew on smoked pork while fishing.

"Elusive, slippery … fish," he joked.

"Speaking of elusive fishes, where is Jakobin?"

"Likely training with Zarx, or the Silver Talons. Much like myself, he dislikes losing. With nothing found in the villages, I imagine his focus has shifted toward tomorrow's festivities."

"He had better focus," Selaphiel said, a sly grin on his face.

"Swordsmanship is just one feature of the tournament," Cordoc said, sitting up and dusting himself off.

"And fishing is not a part of it," he finished.

As he spoke, a horse neighed nearby.

Tomorrow's tournament consisted of five competitions: dueling, archery, jousting, agility, and finally, a test of wisdom.

Cordoc had tried to discover what form the final competition would take, hoping to get an edge but had found it to be a tightly guarded secret.

Selaphiel reached down, grabbed a long piece of hay and put it in his mouth, holding it between his teeth.

Cordoc looked at him with narrowed eyes.

"You do realize that horses relieve themselves here?" Cordoc said.

Selaphiel froze, and with a loud spitting noise the wheat left his mouth like an arrow from a bow.

Cordoc rubbed his nose and snorted.

"I forgot about that," Selaphiel said as a horse neighed again. Selaphiel turned and looked dumbly at the horse standing ten feet away from them.

"I don't suppose you have some water with you to wash my mouth out?" Selaphiel asked.

Cordoc gestured to the water trough.

Selaphiel made a puffing noise.

"Well, I am off to find water," he said as he left the stables. "Clean water."

"I will come with you," Cordoc said. "Gives me a bad taste in my mouth having seen you do that."

Selaphiel did not let Cordoc see him roll his eyes.

They were south of the castle, near a local market they often visited. The large hut was filled with goods, including meats, cheeses, wines, and many other things that were good for purchasing. On the front was a makeshift sign that said "Dalion's," which was also the name of the owner of the humble place.

As they approached, the front door burst open in a quick motion and a scraggly-looking man fell on his face in a puff of dirt and grass.

"And stay out!" came the shout of Dalion, who had thrown the man outside.

The scraggly man struggled to his feet and ran, face as red as an over-ripe apple.

Both Cordoc and Selaphiel paused in a mixture of surprise and confusion. They cautiously entered the hut and saw goods hanging from the ceiling or placed neatly onto shelves with signs signifying their price in gold. Dalion, a large-framed man with a balding head, greeted them with a bow while dusting off his hands. A few men and women were in the shop, browsing the wares.

"My lords, what brings you to my humble shop?" he asked with a northern accent.

"What happened with the man outside?" Cordoc asked curiously.

A mischievous look gleamed in Dalion's eyes.

"He tried to steal some bread."

Selaphiel sighed. "Why not call the guards?"

Dalion looked amused. "Because I enjoy handling it in my way."

"Besides," he said, tossing around a loaf, "they will be informed."

"That could be dangerous. You never know who you might offend," Cordoc said.

"Maybe," Dalion responded. "But I have that there," he said, pointing to a large crossbow resting on top of the doorframe.

"Ah," Cordoc said.

Dalion shifted his weight onto his other leg and grinned.

"I would like some wine, please," Selaphiel said, handing over two gold pieces from his change purse.

Dalion's eyes gleamed. "Of course, Prince. Less for me to drink later," he said with a snort, disappearing into a back room to fetch the wine.

"Dalion has always been an interesting person, hasn't he?" Cordoc whispered.

"Yes," Selaphiel whispered back. "But he means well enough."

Dalion returned with a full wineskin after a few minutes.

"Red dragon brew," he said, placing it on the counter.

"Thank you, Dalion," Selaphiel said, putting down another gold coin.

"You both are always welcome. For you to visit a place as common as this honors me," Dalion said as he scooped up the coins.

"Well, you have some of the finest wares; besides, where would I get the hooks for fishing?" Selaphiel winked and took a sip from the wineskin.

Dalion's eyes darted behind them and he lowered his head like a lion stalking its prey.

"Dalion?" Selaphiel asked.

"My apologies, Prince." Dalion shook his head. "You do not know how often people attempt to steal from me," Dalion said, motioning toward a woman who had her back turned to them.

Cordoc grabbed some smoked pork and gave Dalion a silver piece for it, placing it in a sack he carried at his side.

Selaphiel eyed Cordoc understandingly.

Cordoc thanked Dalion and stood near the door admiring the crossbow.

"Has Jakobin been around here today?" Selaphiel said.

Dalion shook his head. "I have not seen him in a few days."

He scratched behind his ear. "He rarely visits anymore. Though I think it has to do with the coming festival. Your brother is competitive for sure; he always asks if I have a leg up on any new weapons."

"We all are competitive." Cordoc shrugged. "All of the time. And that's interesting. Be sure to inform me before him if you do hear of any new weapons."

Cordoc slyly placed ten pieces of gold onto the table and slid them toward Dalion.

"Well," Dalion said. "I will see what I can do."

"True. Jakobin has always wanted to be the best amongst us," Selaphiel confirmed, ignoring the money exchange. A few more men came inside the shop and bowed to the princes as they entered.

"Well, we will leave you to your trade, friend." Cordoc said.

"Do not be strangers, Princes," Dalion said, bowing.

"Nor you." Selaphiel said, exchanging salutations.

Outside they walked on the marble path, noticing the many people walking around them, but giving them their distance. The archers in their towers were watchful and had their eyes upon them always so they could wander around without worry of an attempt on their lives.

"What would you like to do now?" Cordoc asked, stretching.

Selaphiel pursed his lips in thought.

"Would you like to practice some sword play?" He said as they walked over to the training quarters near the stables.

"Sure," Cordoc mocked. "It would give me a chance to know more strategy on how to beat you."

"Oh?" Selaphiel said. "They say you become more apt to face your fears when you continually put yourself in your fears' way."

"Your name is fear now?" Cordoc jested.

"No," Selaphiel retorted. "I'm just saying you are fearful of loss."

"Let's go," Cordoc responded.

"If you wish."

Cordoc grinned mischievously, as he had been practicing.

CHAPTER 2
AN OLD ENEMY

Elder Derrick flew slowly through the night sky. Ice hung from his long silver-gray claws. He heaved a heated breath. The strain of the temperature at this height made it hard to fly. He felt tired but knew he needed to return to Lifesveil as quickly as possible. His visit to Mavet had provided proof of the monsters now dwelling among them. After arriving at Mavet, he had found the battalion that King Hroth had described in the letter. He searched for some time from the vantage point of the sky but could not determine anything out of order.

The men sent by Alanias arrived a day's time after he did. He had ordered them to search the forests that were common around Mavet. He made sure to emphasize the importance of no detail being left unnoticed, or anything strange not being reported back to him. He wasn't able to gather enough information from his meeting with Hroth. Hroth made the situation more confusing than it should have been. Derrick had wondered while speaking to the king how Hroth could have survived this long. He did not believe that he was being lied to as too many witnesses had seen the events described, but he felt a twinge of doubt.

However, his dragon fragment acted strangely when he visited the area the suspicious battalion had been spotted, which changed his mind immediately. This reaction alone quelled any doubts he had. Upon further investigation, he found fragments of a strange metal spread in the underbrush. The battalion was lost to the depths of the darkened trees, the only thing left behind the strange pieces of discarded metal. If it was intentional, he did not know, but he knew the only source of this particular substance. It was a dark, murky purple and consistent with Taneemian armor of the past.

Derrick's thoughts went back to the War of Stones, the last great battle Yadir had seen. That same demonic metal was found around the dispatched bodies of the Taneems, a sight he would never forget. The armor itself was made of something not found in this realm. Like the monsters, it did not seem to belong in the land of flesh and blood. Taneems were horrifying alive, but they were even more unnerving when dead. Even though they appeared to be lifeless corpses, he knew better. He thought back to how he had dispatched many of them with claw and blade.

I was more energetic then, he thought, keenly aware of his lack of youthful energy. He was tired from flying, but he was also weary in his soul. He thought how unwise he had been, how he had foolishly underestimated the power of an enemy. He had been brilliant in battles in his youth, had fought hard for both Ashenborn and Lifesveil.

And how less painful everything was, he grumbled to himself, the ache moving through his body. *Time has a strange way of taking things from people.*

He blinked his eyes several times, attempting to put his mind back on track.

Lifesveil's guards had come upon a living Taneem. A straggler. The creature had been wounded from Mavet's arrows. The moment he laid eyes upon those soulless sockets of loose skin, he knew his fears had been realized. A terrible growl rose from its narrow throat. Guttural and familiar. Derrick closed his eyes, knowing that as long as he lived, he would never forget the sounds those demonic creatures made. All of the Taneemian shared in inhuman voices, voices that haunted men after they had the misfortune to hear them.

So many bad memories, so many failures. The world was changing, changing back to what it had once been before the great war. The past would not return if what was happening was properly acknowledged, if action was taken and taken swiftly, Derrick thought. The young, inexperienced guard had fallen to the Taneems' murky flames, his screams a memory added to that which would not be forgotten.

They had killed it without hesitation, not out of bravery but from fear. Derrick confirmed its temporary death, for the Ashenborn had not yet discovered how to completely kill the creatures. It is not that they had not tried, but that they lacked the knowledge. The Taneems had disappeared at the death of their summoner, Dothros. It now seemed there was someone new to command them. The creature had melted into a mixture of flame and liquid, its cruel, dark presence disappearing, knowing well to leave the area.

He had hoped it would be left alive but could not blame the quick reaction of his men. He shook his head. Droplets of cold vapor dropped from his jaw.

His sturdy wings labored under him. His wings, an extension of himself, were beginning to turn numb. He shook his scales, and ice fell from him like breaking glass. His muscles rippled, and a cloud of steam rolled from his massive scales. He lowered in altitude, sinking beneath the clouds. A large mountain range appeared below him. He could no longer feel his limbs.

"That's no good," he whispered, and began to descend toward the closest mountain. The peak opened up to a level surface. He landed abruptly, if not gracefully. He breathed a ring of fire into the ground of the mountain. The bright flames stood firm against the roar of the cold and wind as he shrank to human form. Lights flashed as he extended his human arm into the fire. Magic poured into his wrist. The gem housed beneath his skin, looking brighter than usual, ignited in flame and light. Sparks and orbs of radiance cascaded from the flames that engulfed it. Derrick rubbed his palms together and held his hands in front of the fire. He coughed a puff of fog. The wind had subsided some, and he realized he would arrive at Lifesveil within a few hours.

He kicked himself for not rejuvenating his strength sooner. He was aware of how much of his magic he had expended. After warming his hands, he removed his sword from his belt and held it into the fire. The blade sparked and became translucent, and it seemed as though he were peering through a window. The blade was a portal to a distant yet familiar place. The room before him was large; the portal through which he looked was the great mirror inside of

Aaish, the hold of the Ashenborn. This was how Ashenborn passed messages to each other, when matters warranted it. A bird was more commonly used because this form of speaking required them to use so much of their power. Birds were easier, but birds were also easier for unwanted eyes to intercept.

"It is I, Ashen-Elder Derrick of Lifesveil," he said above the roar of the wind.

He turned the blade, looking around the room through which he was communicating. This ancient mirror and other items were used to amplify the Ashenborn's powers but were also used as a form of speaking over long distances. He turned the blade, viewing the room from different angles. He cleared his throat and repeated his name again several times.

What is going on? he thought. He removed the sword, tying it back to his side.

They have not responded in some time now. He tried to shrug it off. This had been his seventh attempt to speak to someone. Perhaps the other elders were busy with other tasks, but he felt deep in his gut something was off. He put his hand back to the fire. The orb in his wrist shone a bright sun glow of topaz. He removed his wrist from the fire, his hand unburned, and placed the vambrace over it.

Should I contact others individually instead of Aiash? he wondered.

He turned northwest, looking in the direction that would eventually lead to the Ashenborn temple, leagues away from these mountains.

Should I head there now?

He attempted the same communication method with the kingdom of Edywin to the north. When the Ashenborn had been more numerous, an Elder had been assigned the duty of protecting each kingdom. The Ashenborn had been fewer now and cared less for this particular duty. Again, he received no answer.

Peculiar.

He shifted back and forth, the soft snow like powder under his feet. He extinguished the fire with the wave of his hand. In a burst of light, he regained dragon form and ascended back into the skies. His form felt full of power, but not of energy. Only sleep could rejuvenate his vitality. He headed south to Lifesveil, his mind made up. His first priority was to his kingdom and those who resided there. He would worry about the Ashenborn later; they would hear his findings in due time. He let himself drift on the breeze for some time before eventually reaching the different climate of Lifesveil. In his exhaustion, he knew his senses were dull and unattentive. He landed near the castle and made his way to the king's quarters. Light slowly began to penetrate the darkness, confirming the sunrise.

Derrick could not believe how long he had been flown.

Regardless, he thought, *the king must know now.* He entered the castle, knowing that despite the early hour, the king would be awake. Derrick found Alanias eating and drinking morning wine. The king looked at him with surprise, his expression of someone not quite awake who had been startled.

Alanias motioned for Derrick to join him, and Derrick sat down without hesitation.

"Wine, my lord?" a servant asked.

Derrick shook his head.

"My apologies for intruding," Derrick said.

Alanias shook his head and waved his hand.

"It is of no concern," he said, putting down his goblet.

"What news do you bring?" Alanias asked, wiping his mouth with a cloth.

Derrick repeated his story to the king with every detail that he could recall, leaving nothing out. For an hour he recalled the tale and his discoveries, and the king was silent throughout. Alanias propped his hands under his beard, intently listening. As Derrick finished, he noticed Alanias no longer was eating his food but had pushed it away, and several men appeared to remove the remains of fish and fruit. The king motioned for the attendants to leave. After the last of the attendants left, Alanias drummed the table, his face unreadable as his thoughts concentrated elsewhere.

"The Taneemian have returned, Alanias. We must do something," Derrick said, breaking the silence.

Alanias cleared his throat.

"Zarx, and Zarx only, will be the only other person to be told this," Alanias finally said. "He must know so as to put the necessary men in place to protect our walls and all those who have traveled here for the Ashen. I will tell them after the competition."

"Don't you think we should cancel the Ashen?" Derrick asked, concerned.

Alanias pushed away from the large table and stood, using the edge of the table to steady himself.

"The people need celebration, and we will not deprive them of it because evil has shown itself once again. Lifesveil needs this."

Derrick nodded, but he asked, "But could it be that the celebrations should be postponed?"

Alanias paused and turned slowly to him.

"You do not think we are in danger of them being in Lifesveil, do you?" Alanias asked, concern in his voice.

"No," Derrick said. "We have only just discovered they have returned. It is doubtful that they have gained much substance to them, but immediate action should be made within the Alliance of Yadir to hunt them down, lest we repeat the War of Stones."

"I will make it our priority," Alanias said. "But the Ashen will not be moved. It means more that we show no fear than fold under. Just because our ears hear of evil does not mean we are unprepared to contend with it."

"But my eyes have seen it. It is true; we have that guarantee of it. Surely a celebration at this time is not warranted," Derrick said.

Alanias looked at him seriously. "A celebration is warranted, regardless of how bad the times are," Alanias said, his eyes shining. "I do not want to stop something that gives hope to our people; that is why no one is to know the Taneemian are back until after the celebration is done."

"Not even your sons are to know?" Derrick said, looking at him in surprise.

"Especially them," the king said, smiling. "Today they celebrate becoming men; tomorrow they put those attributes to the test." At that, Alanias turned his back to the elder, signalling he did not wish to speak about the matter any further.

Derrick stood also.

"I have heard nothing additionally, nor have I been able to speak to my order further. I have even attempted to contact Edywin, but no attempt has been successful."

"You wish to go to Aiash?" Alanias said, following Derrick's thoughts.

"Yes, but only after checking our walls. And guaranteeing all are safe during the Ashen," Derrick said.

Alanias rubbed his beard and paced around the table, the echo of his footsteps resounding through the room.

"Good. Maybe a course of action can be made."

Derrick looked down at the vambrace on his forearm. He hoped that going to Aiash would resolve whatever problem there was, but he could not help but notice the same strange feeling in his stomach.

"As for now," Alanias said, "We must act as though nothing is wrong. The people need not fear for the moment until it is necessary."

Derrick agreed hesitantly, out of respect for his king. He did not fully agree with this course of action.

Alanias called his servants back into the room.

"Bring me Zarx," he commanded.

———————✷———————

The morning of the Ashen dawned brightly. The sun shone and birds sang as Selaphiel trudged slowly to the opposite end of the sword room, which was decorated with numerous weapons, both common and exotic. Some of them he had never used, nor did he know how to use them properly. Standing opposite him was Cordoc, his back also turned. Selaphiel and Cordoc were tired from days of training. They had each poured themselves into preparation for the competitions of the Ashen. They both were aware of the eyes of their younger brother Jakobin, who stood anxiously outside the barrier of the sparring area.

"Begin," the armory attendant said.

Selaphiel gripped the wooden sword tightly, leveling it with his shoulder in an offensive position. He and Cordoc had been training for many hours prior to this event, and both of them were well warmed up for the coming day. Cordoc rolled his arm and tilted his head. Their blood was boiling and both were eager to fight. Of the many spars they had fought, Selaphiel predominantly remained ahead of Cordoc.

He was sure that his brother was getting better with every time they met blades, which concerned him. Selaphiel smiled and closed his eyes. Cordoc chose to tilt his blade slightly, in a perfect position to block him if need be. Selaphiel grinned knowingly and moved forward at a slow pace. Cordoc had used this same stance several times prior in fights, and he was familiar with its use. Selaphiel changed the position of the wooden training sword to adapt. He knew this was his opportunity to take the offensive. As he moved, Cordoc's movements mirrored his, with a loud crack of wood.

"You're too quick," Selaphiel laughed.

Cordoc was a keen observer of most things, and he often caught on to more than even Selaphiel did in swordplay, even though he had a trained eye in swordsmanship himself.

With a blur of movement Selaphiel struck harshly, only to be countered by Cordoc's quickness. Selaphiel circled left and attempted another blow but found it equally unsuccessful. Within a few movements, the rest of the room was a blur to him and all Selaphiel focused on was the exchange of blows. Selaphiel exposed a weakness and was able to land a smack upon Cordoc's wrist. Cordoc's blue eyes squinted, and his mouth scrunched into a scowl. Selaphiel smiled and drove forward but was rewarded with an equivalent bruise on his own hand. Cordoc winked and pushed him back.

"Not so fast," Cordoc goaded.

"You keep getting better," Selaphiel said, acknowledging Cordoc's maneuver. "Eventually I am not going to be able to hit you."

"Can't have my younger brothers getting the best of me," Cordoc said as he glanced toward Jakobin.

"If this is your best, then I'm not worried," Jakobin said coolly from outside the ropes.

Selaphiel smiled cheerfully and called for shields from the attendant. The stout man handed them both shields, which they tightened with leather straps. Selaphiel tied his on as tight as it would allow without cutting off his circulation.

Cordoc shook his head, speaking softly, "Selaphiel, you may be better with a sword, but if I could have a bow …" he trailed off.

"I would look like a porcupine," Selaphiel said, finishing Cordoc's sentence. "However, we are not using bows," he added with a wink.

Cordoc rolled his eyes and lifted his shield. Selaphiel jabbed with his shield this time, pushing Cordoc, and with a swift movement he swung left, bouncing off Cordoc's shield and redirecting his sword to the right. With a narrow margin, Cordoc managed to block his sword with effort and a scowl.

"Too many times you have done this same move," Cordoc mocked. Selaphiel knew it wasn't so much an insult as it was an attempt to throw him off guard. He would not allow it to distract him.

Selaphiel shrugged and lifted his shield to block the swish of Cordoc's sword. Selaphiel doubled back, unable to make an offensive move and finding himself in a corner without room to spare. Selaphiel again took the offensive, pushing forward with his shield, and in one smooth motion, he landed another blow to Cordoc's wrist. He sighed in disappointment. This blow had won Selaphiel the spar. The attendant raised a hand toward Selaphiel. Jakobin clapped slowly, an unamused look on his face.

Cordoc wiped sweat from his brow and unfastened his shield, handing both sword and shield to the attendant. Selaphiel did the same. He struggled to suppress the grin that spread across his face.

"Good spar, Seph," Cordoc said.

Jakobin smiled. "Perhaps we will fight in the Ashen." His eyes flashed.

Selaphiel's eye brightened. "Our strengths complement each other; we are unstoppable when we are together." He and Cordoc grasped arms respectfully.

Jakobin smirked. "But in the Ashen, we will not be fighting beside each other," he said, pushing off the arena.

Cordoc nodded. "A truth for both," he said, examining his bruises. Both his and Selaphiel's arms were painted with fading marks.

The attendant chuckled. "My princes, you each did wonderfully. You are each beyond most of Lifesveil's swordsmen."

They valued these words, as he had trained each of them numerous times in the art of deflection, sword fighting, bow mastery, and other skills essential for those called into battle. Most importantly, though, he had taught them how to fight together, utilizing each other's strengths and covering for each other's weaknesses.

Cordoc bowed to Selaphiel, then to the attendant respectfully. "And a most wonderful teacher you have been."

Selaphiel agreed.

The attendant bowed back and said, "All three of you have my blessings, and I wish you the best of luck."

Cordoc again thanked him, and they moved into the outer hallway.

"At least I have a strategy for the tournament," Jakobin chuckled as they entered the hallway.

Selaphiel rolled his eyes. "So that is why you watched us."

"Always expect Jako to do something to benefit himself," Cordoc said mockingly. "Here I thought he was a fan of watching us clobber each other."

Jakobin looked at them both confidently. "As fun as that is, you can both laugh and make fun, but soon I will be wearing the mask of Archkyris. I won't have to try very hard to do it either."

"There are confident men and then there's Jakobin," Selaphiel laughed, realizing his statement rhymed.

Cordoc shook his head.

"Speaking of which," he said, turning to Selaphiel." "Which dragon mask will you take to represent you?"

Selaphiel shrugged. "I suppose I'll pick it according to the hue of my magic."

Cordoc turned to Jakobin. "What about you?"

"Red, of course."

"Well, I guess that leaves blue for me," Cordoc said. "We never really vary from what is normal. Maybe one day we will do something unexpected of us."

"Maybe," Jakobin said.

Zarx's muscular frame rounded the corner ahead of them, and upon seeing the princes, the general shook his head.

"Practicing even up until the tournament I see," he said with fondness.

"Well, one can never really be too prepared," Cordoc said, rubbing his arm where Selaphiel's blows had landed.

"Says the loser," Jakobin snickered. Cordoc furrowed his brow slightly as he glanced toward his brother.

Selaphiel shrugged.

Zarx grinned. "Well, you need to be with the others at the moment. The masks will be selected soon. Though I do not see them all being taken with only you three choosing them."

"Correctly said; they wait on us," Jakobin said as he walked through the foyer into the larger hall. The hall was decorated with awards and signs of tournaments won by the three princes in previous years. Shelves mounted on the walls held chalices and sculptures that had been awarded to them for their achievements. Most of the wall was covered with the names of Cordoc and Selaphiel. As the youngest, Jakobin's name appeared infrequently, but it was there.

Selaphiel noticed Jakobin looking at the wall as they walked. "Maybe this will be your year, Brother. There's always a chance …" he trailed off. Jakobin didn't reply, his face impassive.

Zarx waved them to the door leading outside. Selaphiel and Cordoc continued, the light making them squint, blinded for a moment. Four horses were tied outside the armory waiting for them. Jakobin had already slipped past the other three and untied the fourth horse. He mounted and took off, leaving a trail of dust behind him on the cobblestone road. The clop of his horse's hooves faded away quickly.

"Your brother is always overly eager, isn't he?" Zarx said, watching the dust swirl.

"Eh," Selaphiel said as he mounted the nearest horse. "Maybe sometimes."

"Always," Cordoc said, as he followed Selaphiel's action. With a huff Zarx also mounted his horse, a large coal-black stallion, which was adorned with white dragon embroidery and a golden talon insignia, representing the highest ranks in the military guard of Lifesveil.

The horses cantered one by one behind the other at a steady pace. The large, ornate temple of the Ashenborn loomed close by, its luminous white marble structure gleaming in the light of the sun, making it hard to look at. The expanse of courtyard that they were heading toward came into view, adorned with multiple flags representing different kingdoms.

The large white dragon of Archkyris was the largest, representing the rule of the High King. Below it flew the flag of Lifesveil, yellow with an eight-pointed silver star. The noise of the arena reached them, causing the horses to hesitate. The horses continued only at the urging of their riders. A loud trumpet called, and they were greeted by several Silver Talons, who bowed as they passed. The door to the inner court opened with a creak. Inside, they spotted Jakobin handing over the reins to his horse, with a satisfied look on his face. After the other three dismounted, servants took the horses. Zarx motioned toward another door to his left.

"This way. I will go now to sit by your father's side. The best of luck to each of you, and do us proud by at least one of you winning," Zarx said, grinning.

"Zarx is in rare form today," Cordoc said, not ever having seen Zarx so expressive.

"He's usually pretty bland, if you ask me," Selaphiel joked.

They entered the room and were embraced by the warmth of the inner quarters. The inner room was decorated with flags identical to those outside, each highlighted with torches. In the center were the masks of the Ashenborn Tournament, known as Ashenveil and reserved for princes or men of Lifesveil. Men stood lounging against the walls, whispering amongst themselves. The whispering stopped when the princes came in.

"Awkward," Selaphiel whispered.

"Anyone you recognize?" Jakobin asked, scanning the room.

Cordoc whispered, "There is Prince Thornbeorn of the northern kingdom of Wulvsbaen." He nodded toward a man with reddish hair and armor that had white fur garnishing it.

"Have you had any contact with him?" Jakobin asked.

"Only in dealings in diplomacy, but nothing so casual or interesting as this," Cordoc said.

"A strange man to wear fur in such a hot climate as Lifesveil," Jakobin said.

"They say ice runs through their veins," Selaphiel said.

Cordoc sighed. "Ice is a solid. Do you not remember our lessons?"

Selaphiel shrugged. "You know how people speak of old wives' tales. Besides, you act like I was not in those exhausting classes with you all these years."

Selaphiel shook his head with disgust. If there was one thing he hated, it was being cramped up in a small room for hours on end.

"People also say they do not feel pain, because the cold has frozen any feeling in them," Jakobin trailed off, a smile forming. "But that is lunacy of course."

Thornbeorn's gaze met theirs with a curt nod. The other attendants continued talking amongst themselves, seeming to no longer be interested in their presence. Every so often a glance would come their way, but they did not make much of it. The center table in the room held the eight dragon masks, each a different color. Each represented those of honor who had once inhabited Lifesveil. Red was once worn by Nathan The Strong; blue by Lekoan The Wise; brown by Galfik The Shield; purple by Goias The Mind; black by Kale The Merciful; gold by Sephora The Kind; green by Dragos The Healer; and finally silver by Tansae The Brave. Each were heroines or heros of the past who had crossed blades with Dothros and had died to protect others from the reaches of the darkness that would otherwise have swallowed all the kingdoms of Archkyris.

Cordoc went first, grabbing the blue dragon mask. The crowd looking around them whispered. Selaphiel grabbed the yellow-gold mask. Jakobin approached and grabbed the red mask, a serious look on his face. The remaining masks were removed, as only princes or men of Lifesveil could wear them. The ones unworn would be displayed as memorials for this special day.

The rest of the attendants carried their own masks, symbolic in some way of house or kingdom. The princes noticed men wearing skulls, a blue fox mask, and even one that appeared to be an owl mask. Selaphiel eyed his own mask suspiciously before strapping it on his head.

"I was worried that it would somehow make it hard to see, but there is not a problem," he said, moving the mask to ensure a snug fit.

Cordoc rubbed his finger across the blue mask and turned it around in his hands. With a loud trumpeting noise, the doors opened, and the light of day rushed into the room.

"Come forward," came the familiar voice of Alanias. They all filed out quietly, awkwardly bumping into one another.

After all the men had exited, the door swung closed behind them, a noise that could not be heard above the roar of people. Around 6,000 people from different kingdoms were housed in the upper seatings, and center was the throne of the king for observation of the events. Men and women cheered, making the air vibrate. The arena encircled them; the flags of Lifesveil decorated it. It stood massive, looking like a giant stone wheel.

"Welcome to the Ashenborn Festival," Alanias said vibrantly, his voice carrying from his throne.

"Today, we will celebrate the lives of the Ashenborn, and those who have given their lives to protect us." His voice continued to grow louder.

The crowd grew silent as Alanias spoke.

"Many know those who died to save us all, and their names are written upon the tapestries hung throughout our kingdom," he said, motioning toward various colored sigils.

"To be Ashenborn is to serve others, and to quench the flames of the wicked."

The crowd was silent, clinging to the aged king's words.

"My sons have chosen to honor them by wearing their masks, but I ask of you, how will you honor them? With just words? Or how we present ourselves with our own lives?"

Alanias smiled, his eyes slightly damp; emotion swelled within him, as his affection for all there could be felt.

"May your fires burn bright! Fight for honor outside of yourselves! Fight diligently for one another!"

The crowd roared, yelling the names of the men and women who had fallen. This was not just a festival for the Ashenborn but for all those who died giving their lives in any conflict.

Alanias closed his eyes for a moment.

"The one to win will receive the white dragon mask, which guarantees title and the promise of trial of Bright Flame, the most sacred ritual of our heroes and heroines."

Jakobin turned to Cordoc while eyeing the competition. "Who do you think will win?"

Cordoc ignored him, paying attention to his father's words.

Alanias cleared his throat.

"Derrick, our Ashenborn Elder, will read the names of those participating in the first round of competition."

The sky darkened as the dragon flew over the sun. The brown dragon glided over the crowds and landed beside Alanias with an earth-shaking thud. Flames flickered from its nostrils as it roared a trumpet of a growl. The dragon turned and spewed a large torrent of bright red flames. The crowd erupted in applause. The dragon began to shrink and within seconds reverted to his familiar human form with a blinding flash of light.

Derrick spoke, not appearing winded at all after his transformation. This was a sign of his power; young dragons needed time to recover after changing. He looked regal, his jeweled sword strapped to his side.

"On behalf of our King Alanias, and the High King Archkyris, we of Lifesveil welcome you to the Ashenveil."

The crowd cheered and clapped their excitement. Derrick paused to allow the noise to settle.

"The Ashenveil is held to celebrate those who gave their lives to protect us in the War of Stones. That was long ago, but it is still relevant to us now." Derrick paused and displayed the various masks, then spoke the name of each fallen Ashenborn that had not been selected by the princes. He recounted the sacrifices of the heroes and heroines of the past, and emphasized how they would be remembered. As he began to finish, his emotion was evident, and his eyes revealed that he had been around to live the stories he was telling.

"We have a free Yadir, and it should never be relinquished, nor should we ever forget the reason we celebrate. With that being said, I present your contestants!" Derrick announced, motioning toward the men in the arena.

The crowd thundered in response.

"The first competition is the crossing of steel. Contestants may not dismember or kill each other. Magical power is permissible, insofar as the same rules are followed. Any killing will be repaid blood for blood. I will see to that myself. Enjoy these matches!"

Derrick's voice echoed through the areana.

He motioned toward where the princes stood.

"The first two contestants are Prince Jakobin, who has chosen the Red Dragon, surname the Strong of Lifesveil. His opponent will be Prince Tsain of Mavet, bearing the skull and symbol of his kingdom."

"That was quick," Selaphiel said.

He was a little surprised that one of them had been chosen for the first fight. The royal horns and drums echoed the excitement in the air. He had hoped none of them would be the first to fight so they could size up the competition.

Jakobin strapped on his dragon mask and accepted a large two-handed sword. Jakobin's neck was tense. Tsain, a large muscular man with stark, silver hair, grabbed two large scimitars, one in each hand. He wore a mask that resembled a black skull with trees for horns. The trees looked as if they grew from the eye sockets of the skull, its roots grasping onto the inner eye. Both participants stepped into the center of the courtyard, and the remaining men were directed to stand on a railed ledge overlooking the scene. Alanias beamed with pride to see his son approach the arena. This meant just as much to him as it did to his sons. Jakobin looked toward his father and raised his sword to him. The crowd cheered in delight.

Jakobin lowered his shoulder and felt the weight of the sword in his hands. He let it rest for a moment and tightened his grip on the pommel. He lifted his sword above him and yelled. He turned to Tsain. He couldn't see the eyes of his opponent because they were hidden by the eye sockets of the black skull. The loud trumpet call sounded, signaling the beginning of the duel. Tsain moved forward clumsily, with raw power rather than skill at his disposal. The way he carried himself was familiar to Jakobin. Dozens of the guards and men he had trained with were less agile than he, and he could always determine by the way they walked how strong they were.

Jakobin couldn't help but notice that the veins in Tsain's neck were visible. With the first move, Tsain danced to his right with both scimitars coming from either side; with a quick side step Jakobin moved away from the blow, blocking the left weapon with a spark of steel. His hands jolted at the first impact. A cheer from the crowd echoed through the arena, even though to him it was a jumbled gargle.

Shaking off the blow, he swung with all his might, catching Tsain off guard only for a moment before he leaped out of reach.

"So much for brutish strength," Jakobin whispered bitterly.

Continuing his swings, Jakobin stepped forward. Tsain quickly crossed his blades in defense, blocking him, before pushing Jacobin backward, causing him to topple into the dirt. Dust floated around him. A downward slash from Tsain slammed against the side of his sword and held him in place. With a push he rolled away from it and moved into a crouching position.

Jakobin could feel how slow he was as he moved to reposition his sword. He could taste steel in his mouth.

"You shouldn't have used such a heavy weapon against me," Tsain said in a crisp foreign accent.

Jakobin laughed and dusted off his back, still able to hold up the sword with one arm, but the motion was nothing more than a feint. He had hoped to go a little longer, but he knew lighter weapons suited him.

"You would do better if you had two more. Besides it's not that heavy," Jakobin said as his magic flashed. Jakobin grabbed and twisted the pommel of his sword, causing the small divot in his blade and hilt to separate into a second smaller sword, which he then removed from the larger blade. Jakobin now had two swords, neither of which were compromised by the division.

Tsain snorted, "A well-crafted weapon. Very deceptive."

Jakobin swung the smaller of the blades around in a circle, making a whistling noise. Tsain sneered and lumbered forward. With a clank and spark from the blades, he pushed Jakobin again. The exchange was quick but ineffective for both. They both backed up and met each other blow for blow in a blur of motion.

Jakobin noticed that Tsain was slipping, and his clumsiness was more pronounced. Jakobin smiled confidently at the change of pace. With a quick correction, Jakobin swung his blades up, hitting the blades out of Tsain's hands completely. He nearly laughed as he imagined the expression beneath the mask. Before Tsain's swords had even settled on the ground a few feet away, Jakobin had already lowered his shoulder and knocked him to the ground. Tsain rolled with ease out of his reach and retrieved one of his swords.

"I had no idea Mavet has such strong swordsmen," Jakobin smiled.

The black skull mask tilted with amusement, clearly aware of the sarcastic nature of the comment.

"There are a few of us who are leagues above the others."

Jakobin rolled his eyes.

"So that makes you what, a foot above the ground?"

Tsain laughed deeply in response.

Jakobin repositioned his mask, which had slipped due to the sweat on his brow.

Tsain moved more smoothly as he walked toward him, holding the single sword.

Jacobin stood in a defensive position, blades along his forearms.

Tsain looked around him and stopped walking, his gaze on something in the crowd.

"Distracted?" Jakobin flicked his blades around.

Tsain moved clumsily into a run, his lips open in a silent roar.

The movement was slow, and Jacobin was able to manueaver under the first would-be strike and parry the second before ripping the sword from Tsain's hands, using both blades in opposite motions. His opponent fell, hard, to the ground.

Jakobin held his blades at Tsain's throat and heaved a sigh. The crowd erupted in cheers. Selaphiel yelled loudly above the others.

Tsain lay sprawled on the ground, removing his mask. Jakobin sheathed his blades and offered his hand. Tsain accepted it gratefully and stood up beside him. Looking at Tsain's face, Jakobin realized Tsain was around the age of Zarx.

"Good fight," Tsain said.

Jakobin nodded and shook Tsain's out-reached gauntlet. The grip was like a clamp, and he felt his fingers go numb. Cheers erupted from around them, the crowd was obviously pleased with the outcome. Tsain still clasped his hand, looking him hard in the face. Jakobin thought his fingers would be broken before he released them.

"Until next meeting," Tsain said, finally releasing Jakobin's hand.

The crowd cheered at the win. Jakobin bowed and could not remove the grin from his face. Cordoc tried not to appear too excited, a quality that seemed to be lost on Selaphiel, as he was jumping up and down. Tsain disappeared under the shadow of the arena, where healers checked him for injuries.

"This is exciting!" Selaphiel exclaimed.

The drums pounded again.

Cordoc chuckled; he could feel himself getting fired up, too.

Elder Derrick approached the upper arena, his hand outstretched toward Jakobin.

"The first round goes to Lifesveil's prince Jakobin." Derrick paused, allowing the crowd's cheers to die down in volume.

"Round Two will begin with yet another prince of our kingdom!"

Elder Derrick winked at Selaphiel.

"I think I am next," Selaphiel said, gripping the edge of the barrier anxiously.

"The next fighters will be Cordoc of Lifesveil, surname the Wise, and Thornbeorn of Wulvsbaen!" The crowd erupted in cheers again.

Selaphiel looked displeased. "Of course, and to think I held out hope I would fight a good opponent such as him."

Cordoc winked. "Perhaps some other time."

With agility, Cordoc jumped into the arena, landing lightly.

"Do not lose!" Selaphiel called down bitterly.

Cordoc shook his head; he knew how his brother often wanted to fight the best swordsmen to get better. He believed this was the reason Selaphiel often won when practicing with his brothers.

Thornbeorn descended the steps, sweat pouring from his forehead. He was garbed in fur armor but was not wearing a mask.

Cordoc noted this with amusement, thinking Thornbeorn's forehead was so shiny it reminded him of the morning sun. Thornbeorn walked unevenly until he was standing in the arena. The familiar pounding of the drums reached Cordoc.

"Why not remove your armor? Also, where is your mask?" Cordoc asked over the noise of the crowd.

Thornbeorn narrowed his eyes. "I cannot, as it has shrunk from the heat." He paused, adding, "As for the mask, I forgot it."

Cordoc laughed and shrugged.

Thornbeorn looked at him stoically.

Cordoc drew his blue-hued sword. It was decorated with ancient symbols and framed in cerulean.

Thornbeorn wiped away sweat, his face red.

"Shall I cut it off for you?" Cordoc said, pointing at the fur as the two men went to their separate fighting corners. He made a sawing motion with his sword.

Thornbeorn rolled his eyes and pulled off the sleeves of the fur he wore. He tossed the fur to the ground.

The starting horn sounded.

Thornbeorn drew a two-handed sword, which looked like a thick, curved icicle.

Cordoc looked down at his own sword and thought his resembled a twig compared to the branch Thornbeorn brandished.

The air seemed to cool off a bit, and Cordoc noticed he had started to shiver, a slight twitch in his arms. Thornbeorn's eyes turned an icy blue color, and what looked like steam rose from his muscles. Cordoc eyed him curiously.

"You have magical abilities as well?"

Thornbeorn smirked. "Does not everyone in Lifesveil?"

Cordoc looked stunned.

"Just a select few of you can use magic of this power, but all in Wulvsbaen can," Thornbeorn said.

Cordoc raised his weapon in front of himself challengingly, and with a burst of magic, an aura formed over his free arm. The air around his arm bent in extreme heat.

"Oh," Thornbeorn acknowledged, "I did not take you for someone who could do that. For many that is complicated to maintain."

Cordoc shifted his feet, the gravel moving noisily underneath him.

"All of my siblings can do this." He closed his eyes, feeling the warm energy rushing through him.

Thornbeorn looked more comfortable; his face had become a more normal shade, and he no longer had sweat beading on his forehead.

Cordoc noticed a chill in the air.

"A bit odd for it to be so cold all of a sudden," Cordoc said, knowing full well what was causing the coolness.

Thornbeorn raised an eyebrow.

"Yes, I am more accustomed to the cold. This sword is forged in the cold water of Wulvsbaen; it allows me to change the temperature at my leisure."

"Northern folks," Cordoc jested. "And here I thought you were doing it of your own ability."

Cordoc kicked up dust and brought the weight of his weapon toward Thornbeorn, who parried it without much effort. Thornbeorn snorted.

"It is of the highest quality. Also, I forged it."

They stood in a gridlock, Thornbeorn's teeth clenched. Their blades rattled as each pushed as hard as they could. Despite his aching muscles, Cordoc was pushed backward in a rough tumble.

"Nice sword, just saying," Thornbeorn said. "I know quality when I see it."

Cordoc wheeled around, nearly catching Thornbeorn by surprise, his movements quick and precise. Thornbeorn backed away a few steps, the scratches on his sword gleaming from the heat of the blows.

"H-how? There's no way you should be even able to scratch it!"

"You're not the only one with clever magic." Steam rose from Cordoc's sword. "Besides, my father gave me this sword. It was forged here, out of our kingdom's metals."

Thornbeorn stood his ground. He changed stances, raising his sword above his head, an offensive move known as the window guard.

Cordoc was familiar with the stance as Selaphiel used it often.

"No wonder Selaphiel was interested in fighting you," he whispered to himself.

"Fire and ice. A battle as old as time."

Cordoc squinted at Thornbeorn's words.

"You're not easy to please?" Thornbeorn asked, tilting his head.

"Just not a fan of clichés," Cordoc sighed.

"Well then …" Thornbeorn said, approaching him slowly. "Let's see how you deal with this cliché."

Cordoc placed his blade slanted across his chest, his other arm free.

"Come on then. If you think to prove me incapable," he said, smacking his chest challengingly.

Thornbeorn growled roughly.

With a great deal of effort, Thornbeorn vaulted toward him. He spun, displaying his back to Cordoc in what could be termed a hazardous move.

Cordoc smiled and moved forward, seizing the opportunity to strike Thornbeorn's back. He had mistaken Thornbeorn's speed, however, and met the familiar vibration of metal on metal, much to his surprise.

The crowd cheered at Thornbeorn's audacious move, then gasped as Cordoc nearly routed him.

"A dangerous maneuver," Cordoc panted.

Thornbeorn shrugged, a wild grin on his face. "The crowds tend to enjoy it."

"You are a glory hog then, I take it?" Cordoc asked.

"A what?"

"A type of pig that migrates south," Cordoc said, answering his rhetorical question.

Thornbeorn shook his head slowly, a small grin showing on his lips.

Cordoc waved his sword. Sparks skidded off his blade, and he drove forward.

"Agh," Thornbeorn sputtered.

They each parried and avoided lick after lick, neither gaining the edge on the other.

"We are well-matched," Cordoc said, his teeth clenched.

"Or we are neither very good," Thornbeorn winced.

"That's what I was thinking," Cordoc said.

Cordoc circled to the left, with Thornbeorn moving opposite him.

Thornbeorn moved first. Cordoc side-stepped the would-be knock-out blow, kicking Thornbeorn's feet out from under him. Thornbeorn fell like a bag of bricks, Cordoc noticed, but he nimbly regained his feet, avoiding a pin. Thornbeorn used his sword to vault forward, and laying the blade on the length of his forearm and across his elbow, he pointed at Cordoc.

"I will have to remember that little maneuver," Cordoc said, impressed.

"As I will yours," Thornbeorn said happily. Cordoc was glad to see Thornbeorn was enjoying the fight as much as he was.

"I would say I am third among my brothers with the blade. If you can't beat me easily, you'll struggle later on."

"You mean you are not the best? I was fooled," Thornbeorn said respectfully.

"I have my own talents, though. I hope you are a good bowman," Cordoc panted, out of breath.

"Not so much," Thornbeorn replied, out of breath as well. "I might as well just throw my sword than fire an arrow from a bow."

They both moved toward each other aggressively but paused at a strange noise from the stands that silenced everyone surrounding them. The sound made their hearts churn in their chests.

It sounded like a girl screaming, but they were unsure until more screams rose. Abandoning their fight, they turned and saw monstrous figures advancing through the stands.

CHAPTER 3
SERVANTS OF FIRE

———※———

Cordoc froze as he heard a yell from the crowd. At first it did not register, and people within the stands did not initially react, seeming to be searching for the source of the noise as well. Thornbeorn turned with a perplexed look on his face. Cordoc scanned the crowd slowly, unsure of what he was looking for. Screams rang out as a torrent of flame shot up into the air above them. A tall, dark figure with fire billowing from its mouth stood as the source of trouble.

Thornbeorn stood in shock, not sure what was going on.

More figures breathing fire emerged from the crowd. Cordoc did not know whether he was dreaming or if this was actually happening.

"What is going on?" Thornbeorn exclaimed, snapping Cordoc back into reality.

Selaphiel and Jakobin turned from the ledge and joined the guards heading toward the disruption. Panicked, people began to run from the courtyard. Lifesveil's guards assembled around the king in a quick and efficient formation. The princes looked around them but did not see any of the contestants hanging around to assist the guards.

"Cowards," Jakobin whispered under his breath as he ran toward the threat, angry that everyone around them had run.

A shrill scream erupted from the mouths of the fire-breathing creatures. The noise was unnatural, and it made his blood stab his veins like icy blades.

One of the creatures turned its gaze toward them and smiled a wicked, needled smile. It turned toward Selaphiel specifically, smiling wider. Its white eyes slowly faded to a coal black, with no visible pupils. Its eye sockets seemed to shrink into its face, which looked like that of a man who had never eaten food before, its skin wound tightly around its eye sockets. Selaphiel's stomach knotted at the sight. The creature looked demonic. He had heard stories but had never seen a creature like this before. For him, this was like seeing something out of a fairy tale, or worse yet, a nightmare.

"A Taneem," Selaphiel mouthed, suddenly realizing what stared back at him with soulless eyes. *But they're extinct,* he thought, stunned.

The guards around Alanias tightened and bellowed orders while moving the king toward the stronghold.

Reaching the creature that was staring at him, Selaphiel's eyes lit with magic as he drove his blade into the creature's throat, severing its head from its body. Its opaque purple blood flowed onto the ground, pooling near his feet. Zarx observed the swift beheading from the side of the courtyard, where he was protecting the king. His silver sword gleamed, unsheathed and ready to shed blood for the king's protection.

Cordoc had his bow trained on the creatures and began firing upon those who ventured too close to their father. He saw the creature fall before Selaphiel and made sure to keep his eyes moving in case he missed one.

"Guards! Get the people away from here! Jakobin and Selaphiel, move to Father!" Cordoc commanded.

He fired arrows that flamed blue as he gave directions. Alanias was pulled through the door by Derrick and Zarx, who stood beside it, ready to fight any of the creatures who dared to go near it.

"Silver Talons, to me!" Zarx yelled.

Members of the guard moved to assist Zarx, fighting desperately to reach him.

Selaphiel moved forward as well, his blood pounding in his ears. Jakobin struck a creature with his smaller blade, removing the cloak from its face in the process. The creature was transparent, its veins and internal organs visible through its pale skin. Selaphiel froze.

"How can this be?" he asked himself. The Taneem's eyes flicked white and a hissing noise escaped its mouth. "Get down!" Jakobin yelled as he ducked.

A sooty crimson flare erupted from the creature's mouth. Selaphiel narrowly ducked underneath it. He was astonished at his near death, if he had even touched the flame he would have been severely injured. His eyes burned as he felt the scalding air that surrounded the fire. A Silver Talon guard drove his blade into the back of the Taneem's neck while it was focused on Selaphiel. Fire bellowed from the new wound the guard had created, engulfing him in fiery light. The guard screamed as the fire engulfed him. Within a few seconds, the man's charred body ceased moving, the fire claiming him with its deadly embrace.

Selaphiel knew the man was dead and winced, looking away. He glanced at Cordoc, who continued firing arrows in quick succession at the remaining Taneems. Cordoc's bow had become covered in blue flames that moved along each arrow as they whisped and flicked the air. The fire from the bow cast a blueish shadow of a straight line beside him as two Taneems were dispatched. It was not often that Cordoc lost control of his magic, but the strain of using so much had made it hard to control.

Most of the people were now gone, and the brothers only needed to worry about the enemies among them. A large Taneem, around eight feet tall, called out in a deep voice. The sound commanded the monsters' attention. Cordoc drew another arrow and fired it at him. The beast lifted its palm. The wooden arrow shattered as it hit the invisible wall of the monster's magic.

Zarx strode forward, sword and shield in hand. Jakobin helped a woman up and pointed her toward a safe path to avoid the fighting. Tears streamed down her face as she hugged Jakobin. She then quickly moved back to her seat and pulled a little boy out from below. She picked him up and ran from the area, not looking back. The child was sobbing, his red face drenched in a mixture of soot and tears.

The remaining Taneems had gathered around the largest one, forming a circle as they snarled. Their stance was that of a pack of ravenous wolves, daring anyone to move closer. The arena was quiet as guards and princes alike made a half circle around them. Jakobin rejoined the group, his face twisted into a grimace.

Suddenly a roar filled the air and the loud sound of glass shattering echoed around them. Sunlight reflected shadows onto the ground in the shapes of large shards of glass. A dark dragon flew by them with a gust of wind, an explosion of air that shook the ground, giving off the sound of hundreds of cannons firing. The large Taneem smiled, looking in the direction of the noise. The remaining Taneems screeched. Selaphiel and his companions fought the urge to hold their ringing ears. The creatures' gaping mouths were filled with molten flame, and rivers of fire flowed from their open maws. The fire liquified and surrounded them in an impervious dome of flames and liquid fire. Selaphiel lost sight of them in the blistering heat and smoke they produced. The brothers and guards were each able to find a spot to hunker down as the monsters covered most of the courtyard in blistering heat and light.

Selaphiel coughed harshly, stumbling toward Derrick.

"No!" Elder Derrick yelled as he leaped into the air. Now in dragon form, he propelled himself from the earth with a great gust of speed. Selaphiel followed Derrick with his eyes, alarmed by the magnitude of Derrick's reaction. For Derrick to react so strongly was cause for worry.

"Archers! Fire volley!" Zarx yelled.

A flurry of arrows blackened the sky, striking the monsters with efficiency. Fire erupted from all directions from the new wounds on the necks of the Taneems. One spray of heat latched itself onto the general's shield. As Zarx threw his flaming shield to the ground, the smell of burned flesh reached Selaphiel.

Suddenly, the smoke disappeared and no live Taneem could be seen. The bodies of Taneems littered the ground, but the large one had disappeared. Cordoc kept his bow ready, scanning the area to be sure none were lurking in the shadows. Selaphiel and Jakobin made their way to Zarx. He looked confused and distressed, looking around as if he were not actually there.

"They used the fire and smoke as a means of escape," Cordoc said, sheathing his arrows angrily.

"Silver Talons," Selaphiel bellowed. "Bring healers and tend to the wounded!"

The men bowed and went about carrying out the command. The princes looked at Zarx, who threw down his sword. It skittered and skipped, a loud metallic noise.

"Send a message to the Ashenborn," he said in a shaky voice to a nearby Silver Talon, who hesitated but carried out the request, running to procure a scroll.

Jakobin looked around for Thornbeorn and Tsain, who were no longer in the courtyard. Cordoc and a few guards checked the bodies of the fallen Taneems, making sure they were dead. Water was fetched to quench the flames, which left black stains across the once white courtyard. The blood of the Taneems burned where it had spilled on the ground, and gallons of water were needed to quench the flames. Above them, the once-proud sigils of the kingdom were burned and torn. Jakobin drew his sword with a grit of his teeth, spotting a Taneem still breathing and clutching a seal with a royal symbol on it.

"I found one alive," Jakobin called behind him. Selaphiel stepped up beside him, and his eyes flashed dangerously.

The Taneem's eyes flicked open.

"Your eyes change and you're dead," Cordoc said, an arrow notched, catching them by surprise at how quickly he was behind them.

Selaphiel raised his hand, his palm beginning to cast a bronze aura.

"Why are you here?" Selaphiel said, hatred in his voice. The Taneem had a wound on its side, which was gushing flaming blood.

"To ..." its voice hissed, "deliver ... the good news." Blood seeped from its mouth as it spoke. The Taneem dropped a scroll from its claws. Jakobin picked it up carefully, keeping his eyes on the dying creature.

He unrolled the scroll and looked unsettled at what he read.

The Taneem's laugh filled its mouth with more blood. Its eyes began to shrink into its sockets, and its mouth remained open as it breathed its final breath. They each relaxed from their stiff positions. Cordoc swiftly shot an arrow through its skull for good measure. Selaphiel turned, a nauseated look on his face.

The creature's face shriveled, and it looked only slightly more dead than it had just moments before. Its eye sockets and skin began to droop. The air filled with an even more foul odor. The smell of the Taneem's lifeless corpse blended with the smell of burning bodies.

Cordoc motioned for Jakobin to hand him the parchment. He read it and handed it to Selaphiel silently. Selaphiel examined it but didn't say a word. There was only one line on the parchment.

Archkyris, the High King, is dead.

He handed it to General Zarx, who had watched the scene unfold. General Zarx's expression was bewildered as he rolled up the letter, now stained with the purple blood of the dead Taneem.

"What did it say?" a Silver Talon asked.

"It's not your concern," Zarx answered. "We will forward this to King Alanias. It is his information to disseminate if he so chooses."

Zarx turned and called to another Silver Talon, one less inquisitive. He gave him the letter and ordered him to take it to the king. "Do not, under any circumstances, barring a direct order from King Alanias himself, open and read this message. Insubordination will result in your death. Is that understood?"

The Silver Talon nodded hesitantly, unable to respond, not prepared to accept such a large responsibility. He took the letter, though, and left quickly. Zarx retrieved his sword and turned toward the remaining Silver Talons.

"Check everywhere to ensure there are no more of those monsters and be prepared to give aid to all injured."

"If we find any alive, shall we capture them and bring them in for more answers?" a Silver Talon questioned.

"No. If you find one alive, kill it without hesitation. You've seen what damage one can do. There would be no gain, only loss, in attempting to capture one."

Turning to Selaphiel, he said, "We shall meet within the inner court room with the king to discuss this."

Jakobin looked around. "Where are Tsain and Thornbeorn?" he asked. From behind him, a voice called out. Thornbeorn trudged up from the lower courtyard, his armor singed. He was favoring one arm and held a sword in the other.

"What happened?" Selaphiel said, running over to him.

Thornbeorn winced and leaned on his sword, breathing heavily.

"What happened, indeed," he asked, looking around wide-eyed at the damage from the battle.

"I left to follow Tsain. He murdered one of your guards from behind before leaving this assault. He seemed to be awfully calm as he left. I thought he was trying to save his own hide, but I was incredibly wrong."

He stopped to catch his breath.

"You may not believe me when I tell you this …"

"What?" Cordoc asked impatiently.

Thornbeorn swallowed, then continued. "His body turned into a dragon. And he lept into the air, flying toward the forest. I encountered several of those monsters. None of them attacked him. It was as if they did not see him at all."

Zarx's face was unnaturally pale.

"All I remember hearing was the shattering of glass and the Light Prison breaking into shards," Thornbeorn continued. "I could not make out entirely what happened, but I believe Tsain is the cause."

Zarx walked away briskly without a word, the cloak he wore flapping behind him. He exited the courtyard through the doors where the contestants had entered. The remaining Silver Talons followed him, unsure of what was going on.

"Those cowards who did not stand with us and fight will not be welcome here ever again," he muttered under his breath.

Cordoc looked concerned. Selaphiel's gaze followed Zarx as he left, an equally confused look on his face. Elder Derrick rejoined the group, dropping in as if out of thin air. His face showed his anguish.

Derrick walked over to the dead body of the Taneem and turned it over with the blade of his sword.

"So that's what they look like," Jakobin said, his voice trailing off. "We have heard stories of Father's conflict with them." The translucence of the creature began to fade, its hide turning an opaque purple and obscuring the internal organs from view. The Taneem's jaw looked out of place, giving it a more sinister appearance. Derrick looked at the creature, then struck the ground with his sword angrily.

"They look different this time, almost sickly. They are Taneemian none the less," Zarx growled.

Derrick made an angry motion in the air with an equally agitated and shocked expression.

"All of the prisoners have escaped," he said.

The shattered remains of the once great prison lay everywhere. Shards of light began to slowly fade in color to dark husks. The bodies of men who had died lay strewn across the desolate battlements. The prisoners' pods were emptied. They were now nothing but dark shells, their former luminescence gone.

Zarx's expression did not change as he examined the cells, checking to see if any prisoners remained or had been killed. Zarx and Cordoc had traveled to the prison, finding Tritus and Daemos alive, but both had been battered in the assault. Tritus had taken a serious laceration above his elbow from the shards of magic glass. Daemos had suffered minor physical injuries by comparison, but he was mumbling incoherently, apparently in shock. The sound of the massive prison shattering had caused both to become partially deaf.

"What did he see?" Cordoc asked, looking at Daemos.

Zarx shook his head. "Daemos is mumbling about a dragon ..." his voice trailed off.

Cordoc raised an eyebrow.

"Considering only the Ashenborn can become dragons, I'd say it's more likely he was hit in the head by a shard of the prison," Cordoc said, amused with himself.

Zarx remained stone-faced, unamused by Cordoc's jest.

"It matches what Thornbeorn said. Two witnesses agree. When Tritus can speak again, he will confirm it as well," Zarx said, grabbing a shard of glass. "The Ashenborn fear these prisoners; they would have never aided in releasing them."

"What of Elder Derrick?" Cordoc asked.

Zarx turned the shard over in his hand.

"He speaks with the king's council now but will arrive here shortly to see what we cannot." Zarx tossed the shard on the ground.

"The king—your father—is not pleased to hear of this news. For good reason at that."

Cordoc nodded. "Jakobin is in his counsel, and Selaphiel is aiding those who are injured. My brothers can quell my father's fears for the time being."

Zarx grimaced. "Alanias wishes that no one know of the message on that parchment. It would bring no good to spread something that cannot be verified as truth."

Cordoc nodded. "Will you search for the prisoners?"

Zarx shook his head. "Anything that was to be found would have been seen on the climb up here. Besides," he nodded toward his group of men standing guard on perimeter around them, "I am much more concerned about them finding us."

Cordoc scanned the area and observed approximately fifteen Silver Talons around them, spread out and in spots of tactical advantage. A few were perched in trees; most stood on the ground. Some had crossbows with arrows already notched, while some had their swords removed from sheaths. One of the Silver Talons sat on a rock. Zarx whistled a sharp, high-pitched note to get his attention. The Silver Talon looked at him nervously, for no one wanted to be called out by their general. Zarx glared at him, and the Silver Talon immediately stood.

"I am proud of you and your brothers," Zarx said, returning his gaze to Cordoc.

"You each stood your ground to fight those creatures. Others ran for cover. You ran to cover others. You have proven yourselves to me," Zarx said, his voice filled with pride. "Even if you did not complete the Ashen, you cannot be faulted for that. You have done better than that. You have shown yourselves brave in actual battle."

Cordoc shook his head. "It was nothing exceptional but was required of us. I hope anyone would do the same."

"Yeah, well, they did not," Zarx said, thinking of the many competitors, armed for battle, who had fled rather than stay and help protect the unarmed spectators.

The dragon form of Elder Derrick flew toward them with exceptional speed. When he landed, glass dust spiraled in all directions. Zarx and Cordoc covered their eyes to avoid having shards embedded in them.

"Must you always land so harshly," Zarx remarked.

The dragon snorted.

With a burst of light, the human form of Elder Derrick stood before them.

"Shall we?" Zarx looked at Derrick with what appeared to be a mixture of fear and annoyance.

Cordoc looked from Derrick and to Zarx.

"It will be alright, Zarx. We've made it through a lot, haven't we? Something as simple as another Taneemian attack can't be too disheartening," Cordoc consoled.

He understood the worry on Zarx's face, though. Zarx had dealt with conflicts and wars with extreme loss of life. He'd watched his own family be consumed by Taneems when he was only twelve years old. He was tough. It was no surprise he was the head of his father's guard.

This situation was different, though. Worse. They were now faced with the possibility of the kingdom's most terrifying enemies once vanquished, again becoming their greatest threat. No one had expected the dire situation they now faced. Everyone had believed the Light Prison would hold their enemies until the end of time itself.

Cordoc, Zarx, and Derrick finished climbing the set of stone steps leading up to the entrance of where the prison once stood. At the crest of the cliffside and steps, they stopped to examine the remains of what was once the most incredible and imposing structure in the realm. Broad, sizeable husks of former sunlight littered the ground. Although the structure was of unimaginable size, it now stood at half its height, with some areas completely leveled. Surprisingly, the different sections of the prison could still be made out. Areas where each prisoner had once been locked away were now destroyed, but the shells of the walls were partially intact.

"Nearly twenty-five years ago, Archkyris guaranteed the safety of everyone in Yadir when he used magic to encase the prisoners within walls of protection. These walls have now failed us," Derrick said.

It had been believed that the Light Prison was impenetrable. Alanias had told Cordoc of the Light Prison when he was younger. He had said that only the most horrid, depraved creatures were locked inside, and that no one ever be allowed in or out of their individual cells. Alanias had also told Cordoc that many believed the Light Prison had such power coursing through it that it prevented the beings inside from even moving, thus also slowing down their regular aging process.

Whether or not that was true though, no one really knew. The Light Prison was a secretive place. Information about it did not circulate amongst anyone but the High King and a few leaders of the lower kingdoms. Cordoc wasn't even sure if Alanias knew anything more than the legends of the Light Prison.

"How many guards stood watch over the prison?" Cordoc asked, directing the question to both Zarx and Derrick. He knew that Zarx was the head of the guard over the prison, but also that Derrick had been involved in overseeing the prison since it was formed.

Zarx wiped beads of sweat from his head with his forearm.

"There were only three guards posted to watch the prison at the time of the attack," Zarx said, his face turning red. His look of despair was replaced with one of anger.

"Agghh!" he bellowed as he kicked a piece of husk directly in front of him. "I knew something like this would happen! Did I not warn you, Derrick?"

Zarx shot Elder Derrick a look of distaste.

"I told you we needed more people to watch the prison, to keep something like this from happening. And you said no." Zarx turned toward Derrick, now pointing a finger in his direction. "You told me that, did you not? This is your fault!" Zarx exclaimed.

"I advised you that we needed to keep the number of people privy to the workings of the prison to a minimum," Derrick responded, unfazed by the sudden outburst.

"So are you agreeing that this is your fault, or no? You forced me to limit the number of guards when more precaution was needed."

Cordoc looked from one man to the other, disturbed by the direction of the conversation.

"The orders of the king are not to be ignored ..." Derrick said.

"Zarx, this isn't Derrick's fault any more or less than it is Father's," Cordoc interrupted. "How could we possibly have known what was going to happen here? Everyone thought the prison was secure and that nothing could change that."

"Let's go. We have work to do." Derrick spoke unemotionally. "We must save this useless banter for another time, General."

Cordoc had by this time stepped between Zarx and Derrick.

"May we continue what we came here to do?" Cordoc asked Zarx.

"Move," Zarx said as he shoved Cordoc out of his way with one arm. He had an anger in his eyes that Cordoc had not seen in him before. He stepped quickly toward Derrick, who had finally turned to fully face Zarx.

"Stop," Derrick ordered, his voice only slightly raised. "This is not wise."

A vein in Zarx's forehead bulged and his jaw muscles tightened.

"You are a general and I would not deem it wise for you to continue, less I have to dishonor you in front of your men," Derrick warned.

Zarx did not stop. Before Cordoc could regain his balance and intervene, Zarx reared back with his right fist and sent it directly at Derrick's face. Derrick's eyes flashed jaspar. He deflected the punch with his right forearm and swept Zarx's legs out from under him, using his own momentum against him. Zarx was thrown to the ground, landing heavily.

Derrick stood straight and turned to Zarx, who had rolled over on his back and sat up on the ground. Cordoc examined Zarx's face. It appeared the impact with the ground had knocked the anger out of him.

"Are you finished?" Derrick asked Zarx with a guarded expression. "Division between us is not something you want right now. It's not something any of us need."

Zarx remained silent, embarrassed as Derrick offered him his hand. Zarx ignored it and stood on his own. Cordoc knew Zarx was sometimes stubborn and prideful, but it wasn't often that he let his emotions overtake his reason. He knew he stood no chance against Derrick, even in a circumstance in which Derrick couldn't fight back. His power wasn't something any of them fully understood.

Derrick turned away, unaffected by the snub. He looked at the debris and stepped inside the entryway. Cordoc followed Derrick. He glanced behind him to see Zarx brushing dirt off his armor before following them in. The sun was setting, and they were losing daylight rapidly. If it became too dark, they would miss clues as to what happened and where the prison's occupants had gone.

There didn't appear much to see inside the prison. Eight cells, all similar in size, were barely discernible to Cordoc's untrained eyes. Derrick stepped over to one particular cell, looking grim.

"Elim," he said, his voice trailing off.

"What?" Cordoc had a puzzled look on his face.

Zarx shook his head.

"Elim was in this cell. A being capable of the greatest evil. He and Tsal had a wicked bond."

Elder Derrick grabbed the fragments in his hands; they lit up at his touch.

"Do you think that the message was correct?" Zarx asked, looking around, acting as though their earlier exchange had not occurred.

Elder Derrick sighed, a look of sadness on his face.

"The only way that the prison could have shattered is the death of Archkyris."

Cordoc's eyes widened.

"So it is true? How do you know?"

Elder Derrick shook his head.

"There is no doubt; the prison is our confirmation."

"Wouldn't a body be the only way to truly confirm that?" Zarx asked plainitively.

"Yes, but this is the same sort of discovery and irrefutable. This is as good as physical evidence," Derrick said quietly.

"Did you know him well?" Cordoc asked, sensing the tension building between the two men again.

"Yes," Derrick paused. "There never will be another like him. He ruled with all the qualities worthy of a High King. With his death, our protection from outside forces has fallen."

Derrick turned away from him, attempting to hide the fear in his eyes.

"And even from ourselves," he said under his breath.

"Magical stones, dragons, Light Prisons …" Zarx trailed off with a snort, noticing Elder Derrick's demeanor.

"You're afraid, aren't you?" Zarx prodded.

Derrick composed himself, turning back to them.

"This is more important than the miraculous; with the High King dead, word will spread even if we try to hide it. And without his leadership, the kingdoms will turn on one another, vying for position."

"Who is qualified to take the crown?" Cordoc asked.

"One of the kings will be elevated to that position, considering Archkyris never took a bride or begot children. It is more likely it will be taken by the sword."

"The sword?" Cordoc asked.

"He means war," Zarx said flatly.

"With Elim and his powerful allies free, the power struggle of kings, and the Taneemian back in the world, we face dark times," Derrick said grimly.

"The position of High King is not given. It is taken. Many will march on Archkyris' throne. Edywen, the kingdom to the east, will no doubt move first, as it should. Because of its proximity to the seat of the High King, Edywyn is chosen as protector of the throne, at least until the new High King is selected."

"But what of Elim? And the Taneemian? Even though they appear to be weakened at this time, they will reach full strength. Then what?" Zarx asked angrily. "Will anyone be concerned with that? An evil that devours everything in its path?"

Derrick pursed his lips and sighed.

"It is true that the Taneemian appear to be different than when we faced them in the past; much like the prisoners, they will regain their old strength once they have had enough time to rest. There is not much that can be done; I am afraid that no one will care about them for now," Derrick said. "Men would rather pursue power than acknowledge they are near their own destruction. But some will listen to reason. The Ashenborn will summon me soon, I hope, and they will establish a plan as to how to deal with this threat."

Zarx huffed and rolled his eyes.

"We have sent word to my brethren," Derrick continued. "Though they may not acknowledge my pleas and will probably regard my words as foolishness, especially in light of Archkyris' death. But I will find out how he died and what is to be done about the Taneemian."

"Who do you think released the prisoners?" Zarx spoke, sounding annoyed.

"Tsal, the war-criminal who escaped us all those years ago. He alone was not bound by the prison," Derrick said.

"Thornbeorn claimed that Tsain did it."

Derrick shook his head.

"He was not who he said he was. That was Tsal."

"Then we must pursue them!" Cordoc exclaimed. "You both surely know where they would have gone."

"No doubt to the Minos Isles, the last realm of Dothros," Derrick replied. "However, they are weak, and it will take days, maybe even weeks, to recover from the effects of the prison."

"Would this not be the best time to strike then?" Cordoc said, gripping the pommel of his sword.

"No," Derrick replied firmly.

"It would lead to our death," Zarx said, agreeing with Derrick. "The Minos Isles are harsh islands; raging storms and the ocean would stop us from pursuing them. The current season would not allow it."

"You're an Ashenborn! Surely these monsters are nothing to you," Cordoc said, standing taller.

Zarx looked over at Derrick, interested in his reply.

"I am Ashenborn, but I am only one. I am sad to say I would not be able to handle all of them," Derrick said. "Even in their weakened state."

Zarx looked at him, his eyes narrowed.

"Could you not call more of those dragon-men?" Zarx said sharply.

"The Ashenborn do not charge into a battle blind," Derrick began.

"They do not charge into battle at all anymore," Zarx interrupted.

Derrick gave him a warning look.

"You forget yourself, General. We are on the same side here; save your anger for more needed subjects," he said, visibly annoyed.

"The Ashenborn were once a great order," Derrick said, turning to Cordoc. "While it's true that all they do now is sit around arguing and eating, they are still powerful. We will need their help to destroy the Taneemian. If they will agree."

Cordoc bowed his head, "Elder, I am sorry for pushing you; I meant no offense."

Elder Derrick put his hand on Cordoc's shoulder.

"Cordoc, you have the best of intentions; these are troublesome times ahead. It is understandable."

Cordoc nodded.

"Zarx," Derrick said, turning back to the general. "The fact all of the prisoners were released means Elim will come for the kingdom of Lifesveil."

"Because Lifesveil enslaved them," Zarx replied. "I would expect no less of someone who wants revenge."

"How long do you think we have?" Cordoc asked.

"Not long enough, but one can only wonder at the effects of being in those cells for twenty-plus years. They will not move on us for some time, though I cannot say exactly how long. Tsal may have already prepared for attack in Elim's stead," Derrick answered. "The focus of his revenge will be Lifesveil, as Alanias was the one who killed Dothros, Elim's father."

"They will come from there," Derrick added, pointing south.

"The harsh environment makes the Minos Isles a good place for them to hide, and a perfect place to attack us from."

Derrick folded his arms, then continued.

"They chose the best time too, because this time of year the rain on the Minos Isles would make tracking impossible. Especially if they are not on foot …"

"You mean there are others besides Ashenborn who can turn into dragons?" Zarx asked.

"Now there are …" Derrick said, his voice trailing off. "I believed it to be impossible without dragon fragments. However, this attack has shown the Ashenborn are not the only ones who can control the dragon power anymore. And Dothros' old armies, the Taneemian, are behind Elim. Our enemy only grows stronger and more prepared as time passes."

"Do you think they killed Archkyris?" Cordoc asked.

"Carnivores separate herds to make it easier to capture each animal individually. I believe they killed him to throw this realm into disarray," Derrick said with certainty.

Zarx looked grim. He walked to the southern edge of the now broken Light Prison and peered over the edge.

"Zarx, inform me whatever added knowledge you discover," Derrick said, walking toward Cordoc.

Zarx snorted but continued to look toward the dimming light of the horizon.

"Cordoc, I will report our findings to the king. Bring your brothers to the Ashen Temple before first light," Derrick said.

With that, Derrick walked off the edge of the prison, falling into the open expanse; from a distance they saw him change into a topaz dragon and slowly glide into the wind. The dragon flapped several times, turning and heading in the direction of the kingdom's walls.

"Think wisely before you accept his offer," Zarx said.

Cordoc ran his fingers through his hair.

The Rite of Bright Flame? he wondered. *Is that what Derrick is planning?*

CHAPTER 4
OLD VOICES
SPEAK ANEW

———※———

Selaphiel stood outside the stone dwelling of the healer, his eyes burning from hours spent assisting the healer repair wounds. Father had often told them privilege did not disqualify the use of one's time, a sentiment he always took to heart no matter what it was that needed to be done. His heart was heavy, and he felt less kind than usual. The effects of seeing someone brutally die bothered him. His fingers were numb, and he was shaking. He himself had only killed large game such as deer or the occasional rabbit when hunting. He had often fought in tournaments, but he had never killed anyone before, and even though the dead had been Taneemian, it still bothered him. To see someone burn to death was a cruel memory, still as fresh as the fires that had caused it.

Selaphiel leaned on the wall and looked at the stars. He noted how silent they were, and that the world went on without his say-so. The sky was filled with celestial beings that were constant and silent. Selaphiel stretched his aching muscles and decided it was best to head to the castle as he was no longer needed by the healer. The only thing left to do now was to wait for healing to occur.

He imagined that most were asleep by now, and he let his magic guide him down the path back to the guarded gates. With a familiar noise, the large doors opened and he ascended the steps toward the royal chambers. Cordoc stood outside of his door, waiting patiently.

"Any news?" Selaphiel asked groggily.

"Yes, but that remains for us tomorrow. You don't look like you are in the mood for any new information. I will tell you though, that Derrick wishes us to meet with him in the temple at sunrise."

"All right, I'll be there. Thank you for keeping it to a minimum."

"None of us could handle any more tonight," Cordoc said, rubbing his neck.

Selaphiel opened his door.

"Selaphiel?"

"Yes?"

Cordoc hesitated.

"I saw how you reacted today. Are you okay?"

"Yeah," Selaphiel said. "I'll be okay. I'm just a little rattled."

"If you ever need to talk …" Cordoc trailed off. "Besides, this is not something that happens every day."

Selaphiel nodded. "Thank you, Brother; I'll be okay. I believe I need time to process it with an added bit of sleep," he said with a tired smile.

"Isn't that right," Cordoc said.

Selaphiel started, just now noticing the shadows under his brother's eyes. "Are you okay?"

Cordoc nodded. "Just tired."

Selaphiel understood that feeling.

"Have you heard from Jakobin?"

Cordoc smirked. "The sleepy-head fell asleep right after I told him about meeting Derrick in the morning."

Selaphiel grinned. "That sounds like him."

"Goodnight, Seph," Cordoc said, turning and letting out a yawn.

"Goodnight, Brother," he responded.

Selaphiel entered the room and closed the door behind him. He looked around at his room, lit by flickering torchlight. His room was medium-sized, plenty of space for his needs. He reached his hide-skin loft, untying the dagger he had on his side and tossing his leather tunic onto the floor nearby.

He lay on top of the bed. It was too warm for him to consider the fur sheets. He closed his eyes but inevitably lay looking at the tapestry on the ceiling. The stone columns appeared to weave back and forth in the firelight, making intricate patterns that he often followed with his eyes when he had trouble sleeping. He sighed, unhappy with his inability to fall asleep quickly.

"Jakobin can fall asleep without a second thought," Selaphiel said, laughing bitterly to himself.

When he closed his eyes, he saw nothing but blood and fire. He slowly moved to a sitting position on the side of the loft. He gripped the red wood posts, running his thumb up and down the smooth surface. Selaphiel stood up and grabbed a nearby pitcher of wine. He found a goblet and poured the rich, dark red liquid into it. The color made him wince, considering all he had seen today, but he drank it nonetheless. It was particularly bitter. He looked at it, displeased, but continued drinking. He suddenly realized that he had hardly drunk anything that day. Or eaten anything for that matter, he thought, as he turned to the bread and cheese that had been set out for him. He bit into this food hungrily.

A noise outside of the door interrupted his chewing. He froze. The scratching continued, and the door handle twisted noiselessly. Selaphiel swallowed, and felt the bread go down his throat awkwardly as he helped it with another sip of wine.

Selaphiel opened the door slowly, the door squeaking as it opened only a crack. He heard shuffling and hasty footsteps. He slung the door open forcefully as someone clumsily fled out of view.

He looked in the direction of the noise, attempting to make out whatever he had seen or heard. He wanted to pursue but knew he was weaponless. He went back inside, considered informing the guards, but instead felt for his dagger, placing it beside his bed. He realized that he would not get much sleep tonight. With a crack of flame, he summoned his magic. He considered going outside, but he was tired, so instead he lay in bed and and watched the door. His eyes were heavy, and he rubbed them. He blinked several times to clear his vision. The door rattled. He stood up, aggravated.

"Jakobin …" he muttered to himself.

Of everyone, he knew Jakobin enjoyed teasing him the most.

"It is late, and I've no time for your games."

He doubted himself for a minute, considering all that had happened. Even for Jakobin, this type of prank was out of place. He pressed his ear against the door.

He heard a low guttural noise. His eyes widened as he backed away from the door. The wood cracked and something pushed through, spewing splinters into the room. The large, needled mouth of the Taneem roared as bright, blinding flames erupted from between its jaws. Selaphiel yelled, desperately grabbing for any weapon he could get his hands on. The fire reached for him like long talons and wrapped around his throat.

He woke up in a cold sweat looking at the ceiling of his room.

He rubbed his face and breathed deeply into his hands, shaking and nauseated. He knew he would not sleep any more tonight.

"These are what are called the Ashenstones, or dragon fragments. They are the source of power for the Ashenborn. You each have your own magical abilities, but these stones enhance them and make them stronger."

Derrick walked with his hands behind his back, looking very scholarly.

"Magic allows you to conjure fire, weapons, heal the wounded, and even change the temperature of your surroundings. Before the War of Stones, magic had no bounds to what it could do. Magic could curse, decay, and entrap. Magic itself was crippled by Dothros, who sought to use magic to imitate the Ashenborn," Derrick said. "If not for the Ashenstones, magic itself would have left this world."

Derrick looked at his wrist.

"Dragons are often revered as the culmination of magic. In the realm of power, the dragon is unarguably the strongest compared to all other creatures. These living stones grant you power, a power that binds to you, lives in you, and transforms you."

He paused his step and looked at the three princes sternly.

"This is not something to be taken lightly. You will be changed forever because of this, if you so choose. There is no turning back. The Ashenborn have not spoken to give permission to the rite of Bright Flame. In exigent circumstances, sometimes action must be taken. I am Ashen Elder and regardless of personal consequence will perform it if you are willing."

He paused, adding, "Many will learn of my treason and call you terrible things because of what you will become …"

He gestured toward the brothers with his hand. "Well, what you must become.

"Each of you harbors individual powers that will manifest themselves in different ways. Your hues also have a lot to do with it. A yellow fragment for instance could be gold or bronze. It is up to the fragment to reveal itself. These are powers like you have never experienced. You all have magical abilities; they will be intensified."

His gaze scanned the princes' faces.

"What do you mean, powers?" Cordoc asked.

"The first is the dragon power; the other is an improvement upon your already learned abilities. For instance, Cordoc, you could have the power of foresight, or prophecy. Maybe even something never seen before. The possibilities are up to you."

"Prophecy? Like telling the future?"

"Yes, well, prophetic dragons usually are more complex than that, often having enhanced wisdom as well."

"What of Selaphiel?" Cordoc asked, guessing Selaphiel was anxiously waiting to ask that same question by the expression on his face. "Our hues are all different. Are you saying that our hues represent our characters?"

"Your soul, more like it. Your character is a part of your soul. Selaphiel and Jakobin will develop differently from you."

Derrick placed his hand on the center of his chest.

"It can be determined Selaphiel will be a truth-seeing dragon, also known as a Gwirion. Though you must realize there is more depth to this than just skimming over your latent powers. There is always more to a thing than can be seen on the surface. This is just the beginning. This will make you different in other ways that are hard to foresee."

"What about Jakobin?" Selaphiel asked.

"The power to see weakness, and to have strength because of it. A dragon of vigor, also known as a Chalus. A dangerous ability, but the fragments choose who is to wield each. Jakobin, if any should be on guard it is you." Derrick looked at him firmly.

"To see someone's weakness can tempt you. What takes true power is to realize people's strengths in spite of their weaknesses."

He paused, searching their faces.

"This goes for all of you. You can be blinded by relying just on yourselves; together you cannot be deceived easily. A rage of three cannot be fooled indeed," Derrick said poetically.

"Rage of three?" Jakobin asked.

"An old saying, meaning three dragons or Ashenborn will not be easily defeated. You see, three is a special number among the Elders. Just remember you have strength together."

He grinned.

"Now to a more interesting topic, the kindling."

"These words aren't very original. Everything is about fire or burning or flames," Cordoc said pointedly.

Derrick pursed his lips.

"Fire is the center of most things. Besides, would you prefer to call it the dragoning, or the giant lizard transformation?" Derrick smiled.

"Ignore Cordoc. What is the kindling?" Jakobin said, impatient as always.

Derrick cleared his throat, answering, "Your fragments, when bonded with you, embed themselves into you, becoming a part of you, until death would separate you. Their magic will never leave you until you no longer live in Yadir."

"What exactly does that mean?" Selaphiel said.

Elder Derrick rolled up the sleeve of his garment and reached his palm outward. His old brown eyes began to illuminate, changing to a topaz color, and shards of the same color shone brightly through his gauntlet. Tendrils of light wrapped around his shoulder.

"The fragments embed themselves into you, becoming the source of your power, as you will become aware once you have been bonded."

The fragment emerged from his skin, as if it were transparent.

"They can be removed if you will it."

The stone moved back without effort into his wrist.

"Guard yourself, as they can be removed by blade. Your magic should more than suffice to block such an attack, however."

Selaphiel looked on with wide eyes.

"I'm not so sure ..." he trailed off.

"Will it hurt?" Jakobin said.

"No, but I dare tell you it will be the most bewildering thing to ever occur to you. Also be warned: the dragon power has side effects," Derrick winked, rolling down his sleeve.

"The stones run out of power after an excess of use. Each person is different; you cannot compare yourselves to each other. Each has his own limits; this is humanity. The only way to revitalize a fragment is to place it in fire to rejuvenate its ability."

"What happens when they are emptied?" Cordoc asked, concerned.

Derrick rubbed his beard.

"The stones will dull to the color of stone, and if not rejuvenated, it will kill the bearer. If the person dies, the bond is broken. You must be sure not to allow this to happen. These are living stones, renewed daily by fire."

"How will we know when we have over used them?" Cordoc inquired.

"As you know," Derrick said, "Magic draws from your blood, and so does your Ashenstone. Magic draws from your stone first, then your own resources."

Derrick cleared his throat.

"Much like shakiness brought on by lack of food due to hunger, you will know the effects. Do not let this happen to you; death in this way is unquestionably painful."

Derrick clapped his hands.

"Your transformation will occur without warning. But after the first time, you will be able to control it on your own. Your abilities will manifest gradually, but then remain constant."

Derrick lifted a single finger, waving it in their faces.

"Beware of the dangers that come with it. To become something so powerful will initially feel bewildering, and your thoughts may be confused. You will gain better control with time. Beware of how powerful you will feel. The feral nature of a dragon will change the way you think. While a dragon you will feel more like a wild animal, and it may even spill into your humanity."

Derrick opened the clear chest and removed three glowing stones from within.

"Having heard all this," he said, turning to them, "What do you choose?"

The three stood silently.

Derrick sighed. "No one will blame you. But ignoring what's going on will shift the blame to us. Fighting darkness with the power we currently hold is a lost cause. I do not ask this of you lightly. Remember, through all of this, you will never be alone."

Selaphiel stepped forward first.

"What do we have to do?"

"Open your hands," Derrick said simply, "And prepare yourself."

The stones floated from his hands, a fragment landing in the palm of each of the three princes. The fragments were jagged and dull.

The three princes looked curiously at the fragments they held.

"Place your fragments under these vambraces." Derrick moved to help tie one onto each of their respective arms.

"I will now bind them with you. Prepare to feel a strange sensation."

Derrick touched his own vambrace and closed his eyes, murmuring quietly.

The stones shot streams of light around the vambraces and into their arms. Their eyes lit up. White flames floated in the air as what appeared to be waves of fire wrapped them in pearlescent light. Sparks skittered around them with the sounds of a crackling bonfire. The old temple shook, and dust floated into the air. Derrick was the only thing not moving. His eyes echoed power as orbs of white floated around him. As a final wave of fire subsided, the princes stood speechless. The white orbs floated all around them. They spun faster and faster, slowly separating into smaller and smaller orbs, until finally they disappeared altogether.

Derrick stood tall as his voice echoed with power. "You are Ashenborn," he said. "This final warning I must give to you. You have chosen a new life, one of sacrifice. Do not abuse it. Because time is of the essence, I cannot train you in the use of your new powers at this time. I wish we had the years you will need to completely learn all you must know. Once you become dragons, there will be more to be learned."

He added sorrowfully, "You do not have that luxury. Instead, you must learn as you are called upon."

Selaphiel turned abruptly as Jakobin popped his knuckles.

"Use the magic sparingly. The Taneems will definitely know who you are, and even more so now," Derrick said. "Use this power when nothing else is possible."

Selaphiel turned his arm, looking at the vambrace.

"Remember, you are now even more of a target than you were originally. There will be those who want to kill you because of what you possess. Guard your hearts earnestly. Each of you holds more importance than you know. When the time comes, I will teach you in more depth. I have simply prepared you for the basics. There will be more for you to experience before more can be taught."

"Are we the last ones to become Ashenborn?"

"No," Derrick said. "You are the first of a new covenant. More will follow after you, as times have changed. The time of our ritualistic and specific nature must change. The Ashenborn will die out unless we do something unselfishly. Believe me, the Ashenborn way of this ritual takes days."

"How will we know how to use these powers?" Cordoc said, still looking at his palms.

"I can only tell you my own. But that would not benefit you. We carry the same power; it will show itself to you more and more with time. I would be remiss not to talk to you about your enemy. You will be facing those who wished to dethrone the power of the Ashenborn, and the kings and queens who supported them.

"Alongside them are the treacherous monstrosities of the Taneemian. Few know this, but the Taneemian are not of this world, so in truth, they cannot be killed in this world. It is not to say they are immortal, but that we have discovered no way to kill them eternally. The Taneemian come from somewhere other than Yadir, though we do not know from where. That they bring their own back from the dead we only know from the return of those killed.

"You should have no fear of it affecting you, because you are Ashenborn, but know for the time being you will face something that cannot be killed, only contended with. The creatures fell when Dothros fell. There is the mystery. Since Dothros is no longer alive, we must discover what or who brings them to walk outside of the shadows."

"Tsal," Jakobin said angrily.

"How are they able to become dragons?" Selaphiel asked.

Derrick sighed, "A person can carry a sword, but that doesn't make him a master of the blade. Imitations will arise, much like has already occurred."

"So they are not as powerful?" Jakobin said with an air of confidence.

"No, fakes do more harm than good. However, imitating power eventually leads to power," Derrick said.

For several hours they discussed all that being an Ashenborn entailed, until Geoff delivered the news of their departure.

"I will teach you more," Elder Derrick said, "when time allows; now there is much for you each to learn without words."

They left the temple in silence, aware in themselves the privilege they carried. Jakobin was the first to leave them, eager to prepare for the coming journey.

Selaphiel and Cordoc watched as Jakobin went out of sight.

"A rage of three …" Selaphiel whispered.

Cordoc kept pace with him.

"Isn't a group of dragons a thunder?"

Selaphiel shrugged. "Either sounds equally intimidating."

———— ❉ ————

Alanias took a deep breath, flustered from lack of sleep. He was preparing to deliver a message, which he had with grief received. He had decided to deliver the news himself, rather than rely on a messenger. Men, women, and children by the thousands had gathered in the square of the mighty hold. The crowd was mostly silent, while a few whispered nervously. The royal purple of the king's clothes drew attention as he walked onto the parapet. The king approached the edge and stopped.

The crowd grew quiet as they noted his somber face. The king surveyed the people below him as he gathered his thoughts. He was disturbed by what he had learned and knew he could not relay the entire contents of the message.

"I have received word of a large horde of Taneems approaching from the plains of Syriane in the south." The old king spoke in an unexpectedly solid voice, which echoed with ease through the distance. His face was wrinkled, but his eyes, however, were full of reassurance, showing nothing but youthful endurance. King Alanias stood straight, taking in the looks of fright and shock. A nervous murmur ran through the crowd.

"No need to fear, my good people, for Lifesveil will prevail. We have all lived a life of plenty, but it is what we do with the plenty that truly matters," the king said as he lifted his right arm and pointed toward the rising sun.

"We have prepared for seasons of peace and war, and now is the time of war. Fight we must and fight we shall, and we are not alone. The world is full of our allies."

Alanias paused and smiled widely.

"We know our enemy, and the rumors are true. The Taneemian are back."

Alanias drew his sword and held it in front of him, silencing the rising sounds of the crowd.

"We cannot fear the darkness; the darkness must fear us. We put down this enemy before, and we will do it again. I give you this promise; if not in my lifetime, then the lifetime of my sons." Alanias' gaze swept across the crowd.

"We are well prepared; we are not a people to sit back idly and await the worst. We will fortify, and we will meet them."

Alanias nodded toward his royal guard, a tough armor-clad group of men who lined the city's massive walls. Adorning each of their cloaks was the familiar symbol.

"These men have stood the test of time throughout Lifesveil's history. They are our preservers, our protectors. They have experienced war and pain throughout their lives. They fight so that we may remain safe. We have no reason to fear the Taneemian, those desolate creatures, for these men are well-trained in the art of combat. But to ensure our survival and preservation, I am sending trusted men to the city of Malfait."

People chatted nervously, but many held onto his words.

"Birds cannot be sent, because this message requires the utmost care. If our enemy were to know our intentions, then more could die. Although we need not fear the Taneemian, we must remember their trickery and deceptive spirit. They are wicked beings that do not allow surrender. And they stop at nothing to accomplish what they are ordered to do and kill without restraint."

Alanias paused to allow them to take in his words. "Those who wish to send their loved ones to our secret holds and allies will be offered an escort with a medium-sized battalion of 300 of our well-seasoned men. As your king, I ask that the men who can wield a sword stay and fight. I demand however, that we be filled with courage and not fear. Pray for us all in this hour and do not think we will leave you in the dark."

With that, the king turned and walked back through the doorway of the castle.

Zarx stepped up to address the crowd. "In one hour's time, those wishing to fight must report to the inner courtyard to receive weapons and armor. Those who wish to find sanctuary should return to their own homes and await the call to leave. Remaining outside will only make you and your family an open target."

He paused, adding, "I leave you in this moment to consider your worth: will you hunker down, or will you fight beside me?"

Zarx turned and followed the king through the doorway, flanked by members of the royal guard.

The noise of the crowd rose as people began talking to their neighbors, discussing what they'd heard and considering their options. The sun filtered through the trees, lighting the courtyard irregularly as the crowd began to disperse, returning to their homes to prepare either to flee or fight.

Alanias fell into his golden throne and began to rub his temples. He waved off several servants who offered him assistance, taking instead a goblet of wine and drinking it thankfully.

Alanias stood up slowly and stepped down from his throne. He began to pace, wondering what would happen should the walls fail to hold back the Taneems. Surely, he thought, Lifesveil couldn't be overrun by even a large force. But what destruction would befall the city in the process of an attack? How many citizens, unprepared and undeserving, would suffer and die in the event the guard could not repel the coming attack?

Alanias scoffed at himself. It wasn't like him to doubt his military men. They had trained since they were young boys, learning the art of combat. Alanias even remembered the many early mornings when he'd awakened his own three boys just to go outside and train in the art of magic and sword. His two blood sons, Cordoc, the eldest, and Jakobin, the youngest, were noble and everything a father could hope for in a child. But Alanias' adopted son, Selaphiel, his middle child, was the most special to him. He knew the importance of honor, discipline, and integrity. Although Cordoc and Jakobin possessed these traits, Selaphiel never strayed from them. He worked twice as hard to gain his father's approval, though Alanias had never required that of him. Alanias did recognize, however, a nature within Selaphiel that made him a trustworthy and loyal heir.

Cordoc and Selaphiel entered, grim looks on their faces.

"So we're heading to Malfait then?" Cordoc asked, somewhat surprised he had even agreed to go in the first place.

"You and Selaphiel both know that the risk of loss is too great for us to not send for aid," Alanias replied in a serious tone. "If we do not get assistance from Malfait, Lifesveil may fall. You heard me attempt to reassure the people that everything will be fine. But if we don't get help, it is very possible that we will be unable to fend off an invasion."

Selaphiel shot his father a look of disbelief.

"You and General Zarx just assured the people that everything would be okay," Selaphiel said, his voice shaking. "Father, what's really going on?"

Zarx walked into the room briskly, shutting the door behind him to ensure that no one would overhear their conversation. He then approached the king and his sons.

"Your Majesty, you know that I support you and your judgment. But at this moment, I cannot tell you that I agree with sending your sons to Malfait. You and I both know the dangers that lie in just traveling to the city."

"I am aware of the risks," Alanias responded, his voice dangerously calm.

"But it's more than that, Your Majesty," Zarx said. "Would they not serve a greater purpose here, protecting this glorious city from the frontlines?"

Cordoc stared at Zarx, trying to understand his true motivation for keeping them here.

Alanias spoke forcefully. "I know what is best, General. I have been leading my men and my kingdom for many years now. Sending my sons to Malfait is the best way to show how serious the situation is, and how desperate it may become. Our allies will recognize our time of need and send us their aid."

"I'm just not sure that the situation is that desperate yet, Your Majesty. I believe we can handle the Taneems. We have many times before," Zarx said in an unsteady voice, his face betraying his unease. Something was bothering him, and Alanias noticed it.

"Besides," Zarx added, "With Derrick away to Aaish, we are more defenseless than is fitting to face them."

"I know. But we must make do with what we have."

Alanias spoke kindly to Zarx, as Zarx had been the age of Cordoc, Selaphiel, and Jakobin when the Taneems had shown themselves last time. They had all trained together, and Zarx came to his position as general for the king because of his friendly relationship to the king's sons and for his veracity and maturity in battle.

"I'm going to be straightforward with you, Your Majesty," Zarx said. "There's another problem." His eyes were rimmed in red and his face was pale, as if he'd not been able to get much sleep. Taking this observation in, Alanias began to worry.

"What is it?" Alanias said in a more urgent tone.

"We will be under attack shortly. You're ready and willing to send off Cordoc and Selaphiel to gain some reinforcements, but there's one problem. Jakobin is missing. No one knows when he left or where he went."

Alanias nodded. He had been informed of his son's disappearance.

"I have sent men to look into it but did not deem it necessary to tell anyone and cause more worry. Jakobin disappeared this morning after promising to go to Malfait." He paused and stared into the distance. The men around him gave him their full attention.

"Jakobin, I fear, took off without his brothers. His brothers are the most fit to find him." He looked at Zarx. "I have faith in that."

Alanias sighed.

"Selaphiel and Cordoc, this is why I am sending you to Malfait as well. You know Jakobin better than anyone. I know you will find him and ensure his safety. I fear the worst as the Taneemian presence is spreading like fire."

Alanias turned to Cordoc.

"Have I not taught you to use the bow?"

He turned to Selaphiel. "And you the art of the sword? I trust what has been instilled in you, and I want that to continue when I am dead and gone."

Cordoc's eyes widened.

"Surely, Father, you do not think Lifesveil will fall?"

Selaphiel remained silent, eyes wide.

"I have no doubts we will succeed with Zarx here. He has proven himself, as have you both," Alanias said. "But I want you to put what you have been taught into practice. Now is the time to do that."

Selaphiel's eyes misted over slightly. He blinked, then stepped forward, saying, "Father, what would you have us do?"

Alanias eyes hinted at tears.

"Find Jakobin and bring us aid."

Selaphiel and Cordoc bowed, both trying to hide the concern on their faces.

"I almost forgot," Alanias said, placing two flat pieces of what looked like mirrors on the table.

"These are windowspeaks. Derrick wanted you two and Zarx to have one so that he could communicate with you each step of the way. He was only able to make two with the remaining magic of the Light Prison. It seems even magic has its limits."

Selaphiel picked one of the pieces up and moved his fingers along its edges.

"How do we communicate with these?" he asked.

"Derrick said to state who you are and who you wish to speak to," Alainis replied.

Zarx picked up his piece of glass with a look of disgust.

"If it is of benefit, I will take it as the king commands." Zarx placed the fragment inside his cloak.

"I wish to speak with my sons alone for a moment, Zarx."

Zarx bowed without speaking and exited the room.

Alanias was quiet for a moment, as if searching for the right words.

"I am proud of all of my sons."

Alanias walked to them and smiled widely, a hint of tears visible at the corners of his eyes.

"You made your father proud by how you ran into the fight, and despite the danger surrounding you, each of you held your ground."

Alanias put a hand on each of their shoulders.

"You both are men; Jakobin also. I am glad to have been able to walk with you on your journey to becoming men. You will never truly know how much you are loved by me, and how I would never trade any of my time with you for anything else."

Alanias paused, fumbling for words, his face reddening with emotion.

"I know you will be safe. Remember to stay out of harm's way so you can return to me."

He pulled them into a hug. The embrace of a father.

———— ❋ ————

Cordoc and Selaphiel stood side by side, dressed for travel with packs on their backs. Zarx nodded toward the brothers as the men around them prepared to open a secret passage in the wall leading to the labyrinth of tunnels below the king's palace. Selaphiel looked at Cordoc.

"They will be okay, Brother. Zarx and our father are able to take care of themselves," Cordoc said.

Selaphiel's face was unreadable.

"Jakobin should be with us," Selaphiel finally said.

Zarx walked forward, giving instructions as if he hadn't heard their exchange.

"Follow the tunnel through until you reach the steps leading up to the trap door. It will be a lot smaller than you remember it." Zarx paused and gripped the hilt of his sword, remembering them as small boys playing in the tunnels.

"The tunnel is approximately two miles long, so you will end up just outside of the Legorith Mountains. There will be no light in the tunnels, so you will have to use your own," Zarx said.

"Take refuge at Delgraph for the night, then continue to Malfait in the morning. The city of Malfait is many leagues from Delgraph, so you may want to locate those horses you two are always leaving at the stables there. You never know who you might have to outrun …" Zarx trailed off.

The door of the secret passage groaned open, dust blowing out from the now visible cracks until before them stood a dark doorway just big enough for a single man to walk through.

"Take heed and know your family waits for your return."
With that, Zarx turned his back, hiding his emotion
from them.

"Zarx?" Selaphiel asked.

Zarx stopped midstep.

"Yes?"

"Do you hate us for choosing to be Ashenborn?"

Zarx sighed. "I may not approve, but you are both more
important than anything I might believe. You make your
own choices, and I will not hate you for them."

Selaphiel smiled. "Thank you."

Zarx nodded.

"Now go. Be safe."

Zarx disappeared around the corner.

Selaphiel let out a sigh and entered the darkness
with Cordoc.

"Do you think we should shed a little light on the subject?"
Selaphiel said as the door closed behind them, robbing the
tunnel of any light. Cordoc rolled his eyes, which could not
be seen in the dark, and laughed.

"When are you gonna stop saying that?" Cordoc lifted his
palm and and blue specks of light began to combine a few
inches above his hand until a fingertip-sized ball of light
hung suspended in air. The blue luminescence lit the tunnel
in the area they stood and a few feet ahead of them.

Cordoc turned, and the pupils of his eyes matched the color
of the sphere, his eyes and the flame both glowing blue.

"We must be going," he said, turning back toward the
tunnel. The walls around them were covered with moss, and
the air was humid and thick with condensation. The width
of the passage was ten feet from their shoulders and several

feet above their heads. The flickering blue flame made the moss appear to move as they passed. A rat ran between them, which did not seem to bother the two as they walked. Selaphiel merely looked at it and shook his head in disgust.

They walked for what seemed like miles, hearing nothing but the trickle of water and their footsteps, and seeing nothing except the occasional rat. Selaphiel stopped to wipe the sweat from his brow.

Suddenly he froze and squinted his eyes. Cordoc turned toward him.

"What is it?" he asked.

Selaphiel shook his head after a moment and shrugged, "I thought I heard something. It could just be the rats down here."

Corodoc shivered. "A very narrow passage to be talking about that," Cordoc said while staring ahead. Selaphiel's smile faded quickly as a scraping noise sounded ahead of them. They stopped just as the tunnel came from a curve to a straight-away in front of them.

Cordoc squinted into the darkness. "What was that?" He whispered, breathing at a slightly faster rate.

Selaphiel grabbed his hunting knife and stood beside Cordoc. Again, the scraping sound reached their ears.

"Send your light up the tunnel," Selaphiel said.

With the flick of his wrist, the suspended light shot forward, stopping several hundred feet ahead at a figure dressed all in black. The figure leaned against the wall, unmoving, but the sound of breathing became louder and faster.

The brothers stood frozen. Neither spoke. Selaphiel drew his sword and sent his own light to join Cordoc's. A light of neon blue and golden yellow filled the tunnel. The figure remained still.

Selaphiel held the blade with one hand in a defensive position and began to step forward. Cordoc shook his head.

"Not yet, Brother," he said, placing a hand on Selaphiel's shoulder. They watched for a minute more and, at Cordoc's nod, began to walk forward. They realized at the same time that the sound of breathing had stopped, and they soon realized what they were looking at was a newly dead body. Selaphiel pulled back the hood of the robe to reveal the face of a Taneem.

Selaphiel examined a wound on its chest. The wound was deep enough to kill, but there was no blood. Cordoc shook his head.

"Is this what was breathing?" Selaphiel said, unsure.

Cordoc shook his head uncertainly.

Selaphiel stared at the wound, finally saying, "Only one thing could have made a wound like that."

"Yes. Magic."

"Do you think it was Jakobin?" Selaphiel said hopefully.

"Let's hope so. Otherwise there may be more to worry about. Its breathing stopped as soon as we approached it," Cordoc said. "I think it just met its demise. This wound is obviously what killed it. It is cruel even for the Taneemian to allow something to die so painfully and slowly," he said, looking disgusted.

Selaphiel stood up straighter, now even more conscious of the possibility of other threats within the tunnel. He looked around, listening carefully.

"What if there are more of them?"

"Calm down, Brother," Cordoc spoke in a collected tone, seeming unworried by the Taneems or anything else that might await them in the tunnel.

"What are you talking about? That's a Taneem! In our tunnel! Who knows if there are more where that one came from!" Selaphiel said, raising his voice. "This could be a lot more trouble than you're considering …"

Cordoc's voice was relaxed as he replied. "It's okay, though. The Taneemian are our enemy. And something killed this one. You know, 'the enemy of my enemy is my friend' sort of thing."

Selaphiel seemed unsure. "Or the enemy of my enemy is just another enemy of our enemy and us …"

Cordoc chuckled to himself. "I think you should concede that you may be overthinking it a little."

"Maybe," Selaphiel admitted, but he remained alert, looking around carefully for evidence of other creatures.

"Would you do the honors?" Cordoc asked.

Selaphiel responded by stretching out his own hand, palm upward. Golden sparks jumped around above his palm, spinning around each other until a nearly solid sphere of light had been formed. The light projected along the walls of the tunnel, reaching far into its depths.

They continued walking, hoping that they would reach the end of the tunnel before sundown. There was no sign of how much time had already gone by. Delgraph would be a short walk from the end of the tunnel, but with Taneemian attacks becoming more and more frequent at night, being outside had become a dangerous prospect.

"I think we should relax a little when we arrive at Delgraph," Cordoc suggested, wanting to rest and perhaps get something to eat. The two had been walking for most of the day.

"Sounds fine to me. I could use something to drink, and definitely some food." Selaphiel's tone shifted into a more concerned voice. "Where do you think Jakobin is?"

Cordoc thought to himself. With all the trouble Jakobin had gotten into growing up, it wasn't unlike him to run away for a while and return with a cooler head. Often, Jakobin would run ahead of them no matter what they were doing, whether it be out of excitement or eagerness.

"Honestly? He could be anywhere. At this moment all I care about is the fact that we need to reach Malfait and retrieve help. Jakobin will show up eventually, as he always does. Father said he may have already taken the path we now take."

"So you're not worried?" Selaphiel seemed to relax some.

"No. It's not worth my time to worry," Cordoc said bluntly. "He has the same training and magic that we do. He can take care of himself."

Selaphiel nodded, realizing Cordoc was right. A short while later, they approached a set of stone steps. The walls narrowed as the steps twisted upward. Selaphiel nodded for Cordoc to go up first. Cordoc began climbing and got about twenty steps before hitting his head on the ceiling.

"Ouch!"

"Are you all right?" Selaphiel asked, holding his light a little higher to see Cordoc rubbing the top of his head.

"I'm fine; I just hit my head on the door."

"I'm not going to lie; that's pretty funny. You'll have a goose egg on your head soon enough," Selaphiel laughed.

"Yeah, yeah. Thanks."

Cordoc shook off the pain and pushed on the door above him. It was heavier than he remembered.

"Hey, I think there's something on top of the door. Come up here and help me push."

Selaphiel joined Cordoc at the top of the steps and put both hands up to the door above his head.

"Maybe you're just a little tired from walking?" Selaphiel joked. He pushed hard on the door himself, but it only shifted a small amount.

"All right," he said, defeated. "Let's open it together."

"You know I could have opened it if I had really tried," Cordoc said, enjoying himself.

He didn't like giving his younger brother the last word all the time, especially since Selaphiel was often right.

Both of them pushed on the door with all their strength. The door groaned and creaked, but eventually swung open and let in a rush of chilly air.

"Kill the light!" Cordoc said hastily. Selaphiel closed the hand the sparks had been circling above while placing his other hand over it. The light dimmed and vanished. Selaphiel suddenly realized why Cordoc had been so quick to command him.

As Zarx walked briskly down an alleyway near the palace, he looked around at the kingdom that held so many memories for him. He had spent more time in the palace than he had at home with his own family. This was where he had grown up. Cordoc, Selaphiel, and Jakobin were like brothers, and Alanias had welcomed him into their family. Alanias had even spent many evenings personally teaching Zarx the art of combat. Sword fighting was a skill that he had developed quickly, but he became a master of hand-to-hand combat. He remembered the day he turned fifteen and joined the first guard initiative. It had been a rapid process to find new recruits for Lifesveil's royal guard. Zarx was the most qualified member and the youngest to apply at the time.

He had advanced through the ranks quickly and made general at thirty, becoming like a big brother to the princes and well-respected by Alanias. To be made general so young was a privilege, and it was something that he continually worked to prove himself worthy of. He was respected among his men, and despite his sternness, they followed any and all orders he gave. He had ordered his men to capture a Taneem if possible, and their efforts had not been in vain. They had finally gotten one restrained. In other circumstances they would have killed it on sight, but Zarx had some questions.

"Geriff, hold him tightly," Zarx said, referring to the Taneem that lay bound, surrounded by several Silver Talons.

"You had better speak, or I will make sure you never speak again," Zarx said as he pulled a short blade from his hip.

The Taneem hissed.

"Now that is the sort of thing I was hoping you would not do." Zarx put the sword to its throat.

"Form a perimeter; I do not want anyone seeing us," Zarx said to the Silver Talons, who bowed and disappeared behind a building. Geriff remained, holding the ropes that bound the Taneem.

"Zarx of Lifesveil," the Taneem growled.

"There we go, useful conversation," Zarx said, lessening the pressure of the sword.

"Why are you and your kin in Lifesveil?" Zarx asked roughly.

The dark ugly eye sockets of the creature fully focused on him, a white speck appearing in them. Zarx could not help but notice that the Taneem looked healthier than the ones they had encountered at the Ashen.

"One change of color in your eyes and you will not live to regret it. We have enough experience with your kind to know your tricks."

The Taneem calmed down for a moment, unaware it was calling on magic.

"I have done this to catch your eye."

Zarx sniffed. "And you have my attention, but I am afraid you have gotten the wrong person's gaze. Do you mean to tell me you were intentionally captured?"

The creature cocked its head and smiled.

"Do you think your mortal men could restrain me if I did not wish to be?"

Zarx looked at it with repugnance.

"Do not flatter yourself. We have torn down many of your kind. Now what do you want? The kingdom? A truce? None of these will be granted."

The Taneem shook its head, blood oozing from the wound on its neck.

"There are those who wish to seek you as an ally," it said in its raspy voice.

"Anyone who is willing to side with you has nothing that I wish to possess," Zarx spat.

Geriff readjusted his grip on the ropes.

"Lifesveil need not fall," the Taneem said flatly.

"And it will never. Who speaks such bold words?" Zarx said, becoming annoyed. "Is it you or someone else?"

"Elim." The Taneem's eyes gleamed.

Zarx's eyes widened.

"Where is he?" Zarx snarled. "Where are the rest of those disgusting war criminals?"

His free hand tightened into a fist.

"Where they wish to be," the creature responded.

Zarx took the ropes binding the Taneem and held the creature before him. He grasped the sword in his other hand and placed it on the neck of the Taneem again.

"You think you can frighten a Taneem? If you kill me, I will be reborn again. You can never truly kill usssss," it hissed.

"Not as I hear it," Zarx said roughly. "Besides, if that is true, you will still be in tremendous pain."

The Taneem laughed.

Zarx threw the creature to the ground, knocking the breath out of it.

"Where can I find Elim?" Zarx walked to where he had thrown the creature. Geriff looked around nervously.

"The Light Prison. In two lights. The eve."

The Taneem spat blood.

"I suppose he wants us to meet in peace. Or is this a trap?" Zarx gritted his teeth, the muscles in his neck bulging.

"You can have your men to make you feel safe," the Taneem replied, cackling.

Zarx grimaced. "So be it. Tell Elim I will meet him."

The Taneem slowly rose as Zarx cut the cords of rope binding the monster.

"Geriff, follow him, and tell the Silver Talons to stand aside. Make sure it leaves without being seen. If it tries anything or even makes an improper movement, kill it." Zarx sheathed his sword angrily.

"A pleasure, Zarxsssss," the Taneem said rudely.

Zarx glared at the monster, contemplating killing it himself.

"Do not even lessen my name by putting it on your lips, creature."

The creature turned and disappeared in a quick movement.

"Why let it go?" Geriff asked, turning to follow.

"Because he has a message to deliver. And I want him followed. So go!"

———————✸———————

Sundown had come and gone. Cordoc and Selaphiel looked around, aided only by the light of the half moon. They stood at the base of cliffs, the doorway they had exited hidden among the boulders that surrounded them.

"We're behind schedule," Selaphiel said, stating the obvious. "We need to keep moving. If we don't reach Delgraph soon …" Selaphiel trailed off.

The wind was blowing gently, sending chills down Cordoc's and Selaphiel's spines.

"Yeah, we'll keep moving. But what happened here?" Cordoc asked. Selaphiel examined the area, not knowing what he was referring to. Then it hit him.

"This whole area," Selaphiel said, "it's been burned!"

Cordoc shushed him. Neither knew who or what might be nearby to hear them. The forest that grew up to the cliffs had been burned almost to the ground. Where once large oak trees and other plant life had grown, only charred rocks and the trunks of dead trees remained.

"Look," Cordoc said, pointing to a large rock lying beside the entrance to the tunnels. "Someone placed the boulder over the entrance. We used to hide the entrance with grass, branches, or roots, but after the forest burned, it must have revealed the stone door."

"And someone noticed it, and put a rock in front of it," Selaphiel finished. "Why would someone do that?"

"I'm less concerned about why than I am about who," Cordoc said thoughtfully. "Depending on who found it, it could be a penetrable weakness that Lifesveil isn't prepared for. That rock was big enough to hide the door completely, which means that whoever found the entrance didn't want anyone else to find it."

"And," Selaphiel said, "they may plan on coming back."

"Precisely. The other thing that strikes me is that boulder is rather large, and it took both of us to get the door open."

"So it probably took more than one person to place it there." Selaphiel shook his head, partly in worry, partly in wonder.

He struggled to understand what this information meant. "What are the ramifications of an enemy knowing the location of our backdoor entrance?"

Cordoc's lips were pursed, not really wanting to think about the dangers that could await Lifesveil if they didn't act quickly.

"Help me," he said. "We need to move the rock back. We can't let anyone else know that we know they know."

"What?" Selaphiel asked.

"Come on!" Cordoc urged.

They pushed the rock with all their weight and the rock slowly moved back into its original position. Cordoc found an unburned branch and brushed the sandy soil with it to hide the evidence of their exit.

"Let's get moving," Cordoc said, dropping the branch.

The two began trekking as quietly but as swiftly as possible through the blackened trees. Cordoc, Selaphiel, and Jakobin had grown up in these woods. They had shared many great memories here together, and its current state made the brothers sad. They had learned how to hunt, particularly larger animals such as bear and boar, and had each had their share of close brushes with death. They considered each other rivals as well as brothers and had built a close bond while learning new skills. It was like erasing a memory, seeing it so empty.

"I see some light ahead!" Selaphiel exclaimed, happy he didn't have to worry about a run-in with the Taneems that night.

"That's Delgraph for sure!" Cordoc said with just as much glee.

They picked up their pace, nearly tripping over roots and twigs as they approached the village. Delgraph wasn't the largest or wealthiest village in the area. Although it fell under the rule and protection of Malfait, it existed so far outside of the main kingdom that it was virtually unguarded. Malfait had made a pact with Lifesveil, whereby Lifesveil guarded Delgraph while being allowed to use it as a sort of outpost. Malfait was happy to agree to the pact.

However, Delgraph was a merchant village, and Malfait imposed steep taxes on the village residents. This meant that many merchants worked all day just to hand over much of their earnings to the kingdom. Although Alanias disagreed with such steep taxes, the benefit of having an outpost for his soldiers outweighed any political sway he might use to change things. It wasn't worth the risk of losing an alliance as important as this one. Malfait received added protection for Delgraph from Lifesveil, and Lifesveil received an outpost. Both viewed it as an equally rewarding deal.

Selaphiel stopped abruptly at the entrance to the village. It wasn't really a gated entrance, but rather an opening between two buildings where a well-worn path led into the village center. Selaphiel looked back and saw Cordoc just behind him. He could not recall a single race where Cordoc had beaten him. On foot, that is. Cordoc had a gift with horses.

Cordoc ran up to Selaphiel, stopping beside him. He adjusted his bow and the arrows that rested in a sheath on his back and placed a hand on the dagger on his belt.

A building stood on either side of the road at the village entrance, and a torch burned beside the buildings' doorways to give light to travelers and visitors. The brothers continued walking down the path toward the center, eager to get to the tower and deliver their message.

As they walked along, Cordoc thought about how proud he was of Selaphiel despite what they were going through. Although Selaphiel had been adopted, he knew that he was truly his brother. Cordoc trusted Selaphiel with his life and knew Selaphiel felt the same.

"Once we reach the tower and deliver the message, will we stay here for the night?" Selaphiel asked, hoping for food and rest before continuing their journey.

"Yeah. I think we should find some food and then maybe find a place to sleep. Perhaps we'll check in on Elgiri. Maybe he'll allow us to stay there," Cordoc said, smiling. "Elgiri is a little crazy. But that comes with the territory, I suppose."

"Definitely," Selaphiel nodded.

As they walked, they passed various stalls lining the street. Many had their own lights or torches to welcome visitors late at night, and men and women watched them hopefully as they made their way past. Unfortunately, many of the owners were forced to work at night as well since their daytime earnings were barely enough to meet the tax quota.

As they passed by, Selaphiel noted the goods in each stand. A jewelry cart contained beautiful sapphires and emeralds placed in artfully designed necklaces, bracelets, and rings. Another stand had multiple baskets of fruit, the majority of which were apples. The stand after that had linens and clothing, all handmade and of excellent quality. Each merchant stared at the passersby, smiling, willing them to come purchase something. It took some effort for Selaphiel not to stop.

Cordoc noticed his brother eyeing everything and said, "If you're that interested in buying something, we can stop by some other time."

Selaphiel laughed. "It's not about buying something. You and I both know we could buy everything they have with what's in my coin bag here," Selaphiel said, motioning to the bag hanging over his shoulder. "Sometimes I like to just stop and admire things. Particularly handmade things that take effort and care."

Cordoc respected Selaphiel for that. He had never known Selaphiel to use a fishing rod he hadn't made himself.

"All right. We'll take a look on our way back so you can drool over everything but not buy any of it."

Selaphiel smirked and adjusted the sword on his hip. Although it was heavy, he liked having it with him wherever he went, just in case. One never knew when the Taneems might be upon them. To be caught off-guard could be a death sentence, and their father had taught them to always be prepared. Always.

After walking for a few more minutes, the tower came into view.

"Care to race?" Cordoc asked Selaphiel.

"Care to make it a challenge?" Selaphiel jested. With that, the two took off running toward the tower.

When Cordoc finally caught up to Selaphiel at the base of the tower, Selaphiel began to reach for the bottom of the ladder. Looking up, he could see the many stars above him, and for a second he was lost in thought about the beauty of the night sky.

"Don't move!" A shout came from a few feet away, where two guards held Selaphiel and Cordoc in their crossbow sights.

A voice spoke harshly, "How dare you point those in the faces of Lifesveil's princes?" A man with short brown hair and a bushy beard appeared and spat toward the first voice.

Elgiri shoved one of the guards, who almost lost his balance.

"My Lords Cordoc and Selaphiel, a pleasure as always," Elgiri said while bowing slightly, holding the pommel of his sword. He waved off the guards, who stepped dutifully away from them. The one who'd been shoved glared before he moved away.

"What, my friends, has brought you here to my humble tower?"

"Our father has sent us to warn you of a Taneemian horde, and for us to garner aid for our kingdom from Malfait."

Elgiri scratched his beard and furrowed his eyebrows.

"He thinks it best for all of those of Malfait to take refuge in Lifesveil or to come to be escorted to a place of safety for the time being," Selaphiel continued.

Elgiri's facial expression remained unreadable as his eyes stared off into the distance.

"To think King Alanias would send those who cannot fight to another location is scary indeed. Does he believe he can win such a fight? Is not Lifesveil the safest? You speak of the Taneemian ..." Elgiri said, appearing unsurprised by their news.

Cordoc shook his head. "Taneems are moving in from— wait how did you know?"

Elgiri continued to look off into the distance, a look of concern on his face.

"Let's get inside," Selaphiel said. He stepped to the ladder, looking around as he did so, scanning the area for possible threats. He grabbed hold and began climbing, while Cordoc and Elgiri followed.

Halfway up the ladder, Elgiri called down to one of the guards standing at his post with his crossbow.

"Make haste and alert all members of the Guard. Tell them to identify anyone who is not showing his face in public. If Taneemian, kill them on sight. Check the south tower and be wary. After you have warned those on watch at the south tower, return here to report. Go!" Elgiri yelled.

"Yes sir!" the guard shouted, slinging his crossbow over his shoulder and taking off in the direction of the town's tavern. He was sure that was where many of the off-duty guards would be found at this time of night.

One by one, Selaphiel, Cordoc, and Elgiri reached the top, climbing up and entering the peak of the tower. The wind sent chills down their spines. Elgiri entered and closed the large, heavy wooden door behind them with a thud. He then maneuvered the locking mechanism into position so that no one could enter unannounced.

The tower itself was large, made mostly of wood but fortified with large stones securing each of the large posts that supported it. There were eight windows, two on each of the four walls. They were large enough to look out of and allow guardsmen to easily spot and repel attackers with crossbows and other tactics. Each window had a large piece of metal covering it, to block out enemy projectiles. The metal could easily be unlatched and allowed to fall, leaving the window open for the guardsmen within the tower. If it was ever necessary, there was also a balcony that encircled the tower at the top, which provided a view of everything within Delgraph.

"Have a seat," Elgiri said, breathing heavily. With a dark look on his face, he spoke. "I'm concerned about you two possibly having been followed here. You both know that they have an innate ability to track. Did either of you notice anyone suspicious on your way here?" Elgiri didn't have to explain who he was talking about. Cordoc and Selaphiel already knew.

Cordoc started, "I don't think we were followed …"

"But we don't know for sure," Selaphiel chimed in. "We made it to the outer reaches of Lifesveil, then continued through the forest until reaching Delgraph."

Selaphiel didn't mention the intricate tunnel system they had used to get to the forest. That was a closely guarded secret that very few knew about. Alanias had ordered Zarx,

Cordoc, Selaphiel, and Jakobin to never share the knowledge of the tunnels with anyone.

"Is it possible," Elgiri pondered aloud, "that they were waiting outside of Lifesveil and followed you once you left the city limits?"

Elgiri was anxious. It could be seen in his eyes and the tenseness of his body. Cordoc and Selaphiel trusted Elgiri. But he was a guard employed by Malfait to protect Malfait's interests in Delgraph. Certain things just could not be shared with him.

Cordoc spoke up. "I highly doubt that we were followed. I'll admit that two princes leaving the kingdom of Lifesveil to summon support from Malfait might draw some attention from the Taneems. But we have to expect that they're more focused on their impending assault on Lifesveil. Selaphiel and I are skilled at evasiveness. We can track very well and therefore know how to cover our trail. I'm fairly certain we weren't followed."

"So you covered your trail on the way to Delgraph then? No one knows you're here?" Elgiri asked, looking directly into Cordoc's eyes.

Cordoc sensed something odd about the way Elgiri posed his questions. "We didn't cover our trail on the way to Delgraph, no," he said. "Lifesveil's guard knows we're here, however, so I suppose someone knows we're here."

"Very well," Elgiri answered. "As long as you two are safe and weren't followed, I believe that Delgraph will be in good shape to sleep peacefully tonight. I'm sure you understand that you are both now officially under my protection as long as you remain in Delgraph. As confident as I am that you two can handle yourselves, the responsibility of protecting everyone in this town falls on my shoulders."

"We certainly appreciate that. Thank you," Selaphiel nodded.

"There is one pressing matter we hoped you could help us with. Have you spoken to Malfait recently?" Cordoc asked.

Elgiri scratched his beard, making a sandpaper-on-wood noise.

"Not currently. I am actually still awaiting payment from them. I have not spoken to my home kingdom in some time," Elgiri said. "Why do you ask?"

Cordoc shrugged and replied, "We haven't been able to find out if the Taneems have attacked there as well, or if it was only Lifesveil."

"I am sorry my princes, but I do not know. Communication has been patchy recently."

"We appreciate your hospitality regardless."

"Don't thank me, it's my job. And you are my dearest friends. You know we've taken good care of your horses since you were here last. It might be a good idea to take them on your trip to Malfait. You can get them in the morning from our stable. For now, how do you two feel about getting some food and then finding a nice place to rest till dawn? Obviously, your quarters will be free of charge."

"We couldn't impose," Cordoc began.

"I insist!" Elgiri urged. "Malfait has special coffers that it uses specifically to provide a place for its guests to stay. You two are guests, so you will be treated as such. No, you two are princes, so you will be treated as such!"

Cordoc and Selaphiel exchanged uncomfortable glances. They weren't always fond of the attention that being princes brought them.

"Well then, we graciously accept. Take us to your finest eatery, and if it is not to our satisfaction, we will order the cook to be executed at once!" Cordoc joked.

CHAPTER 5
A BARRED PATH

———※———

S elaphiel removed his sword and hung it on a post in the room. Rubbing his arms, he sat down on the cot. It was not overly comfortable, but it would do. The feast prepared for them had been plentiful and filling. Everyone had retreated to their rooms right after the meal. Nearly two hours had passed since midnight, and Selaphiel figured everyone else had fallen asleep by now. He laughed as he groaned, "I need to learn when to stop eating."

He lay back on the bed, not bothering to remove his tunic. In times like this it was best to be prepared. Cordoc's room was down the hall. These were probably quarters for higher-ranking guards, Selaphiel thought. The room was small but also large enough that it didn't feel cramped. There was no window, which bothered Selaphiel a little, as the outdoors were an important aspect of his life.

Concentrating hard, Selaphiel's eyes began to light up, until all parts of his eyes were bronze. He lifted his hand,

and several spheres of light drifted to the top of the room and began to spin. After a moment, the orbs split into dots the size of sand and hung at the same height on the ceiling.

"A replica of the sky when we arrived," he said. Their father had always taught them to be aware of their surroundings. He did not go as far as to recreate all the stars but had focused on the important ones, such as guiding stars that helped in determining location. He smiled as he closed his eyes.

He had been asleep for quite some time when a knock at the door made him sit up quickly.

"Who's there?" he said, standing quietly and stepping toward the door. He pinched himself to make sure he wasn't dreaming, remembering the nightmare he had had the night before they left Lifesveil. Cordoc responded in a hushed whisper. Selaphiel opened the door and motioned for Cordoc to enter.

"I believe Elgiri wishes to go with us," Cordoc said as he lit the torch near the doorway.

Selaphiel nodded and sat on the edge of the bed.

"Elgiri has always been the sort to want to provide help when it's needed. It's one of the many qualities I like about him. That and having that creature of a beard on his face."

Cordoc smiled and leaned on the wall. "It's kind of him, yes, but I think we need to travel alone. It may be wise to leave now."

Selaphiel looked around, his eyes landing nowhere in particular as he thought. Finally, he stood and fingered the sheath of his knife.

"Would it be wise regarding the Taneems? Father always warned that they could see in the dark. Any additional aid would be to our own benefit."

Cordoc shook his head. "I imagine the Taneems would not expect us to go out when they are most effective; besides I would not want to risk Elgiri's life or draw more attention to ourselves."

"They are not as strong as we are," Selaphiel spoke matter of factly. "They are not to be underestimated, though. Besides, I imagine word has already spread about princes here in Delgraph."

Cordoc stopped leaning on the wall. "This is true. But still, time is short. We need to get out of here and quickly. We must leave while they still think we are here, if word has traveled that fast."

"What about insulting the hospitality of Elgiri?" Selaphiel said. "He has given us food and a place to sleep without worry. I feel bad considering all he's done for us."

Cordoc nodded. "Maybe, but we must trade offense for the importance of Father's task."

Selaphiel finally shrugged, conceding the wisdom of his brother's words. "I guess it would make more sense to leave."

"We must take better care to not travel main roads, and we need to avoid obvious locations. We should cover our faces to hide our identities. We aren't wearing fine linens as someone would expect princes to wear, so our clothes won't give us away," Cordoc said.

Selaphiel looked at the alluring comfort of the bed. *Guess that will have to wait for later*, he thought.

"Why not let Elgiri come? If anyone is to come with us, he is the most trustworthy. He could be a vital ally."

Cordoc acknowledged this with a nod, adding, "The issue is, like you said, word of our arrival has likely reached wicked ears. Our best option is to leave without anyone knowing."

Selaphiel blinked. "You really took what Elgiri said to heart. He will find that ironic one day. Maybe not particularly funny though."

Selaphiel retrieved his weapons and placed them beside his cot.

"How do you presume we get by the guards?" He spoke knowing well his brother had already orchestrated a plan.

Cordoc smiled. "Elgiri is just down the hallway in his quarters, and he has his guards posted. There is a window that we could drop from. No visibility, especially in the dark."

Selaphiel strapped his weapons to his back as quietly as he could. "Our horses are here, Kira and Liene."

Selaphiel covered his face with the hood on his shoulders. Cordoc silently did as well.

Cordoc's eyes brightened at the mention of Liene, the horse he'd learned to ride on.

"I need to return to my room to retrieve my weapons. I will be only a moment."

Selaphiel adjusted his tunic and exited the room quietly. He watched warily as Cordoc silently walked down the hallway and into his room. Moments later he returned, giving him a signal of approval, his bow and arrows on his back and his sword at his waist. Selaphiel approached the window set in the wall and looked down into the darkness. He gently grabbed the window's lock and slid it open. He pushed the glass and it creaked on its hinges, causing him to squint his eyes and grit his teeth. Cordoc waved at him to continue.

Cordoc whispered, "I will go first, to check to see if there are any eyes watching."

A cool breeze crept through the window. With a step Cordoc was out of view. The wood creaked under his weight as he stood on the ledge.

"It is safe," was all he said.

Selaphiel climbed through and pulled the window closed behind him. Cordoc motioned down toward the route they would take. The narrow ledge led across the walls, with very little room for them to keep their chests to it. Luckily for them, Cordoc thought, the torches below were too far away to illuminate them. Pointing down, Cordoc motioned to the stables and a convenient placement of hay bales. Cordoc jumped down onto the bales of hay and rolled easily onto his feet, stepping into the shadows at the side of the stable. Selaphiel mirrored his movement, then suddenly ducked behind the pile of hay.

Cordoc's eyes widened and Selaphiel froze. A guard walked up to the hay bales, a torch in his hand. The guard looked at it suspiciously and rubbed his eyes. Hours of watching in the darkness had left him tired and may have made him think the dark was playing tricks on him. The brothers held their breath, not daring to move. The soft thump of the guard's metal shoes let them know he had left. Selaphiel peeked out, then joined Cordoc, patting him on the shoulder as they entered the stables.

"We hadn't anticipated guards at the stables," Selaphiel said in a whisper.

Cordoc shrugged and opened the doors quietly. Torches lined the walls. No guards were inside. Selaphiel located Kira, a dark red stallion both muscular and tall, and began strapping items on him, along with a saddle. Cordoc did the same, finding Liene, a silver-gray mare that had seen battle as many times as Cordoc. Cordoc and Selaphiel began leading them out of the stable by their reins. The horses whinnied, excited by the unusual activity.

"You'd better keep your horse quiet or we'll be found out for sure, Selaphiel," Cordoc joked, trying to quiet his own horse. As they reached the wooden gate, Cordoc noticed a cart stopped near one of the other stalls. He walked Liene over to the cart and noticed a few apples resting on top of what appeared in the darkness to be hay.

"You know, these apples were meant for the horses," Cordoc said as he grabbed the few that remained in the cart and placed them in a satchel hanging on Liene's saddle.

"Are you finished yet?" Selaphiel whispered, annoyed. "We really need to move."

He glanced around the stable and realized that there weren't any horses belonging to the guards in the stalls. Selaphiel assumed they were out on patrol or maybe making a trip to Malfait. Either way, it didn't concern him.

"Let's go," Cordoc said. He petted Liene and led her out of the stable.

The two horses quieted down a bit as they walked down a short dirt path leading to the main road through Delgraph. They had somehow managed to avoid any interference from the guards. Selaphiel hoped that no one would bother to check in on them while they slept. Selaphiel felt a little bad about leaving on such short notice, without properly thanking Elgiri for his hospitality. Noticing his downcast face, Cordoc patted him on the back.

"Don't worry, Brother. Elgiri knows we'll be back for a visit soon enough. Besides, he knows we can't stay in one place for too long."

Selaphiel gave Cordoc a genuine smile, grateful that his brother had a way of making him feel better.

When they made it to the main road, they both swiftly mounted the horses with ease. Both Kira and Liene seemed jittery and excited to be ridden, so Cordoc and Selaphiel urged them down the road at a brisk pace. Before long, they had reached Delgraph's city gates. Without hesitating, Cordoc pushed Liene to pick up the pace, flying through the gates. Selaphiel did the same with Kira. They were finally directly enroute to Malfait, and time was of the essence.

Trees were a blur in the dead of night. Neither of them dared use their magic for fear of being spotted or sensed. They had been riding for a few hours, and the forest around them began to thicken with briars and fallen trees. Selaphiel led and Cordoc brought up the rear. Cordoc was the better rider, but he had his bow, so the brothers had agreed that he should be in the rear in case of pursuers. Selaphiel shivered and spurred on Kira, was just fast enough to stay a few feet ahead of Liene. The muffled clop of hooves was the only noise that sounded through the woods. They would reach the end of the forest soon.

Selaphiel held his hand up and came to a slow trot before dismounting. He tied the reins of his horse on a nearby oak branch and walked to the edge of the thinning trees. In the distance was a fire, with several men surrounding it. He could not make out who they were. He returned to Cordoc, who sat with his bow resting on his arm.

"Anything of interest?" Cordoc asked as he drew an arrow, lightly tapping the sharp edge.

"A group of men around a fire, a camp. The path we took was anticipated," Selaphiel said and folded his arms in thought.

"They must not have expected us at night." Cordoc smiled, pleased with himself.

"There is no way around it without them seeing us," Selaphiel stated.

"If we must, we must." Cordoc walked stealthily to the edge of the woods. Some men sat around the fire in dark red robes. Others were sleeping. One man in particular caught his eye. The man was tall, and significantly tall at that. It made Selaphiel feel short by comparison and that was no easy thing to do.

"I see ten altogether," Cordoc whispered.

"How should we approach this?" Selaphiel asked while he studied them. The glow of the scarlet flames entranced him.

"Does that fire look an odd color to you?"

"I'm not sure. I'm going to sneak up and see what I can find out." Cordoc pointed to several tents scattered around the fire.

Selaphiel acknowledged him and pointed toward a closer spot behind a cluster of trees, where he could watch but would not be visible. After settling Selaphiel and the horses in the cluster of trees, Cordoc crouched and made it to the tents unseen. A slight twitching movement from one of the sleeping men alarmed Selaphiel and caused Cordoc to stop. The tallest man stood up and the rest followed.

Selaphiel grasped his sword tighter. The tallest man waved several of the other men toward the tents. Cordoc remained frozen, staying unseen even when they passed within a few feet of where he was. The tall man pointed more men toward the space between Selaphiel's hiding place and the encampment. That left three men and the tall man at the fire.

The way the men walked was awkward, as if they were extremely stiff. And the glint of the fire on their faces interested Selaphiel. It was almost as if they were wearing masks made of metal.

Cordoc stayed frozen, breathing shallowly. These were not men, he realized. They wore masks to guard the true horror of their monstrous faces. They had stumbled on a small group of Taneems. Cordoc was not surprised, considering what they had dealt with before. Cordoc shivered. The tall Taneem wore a mask that covered the top portion of the creature's face, hiding its eyes but not the needle-like teeth and thin-lipped mouth. The mask was decorated with mandibles like an insect that stretched down either side of its cheekbones. Each of the others wore similar masks. The tall creature gurgled, "They will be here tomorrow."

Cordoc remembered this voice with a silent scowl.

Another creature responded in a shrill voice, "The princes will not be expecting such a welcoming party. Especially since we donned these clothes."

The other Taneem spoke, calling the tallest creature Belial.

Belial stood up straighter and tightened his clawed fists.

"No one is to sleep any longer. I want constant attention to this path."

Belial's extraordinarily long fingers twitched. His terrible appearance was only second to his presence and the air it carried. His face was crooked, and his eyes had no color in them. His skin was translucent, like all Taneemian. The veins and arteries pumping blood were visible, along with the major organs and their processes. He was uglier than the rest and more menacing. Belial strapped on a curved sword with spikes protruding from the blade side, a cruel blood-stained silver. He displayed a disturbing smile. Or what could pass as one.

Cordoc moved as quietly as he could back into position with Selaphiel.

"That's the same Taneem from the Ashen."

"Oh, great," Selaphiel said sarcastically.

"We'd better make a move fast, or they might hear the sound of our horses," Selaphiel cautioned in a quiet, nearly inaudible tone. "Especially considering how dangerous that one is," he added.

"We need to separate them. There are ten of them, not counting any that may be inside the tents. If we can separate them, we may be able to scatter them so we can go through." Cordoc spoke just as softly as Selaphiel.

"Shouldn't we find another route?" Selaphiel asked.

"We have no choice," Cordoc replied. "The best way to Malfait is through this pass, because going around would cost us several days."

Selaphiel looked hesitant.

"But Belial …" Selaphiel said, trailing off. "So much for not making our presence known," he finished, realizing they did not have much choice.

They both agreed Cordoc would fire one arrow with his bow from the shelter of the woods, drawing them over, while Selaphiel snuck around the tents and maneuvered out of sight. After that, Selaphiel would provide a second distraction so they both could move in the direction of their horses, giving them a quick escape. They decided their signal would be Selaphiel unsheathing his sword.

"Would it not be better to ride through them?" Selaphiel said, again doubting the idea.

"They can breathe fire, and we are riding sausages with legs," Cordoc said. "Our horses would be horse soup along with ourselves as additional ingredients if we tried that."

Selaphiel scrunched up his nose at the thought of cooked horse meat.

"Just come on. We have no time to discuss this any further," Cordoc said.

Selaphiel got into position and drew his short sword. Cordoc nodded and released an arrow of blue fire.

The arrow whisked through the air and the moment it came into contact with the Taneemian camp, it burst into an inferno of sapphire-colored flames. Cordoc winced as Selaphiel ran quickly behind the tents. The explosion had disoriented the Taneems. They moved around like furious ants whose dirt hill had been disturbed. Several Taneems were wounded by the fire.

"Search the forest!" Belial called out.

Several of those not burned ran wildly into the woods. Selaphiel narrowly slid behind one of the tents before the small garrison ran by him. He breathed a sigh of relief.

Cordoc watched as Selaphiel eyed his position warningly. Cordoc knew Selaphiel could not see him but knew where he was. He had picked a thicket, a dense one at that. The Taneems growled shrilly as they lightly walked over the pine needles around him. He held his breath. He could not help but notice how the Taneems made no noise when they walked. He could see them better now. They each wore masks that resembled different types of arachnids or insects. He even thought he saw a mask that looked like an assassin bug, a long spear-like appendage drooping from the jaw.

Cordoc turned back to Selaphiel, who watched intently. Selaphiel had cut a hole into the tent with his blade and nodded toward Cordoc. Selaphiel's palm glowed dully, and he slightly raised it toward Cordoc's position. With a flick of his wrist, a ball of gold tumbled through the forest and landed a hundred or so feet from Selaphiel. The forest was alight in golden flames. Selaphiel slipped into the tent soundlessly as the Taneems turned and headed to the new source of fire. Cordoc watched as they went out of view. And suddenly he noticed that Belial was nowhere to be seen.

"Where did he go?" he mouthed to himself.

He heard rustling behind him. He felt breath on his neck. Chills went through him as he closed his eyes, trying not to move.

"There you are," the deep, familiar voice growled.

Long, skinny, clawed fingers wrapped around his face and pulled him out of the brush. He felt his neck pop from the sudden jerk of motion. Goosebumps popped up on Cordoc's skin as a wave of fear washed over him.

"Snakes only make noise before they strike," the voice said from behind him. The fingers released him and tossed him to the ground.

"How much of a fool do you think I am?"

Belial held his jagged sword to Cordoc's chest.

"To think you could distract me like some dog," he rumbled.

Cordoc coughed and let his arms lie beside him limply.

"Oh, hey there," Cordoc said, trying not to look scared.

"Greetings, little prince," Belial said, his thin-lipped grin showing his viperous teeth.

"Let me go, and you will live," Cordoc challenged, trying his best not to look toward where Selaphiel was hiding as he scooted himself backward.

Belial cackled. "Ah, so it's as simple as that, is it?" he said, stepping forward and again placing the tip of his sword to Cordoc's chest.

"Yes. It's that simple," Cordoc said confidently, moving slightly.

"Oh?" Belial narrowed his eyes. "Such bold words for someone with such small odds of living."

A blinding gold light burst upward in the distance, and the screech of Taneems filled the air. Belial did not move his attention off Cordoc.

"So you aren't alone," Belial snorted.

The golden light illuminated his sinister features, his white eyes threatening to give way to fire at any moment.

"Tell me, prince of flesh, why shouldn't I burn you until I see nothing but a pile of charred bones?" Belial spat.

Cordoc shrugged. "It would make it easier if you let me go. Besides I'd rather you tell me a reason." Cordoc could feel a lump forming in his throat.

"Or…" Belial pressed down harder as Cordoc grunted, "I skewer you before they arrive. You give me no good reason as to why you should be left breathing."

Cordoc eyed the wound left by the sword; it was minor but uncomfortable.

Belial sniffed. "Selaphiel. So it's just two of you. Odd of Alanias to send such a small group."

A ball of flame exploded into Belial's face, making him tumble over violently with a roar of displeasure.

Cordoc quickly rolled to his feet and brandished his sword. He looked around, unable to see Belial. He blinked repeatedly, trying to regain his eyesight; his vision was riddled with sun spots. The magic had saved him, but it affected him as if he had been staring at light for too long. Selaphiel emerged behind him, his eyes making him appear especially fierce.

"It's time to go," Selaphiel said, his hands shaking.

Cordoc gave one last glance behind him. All he saw were two white orbs in the darkness.

"Move!" he yelled. Liquid fire hissed by them and burned the outer bark of trees near them. Selaphiel screamed as the outer edge of his left hand was singed.

"Go!" Cordoc yelled again. He turned and fired a volley of arrows.

"Are the rest dead?" Cordoc called behind him.

"Most of them, others wounded," Selaphiel said, favoring his hand.

Another torrent of flame whizzed by them; this time it did not reach as far as it had before. Cordoc could see Selaphiel untying both of their horses. The horse's eyes were wide with fear, and they beat the ground with their hooves. Selaphiel mounted and held Cordoc's horse for him. With a flurry of movements, they both rode furiously, putting distance between themselves and the roars of Belial and the other creatures.

Overhead they heard continual thumps of wind. Both Cordoc and Selaphiel look at each other, confused.

A huge mass flew over them. Its body was colossal and silvery. It looked metallic, as if it were made of chain mail. It gurgled a growl, flying past them. Cordoc's mouth was agape as he stared at it.

"What was that?" Selaphiel asked, spurring on his horse.

"I believe that is the dragon that attacked the Light Prison," Cordoc said, watching the dragon fly away.

"Tsal," Selaphiel said, his voice cracking.

"Keep riding. We cannot stay here," Cordoc said breathlessly.

"Cordoc!" Selaphiel yelled, pointing toward dozens of sets of white eyes visible in the darkness in front of them.

Cordoc felt panic setting in as he saw how worried his brother was.

"This was no small group! This is way more than we are capable of handling!"

"What now?"

"Attack them; we have to break through!"

Selaphiel tumbled as he was ripped from his horse. He reached out with his arms but smacked into the ground, the breath knocked out of him.

"Selaphiel!" Cordoc said, turning his horse, which whinnied a scream and toppled over as a black arrow punctured its heart.

Tears of anger filled Cordoc's eyes, and he quickly fastened arrows from his quiver.

Selaphiel was surrounded by the creatures. Selaphiel gritted his teeth as he tore down Taneem after Taneem but for every one he killed, more came. Cordoc loosed arrows where Selaphiel could not strike, the brothers working in perfect unison. Flames spewed from the open darkness of the Taneems' mouths, stopping short of where Selaphiel held his hand up, a small shield of light cascading around him. The Taneems pounded on the wall but it only glowed in response. Belial appeared and gave a hand gesture, telling the others to stop. Selaphiel's eyes returned to normal as he released his energy. He breathed hard.

"You are much stronger than we had anticipated," Belial said with a flat voice. "You are much more than sons of Lifesveil," Belial said, narrowing his eyes.

Selaphiel, still breathing hard, was unable to respond.

"Not just a son of Alanias, I would wager also," Belial said, perplexed.

The surrounding Taneems growled warningly. One slumped over and fell to the ground. An arrow was in his back; the creatures had forgotten Cordoc. He came running up and fired three arrows strung together with his magic. Three blue starlike arrows hit their mark and three more creatures fell with a dull thud. Belial's anger rose.

"Stand down," Belial waved the others away. Belial drew his other sword. Both blades swung next to him. Selaphiel moved toward him, and with this opportunity he took another swipe at Belial. Belial pushed him, which left him a few feet away sprawled on the ground.

How did that happen? Selaphiel thought as Belial's blade came soaring down upon him. He rolled to the right and was on his feet. Cordoc fired an arrow, which Belial easily avoided. Cordoc attempted another shot, but Belial cleared the distance between them with inhuman speed. Cordoc lifted his bow instinctively. It shattered into two pieces as it was ripped from his hand. Cordoc crouched down and ripped his own blade out of its sheath, blocking the incoming slash. Selaphiel drove Belial back from Cordoc, completely focused. Belial's blades vibrated as they struck Selaphiel's. With a sweeping motion, Belial was able to block both Cordoc's and Selaphiel's swords. Belial hissed, a surprisingly deep noise. The silver dragon circled them now, watching the exchange. Cordoc and Selaphiel glanced upward nervously. Selaphiel initiated the attack on Belial and brought his sword on Belial's while Cordoc circled behind him. Belial jeered as they harmlessly passed by him.

"He's too fast," Selaphiel said angrily.

Belial's eyes were whiter than ever.

The silver dragon roared a trumpeting noise, interrupting them.

Belial stared straight toward the sky. A bright red torrent of flame descended, swallowing the group of Taneems. The monsters howled grotesquely as they were incinerated. Belial angrily sheathed his swords. Cordoc and Selaphiel were breathing hard and could not tell if they should be greatful or afraid.

"Tsal mavet …" Belial whispered in a gurgled tone. A distant roar sounded as the silver dragon circled back. The ground rumbled beneath them.

Belial spat, obviously displeased. A sharp noise came from his throat.

Cordoc looked at Selaphiel.

"Run!" Cordoc yelled, as he threw an arrow at Belial, who was momentarily distracted. Belial opened his mouth, spewing a fire that cut off their escape route.

"I do not care what Elim says," Belial said, looking at them as if they were putrid slime. "I will kill you."

Cordoc swung his blade into the empty air.

"Then try it," Cordoc said challengingly

Belial continued to eye him, shaking his head. "You would not want me to try," he said with a cruel hiss.

Selaphiel shook his head and gritted his teeth in anger. The shape of the dragon emerged from the dark night. Belial grimaced, which could be mistaken as a shiver running through him. Selaphiel felt suddenly out of breath again. Cordoc knelt down and gripped his sword, looking at the coming shape. The shape shrank and a man dressed in brilliant silver armor landed on one knee and stood up in human form. He stood behind Belial, his face pale but human. He had a short black beard running along his jaw and black eyes to match. His hair was a dark brown and shone in the firelight.

Belial looked at the man with hatred.

The man looked back, expressionless.

Cordoc felt exhausted and was not eager to see another opponent.

"You killed them." Belial's lips curled. "We are allied; what was the purpose of that?"

The man snorted.

"They were unable to handle two men. They deserved it," the man said harshly, turning from Belial.

Belial flickered his fingers, as if he were visualizing strangling the man.

"I told them to stand down. These are not just two men."

"It does not matter," the man spat. "It was a lesson to them. They are not dead forever. Immortality has made you sloppy. I saw these two make fools of your many Taneems."

"They deserved to die. But not to die uselessly." Belial scowled.

The man shrugged.

"Elim requires your presence; best to attend to him." The man's eyes glinted dangerously.

Belial clawed at his sides, and his body burst into flames. His body dissipated and was gone, but not before he glared at the man one last time.

Selaphiel looked back at the man, slightly lowering his sword.

"You may remember me from the Ashen." The man laughed, looking at the two exhausted brothers before him.

"Do not lower your blade!" Cordoc said to Selaphiel, his face red. "This is not Tsain, or whoever he has told us he is!"

The man stood still and allowed a small smile to play across his lips.

"I am Tsal of the house of Mavet and its heir," he said cooly.

"Tsal? The war criminal!" Selaphiel exclaimed.

Cordoc ground his teeth. "The war criminal our father has searched for all these years, and he who has caused all this."

Tsal shrugged. "Destroying the prison was easy. Waiting all those years to find a way to do so was a test of patience to be sure."

Cordoc began to back away, his sword still between them.

"Let us leave peacefully," he said.

Tsal smiled, his armor making him appear almost angelic. Two dragons were carved into the silver armor, with carved flames curling from their maws. Selaphiel looked toward the forest, contemplating escape.

Tsal motioned to them.

"Very nifty little bracelets you have there," he said.

"What do you want?" Cordoc said, ignoring the man's comment.

He heard his brother shuffle beside him uncomfortably.

"Forgive my lack of formalities, princes. I am Tsal Mavet, a servant of Elim, son of Dothros," he said elegantly.

Cordoc angrily gripped his blade tighter.

"Alanias is King of Lifesveil and our father. You speak of Elim, one who sought to steal that right."

Tsal laughed, sounding strangely friendly.

"Each side has its own understanding of the truth. It is for each of us to decide. Besides, we have bigger ambitions, and other truths to reveal," Tsal said matter of factly as he held out his hands.

"Elim is not so small-minded as to only wish to be a king," Tsal said in a serious tone.

Selaphiel's eyes blinked dangerously with light.

Tsal turned to him, acknowledging him.

"Or a fake. You of course should be as unbiased considering you are not blood. Tell me Selaphiel, what has your adoptive king told you?"

Selaphiel gave him a hard look.

"Father warned that you were still in this world, and that you were an oath-breaker, and a coward," Selaphiel said, the strength of his voice increasing as he spoke.

"Ah, Selaphiel, there are many things you and Cordoc have no clue about. Your true parents for instance," Tsal shot back. "Like children, you believe only what you are told to believe. Such is the attitude of the victor. Leaving out the details of the true story."

Cordoc let blue flames spread into his fingers.

"He bears the name of the king, and so he is blood. Selaphiel knows his family," Cordoc said. "And there are no more details needed besides the fact that you, Elim, and your Taneemian servants are murderers."

Cordoc challenged Tsal with his blade. Tsal stared at it, a smile on his face.

"I could easily kill you," Tsal said, his eyes glowing.

Selaphiel felt the weight of his blade increase and his legs fall out from under him, as if he were carrying a heavy load. Cordoc gagged hard and bent over.

Tsal laughed, "See? You could not lift a sword quickly enough to beat me. Elim offers you a choice. Whatever you wish will be yours if you only ally yourself with him."

He drew a long, curved sword from a sheath on his back. An aura of light outlined him. Selaphiel released a fire spell at him, which was extinguished with a sweep of Tsal's sword. Cordoc wiped his mouth and pushed himself up. Tsal smirked in amusement and casually walked forward, as if in no real hurry.

"Is that all you've been taught? Infantile tricks? You will need more magic than that."

He walked at a quicker pace, his eyes narrowed as he assessed their response.

"So Derrick has not taught you anything. How kind of him. A failure of a great teacher if you ask me. There are many lessons to be learned."

The hilt of his blade connected with Selaphiel's head, leaving him on his back, looking up at the night sky. With a groan Selaphiel moved to turn himself over.

"I am taking him. You can come quietly or with the shattering of teeth," Tsal said. "Either one can be arranged."

Cordoc yelled and slung a fireball at Tsal, which extinguished into dust before it reached its intended target. Tsal frowned and punched Cordoc in the stomach with his free hand.

"Cordoc, you and your brother pose no threat to us; even if you reach Malfait, it is a dead end. I have no desire to kill either of you. That does not mean you should test me."

All Cordoc could do was grasp his stomach and breathe in an attempt to stabilize himself. Tsal touched the tip of his blade to Cordoc's neck, but not hard enough to draw blood. The sword shimmered like water, as if it were made of something other than metal. It seemed to ripple as it touched him.

Selaphiel moved into a crouching position. His eyes were all Cordoc could see.

"Tsal, only a kingdom of light expels darkness," Selaphiel said, breathing shallowly.

"So you're back up after that hit. Maybe I held back too much." Tsal lifted an eyebrow. "One kingdom cannot kill many. Much as two spoiled children could not kill a Nakal."

Selaphiel wasn't sure what Tsal meant.

"Nakal?" he asked, wiping blood from his lip and struggling to stand straight, finally falling back into a crouch.

Tsal rolled his eyes. "Ashenborn are no longer the only ones able to take dragon form. Yadir is balanced once again."

Selaphiel could feel his strength leaving him. He sat down hard on the ground.

"You have no proof ..." he said, his voice trailing off from trying to catch his breath. "Show us what you truly are."

Tsal snapped his head toward him in a quick gesture.

"You are not worthy to see a thing as sacred as that. I have no reason to prove myself to you two, as you are not worthy to use the form yet. I know you saw me before," Tsal mocked. "No need to establish moot points."

Magic illuminated Selaphiel's eyes, and with new-found strength he stood up.

Tsal looked at him, surprised.

"You are the one who is not worthy," Selaphiel spat, a little blood still flowing from the wound on his head.

Tsal's eyes lit up a glowing silver. "Elim wishes you brought before him alive, but your smart mouth makes me want to just take your dragon fragment and be done with it. Children are frustrating."

Cordoc grimaced.

Tsal drew a trickle of blood from Cordoc, whose neck was stiff from the strain of holding still so as to not get cut.

The magical light wrapped itself around Selaphiel.

Tsal and Cordoc looked at him, intrigued. Selaphiel's aura of orbs exploded into shards of light.

Tsal moved from Cordoc and was struck by a shard, sending him flying with a loud thump. Tsal scowled into the dirt, struggling to stand in the heavy silver armor.

Cordoc tried to move, but instead he felt himself being lifted off the ground with tremendous speed. The world around him faded in and out. He heard the distinct roar of a dragon and lost consciousness as golden hues of magic flames wrapped themselves warmly around him.

CHAPTER 6
INTO THE LIGHT

———✦———

Cordoc awoke to a pain in his stomach. He sat up to find Selaphiel passed out beside him. He looked to be in a deep sleep, as he was drooling. His face wasn't as swollen as before. They were in a large expanse of woods and far from where they had been with Tsal, as far as Cordoc could tell.

"How did we end up here?" he asked himself.

Looking around him, he saw the last of night was slowly fading and the sun was beginning to peek through the trees. A game trail wove through the woods, which he recognized because of his hunting experience. He looked down at his sleeping brother. If only there were a way to replicate how Selaphiel looked at this moment, he chuckled to himself. It was amazing to him that both their swords were but a few feet from them. But his bow was gone, shattered in the fight with Belial. He sighed, holding the pieces in his hands. His father had helped him make that bow. He tossed them away disappointedly. He shook Selaphiel, who stirred and groaned. Selaphiel sat up and immediately put his hand to his head.

"So this is what a hangover feels like," he joked, wincing.

Cordoc smiled. "No, that's what a concussion feels like, little brother."

Selaphiel made a movement to stand but Cordoc stopped him.

"Rest awhile, Brother; your hard head took quite a blow."

Selaphiel looked up and nodded, not arguing. He rubbed his mouth and made a noise of disgust at the feel of saliva.

"What happened?"

"You were sleeping."

"No, how did we get here?"

"You don't remember?" Cordoc asked surprised. "I was hoping you could tell me."

Selaphiel shook his head, which he seemed to regret immediately as his hand returned to his forehead.

"All I know is? Tsal called me more than Alanias, son, then he hit me over the head. What do you think that meant?"

"He probably dislikes you."

Selaphiel squinted and blinked.

Cordoc shrugged.

"I don't know what he meant by that. There is no value in the words of a snake."

Selaphiel looked away, perplexed.

Cordoc squinted into the distance, his thoughts very much preoccupied.

"Regardless, you saved us. You made a flash of light with your magic and poof ... here we are." He paused, adding, "You're sure you don't remember anything?"

Selaphiel's eyes looked upward as he struggled to remember.

"No, I mean I believe you, but I don't remember it."

Cordoc watched him carefully, then shrugged. "Well regardless, we were saved by something fortunate. We need to keep going, but maybe Derrick would know more about it. Before we go, I'll contact him with the windowspeak," Cordoc said as his eyes shifted to to the hunting trail.

"I'm going to follow this trail to see if there's a stream nearby; it could lead to the Goblican River."

Selaphiel winced.

"Do you think you'll be okay?" Cordoc asked him, concerned.

Selaphiel nodded and waved him away.

Cordoc nodded. "Okay, but be alert. I don't know if these woods are safe. Whistle if there's trouble. I'll inform you what Derrick says when I return."

Selaphiel nodded. Whistling was a way he and his brothers often used to communicate in the woods. He stretched out and picked up a twig and began to break pieces of it off into smaller pieces and toss them to the side, a habit of his whenever he was thinking. After a few minutes the headache abated. And none too soon, he thought. He stood and leaned against the tree, his vision blackening.

"Got up too fast," he muttered, sitting down again.

The woods around Cordoc were thick. The growth of the coming green of summer spread around him. He was able to make out several patches of poisonous plants. The place they had landed was oddly clear despite the thickness of the trees around him.

The game trail Cordoc was following stretched and wound down a hill. Selaphiel was out of his view in a few hundred feet.

He looked out at the drop in the canyon below him, awed by the beauty surrounding him. He could barely make out Delgraph from where he stood. It looked so small from this distance. Birds and squirrels rustled around him. The birds sang peacefully as Cordoc continued searching for water while speaking with Derrick.

———※———

The broad head of the dragon looked through the windowspeak, the largeness of his eyes taking up most of the space.

"Elder Derrick?" Cordoc asked doubtfully.

"It is I," the dragon replied, the sound of wind coming through. It appeared Derrick was flying.

"I apologize for contacting you, but you wanted us to speak to you if we ran into trouble."

The dragon's brow raised. "Are you both all right? Have you found Jakobin? Where are you?" His voice did not hide his concern.

Cordoc relayed their location and told him how they had encountered Tsal and the Taneems.

Derrick listened quietly, the sound of the wind flowing past him the only noise.

"As for Jakobin, we have found nothing."

Worry showed in Derrick's eyes, but his next words weren't about Jakobin. "You have encountered Tsal? And live to tell about it? Incredible that both of you were able to handle yourselves against a Nakal."

"A Nakal?" Cordoc asked.

Derrick nodded. "In the history of the Ashenborn there has only ever been one Nakal—a person who is able to become a dragon without using the fragments. I would wager the reason Tsal fled was to understand how to do so, and to teach those previously imprisoned."

"So there are potentially more?" Cordoc said, alarmed.

"Yes," Derrick said. "There were more than a handful of our enemies in that prison; who knows the implications. But you and your brother made it out; how did you do so? You said your brother saved both of you?"

Cordoc shook his head. "He doesn't remember, which is odd, but both of us are experiencing weird, er, side effects?"

Derrick nodded. "That is common for new Ashenborn. Though what you speak of is rather interesting. I must advise you both: do not challenge the Taneems or any of the prisoners again openly. I was wrong to send you away without proper training."

"We knew there was no time for that," Cordoc said. "We knew what was required when we left."

Derrick looked unnerved. "Regardless, do not challenge them, and only if you absolutely must. Tsal especially is at my level of power, and he may be even stronger now that he's a Nakal."

"Stronger than you?" Cordoc said, eyes wide.

"It is likely; that is beside the point, however. You both must make it to Malfait quickly. Who knows what the enemy plots. I myself am going to Aiash to speak to my kin as to what direction we are to take."

"We are capable."

"You both are, but my worries lie with Jakobin. I wish we had some word from him, but you should continue to Malfait. There would be the most likely place for him to go."

"We will; we would never abandon finding our brother."

Derrick nodded, adding, "May your fires shine bright. If you need me, do not hesitate. Be ever watchful."

"Thank you, Elder."

"One last thing. Your father sends his regards and love and wishes you to remain safe."

Cordoc smiled, knowing his father would never miss the opportunity to tell them that he loved them.

"Thank you, Elder, and tell him the same when you see him."

Derrick smiled.

The windowspeak went dull.

Cordoc sighed.

"I hope we are capable of this task," he said under his breath.

He filled a canteen with water from the stream he had found and walked back to tell Selaphiel what Derrick had said.

"Your Grace, I will contact Wulvsbaen and speak to my father the king," Thornbeorn said.

Alanias rubbed his beard and stood up from the table where he had been sitting.

"Thank you, Thornbeorn, but I must ask more of you."

Thornbeorn shifted uncomfortably.

"We will need as many men as Wulvsbaen can muster. As quickly as possible."

"It will be done without question."

"It must be."

"What of the others? How fare your sons?" Thornbeorn asked respectfully.

Alanias' face was grim.

"I fear that they have run into trouble. I often doubt having sent them on this mission. But never mind. You have enough to concern yourself with currently."

Thornbeorn nodded as Alanias handed him a scroll with his seal in red wax.

"Take word to your people and see what men we can gather. Normally the High King and his men would come in time to quell incoming armies, but we can't count on that this time. At all costs deliver this message."

"My Lord, we have a long-standing alliance and we shall send what men we can spare," Thornbeorn said as he bowed.

Alanias nodded solemnly, then turned to look out a nearby window, dismissing Thornbeorn.

"It is only fitting that you receive the same aid that you have provided us," Thornbeorn said, turning to go. "I will make haste."

He left at a run, and Alanias went out to the balcony of the throne room. He had not expected to see ships entering Arkyras Rift from the west. The Rift was a perilous passage for inexperienced sailors, with sharp rocks hidden beneath the waves that could easily reduce a ship to nothing but a few floating pieces of wood. He had thought the enemy would come from the southern Mist Isles. His face became grimmer as he thought of his sons, his resolve wavering for a moment. If they returned with Jakobin and reinforcements, then their journey would have not been in vain. Thornbeorn was also an ally who could be trusted to send men in this time of need.

"Lifesveil shall not fall," he said to himself, reassured by the plans he had made. Yet still he looked over the kingdom, committing the view from his window to memory as if he might never see it whole again.

"I am being silly in my old age." He shook his head and rubbed his temples. *I must be strong for the people,* he thought. *Even if it isn't true.*

A bird flew from the south and landed on the bird keep just below him, delivering some news he hoped to be good. His mood was down. He had spent the majority of the night planning with Zarx and his captains to build up the city's fortifications. Lack of sleep had left him tired and irritable. He contemplated taking an hour of rest, knowing appearances were important. He had seen Zarx off to do other things, and this would give him time to renew his strength.

His shaking hands unwrapped the message delivered by the bird, careful not to tear the delicate scroll. He shook his head and threw down the letter. Nothing of dire importance was contained within. Alanias couldn't recall how he found his way to his resting quarters, but he fell asleep nonetheless, his thoughts still upon the trials that faced the kingdom.

———————— ✳ ————————

Thornbeorn pushed past several men as he announced his departure to the captain of the old wooden ship tied in the port. The captain nodded. He was a curt man of forty and had brown hair with a scattering of gray on his head and in his beard that hinted at his age. His eyes were brown, surrounded by creases that told of long days squinting against the glint of the sun on the sea.

The captain turned from Thorbeorn and ordered his crew to prepare for departure while Thornbeorn looked off to the sea.

"Elim's ships will soon be upon us in a few days. We must make haste to avoid them."

"She will take us there," the captain said, smiling. "The Sea Serpent has never failed me."

Thornbeorn snorted in derision at the name of the ship. The Sea Serpent, a name he cared very little for as he considered sea serpents evil creatures.

"Captain Salenair, is my armor for Wulvsbaen still on board?" he asked as the captain's men moved around them, preparing the ship for departure.

"Yes, as you left it, though I had not thought you to stay for such a short amount of time," the captain said, turning to reprimand a sailor who was doing nothing.

Thornbeorn shrugged. "The Ashen ended sooner than I had hoped. You shall be rewarded with coin, I assure you."

This made Salenair brighten up. The wind picked up slightly, a good sign for their travel. As Thornbeorn looked around, he saw warships docked all around him. He took in the giant sails embroidered with the standard of Lifesveil.

This fleet would meet Elim's, and he wanted to be nowhere near when that happened.

These waters will not be as blue then, he thought.

Lifesveil's fleet was few but strong. And more would come to her aid, at least her people hoped. Thornbeorn handed Salenair a small leather bag of gold coins and climbed down to the lower deck to remove the armor he had donned in Lifesveil for the Ashen. He replaced it with a clean tunic. It would be a while before he would need his fur armor again. He sighed and strapped his silver blade to his side. An old habit that he cared not to change. The ship surged forward, causing him to stumble. It creaked like an old man's knees, but the trip here had made him used to the sound. The ship was leaving the port.

Salenair called down immediately afterward, "Prepare yourself."

Thornbeorn shook his head and grimaced. *A little late*, he thought as he climbed back up to the deck and looked toward the sea.

"Now homeward," he said as he examined the new vambrace on his wrist. His voice trailed off as he focused on the quartz shard that had been bonded to him.

"Was this a mistake?" he asked himself. Derrick had approached him earlier that morning and had spoken about a magic beyond that of his people. He had added something about how Thornbeorn would be the first Ashenborn among Wulvsbaen's citizens. It was an opportunity he had accepted gratefully, but he did not know how his father would feel about it. The kingdom of Wulvsbaen was a proud and powerful people. They respected the Ashenborn, but none had ever become one. Derrick had told him that there were three others to become Ashenborn along with him. He assumed that meant Alanias' sons.

He had come to celebrate the Ashen in his father's stead, since his father had had other, more pressing matters to attend to. *Besides,* he thought, *when the opportunity to become as powerful as Elder Derrick was possible, it should not be overlooked.* He touched the skin of his arm.

The ship had cleared the harbor and surged forward as all sails were raised, catching the strengthening wind. Thornbeorn looked across the gray-blue waters toward his home.

His father would send men to aid Lifesveil, he was sure. If nothing else, he knew that much. He smiled. Dragons or no dragons, Wulsvbaen would come to the aid of its sister kingdom.

————◆————

Zarx walked as quietly as he could, passing small houses and huts of varying size. The night was cloudy, the stars obscured. He gripped his fist tightly, feeling the blood in his veins begin to surge with adrenaline. His steps became heavier as he strolled with more determination, entering the woods that led to the Light Prison. He felt the cords in his neck tighten. It was not often he intentionally allowed himself to be put into such a situation. The walk before him was long and hidden. He followed the trail to the broken prison, which had grown even dimmer since his last visit. The magic seemed to be draining away, like the water from a lake with a broken dam.

He stepped through the first and second line of gates that looked more like stone pillars than doors. He decided the center would be the best place for what he had come for, and he stood still, looking sharply around him. The prison was eerily quiet, despite having been inhabited only a short time ago. The remaining light was enough to produce the visibility of a torch. Zarx shuffled uncomfortably, his hand wrapped around the hidden weapon he carried.

"Zarx." A human voice called through the darkness.

Zarx turned toward the call. The figure was dressed in dark clothing, his face covered.

"You know who I am. Who are you?"

The man removed his hood slowly. He had a finely trimmed beard and neat grayish brown hair that was combed back from a widow's peak.

"My name is Bageden." His brown eyes drilled into Zarx.

Zarx crossed his arms, unamused.

"I was told I was meeting Elim. The war criminal," Zarx said, displeased.

Bageden laughed a hollow laugh.

"Elim need not be bothered." Bageden lifted his chin. "He will make an appearance, but not tonight."

Zarx tried not to show his agitation. "You waste my time. I am a general. I did not think my time would be wasted on one of his lessers."

Bageden scowled.

"You should watch your tongue," Bageden said.

Bageden lifted his palm, sending an orb of magic light floating over the two, illuminating the destroyed prison.

"I am capable of doing to you what Tsal did to this prison. Do not forget it."

Zarx kept his eyes on Bageden, grunting. "An overconfident bunch you all are."

"Regardless," Bageden said, "you have not heard Tsal's proposal."

"Oh? What could possibly interest me? You and your friends are not worth eating with," Zarx said angrily.

Bageden smiled slyly.

"The Taneems are heading to Lifesveil. It is not too late for us to ignore your little kingdom and go on our way. We have already captured so much in so little time."

Zarx pretended to be uninterested in this news.

"There are those who already bow to us. Lifesveil was a key combatant in the War of Stones; this mercy will be given only once," Bageden said.

Zarx raised a brow. "Oh, so Elim is in a merciful mood?"

Begaden laughed. "Deny this and we will kill Alanias and his blood. Elim offers mercy when none was given to his father."

"You will do no such thing," Zarx said through clenched teeth.

Begaden closed his eyes, sighing as if searching for patience.

"Elim hopes not to. You see, he is kind and merciful, if others will accept his forgiveness. It is a free gift. Take it." Bageden's eyes snapped open. "I have."

"Accept the words of a conjurer, and a demon?"

"Accept the words of a lord of kings. Or allow Lifesveil's father and sons to pay for the sins of its kingdom."

Zarx shivered, rattled by Bageden's viperous words.

"You will not harm any of them. I will make sure of that."

"Your face betrays you. We know his sons are outside of your protection."

Zarx sprang forward with his short sword in his hand, but it slashed through nothing but air. Begaden had moved inhumanly fast. Zarx held the sword at his side, ready for a counter.

Begaden looked at him, amused, his eyes glowing with magic.

"Of course," Zarx said. "Blasted witchcraft."

"I will ignore that for the sake of Elim. But the day draws near. Consider his words carefully. Surrender your armies and none will be harmed. Elim is not so unjust to spare you for a price." Bageden looked around the prison.

"Your actions determine the fate of many lives. Weigh his words. Present a white flag along with your armies when we reach you."

Bageden flew off into the blackness in a burst of flames.

Zarx rubbed his arm and sighed. He was used to tough situations, but he knew Alanias, and he himself would never accept an offer that involved sending their people to certain death. Their actions in the past war had proven that sentiment.

"Alanias will not be pleased." Zarx said, his voice echoing in the empty prison. He whistled, and his Silver Talons emerged from their hiding places around the prison.

"Do you think he saw us?" one asked Zarx.

"I do not believe he did. Did you get a good look at him?"

"He is Ashenborn," a second soldier said.

Zarx shook his head, wondering what was going on.

"Where is Derrick?" Zarx barked, looking around.

"He was called to Aaish; the Ashenborn summoned him," the first soldier said.

Zarx rubbed his temples. *That can't be good,* he thought. *Derrick could be in danger.*

"It might be too late by the time a bird reached him," Zarx pondered aloud.

"By association, do you think Derrick has something to do with this? Bageden is a known Ashenborn," the second Silver Talon said.

Zarx shook his head. "I have no reason to distrust him, but he needs to know about this one called Bageden and what he proposes."

Zarx waved one of his men over. "Bring me a bird," he commanded.

The man bowed and ran down the path toward the castle.

"Even if it may not make it in time, I must try. For now, Derrick needs to know what has transpired. He may wield magic, but he is loyal to the crown."

"What about Bageden?" the soldier asked.

After the bird was procured and the letter sealed, Zarx called his men back.

"Wait, rip that letter apart and burn it. I have another idea."

He looked down at the small shard of glass that Derrick had given him and paused before answering the soldier.

"As for Bageden, there is not much to be done at this moment; following him is not possible. As much as I would like to."

Zarx presumed that Bageden would not care if he followed him or even that Zarx knew who he was. He had made that feeling clear enough by showing his face and revealing his name.

"They are not afraid anymore. He revealed himself to me as if it were nothing," Zarx said. "It is possible that more of them are nearby. I want every available Silver Talon combing the forests, outlying villages, and even houses within Lifesveil," Zarx commanded. "Anything found is to be reported to me immediately. Taneemian attacks are becoming more frequent; I sense they are trying to test our defenses."

The Silver Talons took their leave, heading off to do his bidding. He continued down the path to the castle accompanied by four guards. As Zarx touched the surface of the mirror, its edge began to vibrate and the glass itself looked like water rippling on the surface.

"Let us hope that Derrick's magic works," he muttered to himself.

CHAPTER 7
OLD GODS
CHOSEN ANEW

---❊---

Floria, the great temple, stood gloriously against the sunrise, the golden tendrils of the sun giving it a pearlescent glow. The temple soared into the air, standing upon walls of overlaid brick and stone. Only the finest materials decorated it, though vines had begun to climb up its sides, reaching toward the sun. It was surrounded by rivers and massive red-barked trees, its presence imperial compared to the overgrowth of nature around it. At its tallest tower was the dragon reach, a large gated door of purest metals, now open awaiting its guests.

Derrick flew slowly downward into the open mouth of the castle, tired from his long flight. Aaish looked as radiant as the day it was constructed, he thought.

He landed silently on the metal door, making no noise despite his sharp claws. He turned his large head to see a bald man with a short, milky white beard waiting for him. A large scar reaching from the man's right brow to his lower cheek could barely be seen on his dark skin. Albion was the leader of the Ashenborn and the order's greatest protector.

"Albion," Derrick said as soon as he was no longer in dragon form.

Albion smiled kindly.

"It is good to see you again, Derrick." He spoke in a surprisingly deep voice.

Derrick rose half way from a bow, almost stretching.

"I have tried to contact each of you, I have much …"

"All will be explained soon. News and questions should be saved until the counsel has gathered." Albion interrupted quickly, as if he had been doing this all day.

Derrick paused.

"Yes, of course."

Albion motioned him inside the castle.

"I apologize for my rudeness, old friend. These are troublesome times. There is much to keep my mind occupied."

Derrick knew that statement to be true.

"It is no issue. I apologize for speaking out of turn."

Albion smiled.

"Your dwelling has been suitably prepared. Others will be arriving soon enough. Everyone will be summoned when we are to meet at the eve of the day."

Derrick grasped Albion's shoulder before walking past him.

"Thank you," he said.

He looked at the familiar ruby-red walls and followed the stairs downward, his steps echoing. Torches lined the walls, making it both bright and warm. Albion disappeared behind him without another word.

"I don't remember so many stairs," Derrick said to himself. As he exited the staircase, he entered his chambers, an ancient study with a large fireplace. He closed the door behind him. A large serpentine dragon was carved into the chimney. Its tail wound around the chimney and its mouth opened at the bottom, where the fire burned. Its popping, crackling noise made him feel tired. He ignored the scrolls and books he had collected and sat down on a comfortable wooden chair.

A knock came at the door.

"Enter," Derrick said.

The door opened.

"Uriaelh," Derrick said and motioned the man inside.

The man who entered had a neatly trimmed beard and hair and was large in stature. He grinned with delight.

"I apologize for bothering you, Derrick. I have been waiting for your arrival and wish to speak with you," Uriaelh said.

Uriaelh was younger than Derrick but showed great wisdom and courage for his age. Uriaelh was also strong but always kind to others. This was the quality Derrick liked most about him. He did for others before himself. Any inquiry made by him had to be serious.

"It is no trouble." Derrick motioned toward a nearby chair. "Please, sit."

Uriaelh complied, straightening his cloak as he sat.

"It is good to see you again, my friend," Derrick said.

Uriaelh nodded.

"And you, Elder." He looked around the study.

"I find it appropriate that you have scrolls and artifacts in your dwellings. Most of the others possess jewelry or weapons, nothing so …" he paused, searching for the right word.

"Fragile?" Derrick said.

Uriaelh shook his head. "Wisdom-filled maybe. Words of knowledge."

Derrick folded his hands.

"There is value hidden in words; treasures are easily obtained."

Uriaelh chuckled. "As I know to be true."

"What do you wish to speak about?" Derrick asked.

Uriaelh immediately became serious. He looked over his shoulder with a guarded gaze before speaking.

"Did you had trouble contacting the rest of our kin before being summoned here?" Uriaelh spoke in an urgent tone.

"Yes. I tried to contact the others multiple times," Derrick responded.

Uriaelh shook his head. "Perhaps it is nothing, but I feel something is going on that we do not quite know. The Taneems have been seen, prisoners escaped."

Uriaelh rubbed his nose.

"And the death of Archkyris," Derrick added. "All of these in a few days of one another."

Derrick had to lean in closely to hear Uriaelh's next words: "Yes. It doesn't add up. The Ashenborn should have been a presence more now than ever. Lady Hoakama even is astounded at the lack of action."

"Is she here?" Derrick asked.

"No." Uriaelh shifted in his chair. "I am here to represent Edywin in Hoakama's stead as she holds the throne until convened otherwise."

"What are you saying?" Derrick asked, wondering what Uriaelh was thinking.

Uriaelh put his hands on his knees.

"Something is going on with the Ashenborn. Their lack of action suggests it. And you know their rules; we cannot actively declare war without Albion's say-so. I understand there are decisions to be made and counsels to hold before we act, but years of silence and now …"

Uriaelh looked as if he were in pain, finally saying, "I have heard rumors of the Ashenborn's intention from Hoakama. They mean to take Yadir for themselves. To profiteer from these disturbing times."

Derrick looked at him with concern. "Have you discussed this with anyone else?"

"No. Just Hoakama and myself."

Derrick slowly stood. "If there is something truly going on, we must act as if we have no suspicion of it," he said.

Derrick stretched and turned toward his friend. "I believe and trust you Uriaelh. I admit I have been confused by the actions of the Ashenborn of late; however, we do not have much proof at the moment. Perhaps they are having us meet to discuss and explain."

Uriehh nodded, but said, "Maybe. You can never tell. Something is shifting. I can feel it."

Derrick's sword suddenly glowed with a white light.

He drew it immediately and looked at the blade. The face of Zarx looked back at him awkwardly.

"Derrick," he said flatly.

"Zarx."

Zarx squinted, trying to see the area around Derrick. "Are you secure enough to speak with me?"

Derrick looked at Uriaelh, motioning him to be quiet.

"Yes. What is it, General?"

Zarx shifted, uncomfortable with the method of communication.

"Do you know of an Ashenborn by the name of Bageden?"

Uriaelh narrowed his eyes.

"Yes. He is our leader Albion's right-hand man," Derrick said.

Zarx pursed his lips.

"He is working alongside the Taneemian. He made me an offer just now on behalf of Elim. He wished for me to rule Lifesveil in exchange for my allegiance and to betray the crown."

Uriaelh and Derrick's gazes met.

"You are sure it was Bageden?"

Zarx gave a description that left no doubt it had been Bageden who had spoken to him.

"He did not seem to care that I knew his name. He used his own title."

Derrick looked very troubled.

"Please keep me informed. I appreciate that you were willing to tell me of this, considering I am at Aaish."

"I have to make preparations for the kingdom. Just be advised of our situation; there is no telling who is our ally and who is our enemy now," Zarx said.

"Thank you, General," Derrick said, ending the conncection.

"Your general can be trusted?" Uriaelhh asked as Derrick put his blade away.

"Yes," Derrick said. "He has no reason to lie."

"Bageden …"

They looked at each other.

"If something is indeed going on," Derrick whispered, "Bageden has an accomplice. And he is Albion's second in command …"

A servant called from outside with summons to the counsel room.

Derrick was sure he saw an unfamiliar look of anger in Uriaelh's eyes.

"Albion could very well be an accomplice, or he may have no knowledge whatsoever of Bageden's intentions," Derrick warned. "Do not be hasty."

———————※———————

Zarx looked curiously at the man before him. Tritus, of some village he could not remember, was not of royal birth but had set out to become a guard of the Light Prison. Zarx admired the man's effort and demeanor despite the wound that crippled him.

Zarx examined the man carefully. This was the man who could give him more answers about the one who had freed the prisoners. He looked at the wound that had caused Tritus to lose his arm just below the elbow. A cost he had incurred because he wished to protect others.

Zarx's eyes fell onto the vambrace on Tritus' upper arm. He recognized it, noticing the weaving of Ashenborn. Zarx's knowledge of the Ashenborn was limited, but he knew a fragment dwelled beneath Tritus' skin, the vambrace merely a covering for something of greater value.

Zarx calmly placed his elbows on the table in front of him. Tritus looked nervous. Zarx relaxed his stern demeanor in an effort to calm him.

"Lifesveil owes you much, not only for what you did but for what you continue to do. Most would have given up and left to retire while others fight; yet here you remain."

Zarx smiled. "You inspire Alanias, myself, and our men with your determination."

Tritus thanked him dutifully.

"I am glad to be alive. I am lucky."

Zarx agreed.

"However, there is more you can do for Lifesveil," Zarx said.

Tritus leaned forward.

"Yes, General?"

"I want you to show me what Elder Derrick has taught you."

Tritus looked at him inquiringly.

"You mean the magic?" Tritus said.

Zarx nodded. "I would like to know your capabilities and how you can protect others."

Tritus looked uncomfortable. "I have not been able to control it very well," he said, reaching to rub his arm.

"Even so I wish to see it. This is an order," Zarx said.

Tritus sighed and stood up from the table, eyeing the place his right arm used to be.

"If you require it of me, sir."

The air in the room felt humid, and Zarx felt his chest shake. The veins in Tritus' temples bulged, and perspiration drenched his forehead.

Shards of orange and yellow energy flaked from Tritus' healed wound. The stream of magic extended into fingers of fire, lengthening and forming into a recognizable shape, ending in fingers and a thumb. Tritus flexed his glowing arm, forming a fist for a moment. He continued to strain, his shoulder muscles twitching. With each movement, a flare of fire erupted from around his arm. Zarx stood and walked over to him, gesturing him to hold it out for him to see better. He reached out and stopped when the temperature would not allow him to get any closer.

"Impressive," Zarx said, pulling his hand back. "Does this mean you are Ashenborn now?" Zarx asked.

"Yes and no. Derrick believes this shard will be able to power this particular magic, but is not likely to allow me to become a dragon."

"This is the limit of it then?" Zarx said, seeming unimpressed.

"Well," Tritus said, "Derrick said I would be able to conjure swords with practice. As you can see, I struggle to hold the simplicity of an arm right now." He pointed with his left hand at the flares of fire forming his right hand.

"Derrick believes there is a small chance I could become Ashenborn completely with time, seeing as I do not normally use magic."

Zarx looked in deep thought.

"Are you of royal blood?" he asked.

"No," Tritus said.

"Interesting."

Tritus released the magic and the arm disappeared.

"It is hard to use a muscle you have never used before," Tritus said.

Zarx folded his arms.

"I consider you still one of my men even though you have chosen to be what you are. I have a request of you specifically," Zarx said.

"What is it?" Tritus said.

"I want you to be my second in command. Daemos is gone, and I need someone I can trust and rely on to get things done that I cannot."

"I serve the crown, and you, General Zarx," Tritus said respectfully.

"Even if it is against the direct order of the king?" Zarx asked, searching his face with his eyes.

Tritus looked at him strangely.

"There may be a point where you must follow my orders even if they do not fall in line with the king's wishes. I do not ask that you openly disobey Alanias, but if I tell you to do something, you will do it. Do you agree?" Zarx said sternly.

Tritus looked conflicted at the request, finally replying, "Yes."

"Good," Zarx said. "First, I want you to become efficient at your … er, hand magic. We will have need of it. Magic itself is becoming a powerful factor in our world again. Magic … outside of the Ashenborn even. I would be a fool to not acknowledge its place."

Zarx turned. "Meet me at the former Light Prison at the mid of night tomorrow."

"Yes, sir," Tritus said.

"And Tritus," Zarx said with an edge in his voice, "bring a blade with you; I do not want to place my trust in something not perfected yet."

Zarx left him alone with his thoughts. Tritus could not help but wonder what Zarx intended.

———————— ✵ ————————

Selaphiel laughed as he threw water at Cordoc.

Cordoc grimaced at the cold.

Selaphiel felt sluggish from the cooked meat they had eaten earlier.

"The Goblican River is colder than I remember," Cordoc said.

Selaphiel stood up and looked down the river. Ahead of them the river curved, hiding what lay before them. The river behind them was moderately straight, the path they'd come visible. There could be some symbolic meaning in here, Selaphiel thought, but he disregarded the idea as being too philosophical.

Cordoc froze in place, his back going rigid.

Selaphiel turned. "Brother, what is it?" he asked.

His brother didn't answer immediately, making Selaphiel frantic.

Cordoc began to shake, his mouth firmly shut.

"Brother?" Selaphiel said, even more alarmed. He ran toward Cordoc, the water slowing his progress.

Cordoc's eyes shone a magical blue, and his mouth opened as he continued to shake. The windowspeak fell from his pocket and splashed into the water. Selaphiel narrowly managed to grab it. He placed it into his pocket, still moving toward Cordoc.

"Cordoc!" Selaphiel said, grabbing his brother by the shoulders and shaking him.

He had heard of seizures but never seen one first hand.

Sapphire blue flames poured from Cordoc's mouth, making Selaphiel jump back in shock. The flames engulfed Cordoc, leaving a white aura around his body. Selaphiel yelled in surprise. The crack of the flames continued to engulf Cordoc, sending out a wind that made the Goblican churn. Selaphiel righted himself and shielded his eyes. The flames hissed and expanded, tongues of fire and wisps of smoke emitting from the fire surrounding Cordoc. Crackling of what sounded like thunder made it hard to not wince. Selaphiel in despair scooped some water and threw it on the fire, but it only caused the fire to spark higher. The white aura faded, and the flames began to take a larger form, now torrents instead of flickers.

Selaphiel stood by feeling helpless, trying to think of what to do. He strained to call upon his magic, but nothing happened.

Eventually, wings emerged from the inferno, and a long topaz tail flailed back and forth, scales of crisp cobalt and lapis lazuli clearly visible. The flames seemed to shatter as scale and muscle emerged. Pearl white spikes erupted from the scales. The creature's wings were brightly formed, with membranes a shade of tourmaline. As the flames faded, the form of a dragon began to appear. Selaphiel realized what was happening, but instinctively he drew his sword.

The form grew bigger and bigger until a massive hulk of scales and muscle stood over him. The thick neck of the dragon glittered, and as the last of the fire dispelled, Selaphiel saw an enormous monster standing before him. The dragon roared a guttural noise, making Selaphiel cover his ears. The horse-like head of the dragon turned to look at him; its eyes glowed a light blue color, the pupil a slit. It had two solid horns and flaps on its cheeks much like a fish fin on either side. The thin membrane of its eyelid blinked, and it bared its teeth, a hint of smoke drifting from its mouth. The dragon was indeed big, with glittering blue scales and pearlescent teeth and claws. It stood massive in comparison to Selaphiel, who looked at it with wide eyes. The muscular frame bulged as the dragon flapped its wings and walked out of the river onto the shore.

Selaphiel stood still, not sure what to do. Should he run? Should he approach the dragon he thought was his brother?

"Cordoc?" he asked hesitantly.

The dragon snorted and a puff of smoke rose from its nostrils, dissipating in the air.

"Yes," the familiar voice of his brother said, though it sounded gruffer, with more volume and depth than his human voice. The dragon's lips curled into what Selaphiel thought was a smile.

"Who else?"

The dragon showed all of its jagged teeth, causing Selaphiel to step back.

"Elder Derrick mentioned this would happen. I didn't think it would happen so abruptly," Cordoc's voice reverberated.

Selaphiel relaxed and eyed him up and down. He stood amazed by the color spectrum of the dragon's scales. Every color of blue he could ever imagine shimmered before him. He sheathed his sword.

"Elder Derrick was right; the first transformation was impressive," Selaphiel said, his body shaking slightly. "I was afraid you would be feral. You are a sight to be sure."

"Oh?" Cordoc said.

"Yes," Selaphiel said. "Fire spewing from your mouth, engulfed by flames …" his voice trailed off. "Very unnerving."

"You would have let me be engulfed?" Cordoc jested, his claws digging into the earth, his booming voice making Selaphiel's chest vibrate.

"No." Selaphiel laughed. "I tried to throw water on you."

As he said it, Selaphiel couldn't help but realize how funny it was.

Cordoc turned to look at his large wings, which were two times the size of his body. With a flap, the veins in the membrane of his wings began to circulate blood, unfurling the wings to their full size. He moved his tail back and forth, testing each part of his new body.

"This feels … different," he said as he walked on all fours around Selaphiel. Selaphiel moved to the side cautiously; even if he tried, he would have only been able to touch the dragon's knee.

"Stand back, Brother," Cordoc said, his throat expanding and glowing a lighter blue in the cracks of his scales. With a breath, a torrent of fire exploded from his mouth, parting the water and making the river bubble and boil. The fire sputtered out in the Goblican, leaving steam rising from the surface.

Selaphiel looked on in astonishment.

"That felt a little warm," Cordoc growled. His wings began to flap, and his back began to rise off the ground.

Selaphiel shook his head.

With a push of his hind legs, Cordoc slowly lifted into the air. Flapping harder, he soared into the air with ease. Clouds reflected in the mirror-like scales, causing Selaphiel to gasp at the beauty of the dragon before him. Going only a little distance, Cordoc circled back around and landed beside Selaphiel gracefully despite his size.

"Flying," he said and smiled, "is a like a dream."

Cordoc laughed, unable to contain his exhilaration.

Selaphiel grinned. "I have to say, I am a little jealous of you right now."

"Would you care for a ride?" Cordoc asked.

Selaphiel shook his head. "I think it would be kind of weird. Besides, I'll be able to do it eventually. The wait will be worth it."

An odd gleam shone in Cordoc's eyes.

"Hold still, Brother," the dragon said as it pounced on him and grabbed him with its massive claws.

Selaphiel yelped in protest, unprepared for the movement. He felt like a helpless animal at the will of a powerful predator. With a burst of strength, they were in the air, Cordoc clutching Selaphiel tightly with one claw. Selaphiel shivered as the cold air hit them and struggled to keep his eyes open, his eyes rimmed with tears from the wind. The silver ribbon of the river turned into a line of ink after a few minutes, and the trees below looked like small twigs.

Cordoc glided for a moment, almost hovering in place.

"I'll get you for this!" Selaphiel yelled, half laughing.

"Oh? How so?" Cordoc questioned as he pivoted and shot down like a falling arrow. Selaphiel felt his stomach churn, and he was aware he could not feel his face anymore.

"I don't feel alarmed by your threats right now," Cordoc laughed, the sound a low pleasant hum.

Selaphiel held on tighter, blinking from the wind in his eyes. Gusts of wind whistled by them like the howls of a wild dog.

"I think we should go faster," Cordoc rumbled.

Selaphiel shook his head, aware that he was a rag doll in Cordoc's talons.

"Okay, I guess I've tortured you enough," Cordoc said, taking pity on his brother.

He landed softly landed on the ground, releasing Selaphiel. Selaphiel sat, breathing heavily as he tried to recover from the experience. Suddenly, Cordoc's head snapped toward the sky. He began to growl, his snout tilted upward. He curled his wings into his back and hunkered close to the ground.

"What is it?" Selaphiel whispered, rolling away from Cordoc's claws. He noticed they had landed under the safety of some nearby trees.

"I saw something," Cordoc said, scanning the skies.

"I didn't. Your new eyes have you seeing things."

"My vision is keener now, I could not be mis-"

A bellowing roar broke the silence around them.

"What in Yadir?" Selaphiel gasped.

"Another dragon," Cordoc said softly as a dark purple dragon broke through the clouds and circled above them.

"I should not have flown so high," Cordoc said, regret in his voice.

Selaphiel ducked under some trees.

"You should change back," Selaphiel said, eyeing his bright scales.

Cordoc shook his head. "Each time Elder Derrick reverts to human form, he makes a blinding bright light. That would surely attract our guest even more."

"We will be found," Selaphiel said. "At least you are smaller as a human; we can hide."

Cordoc replied, "In an attack, I still have more advantage as a dragon."

Selaphiel look at him, confused.

"You've just become a dragon; you cannot go toe-to-toe with that thing. There are still more things we need to learn about being dragons. Powerful or not, you don't understand everything there is to know. What good is a sword unless you have knowledge of its use?" Selaphiel said quickly.

"It's just one. Besides, there are two of us. You will be well-hidden. There is little to understand about teeth and fire," Cordoc said anxiously.

"You just flew for the first time. You cannot expect to understand everything just because you have something newly given to you," Selaphiel said, alarmed. "Besides, this doesn't sound like you; we should continue to stay hidden in case there are more of them. We may only see one, but that doesn't mean there aren't others."

The dragon in the sky flew away a measure and hovered in place, obviously searching.

Cordoc looked around the forest, then up at the sky again.

"Stay here. I'm going to fight him. I can beat him," he said arrogantly.

Selaphiel's face reddened with frustration. "I won't be able to help you up there. You shouldn't do this. Your power blinds you."

Cordoc winked a reptilian eyelid, saying, "Stay hidden. I can take him."

"At least bring me with you, if you must go don't go alone!" Selaphiel said desperately.

With a burst of wind, Cordoc emerged from the forest with a boisterous roar. Selaphiel shook his head, knowing

Cordoc had heard him but had simply ignored him. Cordoc's tail flailed around like a snake as he rose. Selaphiel glared at his brother and kicked at the ground in anger.

"I cannot believe this," Selaphiel said, a sick feeling in his stomach.

The blue dragon emerged from the trees and flapped his wings, holding himself in place. The purple dragon was much larger than he had originally thought.

The other dragon hissed like a serpent. Cordoc noticed the dragon had a shorter snout than he did and that its spikes were narrower and looked like white needles. Its posture suggested it stood on two legs as opposed to his four, as its rear legs hung limply.

"Who are you?" the dragon questioned.

"No need for introductions," Cordoc growled.

The dragon smiled, an amused expression on its face.

"Are you Selaphiel?"

"No."

The dragon laughed puffs of smoke.

"So Cordoc then," the dragon affirmed to itself.

"Where is Selaphiel?" it asked.

Cordoc tried not to look back from where he had emerged.

"I am alone, and I've come to fight you."

"Fight me?" The voice of the dragon deepened.

"You want to fight with me?" Its eyes glowed a bright purple.

"I am Malakh of Mavet. Servant of the Seraph." Malakh roared and gilded toward him Cordoc, slamming into him with his claws.

Cordoc reeled, then straightened himself with a strong flap of his wings.

"Seraph?" he growled.

"Yes," Malakh spat. "Also brother of Tsal."

Cordoc sneered. "You are just a war criminal, like your brother."

Malakh hissed and blew smoke from his nostrils. He struck his head out at Cordoc with a quick snake-like motion. Cordoc did not expect the strike and had no time to react or figure out how to maneuver to avoid the impact.

———✳———

Selaphiel saw the dragon hit Cordoc in a crash of fury. It sounded like a storm above him.

"Cordoc," he said in an angry whisper.

He brought forth his magic with a spark and ran while looking upward.

"Why?" he asked himself. "Why did Cordoc not listen to me?"

Derrick's words, warning them about the feelings of power and impetuousness that would come with being a dragon, echoed in his head.

Derrick knew what he was talking about, he thought.

Selaphiel shook his head and froze, looking down. The ground dropped steeply off. If he had not stopped, he would have fallen several hundred feet. He could see swift blurs of movement below him. The echoes of scale on scale reached him and he couldn't help but look up. He followed the tree line, searching for something that would provide more height. Whatever was below him was a problem, but he knew he needed to help his brother. A sharp pain shot through his arm. An arrow lodged into his shoulder, fresh blood pouring from the wound.

Selaphiel hit the ground hard, gripping the arrow in agony.

He let out a gasp of pain, then bit down hard. He fought not to cry out even though his head was filled with his own yells. He flinched at the arrow's cold, stabbing pain. With a hard heave he pulled out the arrow, letting out a yell despite his best efforts. He tried to muffle his own continued gasps of pain with his unharmed arm. He lay down, sword beside him, unsure where the arrow had come from.

He heard voices below; from the frequency he knew they were not human. With a deep breath he opened his eyes and looked at the arrow that he had pulled from his arm. The arrow was silver with a black stone for an arrowhead. It looked like those found at the Ashen after the attack.

"Taneems," he mouthed.

"Did you hit him?" a shrill voice said a few hundred feet from him.

"Yes, I wounded his arm," a deeper voice responded. "He lucked out because of my poor aim."

"You know he is to be brought in alive," the first voice responded.

"Alive? Well, now you tell me." The first voice gave a horrible laugh.

Selaphiel gulped and remained still.

"The Seraph will kill any who do not follow his orders," the shrill voice said vehemently.

"A Seraph?" Selaphiel mouthed, knowing he had heard this name a long time ago during his studies as a young prince. *I wish I had paid more attention,* he thought as he quietly tore a piece of cloth from the bottom of his shirt to tie around the wound. The cloth darkened with blood; it would do for the moment, however. He managed to crawl to a group of large trees and lay behind a rotting log. He heard heavy footsteps go by. He rose slowly, eyes scanning, making certain not to turn his head. Blood quickly drenched the makeshift bandage and trickled down his arm. The grotesque sight of the Taneems made him shiver; despite having dealt with them before, he could never quite shake the queasiness he felt around them.

———— ❋ ————

Cordoc flew a half circle and lashed his tail out at Malakh's wings. Maneuvering past him, Malakh spewed black fire into Cordoc's eyes, blinding him. Cordoc roared and clawed at his eyes. It felt like spears piercing deep into his skull. Unable to see, he began falling toward the ground. He felt the wind around him pick up as he descended. Cordoc felt his body tense as Malakh headbutted his side, making him lose his breath. He scratched at Malakh with his back legs, attempting to push him away. Cordoc's head snapped to the side as Malakh's tail struck him, the temporary blindness fading. His mind raced as he tried to respond with his limited vision, striking out at random in an attempt to hit the other dragon.

The smokey figure in front of him seemed to move irregularly, anticipating his attacks. The spear-like tail had drawn blood from him, and he felt himself losing control. Malakh's jagged teeth ripped into his neck. Cordoc felt blood in his mouth as he struggled for breath. He coughed and reached up with his legs and claws to remove the dragon's grip on his neck. Malakh bore down harder, not allowing him any chance to free himself despite his attempts. Like a trap, the dragon's jaws clenched and bore deeper into his neck. Cordoc shook like an animal in the snare of a trap, unable to get away from Malakh's binding hold. With each movement, teeth ripped further into him.

The struggle was causing both dragons to descend. Taking a shallow breath, Cordoc shot fire directly into Malakh's wings. Malakh released his grip, his teeth bloodied. His scales were burnt a black sooty color. Malakh glided away from him, his face in a snarl. Forcing the fire through his wounded throat had hurt Cordoc; he could feel the strain it had caused in his chest. The wound on his neck was so deep he felt only a slight relief at the release of pressure.

"I was foolish," Cordoc said to himself. More than his pride was wounded. He felt the burn of the wound in his neck as his vision flickered in and out.

Malakh chuckled, his white teeth stained red with Cordoc's blood.

"Is this, what, your first time in a fight as a dragon?"

Cordoc looked at him, confused; he worked on breathing slowly so as not to aggravate his wounds further.

"It's apparent. You do not fly as one who has mastered the craft. You are new, meaning you have only recently become an Ashenborn. It is as apparent as the sun is bright." Malakh snarled. "Or by how dead you are."

A constant trickle of red was falling from his neck wound, and Cordoc could feel throbs of pain with each breath he took.

Cordoc slowly flapped backward, putting distance between himself and the other dragon but making sure not to put his back to him.

"You and your brother are exceptional. The stones would not have chosen otherwise," Malakh said, seemingly impressed.

Cordoc let the wind hold him in place as he tried to calm down, flapping his wings every so often to hold him in place.

Malakh seemed to hang in the air, as if strings were wrapped around him. Even with the wind he did not move.

"How do you know this?" Cordoc coughed.

Malakh smiled. "We have informants. You seriously believe that all were loyal to Archkyris, and that even after his death everyone would remain loyal to him? There are those who serve us. There are those who already fight us, or …"

Malkah paused and shook his head. "Were fighting us," he corrected himself.

"After I kill you, I will find your brother," Malakh said, looking at Cordoc.

Cordoc's eyes widened.

"Yes," Malakh said, his expression intense. "I know he is down there somewhere."

Cordoc fought the urge to look down.

He dove at Malakh, fear for his brother overcoming his pain. Malakh's eyes flashed with a blinding light. A strange magic shot into Cordoc, making his muscles convulse. He was aware that Tsal had done the same thing when he and his brother had faced him. Cordoc felt his breath leave him again, and he spiraled toward the ground. He panicked as he fought for control. This magic was more potent and more powerful than any he had encountered before. The more he fell, the more hopeless he felt. The world around him was a blur, and he closed his eyes in defeat.

The smack of branches jolted him, breaking his descent somewhat as he continued falling. He felt himself fall into the harsh cold water of the river with a loud splash. He sank like a rag doll into the powerful current. Wave upon wave washed over him. The cold chilled him, and his large muscles went numb. He felt his body begin to shrink as he saw a mixture of brown and red in the water. He panicked as he felt his consciousness leaving him. He resisted but had little strength left. The cold of the river made him wonder if he was already dead. His body felt like an empty vessel. He finally let go as he felt the river sweep him away. All he could see were bright flecks of light as he was swept away. Panic filled him as the current pushed him further away from his brother, Selaphiel's face the last image he saw before his vision faded to black.

———❖———

"No," Selaphiel said as the giant blue form of his brother fell from the sky, out of his view, like a large star falling from the heavens. His blood pounded in his head.

"No …" He felt outside of himself.

"No, no, no!"

He lay still, uncertain of what to do, but waves of anger sent fresh fire into his veins. With his magic, he summoned an aura on his wounded arm.

It's worth a shot, he thought to himself.

He stood up fiercely and realized with a start that he was surrounded by twenty Taneems.

He felt his body shake as if he were suddenly made of liquid.

The Taneems turned from their search, assembling before him.

There's no way I can take on this many all at once, he thought, glancing back to the spot where Cordoc had fallen. *Not again.*

He could not help but think it would be great if he were able to change into a dragon at this moment.

He clenched his fists, gritting his teeth and concentrating. The vein in his forehead bulged. He imagined himself turning into a dragon. He envisioned wings sprouting, flames shooting from his mouth. He shook his head. Nothing. It would not come from just a thought right now. His brain was spinning; he knew he could not rely on a transformation to help him. He had to come up with something and quickly.

The Goblican.

The river would not only put distance between the Taneems and himself, but it would enable him to fight in the open.

Half of the Taneems had bows trained upon him.

"Drop your sword, flesh."

It was Belial who stood behind him, his blade drawn. Belial looked agitated, his scar from their last encounter still fresh and raw.

The light in Selaphiel's eyes intensified, and he lifted his sword arm unsteadily. Belial looked as intimidating as ever. His clawed hand stretched out, ready for anything Selaphiel could conjure.

"Your brother is dead. Malakh is not one to show anyone mercy." Belial smiled darkly.

"Belial," Selaphiel said with as much hate as he could muster.

Belial ground his teeth. "Drop your weapon."

"Why the interest in me?" Selaphiel spat. "I am but an illegitimate prince to you creatures."

Belial's eyes flickered.

"Elim is always looking for fragments. Even if that is all you are worth, you are worth something."

So Elim is the Seraph they are talking about, Selaphiel thought.

Selaphiel glared at him, contemplating his next move.

As if reading his mind, Belial's eyes gleamed.

"You won't live if you try anything. You narrowly escaped last time. Come quietly. Do us all a favor."

With a kick from the ground, Selaphiel cleared the distance between himself and Belial as a flurry of arrows whistled around him. Selaphiel met blades with Belial, and with a hard push from his aura arm, knocked Belial over in a crude tackle.

Belial snarled and crumpled to the ground in surprise but managed to hit Selaphiel's left leg with his curved weapon.

Selaphiel felt the pain in his shin but knew it would not be enough to stop him at that moment as he stood and ran.

"After him!" Belial's voice said behind him.

Selaphiel ran as quickly as his feet could carry him, stopping behind trees whenever arrows began pouring in. He knew he would be okay if he could get to his brother in time. He turned and let loose an aura of fire on a pursuing Taneem, and golden flames started to burn the underbrush. He felt his aura blink once and noticed a suspended arrow fall away from his neck as another thumped loudly into a nearby tree trunk. It would have been a mortal blow.

Selaphiel pushed himself, despite his wounds and the difficult landscape. He felt his body tingle and the hairs on the back of his neck stand on end. He had been in fights, but never like this. His limbs began to feel heavy, and he knew he couldn't keep up this pace forever. He could tell the strain on his body was taking its toll. Even if he had the mental strength, physically his body would not hold much longer. Belial barked orders behind him. Even though Selaphiel was tiring, the sound made him put on a burst of speed.

"You have made a huge mistake!" Belial yelled at Selaphiel.

"Faster!" he yelled to his Taneems. "Kill him!"

Selaphiel burst out of the forest and hid within the roots of an overturned tree just as Belial came into view. He was so close to the river, he could hear the water pounding on the rocks. Selaphiel held his breath and released his magic, attempting to blend in with the leaves and soil. He steadied himself on the roots of the tree, breathing shallowly. Luckily for him, the roots had been dug up by some creature, leaving a hole large enough for him to squeeze into. He curled awkwardly into a ball.

The Taneem stood in the sunlight flickering through the trees, making Selaphiel shiver at their closeness.

Belial growled, an unearthly noise. He sounded like a wounded wolf intent on revenge. Belial made a violent gesture in the air.

"Spread out," Belial said. "There is no way he made it far enough to get away again."

Selaphiel shook, his thoughts on Cordoc.

"Lord Belial," said an ugly Taneem.

Belial turned in agitation. "Yes," he snapped.

The Taneems pointed to something on the ground.

Belial smirked. "Our prey is bleeding. I thought he had been cut," he said with satisfaction.

Selaphiel tensed, his eyes wide.

Belial followed the trail of blood left by the wound on Selaphiel's leg. Though faint, it was enough for Belial to track. Holding his breath, Selaphiel saw the trail didn't lead to the tree, but stopped a few fet from it. Belial's black sockets reached the overturned tree, then turned away.

"Burn the forest," Belial said. "I would rather not waste time searching. The trouble of bringing him in is not worth it to me."

With a loud thump, Malakh landed in the middle of the Taneems, turning into a human in an instant. The Taneems leaped out of his way. As a human, Malakh was medium height, with black hair down to his shoulders and a full beard barely off his chin.

"So impatient," Malakh hissed at Belial. "Elim would not be pleased with your words," he said, smirking.

"What are you looking for?" he inquired, dusting himself off from the landing.

"You know who we are looking for. He has just evaded us," Belial said with a sneer.

Malakh snorted in amusement.

"Obviously," he laughed. "I have handled Cordoc and you struggle with someone who isn't even Ashenborn?"

Belial looked grim. "He still has a fragment, even if he is not Ashenborn. Besides, you know we are not at full strength yet."

Malakh looked impatient. "Elim instructed him to be brought alive, and the one with Alanias' blood be extinguished. Do not so brazenly disregard orders. Use whatever excuse you wish, but it still doesn't explain your lack of results."

"I do not see Cordoc's body nor his fragment," Belial replied disrespectfully. "Where are your results?"

Malakh looked at him dangerously.

"You are overcome with impatience, and you miss key details in your fuss." Malakh glared. "The prince has wounds that he will die from soon if he has not already. The Goblican can have him and his fragment. I am not concerned with him."

"Elim will be interested to hear that," Belial remarked.

Malakh paused then answered, "As I said, Elim is not interested in him. It would be unwise to say more, if your recovering mind can understand my meaning."

Belial cocked his head to the side, a gratified smile on his face despite the threat.

"Do you wish me to continue to search?" he said insolently.

Malakh rolled his eyes. "He is under that fallen tree. Are you so blind?"

He pointed.

Selaphiel stopped breathing. Several unbecoming words flashed through his mind.

"I saw him when I landed," Malakh said. "A different perspective makes a huge difference. I would have expected better of a Veltris."

Belial called his creatures and gave him a bitter look.

"You beasts prove your own ineptitude," Malakh said.

The Taneems surrounded the tree, eyes white with magic.

Belial lifted a palm.

Selaphiel allowed his magic to surround him, in preparation for the flames.

"Someone help me," he whispered as the dark crimson flames spewed from the Taneems' mouths, surrounding him.

A shrill ringing echoed in his ears. He felt the heat begin to singe him and cried out as a flaming coal burned his neck, turning it a bright red. He dove out of the burning tree and threw off the tunic he had been wearing, panting as flames consumed it. He drew within himself to unleash more magic but saw he was surrounded.

Malakh tilted his head back and folded his arms. "Selaphiel, thank you for joining us. We were close to turning your hiding spot into a pyre," Malakh said in a normal voice, as if they'd met at the market or some other common spot.

Selaphiel looked around like a cornered animal.

"I hear you met my brother Tsal," Malakh said. "And of course, Belial, seeing as you have that burn mark on you hand," Malakh said, motioning toward Belial. The Taneem's eyes flickered white.

"But it appears Belial has a burn of his own now. How nice." Malakh chuckled.

Selaphiel looked at him, bewildered as to why Malakh was talking to him as if they were friends.

"You killed Cordoc." Selaphiel's face was crimson with anger. "I will not speak to you as someone of value."

"Did I say kill? I sometimes use harsher words than I really intend." Malakh grinned at him. "You have not angered me in particular."

"I will kill all of you. You will pay for what you have done," Selaphiel said through gritted teeth.

"No one is killing anyone today," Malakh said, scratching his beard.

"You should have stayed in the Light Prison," Selaphiel said. "Then Cordoc would be safe."

"As I told you, he is not dead, but if you must know, this land could use fewer useless humans on it. Too many mouths to feed and too many mouths eating everything. I do find crowds deplorable."

"Then here is your chance. Fight me right now." Selaphiel glared at him.

"Believe me, boy, you do not want that. I have another solution in mind," Malakh chuckled, then sobered.

"Listen to me, because your only option is to cooperate with us," Malakh said, gesturing to the needle-mouthed monsters behind him. "Belial wanted to kill you; I am showing you mercy."

"Why should I listen to anything you have to say?" Selaphiel said.

"Because, if you do not cooperate, I will find your brother, in whatever state he is in, and make sure there is nothing in creation that can save him."

Malakh lifted an open hand to him.

"Or make him how you think he is—dead. You choose his life or death. His blood would not be on my hands but on yours."

Selaphiel suddenly froze; time seemed to stand still. In Malakh's outstretched hand was Cordoc's golden talon. It dangled from Malakh's fingers, winking in the light of the dying flames.

"What do you want?" Selaphiel said tiredly, his body shaking with exhaustion. Malakh closed his fingers, concealing the necklace once again.

"Surrender, and we will take you prisoner. And I will not kill your foolish brother. Whether he deserves it or not."

Selaphiel looked down, knowing he was trapped.

"How do I know he isn't already dead?"

"I guess you won't know, but not knowing is better than having a guarantee of death. At the very least you will have some shred of hope," Malakh said with finality.

"I could use the power of the Ashenborn to find him," Selaphiel said, looking up. He was bluffing, but he hoped Malakh wouldn't know it.

"You don't have that power; if you did, I imagine your brother's and my meeting would have been much more entertaining," Malakh said, a strange gleam in his eyes.

Selaphiel's mind was racing. He sighed with frustration, realizing he was out of options. "If I agree, will you make sure he lives?"

"Yes, I will even let you see your brother one last time," Malakh said, his voice warm with false empathy.

Selaphiel's eyes teared up, and he released his magic, dropping his sword to the ground.

"Do what you will then."

"Very noble of you," Malakh said, twirling a strand of his long hair.

The Taneems surrounded Selaphiel and placed him in chains, removing his weapons and tying his arms painfully behind him. One Taneem jammed the hilt of a sword into his side, making Selaphiel cough roughly.

"Take him to the prison," Malakh ordered.

Selaphiel looked at him, confused, his eyes watering from the blow. Malakh looked back at him.

"Our verbal contract, yes," he said as he flicked his wrist. "You may see your brother, and he may live on in whatever world is after death."

Malakh hit Selaphiel in the back of the head, knocking him unconscious. Selaphiel's head hung limply as he was dragged away.

"Our sources were right. What use is the seed of Alanias? I am not even sure what all the fuss is about," Belial cackled.

"You will escort him to the Prison of Elos, and I will go and give Tsal the news to pass on to Elim," Malakh said, changing tone.

"Very well, but what of the other?"

"What? The armor?" Malakh asked. "Tsal still carries one, but the rest we have been unable to locate as of yet."

Malakh looked around the forest, a small smile on his lips.

"The pieces will reveal themselves with time."

"Is Lord Elim fully recovered?"

"He is; he makes preparations to move on the Lifesveil."

CHAPTER 8
THE TRUTH

———※———

Thornbeorn leaned dangerously off the bow of the ship. He enjoyed the way the ocean sent sprays of water upward from the wind and waves. He closed his eyes as the cool of the night and salty air washed over him. Summer had indeed arrived; it could be smelled in the air. The dark had been their ally in sailing undetected.

They had been lucky earlier; someone was definitely searching for him, but to what purpose he did not know. Salenair had informed him earlier that men who claimed to be remnants of the guard of Archkyris had asked about Thornbeorn specifically. The men had not stated a reason, making both the captain and Thornbeorn especially suspicious. Thornbeorn sighed; he knew he would be limited to walking around at his leisure in the dark, as he might be spotted in daylight. Especially now that he was being looked for by men he did not know nor trust. He remembered that when he was young, it had scared him to see only darkness in all directions, as if some unknown monster could swim upon him without him knowing.

Except there are monsters out there. Monsters in human clothes, he thought. The splash of the water against the ship soothed him. And he forgot for a moment where he was, and that he was being hunted. *I could live on the water,* he thought.

"Enjoying the stars?" Salenair said behind him, interrupting his thoughts.

"Yes." Thornbeorn said.

"Stars are much more pleasant; you cannot get burned by them," he said, thinking of the Taneems.

Salenair chuckled. "But stars can fall and hit you, or so I've heard."

Thornbeorn considered for a moment the possibility of a star falling on his head.

"I think that would be impossible."

"A friend's cousin says that his brother met with a king and was star-struck. It literally hit him in the head."

Salenair knocked his head with his fist. "Just like that."

Thornbeorn doubted Salenair's story about a star striking someone on the head, but he shrugged, unwilling to argue.

"You see many oddities on the sea," Salenair said. "More than those that live on land."

"I can imagine. I'm sure you have many good stories. I believe there are people who would like to hear them," Thornbeorn said politely. "Maybe you should write them down."

Salenair considered this proposition.

"I don't think anyone would like to hear about my adventures," Salenair said. "Besides, it would be a very long book."

"Our stories make us who we are," Thornbeorn said, thinking of his own story.

"Maybe," Salenair shrugged, then added, "There are many creatures to encounter on the open sea."

"Have you ever encountered Akull serpents?" Thornbeorn asked, curious.

"Sadly, yes," Salenair said patting a large hook that was tied on his side where another man might carry a sword. "This is a precaution. He was a great big beast at that. I hope to never run into one of that size again as long as I live."

Thornbeorn eyed the makeshift weapon.

"A hook?"

Salenair looked offended.

"Not *just* a hook. The hook is so I can entrap it with the sharp edge, hold onto it, and kill it with this."

Salenair pulled out a short narrow blade. It shone in the starlight.

"Ah, an interesting strategy," Thornbeorn said.

Salenair rolled his eyes, shoving the blade into its sheath. "Do you have a better way?"

Thornbeorn pulled his icicle-shaped sword from his side.

"A big piece of metal," Salenair said, amused. "Swordsmen," he said, laughing.

"Not just a sword," Thornbeorn replied. "It's an Akull blade of Wulvsbaen."

He held it out to allow the captain to examine it closely.

"So a big *magical* piece of metal," Salenair said and chuckled.

Thornbeorn sheathed his sword, aware he would not get praise from the captain.

"Well, your way is probably best on the open sea. If they come to land, the Akull blade is more apt," Thornbeorn said, seeking middle ground.

The captain agreed.

"Where are you from?" Thornbeorn asked. "You know where I'm from. I'd like to know your home."

"Jayden, but I have not returned there for many years."

Water splashed in the darkness. Thornbeorn turned toward the sound.

"There are no serpents here," Salenair said with amusement. "Probably just a fish jumping."

Thornbeorn chuckled. "I guess I'm on edge considering we were just talking about them."

"Wait …" Salenair looked hard into the darkness.

Thornbeorn rolled his eyes.

"Don't mess with me."

Salenair looked around quickly.

"How can you even see in that pitch black?" Thornbeorn said, squinting into the darkness and feeling a little foolish.

"Get down below, now!" the captain said, opening the door to the lower deck.

"What is it?" Thornbeorn said, ignoring his order.

"Something is flying over us," Salenair said.

Thornbeorn glanced up quickly, "If you need me, I'll be watching through the holes in the wood."

"It will be fine," Salenair said, and shut the door quietly. A heavy thud sounded behind him.

"Who's down there?" A voice asked.

Salenair turned slowly.

"An easily frightened ship hand," Salenair said. "He is not a fan of things dropping in out of the night sky."

Thornbeorn fumed as he watched.

The man who appeared out of the darkness was heavier than the captain, with the protruding belly of the well-fed and indolent. He had a clean-shaven face and short dark hair.

"What is your business here?" the captain asked.

"Nothing in particular; just interested to know why a lone ship is heading toward the northern wildernesses … or … Wulvsbaen perhaps?"

The captain remained calm and folded his arms, a tight smile on his face.

"I hear the ice is good this time of year."

The man looked annoyed.

"Ice is always cold, and that barren wasteland of a kingdom never changes seasons. It's too cold even for birds to dwell there. And you are headed there why?"

Salenair smirked.

"Don't tell me it's to go ice fishing either," the man said, sneering.

"Wouldn't you like to know."

"A master of philosophy, I see." The man fumed for a moment, then tried another tactic. "Who is below deck?"

"Most of my crew. I'm sure that many of them are sleeping as it's nighttime."

"Salenair, do not be smart with me," the man said, an edge to his voice.

"I am merely answering your questions at the level at which they are delivered," Salenair said, stroking his beard.

The man's eyes illuminated, casting a glow on the darkness of the ocean.

"There is no need for that. If you wish to check, you're welcome to; I have nothing to hide," Salenair said, waving his hand toward the doorway that led below deck. The light in the man's eyes extinguished.

"I am only guilty of smuggling items to Wulvsbaen."

The man looked at him angrily and took a few deep breaths to compose himself.

"Then why so secretive? You have smuggled a lot to our benefit. But you really should mind your manners." The man turned as if leaving, then added, "You are lucky it was not another who found you."

"I consider myself lucky," Salenair said, surprised at how grateful his voice sounded.

Salenair untied a coin purse from his side and threw it to the man.

"I have nothing to hide, but take this so we can avoid awkward meetings in the future." The man looked at the coins hungrily and grinned with satisfaction.

"This is why I tolerate your rude remarks."

Salenair lifted a finger. "Men often tolerate a lot for coin."

"Yes. Well, I'll leave you to your damp piece of driftwood."

With a quick movement, the man disappeared.

Salenair shook his head. "He always has to get the final word," he said to himself.

Thornbeorn cautiously opened the door.

"Come on up; it's safe," the captain called to him.

Thornbeorn climbed out of the entrance.

"Who was that?" he asked.

Salenair snorted. "That was a slimy snake known as Veles."

"He is an Ashenborn?"

"Yes and no. Veles is Ashenborn by transformation only. He shares no other qualities with their nobility. Veles has his own dealings for his own gain."

"Why did you speak so boldly to him?" Thornbeorn asked, then hesitated. "I mean no offense, but he could kill you if he wished to."

Salenair smiled a crooked smile. "And kill a smuggler that he deals with? No, Veles would not wish to do without his coin. He enjoys his delicacies. You should have seen his belly. Veles often will not search a ship if I tell him he can. He has an odd distrust of me, but he tolerates me. The coin I give him helps."

"I see. I hadn't realized I was on a smuggler's ship until now," Thornbeorn said, looking at the captain appraisingly.

Salenair shrugged. "There are more evil things out there. Besides, this smuggler is helping to get you home. I am smuggling you."

"I didn't say I was ungrateful you didn't give me up."

Salenair tugged at the other coin purse hanging at his side.

"You gave me coin; I do not betray the highest bidder." He winked mischievously.

"Ah," Thornbeorn said, unsure if he was joking.

"We should be within the ice of Wulvsbaen by the mid of tomorrow."

Thornbeorn knew what that meant, as the water around the land mass of Wulvsbaen had been frozen for thousands of years. Its thickness could not be broken by ship or man. His people often hunted the frozen tundra, for most animals frequented it as a place for food.

"I will go alone from there."

"I had no intentions of leaving the ship," Salenair said.

Thornbeorn snorted. "Well, I would not expect an outsider to be able to handle the harsh trip to the ice walls."

"You mean to offend me, but I take no offense. A fish knows it's best at being in the water. And my preference is the water," Salenair said, shrugging. "A fish would not be so excited to be in frozen water."

"I see your point. Only those with ice in their veins can make that journey anyway," Thornbeorn said.

The captain looked at him mutely.

"It's not literal; it's just a saying among our people." Thornbeorn laughed. "Does Jayden not have such sayings?"

Salenair shrugged again.

"I guess you would have to be of royal birth to know something of such depth. Being a simple boat captain, I have not had such benefit."

Thornbeorn huffed and shook his head.

"I will be glad to be home," he muttered.

Salenair walked away with a chuckle.

———※———

The body drifted down the river. Daemos spotted it just as the large purple dragon flew away from the forest. For a few minutes he watched from the shelter of the woods, waiting to see if the area had cleared of Taneems. He made a note of the direction they had gone, so as to track them later.

He ran onto the bank and approached the body of Cordoc, which had become entangled in plants growing along the river. Daemos' eyes filled with tears, and he placed his hands under Cordoc's shoulders and dragged him out of the frigid water.

Cordoc's eyes flickered, and he let out a small noise, his breathing labored. He choked as he coughed up water.

"You're alive," Daemos said, relieved. He adjusted his grip, picked Cordoc up, and trudged into the forest as quickly as he could.

"Where is Selaphiel?" he asked, but Cordoc had slipped back into unconsciousness.

From the safety of the forest, Daemos watched as the purple dragon flew along the river. It landed not far from where Cordoc had been trapped in the weeds. The dragon breathed in, its eyes scanning the area. Suddenly it flew into the air without a sound. The lizard-like form disappeared after a moment, disappearing into the distance with just a few flaps of its enormous wings. Daemos breathed a sigh of relief.

"That was close," he muttered to himself.

He examined Cordoc's wounds and noted they were not fatal. Daemos had been prepared to administer life-saving herbs, but he decided it was more important to get Cordoc away from the river. He wrapped Cordoc's neck wound and a few less serious wounds on his arm. Gently lifting Cordoc, he walked deeper into the forest, heading toward a trail he had marked. He had been following the brothers for some time, and he had struggled to catch them. He had been sent ahead to guard the princes, to make sure that no Taneemian reached them, but he hadn't found them in time.

"I shouldn't have taken my eyes off of them," he castigated himself.

He looked back over his shoulder, agonized at the thought of not being able to chase after Selaphiel immediately. He planned to drop Cordoc off in a local village with a trusted friend, then go after Selaphiel.

He quickened his pace, checking Cordoc's comfort and stability as he walked.

After walking what felt like leagues, he gently placed Cordoc on a soft patch of pine needles. Cordoc groaned a little.

Daemos watched him curiously, drinking from a flask. Tied up near them was a brown horse, which snorted when Daemos arrived.

"Aye, girl," he said, patting the side of its neck.

He lifted Cordoc onto the horse, making sure he was secured in front of him. He spurred the horse into a gallop. Cordoc groaned again.

"We will have help soon," Daemos said.

"Se-" Cordoc murmured, only half conscious.

"Selaphiel," Daemos finished.

His thoughts raced. Selaphiel, he knew, had been taken. Even though he had wanted to fight those monsters, he knew that he, Selaphiel, and Cordoc could all have died.

"Knowing Cordoc, he will curse me for saving him instead of his brother," Daemos muttered to himself.

Malfait still needed to know Lifesveil's situation, and Daemos knew that time was of the essence.

His eyes fell back to Cordoc.

"It has to start with saving you."

He gritted his teeth.

"Selaphiel, I *will* find you," Daemos whispered.

After a time, a small village came into view and he reined in the horse at an outlying hut. An elderly lady greeted him from the doorway.

"I need bandages and care for this man. I can pay," Daemos said, throwing her a purse of gold coin.

The old woman caught it and looked at him, a questioning look on her face.

"I cannot stay." Daemos took Cordoc into the woman's dwelling and lay him gently on the bed. The covers were freshly folded, as if the woman had been expecting a guest.

"I have heard from those I trust that you will take care of him," Daemos said, eyes narrowed. "Do not make my friends liars."

The woman nodded silently, and Daemos left quickly, his horse's hooves throwing up a cloud of dust. The old woman looked around, stunned by the speed of his departure. She shrugged and rubbed her hands on the apron tied around her waist and turned her attention to the stranger who had been left in her care.

———✶———

Daemos followed the path with his eyes. His horse's nostrils flared as it sucked in air. Daemos patted the neck of the laboring horse.

"Only a little further."

Daemos knew that Selaphiel could be anywhere. His first concern had been for Cordoc, who had needed immediate attention, but he now was focused on Selaphiel.

"I will not fail him," Daemos said under his breath, spurring his horse on. Within a few moments he arrived at the river. He dismounted and squatted beside his horse, examining claw marks left in the sand by the purple dragon. One set was deeper than the rest, indicating where the dragon had taken flight. He pointed himself in that direction and remounted, shivering as he and his horse swam through the cold current.

"Mountain water," Daemos muttered.

His horse whinnied as they traversed the river. He felt his horse tense and then relax as they came out of the cold river. Daemos looked around carefully and spotted burned grass and foliage and what looked like blood.

His stomach clenched.

"Taneemian are not subtle," he said to himself.

Tracks moved into the forest. He followed slowly, ever watchful of his surroundings. He passed an uprooted tree, still following the trail of destruction left by the Taneems. He circled around bushes and trees, being careful to not miss a single detail. He knew he could see more if he took his time, even though he was desperate to move quickly. The tracks stopped suddenly. He searched the area but could find no traces of the horde of Taneems. He reined in his horse and sat in place, pondering. A glint of gold caught his eye. He glimpsed a golden talon chain lying on the ground.

He grabbed it, brushing off dirt, and turned it around in his hands. Each talon was unique, and this one's crest belonged to Selaphiel.

"Whoever has him does not want him to be recognized," Daemos said, stroking his horse's head. He tossed the talon around in his hand, thinking.

He looked back to where he had found it. He could see nothing but leaves and briars. The wind changed directions, bringing a familiar stench to his nose. The smell of something dead. He looked around to discover a body sprawled on the ground a little from him, partially hidden in the underbrush. He tied his horse to a tree and cautiously approached the form. A Taneem. Its body was a husk and began shrinking as Daemos watched, dissolving into a puddle of dark viscous liquid. Daemos squinted through the stench as he put his blade into the hissing liquid. He knew that finding one before it had completely disappeared was rare, as it would be reborn in its mysterious way. No one knew how, only that they never saw the last of these creatures. He poked and searched the area around the dissolving body, hearing the sound of metal on metal after a few moments of prying. He lifted his blade to find a set of keys hanging from the tip. With a popping noise, the liquid ebbed away with a hiss, dissolving into smoke and steam. The remains were gone, leaving no trace.

Daemos took the keys in his hand, noticing the different shapes in their metal arrangements. Keys like that were often meant to keep something safe or locked away, Daemos knew. Daemos noted one long skeleton key, which he tied to his side. Struggling through the undergrowth beyond where the body had been, Daemos observed deep tracks, made by something heavy, and a long gouge between them, as if something—or someone—had been pulled along the ground. He followed the tracks, but they ended where the ground became rocky.

"A chain and key," he said. He found his way back to his horse, who was munching on some weeds.

"I need to find out what lies around this village," he said, vexed.

With a spur of his heel, Daemos galloped forward in a surge of energy. He had spent half of the day searching, he noted by the location of the sun. Too much time had been spent, but it was not in vain.

The princes of Lifesveil were not done just yet.

————❋————

The old woman shakily but efficiently wrapped his wounds, being careful not to cause him further pain. Cordoc clamped his teeth together, biting down on an old piece of leather. She finished up, throwing away scraps of bloody cloth and disposing of reddish water in a small pan. A small brown and white hound dog lounged on a rug near them, eyeing them lazily. It yawned and licked its nose before closing its eyes again.

"Ignore ol' Copper. He's a good watch dog but a very lazy one," she said, smiling at the dog fondly.

Copper did not stir under his droopy ears.

"You are lucky," she said, turning her attention back to Cordoc. "Wounds like that would have killed most people," she said, nodding toward the vambrace on the small table beside the bed. "My name is Ruth," she added.

Cordoc breathed in slowly.

"Would you help me to the fire?" he asked, pointing.

She huffed and shook her head.

"And risk you bleeding all over my floors?" she said, exasperated. "I've already had to clean several tunics."

Cordoc stood up shakily, his hand bracing his wound.

She gently pushed him back down.

"You must not move, or I will tie you down. You are not as stubborn as I. Nor should you try to be," she said in a tone of warning.

Still Cordoc fought against her.

"Would you bring me a coal?" he finally asked, wincing.

"Are you cold? Because I can bring more blankets."

"No, the coal please," he said.

She shrugged and grabbed an iron ash shovel and forced glowing coals from the hearth into it.

"I do not understand why you would want me to do this, but here." She moved it close to him.

Cordoc reached out with his arm. The coals brightened a cherry red, and sparks of fire circled his arm. A blue light began to glow beneath his skin. Blue flecks of magic began to course through his body, finally stopping between the bandages and his skin. He sighed and lay still.

Ruth looked at him in awe, ignoring the shovel. As she stood stunned, the ash and coal fell from it, and the shovel clanking on the ground. She growled angrily, stamping on the glowing coals. She snatched up the shovel and went to grab a broom.

Copper roused, tilting his head at the commotion before nodding back off.

Cordoc took a deep breath and rose easily. He removed the bandages, revealing smooth skin underneath. Ruth looked on, her eyes wide. He walked to the fire, as more flames poured into his fragment.

"In all my years, I have never seen magic. To me it was just stories," Ruth said. "It makes one's own bandages seem useless when you can just heal wounds with a little magic."

Cordoc rubbed his forearms.

"I have known this all my life. Thank you for showing me kindness. I am in your debt," Cordoc said, turning toward her. "You didn't know me but still treated me with kindness."

Ruth grinned, showing several missing teeth, and pointed to the bag of money. "The man gave me this, but I want you to take it with you," Ruth said.

"Surely not. You need to be rewarded for your hospitality," Cordoc said.

Ruth smiled and turned her head slowly from side to side.

"I do not need gold. I am content as I am."

Cordoc opened his mouth to argue, but his fragment suddenly illuminated the room, signaling it had reached full strength.

"You got a lantern under your skin?" Ruth asked.

Cordoc snickered and considered it a moment.

"I guess you could call it that."

Cordoc laughed again, thinking it was something Selaphiel might have said.

"Where am I?"

"Clipper," Ruth said. "A small village on the edge of the kingdom."

Cordoc knew where he was. Their father had made it a priority for them to know all within Yadir.

"You need rest," Ruth said. "You youngins are too determined to go go go."

"I must go. I need to find Daemos," Cordoc said. "I can only rest when I've found my brother."

Ruth nodded understandingly.

"Did Daemos say where he was going?"

"No. He seemed in a hurry, whatever he was doing," Ruth said, adding, "Who is your brother?"

"Selaphiel," he responded, feeling his stomach clench. "He either was killed or captured."

Ruth's eyes widened as she bowed.

"A prince. In my house!" she exclaimed. Copper lifted his head and huffed at the noise. She gave him a look and he dropped his head to his paws again.

Cordoc lifted his hands, motioning for her to stand.

"I cannot let others know who I am, so please keep my secret. And your bowing is unnecessary. It is I who should bow to you."

"A prince ..." Ruth trailed off. "I am sorry to hear of Your Highness' brother. I hope the best."

"Thank you for your hospitality," Cordoc said respectfully, grabbing his sword from beside the bed. "And I do believe my brother is alive."

"What should I tell Daemos?" Ruth said, realizing he was leaving. "Surely you need more time to heal?"

"No need to worry about it. I will find them," Cordoc said before lifting his hand as a sign of respect. "May your fire always bring you warmth."

Ruth stood stunned, suddenly alone in her house. She turned to see the bag of gold still sitting on the table.

"He left it." She smiled. "If he isn't a dairy cow."

She sat down in her chair, thinking of how lucky she was to have met him.

"Selaphiel and Jakobin?" she said, realizing she did not know his name.

"Or was it Cordoc?" she said, shaking her head.

Copper began to snore softly as she tended to the mess made by the bandages.

———※———

Cordoc strolled through the village of Clipper. It was small, with only a few shops around the town square, but he could sense a feeling of warmth and kindness that was unexplainable. He smelled the odor of smoking meat and the sharp scent of pine sap. His mouth watered. If he had more time, he would have liked to spend the day here, but he knew there was no time for delay.

"Where should I start?" he said out loud.

He looked along the trail that went through the village. Trees surrounded the village, much of it looking the same to him. He noticed a few villagers cutting logs. Despite the looks he was given, he trotted into the forest until he reached a dense cover of woods that made it hard for anyone to see him. There was an opening in the top—that way he could fly upward and view the landscape undetected.

The change to dragon was easier this time. He flew into the air, enjoying the feeling of the wind. He flew high within a few seconds and began to glide in an attempt not to make much noise, lest he spook the villagers.

He soared into the azure sky and tilted his shoulder, angling his wings to coast on the wind current. He had seen birds do it. A weird scratching feeling came into his gullet. A rutting noise came out of his throat as he attempted to clear it. It only resulted in him getting more choked. He tried to swallow, but he felt whatever it was coming out of his maw.

Blue fire surrounded him. He was not consumed but he felt his consciousness take him somewhere else.

He looked around. He was no longer in the sky but at an old prison. He watched as Taneems ran along the walls, evading a bronze dragon that roared and spat flames. There was a giant hole in the top of the ancient prison. The dragon strained against its restraints and flapped furiously into the air, violently whipping its tail to and fro.

"Selaphiel?" Cordoc asked, confused.

Neither the dragon nor the Taneems seemed aware of him. Cordoc could not move a muscle as he watched the fight ensue. Flame and claw tore through trees and stone. Cordoc's throat began to itch again, and his vision faded in and out. He squinted and thought he saw himself running toward the prison.

"What?" he said, perplexed.

The images tore away from him like paper and once again he was gliding above the trees around Clipper.

"What?" he said louder, not sure what happened.

He floated down softly and landed in an open area. His scales rubbed against trees, ripping the bark off them. He changed back to human and looked through the sunspots in his vision, blinking until they disappeared.

He needed to figure out the meaning of his vision. He turned back toward the direction of Clipper. Maybe someone there could help him. At least it would be a start. *I wonder if there is an old prison around here,* he thought as he walked back to the village.

CHAPTER 9
THE PRISON OF ELOS

———————✳———————

Cordoc flew as quickly as he could, searching the trees below him. He was like an arrow soaring through the air. In his desperation, he had figured out he could double his speed by narrowing his wings into an arrow shape, flapping here and there to increase elevation. He had been searching since early that morning, and it was nearly sunset. He had begun to lose hope of finding the ancient prison a villager had said still stood but was no longer inhabited. What had truly caught his attention was the villager's comment that the prison had been unused for nearly twenty years.

"Meaning," he said to himself, "it would have been around during the War of Stones. Making Malakh aware of its location."

Or so he thought, but he had nothing else to go on. He had searched the place he and Selaphiel had done battle with Malakh and the Taneems but had no luck. He closed his eyes, angry with himself.

"If only I had not been blinded by this power."

He squinted his eyes at the brush below him. He circled back and forth, searching in the fading light.

How hard could it be to find a prison?

He flew lower to the ground and grabbed onto the tops of the great trees. They creaked beneath his weight, but they did not break. He sat on his haunches and huffed smoke, and a frustrated growl broke through his teeth.

"If only I had something to go by."

His vision blinked in and out and a soft voice spoke to him, too faint to understand at first. As he strained to hear it, it became audible.

"Stay still," it said.

Cordoc's vision returned, and he felt a chill despite his insulating scales. He was alarmed but doubted it would be a good idea to ignore such a clear command. He froze as he heard the clop of hooves. He turned quickly and saw a small dust trail rising over the hill below him. He heard a horse whinney in the distance.

"Whoever it is, they are about to have an unlucky day," he said, launching himself into the sky and gliding around the open width of trees. He wondered who the voice was or how it could speak in his head. That voice made him think he was crazy, which to him was not surprising considering all he had seen and done recently.

"If it helps me find my brother, then I embrace it," he finally decided.

He soared above the hill and peered down through the clouds. He saw a horse running off into the distance, leaving its rider sprawled on the ground.

Cordoc roared loudly and reached out with his talons like a hawk.

"This should be amusing," he laughed. He had never thought he would enjoy doing something like this.

The man's face was pale, and he stumbled backward, hastily drawing his sword. Cordoc lowered his claws and landed softly several feet from the man. He flared out the fins on the sides of his cheeks.

"Going to strike down a prince of Lifesveil, aye?" Cordoc grumbled.

Daemos shuddered and threw his sword to the ground.

"You have some nerve doing that to me, considering how many dangerous dragons could be lurking about!"

Cordoc allowed a small smile to spread across his face, which looked unnerving to Daemos.

"I'm sorry; I didn't know it was you that I was following."

Cordoc shifted to his human form and held out his hand to help Daemos up.

"I thought all of Yadir was breaking in half," Daemos said bitterly as he accepted Cordoc's hand. He picked up his sword and sheathed it.

"I am very sorry, friend."

Daemos shook his head. "I am the one who is sorry, Prince. It was unbecoming of me to greet you in such a hostile manner."

"It doesn't bother me; I would have probably done the same thing. It is unnerving to see something that big coming at you so fast. Even a seasoned warrior would likely dirty his pants at the sight."

Daemos face turned red. "It is not like me to be so easily frightened—and my trousers are fine, but I am glad to see you, although a little suprised to have your company so soon."

Daemos looked Cordoc up and down, confused.

"You do not look to be hurt anymore; that Ruth sure does know how to heal," Daemos said, walking around Cordoc.

"I may very well have to consult her on my bad back."

Cordoc shrugged. "The power of the Ashenborn enhanced my own magical capabilities. I am as suprised as you that I was able to heal so quickly. I could barely heal a broken arm before this."

Daemos shook his head and chuckled. "I am certainly going to have to learn magic one day in that case."

He turned around and sighed.

"Well, my horse has left me. She never really was a fan of things that could eat her."

Cordoc noted, "You don't need to worry about her; I'm sure she'll return home. Besides, I'm a dragon now, so a steed is no longer required." He paused, then asked, "Have you had any luck tracking Selaphiel and the Taneems?"

"Yes! I'm heading toward the prison of Elos. I found several items that point to him having been taken there," Daemos said, holding out the skeleton keys. "Though there is only a ghost of a chance he'll be there."

Cordoc looked hopeful.

"I spoke to several villagers in Clipper. They recall that prison as being in use around the time of the war."

He considered telling Daemos about his vision but didn't know how he would take it, so he left it at that.

Daemos nodded in agreement.

"All roads seem to point there. And if nothing else, it's a place to start. I don't believe he would have been taken far."

"What makes you so certain?" Cordoc inquired.

"I don't ..." Daemos began, then paused and took a deep breath. "I am merely trying to be optimistic, because if your brother has been taken far away, there is very little chance of finding him before he is turned over to Elim."

Cordoc closed his eyes as guilt washed over him once again. Selaphiel's capture was his fault, and he knew it.

"Then let us remain optimistic. How long until we reach Elos?"

"Morning at least."

Cordoc clenched his fists.

"Then lead the way. We are going to find my brother—or would you care to fly?" Cordoc asked.

"No, by foot is fine," Daemos said, already walking.

Cordoc laughed and followed behind him.

"It would probably be a good idea not to draw attention to ourselves," he said, chuckling.

———※———

Selaphiel felt his throat throb with pain; he hadn't had anything to drink for some time. The Taneem attending to him looked nearly asleep.

"Could I have some water?" he asked, his voice raspy.

The Taneem's eyes snapped open and it shook its head to wake itself. It grabbed a large wineskin and threw it through the openings of the bars. It sloshed onto the ground, some of its contents spilling onto the floor.

Selaphiel drank it quickly, the cool water soothing his scratchy throat.

"Are you content or do you need more?" the Taneem said, looking at him flatly.

Selaphiel shook his head, wiping his mouth. "Your gesture is appreciated," he coughed.

It tilted its head inquisitively.

"What do you mean?"

Selaphiel attempted a shrug.

"I don't think everyone is bound to be evil. The same as I do not believe one is forced to be kind; they are each a choice."

The Taneem grinned a needled smile. "It is not out of kindness that I give you water, but so you can be kept alive. Nothing more. Besides, all Taneemian are the same. We are what we are."

"You gave me water," Selaphiel said, an edge to his voice, "So I will only tell you this once. Let me out or else."

The Taneem rolled its black orbs of eyes.

"Or else? That sounds like fun."

Selaphiel's eyes glowed yellow, the golden hue cascading across the room, illuminating the Taneem, who grabbed his weapon and stepped back. The weapon was a long metal rod with a sharp blade on the end resembling a reaper's scythe. He raised his scythe to strike at Selaphiel through the bars, but a blinding light erupted from Selaphiel. The Taneem stumbled backward, blinded. His keys dropped from his hand, and a tendril of light reached out and grabbed the key, pulling them into the cell.

"Fool!" the creature growled, scratching at its eyes furiously.

Selaphiel put the key in the lock and popped the door open.

The Taneem began to flail his weapon aimlessly in the air around Selaphiel.

"Perhaps ..." Selaphiel said as he crouched, drawing with his fingers in the air at his side. Yellowish flame flowed through his fingertips and formed into a sword; the blade materialized as a bronze luminescence. With a swift motion, he struck the Taneem below the ribs, the blade sizzling at the contact.

The Taneem fell silent and black globs of blood spilled out of his mouth.

"Fool of a ..." was all the creature could manage as Selaphiel pushed it off the blade, the body landing with a soft thump. It lay in a pool of its own blood, which hissed familiarly as it spread on the prison floor. Selaphiel leaned on the wall, using his sword to balance himself. He hadn't known he was capable of making a sword appear out of nothing.

"What in Yadir?" he whispered, ducking into an empty cell. He had always been able to control his magic, but this time something was different. This time his magic had acted of its own accord. He reached into his pocket and felt the windowspeak, tensing as he pulled out several broken pieces.

"So much for that."

He dropped the smaller shards of broken glass onto the cell floor and kept the largest piece. No doubt his recent battles had been the cause of the broken item.

"I am Selaphiel; I wish to speak to Derrick of the Ashenborn."

The surface of the broken glass did nothing but show his reflection.

"Great. Derrick gives me one item, and I break it," he said, unhappy with himself.

At the very least I have a mirror now, he thought.

A short Taneem entered the passageway. It sniffed the air, its dark eyes scanning the cells until it landed on the other Taneem's body.

"Lord Belial," the creature called back to his master.

"Oh, that's just great," Selaphiel muttered. "Fantastic news."

A tall menacing figure covered the light of the doorway.

"Yes, Darcre?" a familiar voice growled.

Darcre motioned to the dead body.

Selaphiel sighed.

I bet Cordoc would have had no trouble getting out of here, he thought, wishing his brother were with him.

"Selaphiel," Belial called into the prison, "return to your cell and we will overlook your transgression. He was a meaningless pawn. You will be forgiven for the murder of this Taneem."

Selaphiel began to sweat. As he leaned against the wall, he noticed his flame sword quivering and white sparks beginning to shoot from the blade.

Belial saw the sparks and moved toward the cell, Darcre behind him.

"Cease what you are doing," Belial said menacingly.

The power surrounding Selaphiel streamed into the sword.

Selaphiel tried to shield his sword, but as he did, the yellow flame solidified into crystal-clear glass. Selaphiel's eyes began to glow a tawny bronze.

Belial growled, "Selaphiel, come out."

Selaphiel felt the same call to action he had felt when summoning the sword. He knew what to do now. With all his strength, he stabbed the floor of the prison. A gold tidal wave of magic flew through the prison, and lightning cascaded from the point of contact. White sparks bounced off the shaking walls, making popping noises. The power surrounded him, and the power shot into him. Selaphiel felt strength erupt through the wave of magic. White light formed around him, and his body began to elongate, new limbs began to form on his back, and a tail began to take shape.

As light sparked and energy poured out of him, he grew to four times his original size. Selaphiel let out a yell that turned into a roar. The energy burst out a final wave, cracking the prison in half and sending rubble flying in all directions.

Selaphiel opened his newly enlarged eyes. The magic sparked and dissipated until only a magnificent gold and bronze dragon remained. Selaphiel realized he was now a massive two-winged dragon, with bronze teeth and horns. Glowing golden scales protected him like the massive shields of knights prepared for battle. He twisted his long tail and unfurled his yellow wings. He felt a burning in his chest, so Selaphiel opened his mouth and a river of fire spewed out.

"No!" Belial yelled, holding a sizable wound on his side caused by falling rubble.

"Attack!" Belial cried, pulling his sword. "Forget about keeping him alive!"

With a shout, Belial and several other Taneems charged Selaphiel.

As Belial ran, he threw a black orb of magic, striking Selaphiel on the side. The orb shattered against his golden scales and fell harmlessly to the ground.

Selaphiel smiled. Pushing of the ground with his four powerful legs, Selaphiel was airborne. His massive wings thrust him through the new opening in the prison roof. Turning, Selaphiel roared and breathed a fireball of yellow flame at the prison. The flames streamed through the cracks of stone, demolishing it more. The heart of the blast struck Belial, who catapulted into a wall, falling to the ground. His body lay motionless.

Selaphiel turned to leave and felt hot fire strike him with a jolt on his jaw. Selaphiel spiraled but righted himself with a few flaps of his wings. He looked around, unsure where the blow had come from. Another one hit him, making him lose control and sending him crashing into a dense group of trees, the large trunks snapping like twigs as he hit them. He rolled to his feet and clawed the ground, exposing mud and damp ground from the night before.

Malakh's voice rang through the forest, "Strike him now, fools, before he escapes!"

Red flames erupted all around him, forming a circled dome of flame. Selaphiel growled. He had been easily captured before, but now, his enemy did not have as much of an advantage. He roared a challenge and met the flame with flames of his own. He propelled into the sky, the flames flowing from his mouth and exhilarating him.

---❀---

The monstrous roar tore through the forest.

"What was that?" Daemos asked, his hand on his axe.

Cordoc strained to see ahead. His eyes seemed to brighten a little.

"I don't know, but whatever it is, Selaphiel must have something to do with it."

Daemos gave him a bewildered look.

"It could be a Scorian; it is foolish to head toward a noise we don't recognize."

Cordoc nodded as a golden torrent of flame flew from the forest a mile away.

"A dragon with golden flame!" Cordoc yelled as he took off at a sprint. The flames illuminated the shadows where they stood.

"Not a Scorian, then," Daemos called ahead, out of breath as he tried to keep up. Cordoc, looking excited, didn't slow his pace.

The forest shook around them as a giant object fell from the sky, scorching trees and sending smoke spiraling into the blue sky. Cordoc let his magic flow through him, and he notched an arrow with a magical energy burning from the tips of his fingers. Daemos stopped, bending over to breathe as he caught up to Cordoc.

They were close enough to see the prison. Flames had torn through a small fortress in the center of the garrison, and there was a hole in the roof that looked fresh. Cordoc noticed several Taneems dazedly attempting to recover from the blast. Cordoc froze when he saw the large form of Belial rise from the flames, black flames of his own encircling him. Cordoc and Daemos crouched behind a large boulder, watching cautiously. Daemos pulled out his hunting knife.

A voice called out commands, though neither Daemos nor Cordoc could understand its meaning. Belial growled angrily with needled teeth and breathed scarlet flames, dispelling the golden flames still flickering around him. He unsheathed his wicked sword and angrily growled out more orders.

Daemos gripped his blade tightly.

"Shall we head in the direction the enemy is going?" he asked.

Cordoc nodded, his gaze moving toward the scorched trees.

Belial's eyes turned white, and he followed the other Taneem from view. Cordoc and Daemos followed cautiously. Crimson fingers of fire licked the trees, and Cordock could see the Taneems gathered in a circle around a massive creature. Cordoc hid behind an old tree and Daemos fell back, finding a bush to crouch behind. The Taneems used their dark flames to encircle the dragon. Another figure floated above the dome of flame. Its voice reverberated. A voice Cordoc remembered.

"Selaphiel, you have nowhere to go!" Malakh said loudly.

The golden dragon tucked in its wings and opened its maw to roar a challenge. Cordoc watched, admiring Selaphiel's transformation. He had no doubt this was his brother. Daemos watched the scene for a moment before saying, "Shoot Malakh."

Cordoc nodded.

With all his strength he pulled back his bow, and the arrow flew though the air with a whistle, straight for Malakh. Malakh turned at the noise and was struck in the arm, causing him to drop his sword. Malakh yelled, and the Taneems around Selaphiel lost focus on their spells and the dome failed.

"Attack Malakh, Selaphiel! It is Daemos and Cordoc!" Cordoc yelled and fired two more arrows at nearby Taneems. Daemos charged at the monsters as well. With a burst of wind, Selaphiel cleared the distance between him and Malakh. He was overjoyed to know that his brother and Daemos were now here to help him take on the insurmountable odds. He spewed a torrent of flame upon his enemy, his rage palpable. Malakh howled in pain, stumbling back, a fresh bubbling burn on his exposed arm. Cordoc fired again, his arrow flying straight and true. Malakh dropped to the ground and glared at the arrow protruding from his chest.

Cordoc eyed him with caution, knowing full well that though well-placed, the blow would not be the end of it. Selaphiel landed and struck like a cobra as Malakh ripped the arrow from his chest, blood staining his clothes. Malakh avoided Selaphiel's fangs with a backward movement but was thrown off balance. Selaphiel followed with a tail swipe, which sent Malakh tumbling violently to the ground. Malakh rolled desperately and grabbed the sword he had dropped, jabbing at the dragon's head. Selaphiel retreated, the inside of his mouth bleeding where Malakh had landed a lucky blow.

Malakh wiped his own blood from his head as he brushed his hair out of his face.

"Bloody child!" he yelled. Malakh struck the ground with his blade. Dark shadowy tentacles emerged from the blade and wrapped around Malakh. Selaphiel took a deep breath and exhaled as much flame as he could. The flames sparked off of Malakh uselessly.

"You have only just found this form, but I have perfected it," Malakh goaded, his voice deepening. With that, dark purple lesions began to sprout from his hands and feet.

Selaphiel winced at the revolting sight before him.

Malakh's dragon was equal to the size of Selaphiel, but stood on two legs. His back legs bent slightly as he hovered in place. Spikes adorned his brow and joints, and dark crimson wings larger than his body sprouted from his back. The amaranthine dragon growled and purple flames flickered from its mouth and claws. The transformation was grotesque, as Malakh writhed like a snake that had just shed its skin.

"Behold," the beast gurgled.

Selaphiel charged and flung himself at the monster, his mouth open in a roar. Malakh moved aside and struck him on the jaw with his jagged tail.

Selaphiel felt his teeth snap together and his ears rang.

"You are an inferior creature," Malakh said as more purple flames erupted from his claws and wrapped around Selaphiel like a chain. The chain tightened around Selaphiel's neck like a noose. Selaphiel struggled to remove it, but each movement made the chain grow tighter. It became harder and harder to breath. Another of Cordoc's arrows flew at Malakh but bounced off harmlessly. Malakh rumbled a chuckle. He slung Selaphiel to the ground, breaking the magic chain, and lifted the other claw to send Cordoc flying. Selaphiel coughed sparks and struggled to lift himself. He felt light-headed.

"It is ironic," Malakh said and struck Selaphiel as he was getting up. "You are acting as though you are some sort of deity." Malakh shrugged and shot another spell at Selaphiel. "In the face of the true power you are as mere children only dreaming of strength."

Malakh laughed and shook his head when he realized that all of his Taneemian servants were dead.

"So you killed them," he said, sneering. "Truthfully, I do not need them. Their failures are as numerous as their abilities to rebirth themselves."

Selaphiel rose slowly, still feeling groggy. He stepped between Malakh and where he knew Cordoc was hiding in the woods. Malakh flapped his wings and turned his head to the side.

"Stubborn children at that. Spoiled even. Good children know how to take their punishment."

Cordoc suddenly appeared in dragon form, breathing fire as he advanced on Malakh.

"Children of Fire," Cordoc said, his eyes shining.

The sapphire dragon stood up with its wings flaired. Both bronze and blue behemoths stood on either side of Daemos.

"Imagine that," came the familiar voice of Belial. "More Ashenborn."

"Yes, and now that there are two, you'd better run, little flea," Cordoc said in his newly deep voice.

Malakh laughed. "Just more targets for me." He crouched, saying, "Do not get in my way, Belial."

Selaphiel cannoned into the air, while Cordoc stayed on the ground. Blue flames jetted at Malakh. He looked aggravated as he used magic to defend himself, then swiped his tail across Cordoc's face. Selaphiel clamped his jaws down on Malakh's tail and held on tightly. Malakh screeched but couldn't move as Selaphiel dug into the earth below, pinning him to the spot. Belial ran at Selaphiel but was tripped by Daemos.

"Forgetting someone?" Daemos said.

"Blasted flesh!"

Daemos circled him with his sword, challenging him.

Cordoc was happy for the distraction. He pounced on Malakh, roaring like a lion. Malkah tumbled to the ground at the impact. Selaphiel let go of his tail and joined the terrible brawl.

Malakh's teeth flared purple flame as Selaphiel and Cordoc tore at his wings with their fangs.

A shockwave of fire sent the brothers tumbling backward into the dirt. Malakh's wings dangled uselessly beside him. They were broken, the membranes ripped like parchment.

Malakh was breathing hard but never took his slits of eyes off them.

"Do not think you have won," he said, gasping for breath.

"I didn't think gods got tired," Cordoc said mockingly.

Selaphiel growled. "Come on then. We're ready for you."

Malakh moved forward but his legs gave out beneath him, and he hissed in frustration. His clawed hand shook, and he glared down at it angrily.

"He's finished," Cordoc said circling him.

Selaphiel nodded.

Daemos pinned Belial to the ground beside them.

"You all are fools! You will pay—" A hit from the side of Daemos's blade silenced Belial, knocking him out.

"Thank you," Cordoc said.

"Why are you interested in Selaphiel?" Cordoc said, addressing Malakh.

Malakh spit blood and flexed his hand.

"Wouldn't you like to know."

"We will kill you right here," Cordoc said. "Or you can start talking."

Selaphiel gave his brother a concerned look.

Malakh's mouth curved up in a sly smile.

"You wouldn't do it."

Purple flames slowly moved their way over Malakh's body, and the torn membrane of his wings began to stitch itself together.

"Wouldn't I?" Cordoc's eyes glowed sapphire.

"Brother," Selaphiel said softly.

Cordoc turned to him and shook his head.

"He took you and tortured you. He nearly killed me. He cannot be left alive."

"He should be given mercy. We don't have to kill him," Selaphiel said.

Malakh shook his head and chuckled.

"Don't follow us. Next time you will not be so lucky," Selaphiel said sternly.

Malakh hissed, "I will kill you next time. Regardless of my Lord's wishes."

Selaphiel floated into the air.

"Do not speak prophecy that you cannot fulfill."

Cordoc picked up Daemos in his claws. He watched as Selaphiel flew into the open air.

Cordoc narrowed his eyes. An image of a dead dragon flashed across his vision.

"I may have underestimated you once. But I assure you if you do try anything against us in the future, you will die; this is a true prophecy. I have seen it."

Malakh tensed at Cordoc's words.

"The only truth, boy, is that my master will adorn his crown with your and your brother's scales."

Cordoc hovered above him.

"I do not doubt he would try."

Malakh kept talking, but Cordoc ignored him as he followed after Selaphiel.

The day had turned to night. They were able to hide in the clouds, the cool dampness keeping them awake. Selaphiel saw an opening in the forest beside a lake. Cordoc spotted it at the same time and they began to descend, their strength failing. Cordoc could feel the dragon power leaving him, and quickly they landed on the beach of the lake. Their magic left them and they both crumpled to the ground.

Daemos watched over them as they slept, his muscles tired but his mind alert.

———— ❋ ————

Selaphiel awoke to the aroma of cooking meat. Opening his eyes, he saw Daemos sitting on the opposite side of a fire, two rabbits roasting on a makeshift spit. With a groan he moved to a sitting position. He noticed Cordoc was gone.

"He's checking to make sure we weren't followed," Daemos said, poking at the browning meat, to answer Selaphiel's thought.

Selaphiel groaned. "I feel like I've been trampled on by a herd of cows."

Daemos nodded, replying, "I suppose that would make you ground beef."

Selaphiel stared at him for a moment and shook his head.

"You make terrible jokes, like Thornbeorn," Selaphiel said.

Daemos winked, pulled a rabbit off the spit, and handed it to Selaphiel. Its meat was a light golden brown.

"Cordoc has already eaten; I caught these earlier this morning."

Selaphiel took it thankfully, looking around the wooded area they were in as he chewed. He ate ravenously, the sweet gamey taste welcome, as he had not been given food during his capture.

"Scorian territory," Daemos said, a grim look on his face.

Selaphiel stopped chewing and swallowed the bite in his mouth.

"How far in are we?" he questioned.

Daemos shrugged. "On the outer edge. Scorians have not been seen for years. Large ravenous beasts, they are."

Selaphiel nodded. "I recall having heard of one on the outskirts of some northern kingdom when I was younger. It was seen leagues away, though," he said finishing his meat.

"Do you want the other? Speaking of ravenous beasts," Daemos said, aware of how quickly Selaphiel had stripped the rabbit.

Selaphiel shook his head. He stretched and groaned at how sore he was.

"Thank you," he said, wiping the grease from his lips with his sleeve. "That was a close call with Malakh; without you two I would have never escaped."

Selaphiel looked at his wounds, which had healed to light purple scars while he slept.

"I am healed already?" he said, amazed at how quickly the wounds from yesterday's battle had disappeared.

Daemos laughed. "The dragon power is full of mysteries. And it was our pleasure, but without Cordoc ..."

"You would have done just fine, Daemos," Cordoc said, interrupting.

Selaphiel jumped up at the sound of his brother's voice.

Cordoc looked at him, ashamed.

"What is it, Brother?" Selaphiel asked.

Cordoc stared at the ground.

"If it had not been for my arrogance, you and Daemos would have not had to deal with this pain," Cordoc said. "I foolishly challenged an opponent I wasn't prepared to face on my own. I do not deserve to be your brother. What I put you through cannot be forgiven."

Selaphiel shook his head.

"Our enemy would have gotten me even if that had not happened. I thought you were dead. No apology is necessary. I'm just glad you're alive."

Daemos smiled as Cordoc hugged Selaphiel.

"Thank you for coming to save me," Selaphiel said. "Both of you."

"You are much too forgiving," Cordoc said gratefully.

Daemos put a closed fist to his chest.

"We would not have stood a chance if not for you, Selaphiel. That was impressive," Daemos said.

Cordoc smiled. "You have ascended to an Ashenborn. Only royal blood can do that."

He knew what he was saying as he said it. As an adopted son, Selaphiel had often doubted his own importance.

Selaphiel lifted an eyebrow.

"The fragment senses it in you, Brother," Cordoc said. "You are no less royal than I or Jakobin."

Selaphiel nodded.

"You have never been," Cordoc added.

Daemos shook his head. "I can't say I'm not jealous of the power within you both. That was spectacular."

Daemos took the last of the rabbit and began to eat it.

"What is it like? To be Ashenborn?" he asked around a mouthful of roasted meat.

Selaphiel and Cordoc were silent, thinking over his question.

"Like ..." Cordoc trailed off.

"... being a giant raging bonfire," Selaphiel ventured.

"Perhaps that's accurate; it's like nothing I can describe. It isn't initially a pleasant experience. Besides, having wings feels like having an extra pair of arms on your back," Cordoc affirmed.

"Same for the tail," Selaphiel laughed.

Daemos coughed, choking on rabbit as he tried to hold back a laugh.

Cordoc scratched his head.

"Though we have more issues, it seems. Malfait is not far from here, and we have several men after us."

"Tsal, Malakh, and Belial," Selaphiel said. "Hopefully Malakh is too badly wounded to follow us, but I feel he won't give up. And they'll bring more Taneems with them this time."

"Each of them is high-ranking in Elim's army. For all three to be sent after you two is serious," Daemos added.

"I wish we could have discerned their purpose for wanting you. Do you remember anything they might have said that would help us figure it out?" Cordoc said to Selaphiel.

"Nothing. They spoke of killing me, but they planned to take me to Elim. They said he wanted me alive. I'm unsure why. Whatever it is, I'm sure I'll get an audience with Elim sooner or later, despite it being unwanted."

"Why Selaphiel specifically?" Daemos asked.

Cordoc rubbed his nose, a common gesture when he was thinking.

"Who knows," he replied.

"There was one thing that struck me as odd. Malakh said, *'The three of us.'* Meaning Jakobin is alive," Selaphiel said, recalling the comment.

"I hope so." Cordoc said.

"He said he intended to eliminate the blood of Alanias. But that did not include me for some reason," Selaphiel said.

Daemos poked the fire with a stick.

"Because you are not blood to Alanias, though you are his son. Which means Cordoc, then Jakobin would inherit the throne first ..."

Daemos stood up abruptly.

"When Father dies," Cordoc said.

"Elim does hate Lifesveil. Not surprising considering it contained his prison," Selaphiel said.

"Alanias got word the two of you were being followed, so he sent me to help protect you. He didn't know who was following you, though, or why," Daemos added.

"We must go to Malfait now; if Elim is trying to eradicate your bloodline he would have to start with Lifesveil," Selaphiel said.

"Or the High King," Cordoc said in a moment of realization.

"It makes sense," Daemos said angrily, throwing the rest of the stick in the fire. "Alanias never said you two specifically were headed to Malfait. Someone had to inform him. Perhaps one of our own."

Selaphiel clenched his fists.

"That means where ever Jakobin is, he is not safe," Selaphiel said.

"Your brother is smart. Our best bet is like you said, stick to what Alanias told you and go to Malfait. No doubt your brother knew of the importance of getting there."

"True. So we need to go now," Cordoc agreed.

"Wait. Did Father explain his plans for us to go to Malfait to you?" Selaphiel asked Daemos.

Daemos slowly shook his head.

"No and yes. He told me you were going there for aid, and that it would require royalty to speak to the king there." Daemos paused. "I imagined it was because it was sensitive information. It's not smart for someone of my rank to question the decisions of a king. Besides, it's not unknown for a father to send his son to represent him."

Cordoc looked grim.

Selaphiel noticed his expression.

"What is it?"

"Have you given thought as to why Father sent us?" Cordoc said. "And not someone else?"

"It's like Daemos said; the severity of the situation is best conveyed by sending one's own family."

"Maybe," Cordoc said. "But why not send just one of us? He sent all three of us."

"Questioning this will do no good at the moment; for now, let's proceed with what the king has told us," Daemos said, although he understood the point Cordoc was trying to make.

"Okay," Selaphiel said absentmindedly and checked the fragment in his wrist. It looked as bright as it had before.

"I placed your hand in the fire to replenish it. Yours looks as though it has full strength," Cordoc said, noticing him examining his wrist.

"Thank you," Selaphiel said.

"I have just thought of it, but why not contact Derrick? Do you still have the windowspeak?" Cordoc asked.

Selaphiel gave him an embarrased look as he produced the one small piece that had been left over after finding it broken.

"Does it still work?" Cordoc asked with hope.

"No," Selaphiel said sadly. "I guess it broke during the fight or when they transported me to the prison."

"It cannot be helped at the moment, though it is a setback for sure."

"What would be our best way to travel to leave here?" Selaphiel asked.

Cordoc turned to observe the skies.

"Daemos, we will glide low and follow you as you are on the ground." Cordoc noticed that mist had surrounded the trees, making it hard to see.

"With the mist, if we fly low we should be able to stay hidden."

Daemos grabbed his knife and tied it to his side.

"It is not very far. Only a few hours on horseback."

"Less with wings." Cordoc winked.

Daemos glared. "I will not be carried when I can ride. I am a soldier, not a parcel."

Selaphiel threw his hands up.

"I know, right?" he said sarcastically.

Cordoc laughed.

"You enjoyed that ride," Cordoc said, laughing. "Besides, this time you can fly on your own."

"Or carry you …" Selaphiel looked at him with a challenging expression.

"Regardless," Daemos said, "we must leave immediately. There is no time to delay."

Cordoc and Selaphiel agreed.

"What from the scouts?"

"Ten thousand or more. Truly it is hard to count an enemy that doesn't really die," Zarx replied.

Alanias rubbed his temples, feeling the prelude to a massive headache.

"We haven't received word of any reinforcements. We only have what is available to us here," Alanias said, exasperated, now rubbing his forehead.

"Don't worry, King. We will hold them," Zarx said assuredly.

Alanias' thoughts went to his sons.

"Do you think I chose well to send my sons away?"

"I cannot speak on your decisions because I stand by them, but I know this: protecting the future is always a priority. Your children fall under that category," Zarx said.

Alanias gave a brief smile.

"What are your orders?" Zarx said, hoping to distract the king from his worry for his sons.

Alanias pointed at several maps of the kingdom laid out on a large table.

As he moved steel figures that represented his armies into various locations, the king and Zarx discussed placement and the most likely areas of attack.

"It will be done," Zarx said. "We won't lose."

The dull short call of a horn echoed through the walls.

"The archers are in place," Zarx said.

Alanias' face hardened.

"How long until they are here?" Alanias asked.

"Within two days."

Zarx folded his arms.

"How can this enemy have so many already?"

Alanias put both his hands on the map, not looking at Zarx, his face downcast.

"This enemy has always been there. It is just now that they are making their move. We thought we had broken the power of the Taneemian, but we could never be completely sure of it."

Zarx eyed him curiously.

"Always been here?" Zarx asked, wondering what the king meant by those words.

Alanias pushed himself to his feet.

"Enemies do not allow those they wish to destroy to know their full strength; they only allow us glimpses of their true nature in order to let us think we have the upper hand."

"And then they overtake us," Zarx said. "So you think there are more than we see."

"Yes."

"I will send another Silver Talon to verify," Zarx said.

"Good. We will hold a counsel at first light tomorrow."

"Yes, King," Zarx replied. "I also have additional news."

Alanias paused, waiting for Zarx to continue.

"The situation of which we spoke has been seen to. Derrick is aware."

CHAPTER 10
DECEPTION OF A DRAGON

———— ✳ ————

D errick looked around, noting who was present in the grand room. On the signal middle platform stood the one who was to address the counsel of Ashenborn. The middle platform was of intricate design. Elaborate patterns and jewels adorned it, giving emphasis to whoever was speaking, making them taller than those congregated below. Behind it was a massive mirror; an eye was carved into the magical substance. The eye was surrounded by ancient symbols. The mirror was by all accounts the most ancient object in the room and quite possibly in all of Yadir. To speak in its presence to a gathering of the Ashenborn was incredibly symbolic.

Each member of the Order stood in a half circle around the one speaking into compartments that resembled dragon heads. The dragons had been carved with their mouths agape, as if breathing fire toward an adversary. The compartments were not as gloriously decorated as the center dias, but they still held importance by their placement within the big room. In total there were eleven compartments. Derrick felt uncomfortable, his eyes searching for a friend. He saw the familiar face of Etghar, whose untrimmed eyebrows contrasted wildly with his well-kempt beard. Near him was Keirfen, the youngest member of the assembly. Her blonde hair shone brightly, and she had a concerned expression on her normally smiling face. Derrick continued to scan the room. He frowned as eventually his eyes landed on Bageden's empty spot.

Albion took the platform first. Everyone became silent as he stood above them. Uriaelh stood next to Derrick, their eyes meeting in mutual concern.

Albion stood motionless upon the platform, smiling at them as old friends.

Derrick's stomach knotted with unease, but he felt he could trust Albion at least. He was sure everything would be explained, and all would eventually make sense.

Albion greeted them, placing his sword into the slot in the foremost position of the platform, signifying both his status and his right to speak. The other Ashenborn did likewise in their respective locations. Derrick relinquished his sword grudgingly, uncomfortable at the idea of being weaponless.

"In all the ages of the rule of the Ashenborn we have never been as powerless as we are today," Albion's voice echoed and boomed in the immense room. "We have become less and less involved with this world, shirking our responsibilities for our own wealth."

Albion looked down, shame on his face. "As your leader, the fault is mine. I have been more concerned with peace than actually maintaining peace."

The room was silent as Derrick and the others attempted to make sense of Albion's words.

"We have lost our value. We shone through the War of Stones by defeating an enemy without boundaries, without restraint, or without respect for life." Albion paused and looked each of them squarely in the face.

"It is time we do more than be religious teachers, sages, and old magicians hiding within the confines of this garnished tower." Albion pointed to the platform on which he stood.

"Long have we considered ourselves as gods, with decorations of jewels and piles of hidden treasure. We make ourselves higher than gods and have limited ourselves to old ways. We may not have stated our divinity aloud, but our actions suggest we feel this way. When in reality we act as mere babes, entranced by anything that shines brighter than the jewels we own."

Albion paused and turned to face the mirror, his reflection looking back at him.

"We may be Ashenborn, but we are all mortal inhabitants of Yadir," Albion said, peeling his gaze from the glass.

"Archkyris is indeed dead. The Taneemian have returned, and former captives of the War of Stones are free to do as they please. I have been busy in the kingdom of Archkyris and can verify the High King was murdered by one of Elim's men."

Albion looked at them with hard eyes.

"I ask, what will you do now?"

The crowd of men and women murmured among each other. Albion pointed a finger upward.

"The old Ashenborn ways must end, and a new era must begin for us."

Derrick squinted his eyes, wondering where this was going.

Albion paced.

"A new High King will be selected, but that is the least of our worries currently. Edywin will regulate the throne for now. We must focus our efforts on quelling the massive threat of Elim and the Taneemian." The murmurs grew louder.

"Hoakama, the stewardess of the new king, shares our ideals. She will guard the throne and rule justly for the time being. I know it makes everyone nervous to entrust so much power to one person, but to me there is no better person in whom to put that hope."

Etghar lifted his sword, signaling he would like to speak.

Albion nodded, acknowledging him and ceeding the floor.

"I believe I speak for most of us when I say that we trust you, Albion. We trust in your ability to lead us, but most of us feel misguided with your trust in Edywin and Hoakama."

Etghar rubbed his eyebrow, not answering.

"You speak for everyone?" Albion asked.

Albion looked around and noticed the perplexed looks on Derrick's and Uriaelh's faces.

"The majority," Etghar said, spreading his hands out.

"Ah," Albion said. "Please state your reasoning."

Etghar nodded.

"You see, many of us did not truly care for the High King Archkyris. We followed him merely because he provided the things that anyone needs, such as prosperity and peace. We find ourselves in a situation where we could remain prosperous and peaceful. By allowing Hoakama the throne for the time being, many will lose their lives."

"And what is your solution? Do nothing?" Uriaelh said angrily.

Albion held up his hand and turned to Uriaelh.

"He has the floor for now. I understand your anger at his words but let us hear what he has to say. It is never wise to consider just one option."

Uriaelh apologized for the outburst and quieted himself. Etghar shot him an aggravated look.

"As I was saying. We seek peace. There would be no lives lost."

Albion rubbed his beard, considering Etghar's meaning.

"How would you do such a thing? The Taneemian would not simply disregard their master's bidding."

Etghar raised a brow.

"What if their master's bidding had changed?"

Albion furrowed his brow. Everyone was quiet.

"Changed how?"

"What if we made a truce. Even allied ourselves with Elim. Archkyris is dead, and so we must change as you so aptly put it."

Albion rubbed his temples. The crowd muttered nervously.

Derrick's face reddened, but he dared not break the sacredness of tradition by speaking out of turn.

"You mean we would ally ourselves with one whose father slaughtered hundreds of thousands, and with his son who slaughtered thousands? Have you forgotten that?" Albion said, his voice shaking.

Albion was trying hard to restrain his anger, Derrick could tell.

The room was tense. All eyes were on Etghar.

"No one has forgotten. But in the face of sure destruction, and for the good of Yadir, things must be compromised, overlooked even, for the betterment—nay, safety—of its people. Even if we may be uncomfortable with it. Decisions need to be made."

Albion's face reddened as well.

"Forget … how could we forget?" Albion paused. "There are families who were torn apart because of those monsters. Mothers who will never see their sons become fathers. You want us to compromise? our souls? You have disguised reason as foolishness. You speak with your viperous tongue about peace and prosperity. Truthfully, in life these things are second to calling out evil when it appears."

Etghar folded his arms.

"It is not about our feelings, Albion. We have already voted on the decision."

"Voted?" Derrick blurted out.

Uriaelh gripped the side of the platform.

"There was no such vote."

Mara, a senior member of the council, stood up, enraged.

"You did so behind all of our backs!" she shouted.

"You should speak in turn; our rules dictate …"

"Forget tradition," Albion said angrily. "You would go behind the back of your leader …"

"To make the best decision," Etghar asserted, glaring.

A figure entered the room slowly, his footsteps echoing through the large chamber. Derrick felt a chill in the air, one he had not felt in a long time. His body stiffened, and a thread of doubt grew within him.

"We fought a war to destroy the power of Dothros. His son Elim now wields the same power as his father. The Taneemian can be swayed to serve new masters," Etghar said.

Derrick, Uriaelh, and Mara looked at him as one would look at something putrid. The cloaked man approached the podium, slowly removing the hood covering his head.

Derrick stared in disbelief, his breath caught in his throat. "Tsal ..."

The tall silver-haired man smiled chillingly as Etghar stood behind him. By all accounts, he stood as a triumphant warrior that had defeated an army with his raw prowess, defeating them without lifting a finger.

Derrick's blood boiled at the atrocity he saw before him.

"The Nakal," Tsal began, removing a scythe from his side. "Have made an agreement to assist the Ashenborn," he continued, casually leaning on the weapon's handle.

"The Nakal!" Uriaelh said, stricken.

Derrick stood stunned, palms open as if grasping for something.

"False Ashenborn," Derrick whispered. A word that had not been used in a long time. Manipulators of the dragon form through secret means outside of the pure magic possessed by the Ashenborn.

"Traitor!" Uriaelh yelled. His magic flamed from his fingers and he moved forward, gritting his teeth.

Mara put a hand behind her to steady herself. She could only stare at Tsal, mouth open in horror.

What confused Derrick most was the lack of reaction from the rest of the order. They acted as though none of this were new information.

"We convened you here because of your association with Hoakama and Uriaelh," Etghar spat. "You may have summoned us, Albion, but we have used your meeting for our own purposes."

Albion glanced at Etghar.

"Elder Derrick. You are the oldest and strongest among us; you should know the precautions we had to make …" Etghar began.

"Precautions?" Derrick said. "You meant to force us to choose. Call this what it is, a coup."

Derrick's magic could not be contained as flames began to pulsate from his palms.

"Precautions!" Derrick said loudly, his calm demeanor gone.

"You have decided for yourselves. You have pulled us away from our kingdoms so that numbers will be on your side to kill us if you find our answer unsatisfactory." Albion growled.

Tsal shook his head.

"We knew there might be some convincing with our histories, but I did not think you would display so much hatred," Tsal said, his voice calm and soothing, like a viper luring its prey. "This is not the demeanor of someone who supposedly has the best interests of his people in mind."

Derrick could feel fire forming into a small sphere in his palm. He hoped others would stand with them, but only Mara, Uriaelh, and Albion seemed outraged at Etghar's treachery.

Mara lifted her sword and pointed it toward Tsal.

"You killed hundreds of our people and kin! You are beyond reconciliation!"

Tsal lifted the reaper's hammer, tightening his grip.

"Please do not do that," Etghar said, noticing his movement.

"You either choose to follow us or you leave," Etghar said, turning back to the crowd.

Tsal looked at him for a moment, and chuckled.

"They will not join Elim. Their chance is up. They do not have the choice to leave."

Tsal swung the scythe, the hammer side striking the mirror in the center of the eye's pupil. Cracks spread from the center of the eye, and the mirror shattered into a thousand shards of glass.

The spikes of glass flew through the air like weapons. Derrick stood frozen as a long narrow shard plunged into Mara's chest. She gasped as her breath caught in her throat. Uriaelh turned toward her in horror. The others covered themselves in magic to deflect the sharp edges of the glass. Mara fell slowly, giving a harsh cough. A trickle of blood flowed from her mouth. The room was quiet as smaller grains of glass fell at their feet. No one spoke as Mara's body twitched, then lay still. Derrick knelt beside the pool of blood to confirm her death himself.

"She is … dead," Derrick said in disbelief.

"Murderer," Albion growled.

"Raaaaaaa!" Uriaelh yelled, throwing a bolt of fire at the dais.

Masterfully, Tsal avoided the bolt and sliced the fire in half with the blade of his weapon. Tsal smiled confidently as the flames extinguished at the edge of the Mavetian weapon. Etghar, along with the remaining Ashenborn, stood behind Tsal now. Etghar's laugh echoed with pleasure.

Uriaelh looked at them, confused, as he, Derrick, and Albion were the only ones who stood bottlenecked in front of them. Uriaelh breathed harshly as anger coursed through him, and he lifted his arm to deliver another bolt of lightning. Derrick held up his hand, making Uriaelh pause.

"So, we were to bend our knee before you, like the rest," Albion said as his eyes filled with anger.

Albion looked at Etghar.

"We know what needs to be done."

Tsal said, "Do you?"

Uriaelh's eyes were full of tears, his breathing uneven.

"You mean to murder us. Murder the innocent for your own gain."

"Let us go," Albion said, aware of how outnumbered they were and where this confrontation was heading. He searched each of their faces for compassion or guilt; the only one to look away from his gaze was Keirfen. The rest met him with eyes full of hatred and malice.

Uriaelh shifted uneasily.

"You mean to end all wars, with your own hands, by starting one. You truly are monsters," Uriaelh said. An unnatural feeling was in the air.

"We were at peace," Derrick said, still shaken by Mara's death.

"There can never truly be peace," Tsal said, "When a king has died."

"Killed like Mara," Uriaelh said through gritted teeth. "An act of war on your part."

Derrick shook his head in disbelief.

"Why?" Derrick said, looking around at his friends, his kinsmen. "When did you become so obsessed with power that you would give up Yadir's freedom and ignore the acts of a murderer to follow him instead?"

Etghar shrank before Derrick's words, answering him in a small voice.

"Yadir needs us to take over. To make unity where there is separation. Lives must be lost to secure it, as in any war."

Derrick's frustration and anger boiled to the top as the transformation overtook him. Uriaelh and Derrick became infernos of devouring heat as their bodies changed into dragons. Albion's body shone brightly as he began to transform as well.

Uriaelh's copper-colored scales gleamed like snakeskin. Derrick thundered a roar through the tower, the walls vibrating from its sonorous tone.

"Fools!" Etghar raged. "You are cast out from our kind!"

Albion transformed into a golden-bronze dragon and trumpeted a roar.

Derrick reared back and rammed into the far wall, bursting through the stone as if it were made of rotting wood. Smoke and dust tarnished the once-clean temple. Uriaelh, close behind Derrick, slashed at the floor, causing it to crack and sway. The three dragons filled the room with flames and choking smoke. The other Ashenborn could not transform in response because the room was too small.

"Fire magic! There is no room to transform!" one of them yelled as he avoided a falling beam. Tsal ran along the cracking floor and held his scythe high above his head, ready to deal a blow.

"Hold them in!" Albion bellowed, flapping his wings furiously. He kicked the side wall with a vigorous movement, making shockwaves of cracks and causing more debris to fall. The Ashenborn and Tsal stumbled and struggled to remain on their feet.

Uriaelh exited the opening created by Albion and was followed by Derrick, who turned to look at Albion.

"Go!" Albion yelled as he breathed fire into the room.

Derrick acknowledged the command but stayed to strike a beam on the outside of the temple, causing the structure to rock and creak loudly. With another slam from his tail, the far tower crumbled like wood, snapping and groaning as it fell.

"Albion! Come now!" Derrick yelled as the temple began to collapse, a pillar of fire and smoke billowing into the air. Derrick vaulted off the side of the temple into the sky. He turned to see Albion contending with magical blasts while Tsal dealt him blow after blow, each one closer to Albion's exposed underside.

"Albion!"

Derrick tried to reach his friend, but flames and smoke blocked him.

"Get out of here now!" Albion called over the fire.

With an agile leap, Tsal hit Albion on the temple with the hammer end of his scythe. Derrick's heart stopped, and he could do nothing but stare at what was unfolding in front of him.

Albion huffed as he stumbled backward. Magic pelted him from all sides. The scythe end of the blade cut through his neck, spewing fire and blood.

Tsal grinned wickedly and let the reaper's hammer hang at his side. He seemed mesmerized by the blood.

Albion struggled to breathe, and gathering his strength, he burst through the wall and flew into the sky, tumbling and falling into the dense forest, fire spewing from his wound.

Magical blasts bounced off Derrick as he followed Uriaelh. Derrick turned to look back as they flew, tears in his eyes.

"We must look for Albion!" Uriaelh said, watching the golden form disappear into the darkness.

They flew downward to where they thought he had fallen. They looked, desperately trying to find any sign of their leader. Magical attacks continued to rain down after them as they flew. One struck Uriaelh, causing him to wince in pain.

They heard the massive temple fall, breaking and crumbling into the ground. Dragons were in the air, circling the temple as they attempted to stop its fall.

Derrick knew they could not stay, for soon those same dragons would turn their attention to them. He knew it meant abandoning their leader, but right now they had to leave.

"He will die if we cannot find him!" Uriaelh said, dazed.

"We will search for him at nightfall. We cannot risk dying here ourselves," Derrick said.

Derrick wanted to stay, too, but he knew that staying would bring higher risk for Yadir. He frowned as he noticed the dragons were no longer chasing them but were far too concerned with their jeweled tower. A wave of dust flew into the sky, the sound of its fall echoing outward.

"So this is what becomes of the Ashenborn," Derrick whispered.

Uriaelh did not look back as the bricks of stone and decorated towers collapsed. Derrick turned away from the sight, unable to watch. He heard it continue to fall, without having to watch it. The sound of destruction made him feel hopeless.

"Mara … Albion …" Derrick said.

Uriaelh had a snarl on his face, his wings a blur of motion next to him.

Derrick had a sudden realization.

"Lifesveil."

He shuddered as he realized that his kingdom was in more danger than ever. He knew their only hope was to find Hoakama. He flew faster as smoke billowed up behind him. All of Yadir was in grave danger.

CHAPTER 11
AN ENGULFING DARKNESS

———✦———

Zarx shoved the bloodied body off the end of his sword with a kick of his leg. The next Taneem rushed him, but he ducked under the attempted death blow and delivered one of his own. His harsh efficiency could be seen all around. There were several bodies lying on the floor near him. Zarx snarled as Taneemian blood splattered onto the ground. Tritus stood next to him, a shield on one arm and his glowing magic on the other. He stood staunchly, shield raised.

"Why are there so many making it through?" Tritus panted, fending off an attack.

Zarx growled like a wild animal as he sliced the head off another attacker.

A weathered Silver Talon beside Tritus cleared his throat.

"Many are not accustomed to fighting such an enemy. They are beyond count."

Tritus kicked at the freshly dispatched foe, which disintegrated with a repulsive pop.

Zarx noted the Talons in clusters fighting around them in sporadic patterns, giving the three of them a brief respite.

"And Derrick?" he said.

"No news, General," the Talon replied.

Zarx snorted.

Tritus struck a Taneem near them with the force of his magical fist. Its body flew into the air, hitting the wall with a loud crack. Blackened arrows littered the ground, with bodies of Taneems and men lying lifeless all around.

Zarx was pleased at how Tritus had progressed. There was something about the rudimentary magic that Tritus possessed that did not bother him as much—unlike the grandiose magic of the Ashenborn.

"And the king?" Zarx asked.

"He is secure within his chambers."

"Good," Zarx relaxed. "We must deal with the first wall's breach. Send all Bronze Talons to reinforce them. Put archers on the innermost wall and Silver Talons in the courtyard."

Zarx's armor clanked as he turned to Tritus.

"As for you, I want to give all magical advantage to the king that we can."

Tritus nodded as he adjusted his shield. Silver Talons left them in a rush as the sounds of war and battle echoed around them.

They traversed the stairs into the courtyard and toward the overlook of Alanias. The king looked concerned as they reached him.

"They have broken through the wall faster than expected," Alanias said.

Zarx nodded, acknowledging the White Dragon guard surrounding the king.

"Perhaps for now, but we have skill to their numbers. An enemy that has no fear of dying is a reckless one."

Alanias agreed.

"I should be down there fighting with my people …" he said, his voice trailing off.

"You are the king. We need you alive; besides, you have your health to consider. You fight with them even if you are not in the fray. You have already given so much," Zarx said.

Alanias shook as he held on to the railing.

"Do you need my shoulder, Your Majesty?" Tritus offered.

Alanias lifted a hand and shook his head.

"Thank you, I am merely old in body, not in spirit. I am fine."

An explosion in the distance made each of them tense up and turn quickly in the direction of the noise.

"Blasted Taneems," Zarx said.

Alanias closed his eyes. His face was very pale.

A loud cry echoed as a phalanx of Talons charged into a line of Taneems that had made another entry point in the wall. The men looked like a river of swords and shields in the haze of full-on assault.

"Tritus will stay with you," Zarx said, "to ensure you are amply protected. He is trustworthy. I am going down to join my men."

Alanias nodded curtly.

"Do not allow anything to become of you. Too much blood has been spilled before this enemy," the king said.

Tritus watched as Zarx ran into the fray of battle, a group of several dozen Talons behind him.

"I hope my sons are safe. I both regret and am relieved they are not here," Alanias said to Tritus. "You are their age."

"They are your sons; you have nothing to fear, for you raised them to be good men, I am sure," Tritus said, not sure how to comfort him.

Alanias looked solemn.

"It is the wretchedly raised men who pursue my sons that concern me."

"Archkyris protect them," Tritus whispered.

Alanias looked at him and tilted his head.

The smell of soot reached them; Tritus had to resist the temptation to scrunch his nose.

"You're an Ashenborn," Alanias said, pointing toward Tritus' fragment. "You are their brother now; my sons are also of this order," Alanias smiled. "I am glad to know that they are not going to be alone in this world."

Tritus wondered what he meant by that.

The Silver Talons stirred around them nervously. A lone figure was climbing the steps.

"Halt!" a Talon yelled, aiming his crossbow.

The figure continued to climb.

Tritus put himself between the king and the figure.

"Identify yourself!" the Talon yelled.

The figure continued its movement, slowly and in no hurry.

Tritus felt a knot in his stomach as he saw the silvery mask. Its carvings possessed eight eyes, giving it the countenance of a spider.

"Fire now!" Tritus yelled as he thrust his hand forward. The air whistled with bolts and arrows. The projectiles bounced off of the form's cloak. Heavily clad armor showed through a rip of the cloak. There was one spot where an arrow nicked skin. Black blood dripped on the ground.

"That's a Taneemian assassin," Alanias said.

The Taneem drew a khopesh, a short, curved sword. It looked ancient in make, despite the fact its blade reflected a bright metallic sheen.

"Assassin?" Tritus said as men yelled around him.

The Taneem merely side-stepped arrow after arrow, using the hilt of the blade to stop the arc of the projectiles where needed.

"They wear masks resembling insects, or arachnids, predators of those less powerful than themselves," Alanias said as he drew a sword from his scepter. "And they never fail in getting their kill."

Tritus felt a surge of fire go through his veins as the magic within him responded to the approaching danger. The khopesh sliced through a Talon with cruel intent. The man was dead before he hit the floor.

Tritus could hear the clank of its boots with each step after each defeated warrior.

Clank. Another Talon yelled as he fell onto the ground.

Clank. The Talon breathed his last breath, his eyes wide with fear as he died.

The assassin knew where to put his weapon, easily finding the weaker parts of Lifesveil's armor. With rapid succession, it decapitated victim after victim.

Clank. Another step closer.

"Your Highness, you need to retreat. He is making our defenses look useless. I will fight him, but I cannot both protect you and fight him!"

The king stood his ground, a resigned look on his face.

"Your Majesty!" Tritus said with more urgency.

"I know this Taneem," Alanias said. "He is one of the Veltris, named Arius. You would do well to retreat with me. Fighting him alone will do you no good."

"We have no time. We need you alive." Tritus motioned at the remaining Talons, who escorted the king into the inner chambers.

Tritus stared as the door closed. His fear was palpable.

One final *clank* sounded behind him.

Tritus turned to see Arius standing completely still, his blade still dripping fresh blood. With a flick, the blood was gone.

All the defenders were dead, and Tritus was alone with the assassin.

Tritus pulled out his weapon, the fire of his hand heating his blade to a rosy color.

Arius tilted his head and pointed with his khopesh.

"You are Ashenborn?" his deep raspy voice inquired.

Tritus lifted his shield in preparedness.

Arius ignored his silence and moved to strike him. Tritus felt his teeth rattle from the impact, and he stumbled backward. His ears rang as he righted himself.

"Ashenborn. Weak pyromancers if you ask me," the Taneem said forebodingly.

Tritus' arm itched as smoke bent around the now cherry-red blade. He struck out and swung into the open air. Arius back stepped and grunted laughter.

"The kindled dragons, that's what they call themselves."

Tritus gritted his teeth, the veins in his neck bulging.

"You are incredibly young, to face someone as old as I," Arius said slowly.

Arius' cloak rippled in the wind.

"You think this is trivial?" Tritus said, pointing at the bodies around them. "I have no desire to leave your debt unpaid."

Arius grunted. "You, a youth, understand debts?"

Arius sighed, tiring of their banter. "Leave and allow me to have an audience with your king. Ashenborn, whether corrupt or not, may be of use in the age to come. I believe I have proven that I can tear down anyone or anything that stands in my path."

Tritus stood his ground.

"I would die before I would allow it."

A cheer sounded from the outer wall, sparking a flame of hope in Tritus.

"The first wave was our least powerful; it's meant to flush out your weaknesses," Arius said, noticing the hope in Tritus' eyes.

Tritus struck out in a quick movement. "What does that make you then?"

Arius countered and nicked him on his cheek, drawing blood.

"Overly anxious, I suppose."

Tritus grimaced at the sting. With as much resolve as he could muster, he charged headlong into Arius.

Arius ducked and Tritus rolled over him in a flurry of arms and legs.

He hit the ground roughly, knocking the breath out of him. His head pounded. He rolled onto one knee, lifting his shield back into place.

"You can't even hit me," Arius said, unamused.

Sweat beaded on Tritus' face as he felt his body shake at the realization. He steadied his breathing, still shaking.

"Your swordplay needs work," Arius said turning his back to him.

"Get back here," Tritus coughed.

"Tritus!"

He turned and saw Zarx running up the steps, red-faced.

"Zarx," Arius said as he turned toward the sound. "Someone worthy of my time."

Zarx moved to stand between Tritus and Arius.

"Is the king safe?" he said without turning to Tritus.

"He is."

"And you?"

"Worn out from using the fragment," he said as his flaming arm disappeared and he lowered his shield.

"Stay here," Zarx said as he strode forward, his sword held in front of him.

"Zarx, General of Lifesveil. You killed many Taneems in the last war. I congratulate you," Arius said, bowing. "I have been eager to fight you since then."

Zarx looked at him angrily.

"At least some have enough sense to remain dead when they are killed. Unlike your kin."

"No one can kill the Veltris. That is why we bear the name."

Zarx clenched his teeth.

"We have successfully defended against you. We will always. If more come, we will have the same result."

Arius stood quietly, his expression unreadable under his mask.

"No more words?" Zarx inquired.

Arius moved quickly toward him, lowering his shoulder with his khopesh held low. Zarx side-stepped and sword met sword in a metallic crash.

Swords rattled as each pushed back and forth in a deadly rhythm.

Zarx growled through sweat and blood, the veins in his forearms bulging.

"Impressive. No doubt the average Taneem would struggle with you," Arius said, pushing him away with a sweeping motion.

Tritus watched but knew he could do nothing to help as the magic he had used had sapped him. He lay in wait, checking to be sure no other enemy approached them. The sword he had used was melted into a metallic heap.

Zarx ducked and kicked at Arius' legs. Arius jumped backward on one foot and steadied himself with the other. Zarx could feel the weight of his weapon; he was not as fresh as his opponent.

Arius spun his weapon slowly, not taking his attention off Zarx. Zarx tilted his sword sideways, blocking the serpent-like strike from the khopesh, which left a long scratch on the face of his sword.

Zarx was slower to block the next flurry of blows but held his ground impressively. Arius could tell Zarx was tiring and dealt quicker and more decisive blows. Each was deflected by Zarx's sword, but with a great deal of effort on his part.

Zarx now held his ribs with his free arm, his breathing strained. Every movement had become a struggle.

The mandibles on Arius' mask began to glow like molten metal.

Zarx took a step backward, narrowly avoiding being roasted by a blue inferno of flame from the mouth of the arachnid mask. The stream of fire left a black stain on the stone. Smoke poured out of the mask's eight eyes.

Tritus tried to lift himself but didn't have the strength to push himself off the ground.

"I was foolish to have overspent myself," Tritus said, quietly kicking himself.

"Men either rot or burn," Arius said to Zarx as he stepped closer, sending blue flames in front of him with each breath.

Zarx yelled as fire licked at his arm, making him roll back. He saw a red streak appear on his arm even though the flame had not touched him and winced with pain.

Arius stopped as more cheers erupted behind him.

"Lifesveil has prevailed," Zarx said, sweat dripping down his neck.

"For now," Arius said with disgust.

The sound of metal footsteps hammered on the steps below them.

Talons ran up behind them, weapons raised.

"Stay back," Zarx said, waving them back.

A horn sounded outside of the walls of Lifesveil with three long blasts.

Arius snorted. "The next wave."

The sound of a different horn echoed from the edge of the kingdom.

"Mavet finally arrives."

———————— ✳ ————————

"Well, it looks like a bunch of ice and rocks. The cold wind that stings your face is a nice touch. Not my goblet of ale if you ask me," Salenair said. "But if it suits you, who am I to say different."

"It's about as inviting as the sea."

"Not true," Salenair said. "The sea is a beautiful blue; this is a boring gray-white."

"We're close to the shore; you'll be able to leave soon enough," Thornbeorn said, his cloaked armor already on.

"Have you never been here before?"

Salenair shook his head.

"Not much for a smuggler to do here, really. What do you have here for me to smuggle? Ice?"

Thornbeorn sighed.

"We have many resources of value to give to Yadir. Like wood …"

"Where?" The captain joked.

"Further back. We also have fish, and fine gems."

Salenair chuckled to himself.

"If you say so. I'm a pretty popular smuggler, and I've never seen anything of value come out of this place."

Thornbeorn was unamused.

"Would it not be bad for business to be considered a popular smuggler? Like a thief, I would not want anyone knowing my dealings. Besides, Wulvsbaen deals in honest trade."

Salenair clapped his hands.

"A good jab, I must say. But those with influence," he said, rubbing his fingers together, "know who I am."

"Ah."

"Such as yourself. You are being smuggled here, so keep your complaints to a minimum, Prince," Salenair said with a smile.

"I would in no way devalue your, er, service," Thornbeorn replied.

"That's more like it," Salenair said as he lit his pipe.

Thornbeorn motioned toward the pipe.

"Care for some?" Salenair asked.

"No," he responded. "There are many in our village who possess this same type of pipe."

Salenair blew a smoke ring and looked at the ivory pipe he held. It was covered with masterful etchings of the ocean and sky.

"Actually, that was made here in Wulvsbaen," Thornbeorn said proudly.

Salenair looked displeased.

"What? I was told this was made in Jayden, and that it was worth a lot of coin."

Thornbeorn chuckled.

"You were lied to. That particular pipe is incredibly common. Some smuggler you are to not know what you possess."

Salenair rolled his eyes.

"I got this some time ago, but that figures."

Thornbeorn folded his arms. He had enjoyed his time on the sea but knew he was ready to get home.

Salenair muttered to himself as he went to a corner of the ship to smoke by himself.

Thornbeorn chuckled. He had not realized how fond he was of the captain.

———※———

After what seemed like hours, they arrived at the walls of Malfait. Cordoc landed beside Daemos and Selaphiel glided toward them, landing softly.

"Quite the distance," Cordoc said with a huff.

"Yes," Daemos agreed.

Selaphiel noted the grand walls surrounding the city, not unlike Lifesveil's. He could not help but notice how empty they felt. His eyes illuminated without his willing them to. The kingdom often had archers patrolling its walls, but there were none apparent today. The gray stone columns looked unnatural against the trees and vines that surrounded the wall. He had visited Malfait several times as a child, accompanying his father on state visits.

"Seph?" Cordoc asked, slightly alarmed.

He waved his hand in front of Selaphiel's eyes. Selaphiel's eyes raked back and forth across the walls, seemingly unable to hear him.

"What's going on?" Daemos asked.

"He does this every so often," Cordoc said. "Like a trance, almost."

Selaphiel blinked.

"I'm still here."

Cordoc looked dumbfounded.

"I can see inside the city," Selaphiel said, rubbing his eyes. "Though I'm not sure what I'm seeing."

"What is it you do see?" Daemos said.

"Dead," he turned, eyes still aflame. "Everywhere."

"Dead?" Cordoc said, alarmed. "Surely you are mistaken."

With a flash Selaphiel's blue eyes returned.

"I am sure of it. I didn't believe it myself at first, but it's true. Nothing behind those walls is still alive."

The walls looked peaceful and well-maintained, no evidence of the sinister vision Selaphiel had seen seemed to lie beyond them.

"We will see if his words hold true," Daemos said. "Your brother isn't someone who lies."

"We should be able to smell the dead, right?" Selaphiel asked, thinking back to their battles with the Taneemian.

"We should," Cordoc said skeptically.

They followed the wall until they reached the great wooden door that was the entrance of the large kingdom. Normally guarded, the door stood unmanned and open, the center of it shredded and damaged as if entry had been forced. As they carefully stepped past the splintered door, a sour, rotting odor reached them.

Daemos was the first to turn his nose up.

"It is as you said. No one could forget that smell."

The expanse of buildings bore evidence that a battle had been fought here. Houses were burned, and stones lay scattered among them. Worse was the reddish-hued and bloated dead that lay lifeless among the broken buildings.

Selaphiel was pale, and he caught himself by bending over and holding onto the ruins of a nearby house. He gagged and covered his mouth with his fist.

"There is a difference in just seeing a few dead and seeing something like this," Daemos whispered. "This was a massacre."

Cordoc did not look at Selaphiel as he took in the sight. A chill spread through him.

"These poor people ..." he said as his voice faltered.

Tears welled up in Selaphiel's eyes as he looked at the faces of the deceased. They looked less human from having been exposed to the weather. He wanted to look away, but he could not. He could feel nausea boiling in his throat and took a deep breath, choking as he realized he was breathing in the odor of death.

Daemos' face was blank as he walked between rows of cluttered ruins, his eyes on the castle. "Taneems," Daemos said, his voice strangely calm. "They made it here too."

"Maybe there's someone left alive," Cordoc said. "It's worth looking."

"I'm afraid that isn't the case," Selaphiel gulped. "I know there is no one alive here."

The castle was the only thing whole; it stood like a sorrowful soldier above the ruins of the town.

"Monsters ...." Selaphiel's queasiness was replaced by anger.

Daemos examined some of the bloated bodies.

"These have been dead for some time now."

"H-how long?" Selaphiel stuttered.

"A week or so, I'd say."

"How can you be sure?" Cordoc asked.

"Serving Lifesveil," Daemos said, "I have seen many things that no one should ever have to see. I have become familiar with death. The bodies are bloated and have taken on a yellowish-green color."

Selaphiel coughed.

"Then ..." Cordoc said, "that means Father lied to us."

"What do you mean?" Selaphiel choked out, confused.

Cordoc fell to his knees. He punched the broken ground.

"Cordoc?"

"Father," Cordoc choked as tears brimmed in his eyes.

Daemos turned to him. "What do you mean?"

"Father did not send us to find an ally. He sent us to get us away from the oncoming army. A bird cannot bring a message to the dead," he yelled.

Cordoc turned slowly to Daemos.

"Did you know?"

Daemos shook his head, his expression solemn. He realized now what Cordoc was saying. Cordoc looked down as tears dropped onto the stones beneath him.

Selaphiel knelt beside him. His brother's eyes were pink.

"Father may not have known."

"Do you truly believe it yourself? You saw the bodies. How does anyone not notice a dead kingdom like this?" Cordoc said sharply.

"The deception of the enemy is a possibility," Daemos pondered out loud.

"Whether Father intended it or not, we have to go back to Lifesveil," Cordoc said.

"We can't leave them all like this!" Selaphiel said, looking around at the bodies.

"We must return to Lifesveil," Cordoc said. "They are dead; there is no more we can do for them. We have a chance to prevent others from dying by going as quickly as we can."

"It may already be too late," Daemos said in a hushed tone. "Besides, King Alanias wanted the help of Malfait; we would be better served calling on the aid of another kingdom."

Daemos eyed the brothers with concern, adding, "Both of you need rest before we travel such a distance. You both have seen too much to carry on immediately."

"I do not care if it is a thousand—" Cordoc stopped speaking as a sound interrupted him.

They looked around for the source of the noise. Daemos motioned them to follow him. They took refuge in a nearby house that was less damaged than the rest.

"It sounds like a storm is coming," Daemos said.

Dark clouds covered the sky, making it look like nighttime. A lighting bolt struck some distance away, the crack of thunder reaching them in a few seconds. A flood of rain followed.

Selaphiel could tell that Cordoc was silently fuming.

"What do we do?" Selaphiel said.

Daemos scratched his chin.

"We make our way back toward Lifesveil, and on the way, we stop at the kingdom of Melib; we have friends there."

"We need to go to Lifesveil. We can send a bird to Melib," Cordoc spat. "It is too far out of the way to go there—by then, there might be no one to save."

"We can't be sure the Taneemian will not kill any birds we find to send; besides we are only three men," Selaphiel said.

"Two Ashenborn and a captain," Cordoc said sternly.

Daemos nodded, agreeing with Selaphiel. "As much as I dislike the idea, we don't have much choice, though it may be wise to wait out this storm. I know the situation is desperate, but it would be better not to lose our way. We need numbers."

"We don't have time to discuss this or talk about why we shouldn't leave now. Or wait for it to stop raining!" Cordoc said, aggravated. Without another word, Cordoc ran into the rain and with a flash of magic disappeared into the storm.

"Cordoc!" Selaphiel yelled.

Rain blinded him as he stood in the middle of the torrential downpour. He looked around frantically but could not see anything. Selaphiel tried to use his magic to see through the rain as he had through the wall, but with no success.

"We must go after him!" he said.

Daemos looked grave.

"We must," he agreed. "He is bound to get himself killed."

"I know. Cordoc has acted so unlike himself lately. I cannot help but think it is because of these powers," Selaphiel said. "Let's go."

Daemos nodded.

They were in the air in an instant. Selaphiel held Daemos in his claws as he searched the skies for signs of Cordoc.

"Which way to Lifesveil?" he finally said, knowing full well he had no idea where to go in the storm. Its denseness made him reel.

Daemos pointed south, using his other hand to block the wind and rain. He had made sure to not forget how they had come into Malfait.

Daemos looked down dolefully and shook his head in regret.

"This will not be the end."

Selaphiel exploded forward in a rush of wind as fast as his wings would carry them.

"No, it won't." His dragon voice reverberated in the wind.

———— ✦ ————

Uriaelh stood next to Derrick, overwrought. Their situation was pressing upon his mind.

"Maybe something happened to her," Uriaelh said. "We do not know how far those traitors have extended their reach."

Derrick didn't speak; he hadn't quite processed the events of less than a day ago. His face looked suddenly older, the short time in Aiash had aged him what felt like a hundred years. His worry was for Albion. They had searched the previous night but only found traces of golden scales and blood, which boded the worst.

"Derrick?"

He turned, pulling himself back to reality, finally realizing that Uriaelh had spoken to him.

"Yes?"

"Are you all right?" Uriaelh repeated, noticing Derrick's pinched expression.

"As good as one can be. It still has not set in my mind," Derrick said. "I worry for Albion."

For them to kill Mara ... and who knows what happened ultimately to Albion ... Uriaelh thought out loud in a low voice, somber.

"Hoakama should arrive at any moment. Edwin is not far from us," he said, kicking at the cold ground. "She should be able to assist us in finding what remains of him."

Derrick tried to calm himself. So many thoughts were racing through his head. The princes were headed toward Malfait, and he did not know if they were okay. He hated not knowing. It was not knowing that truly disturbed him. Even the worst would be better than what the imagination conjured.

Maybe we were wrong to send them off on their own, he thought.

King Alanias had been sure it was the best thing for them, but Derrick wasn't sure he agreed. Lifesveil itself was under threat of attack, the Kingdom of Yadir divided over the death of Archkyris, and no one knew Jakobin's whereabouts.

They stood under the branches of a giant willow tree. The tree arched and grunted before the gusts of wind, branches thrashing in the air above them.

"The sentry should have reached her by now," Uriaelh said, rubbing his hands together for warmth.

"Breathe. Give it time," Derrick said, trying to soothe Uriaelh's anxiety.

They had chosen this place to meet because the willow tree provided both shelter and protection from being seen. Both knew it was only a matter of time before the Ashenborn made a move on Edywin. They knew they must plan accordingly and act quickly.

Trees stirred around them as men clad in blue armor approached. On their chests was the emblem of Edywin, the crest of a white-faced owl. Derrick and Uriaelh relaxed and gave curt bows. Behind them, a beautiful woman dressed in white lace and pearls approached. Under the lace, the woman was clad in white chainmail armor, giving her a magnificent yet formidable appearance. Her features were delicate and her black hair stood in stark contrast to the white attire. Kindness shone from her warm brown eyes.

"Hoakama, Queen of Edywin, Stewardess of the High Kingdom of Yadir, and Queen of Treasured Wisdom," one of the guards said, announcing her arrival.

Derrick and Uriaelh bowed and responded as was appropriate with customary greetings.

"Elder Derrick of Lifesveil," Hoakama's soothing voice said. "And Uriaelh, my dear friend." She smiled briefly, then got down to business.

"What happened at the counsel of Aiash?"

"We bring bad news," Uriaelh began, steadying his voice.

Uriaelh recounted all that had happened, not leaving out a single detail.

Hoakama's expression changed from horror to sadness as she listened. The guards that surrounded them seemed equally in shock. Hoakama remained silent, her eyes sharp. After what seemed like an hour, Uriaelh completed his tale of their journey from Aiash to Edywin.

"How could this happen?" Hoakama finally spoke.

"The Light Prison no doubt failed after the death of Archkyris," Derrick said. "Tsal freed them when the defenses were weakest. Not only are they free, but their ancient servants the Taneemian have come with them."

Hoakama shook her head, tears appearing in the corners of her eyes.

"It is the War of Stones all over again. Who among us is still for us?"

"Just us as far as we know," Uriaelh said. "Elim and his servants have imitated the power of the Ashenborn; so not only do we have to contend with other Ashenborn powers, but we must also contend with new powers. Powers we thought were specific to us."

"How many dragon fragments do we have in our possession?" Hoakama asked.

"None as of this moment," Uriaelh said, concerned. "I am not sure how they were able to break the seals upon the stones to make themselves counterfeit."

"Tsal was at harder work than we realized. Then we stand before a nearly impossible task of fighting them for Yadir," Hoakama said solemnly.

"There is still hope," Derrick said. "There are those who remain true to our order. We may be outnumbered, but we have resolve."

"Who else is there? The stones have not kindled in years. Do you mean you found those to whom the stones responded?" Hoakama asked, surprised.

"Yes," Derrick said. "Thornbeorn of Wulvsbaen, Tritus of Lifesveil, and Alanias' sons. Five in total."

Hoakama's eyes lit up with hope.

"It doesn't matter that you didn't have permission from our now traitorous order. However, youth have a tendency to follow blindly without consideration. Do you truly believe we can have faith in these newly made dragons?" Hoakama said. "Or that they will be willing to engage in a war in which they may die?"

"As far as experienced Ashenborn, that is true. We are low in number. But these are Ashenborn who are newly kindled; the fragments would not have chosen them if they weren't worthy after being dormant since the war. They will choose as they have chosen before. One cannot be Ashenborn and not fight. The time of silence has ended," Derrick said.

"The fragments chose wrong with the other Ashenborn," Uriaelh said with a sense of foreboding. "Hopefully that is not a cause for concern in this case."

"Perhaps, but who is to tell if those who betray us truly were chosen by the fragments. But that's beside the point. What's important is this: the next generation must be equipped. Otherwise the Ashenborn name will fade with the rise of this new corruption."

Hoakama closed her eyes.

"We must secure more fragments so that they cannot be used against us in the coming war, as well as whatever ancient relics that we may knowingly hold," Derrick said.

"Most of them lie within the temple," Uriaelh said. "Whatever is left of it will have been taken by Etghar."

"I have some hidden beneath that tower," Derrick said, a sharp look in his eyes. "They will believe they have gathered all they need."

Hoakama folded her arms in thought.

"All I have are hidden in the outer caves of the kingdom of Melib."

"There are none that I could recount," Uriaelh said.

"Did you distrust any of our kinsmen before this?" Hoakama asked.

"No, I just thought it would be unwise to leave the fragments out in the open, considering their worth," Derrick replied.

Hoakama placed her finger under her chin as she considered his words.

"There is much to be done," Hoakama finally said. "We must get those fragments first. Edywin will prepare its forces as well."

"I will go to Aiash," Uriaelh said. "I am the youngest among us, and there is no telling what remains behind guarding it. I can also continue to search for Albion on the way."

Derrick started to argue but realized Uriaelh was right. Derrick was the oldest and most powerful dragon there, but he knew this task would require speed over raw power.

"What of Wulvsbaen? Are they behind us?" Hoakama said.

"Thornbeorn of Wulvsbaen is our hope for bringing the kingdom to our side. He travels there now in secret," Derrick said.

"We must prepare Uriaelh. Tell him how to get to your fragments and I will make sure Edywin and this mission goes according to our advantage. What will you do, Derrick?"

"I will find the princes," Derrick said, "and make for Lifesveil."

"I will remain here and prepare my forces. The capital of Archkyris has already been taken by our enemy. I would rather fight them here than where they are fortified."

"Will you have ample defenses?" Derrick asked.

"Yes," she said. "We are a strong people. We were made strong by Archkyris' rule."

"Then let us be on our separate ways," Uriaelh said.

"Then we can scatter our enemies," Hoakama said with fire in her voice.

———※———

Selaphiel felt worry creep in as they lost sight of Cordoc, who had flown far ahead of them.

"Blasted storm," Selaphiel said. So many things were bothering him that he could hardly think straight. His father was now in danger, Cordoc had flown off blinded by anger, and Jakobin was missing.

The sky in front of them was darker than a dungeon. If not for the silver thread of river below them and Daemos' knowledge of the terrain, they would be completely lost. He wished he could summon the stars but knew it would slow them down too much.

"Keep your course. Cordoc is still no doubt ahead of us," Daemos yelled over a crack of thunder.

Selaphiel struggled against the wind, peering through his plate-sized eyes.

"I'm not sure how much farther I can go," he said, adjusting his grip on Daemos.

"Nor I. Your scales are rubbing me to the bone."

Selaphiel hated to stop, but he landed in a clearing beside a lake. His scales felt soaked to the bone and he knew the trip was rough on Daemos. He extended his wings as he released Daemos to provide a roof above them, interlocking his wings to make sure no water got through.

The rain ran around them, allowing them to dry off.

Selaphiel, with a sneeze, made a fire.

Daemos warmed himself beside it, tending to the wounds on his back made by Selaphiel's scales.

"Sorry," Selaphiel said apologetically.

He looked around with his enhanced vision.

"Where are we?"

Daemos sat on his knees.

"Scorian territory," he said, wrapping the raw places on his back with cloth.

"I could heal those."

"It's fine for now. We do not have much longer to travel and we will be at the mountains that surround Lifesveil. I will survive until then."

Selaphiel sighed a spark of fire.

"Cordoc—"

"—will be fine as long as we keep up the same pace. Knowing your brother, he will stop before he drains himself of energy."

"I hope so," Selaphiel said, thinking of how their new-found powers had changed them. It was never normal for the three of them to travel separately. People often considered them a trio in whatever they did.

Daemos finished his wrappings.

"Done."

"Daemos?" Selaphiel started.

"Yeah?"

"Did you know that Father was just sending us away to stop us from being in the kingdom when the Taneems attacked?"

"No. I did not know."

Selaphiel turned his head sideways as if glaring at him.

Daemos looked back at him without flinching.

"I had no idea. Those bodies had been dead for some time. It's hard to understand why Malfait is in the condition it was. If I had known anything about their current state, I would have surely requested aid to prevent something of this magnitude," Daemos said.

"Hmm," Selaphiel hummed.

"You do not believe me?" Daemos said, looking up.

"Whether I knew your father's intent or not means nothing. What I do know is that we were sent to Malfait and found them all to be dead."

His eyes glazed over as he remembered what they had seen.

"Not to speak unfondly of the deceased," Selaphiel added. "That's something I'll never be able to forget. All those people … lost to decay, open to the elements for any traveler to see."

He sighed, wishing he could have done something for them.

"Who could have done such a thing?"

Daemos shrugged, unsure.

"The same one who murdered the High King," he replied, swaying his head back and forth in thought.

"Which kingdoms were loyal to Archkyris?" Selaphiel inquired.

Daemos gave him an interested look.

"I would say Lifesveil, of course, and Edywin, Melib, Wulvsbaen, and Malfait. The others were neutral at best."

Daemos stopped for a second.

"What?" Selaphiel pried.

"It's strange. That sigil at Malfait I found is not identified with any other kingdom in existence. It's almost like a new one. I thought I was just too tired to recognize it, but now I'm sure I've never seen it before."

He removed the piece of cloth from his tunic that he had taken from the dead city.

"I'd forgotten about it until now. We were worried about Cordoc and it slipped my mind."

The rain slowed to a sprinkle and the clouds lightened.

"We can talk on the way. Are you ready?"

"Yes," Daemos said, still thinking.

A loud roar cut through the forest. The trees shook so violently that leaves fell to the ground.

"Uh-oh," Selaphiel started. "What's that?"

Selaphiel turned his neck, straining to look as trees crumbled into cracks and splinters. Groups of trees continued to shake as if a great wind were underneath them. Neither Daemos or Selaphiel moved. The ground pounded like war drums. Each thump sounded heavier and closer.

"A dragon?" Selaphiel questioned.

He arched his elongated neck to look over the tree line, even though the remaining rain made it difficult to see much. They both concentrated on listening. The sound was more a clicking noise than a growl now. The trees were still.

Daemos' face whitened.

"Fly."

"What is it?"

"Just go!" Daemos yelled.

Selaphiel obliged and floated into the air, flapping his wings with Daemos in his claws. He narrowly evaded a barbed tail that crashed into a nearby tree instead. A pale green liquid poured from the barb as it hissed by them like an arrow. The form below them growled with anger.

Selaphiel's breath caught in his throat as he saw an eight-eyed dragon head appear below him. The creature hissed and crackled at them, its fangs dripping hungrily. Its black and red eyes were terrible to look at, the rest of its body hidden in the underbrush.

"What in Yadir is that? Selaphiel rumbled hysterically.

"A Scorian," Daemos said. "We are lucky it didn't reach us in time."

A shiver went down Selphiel's spine as he realized how closed they had been to death.

He looked down and saw the trees shaking below them. The long scorpion-like tail waved above the trees.

"A Scorian?" Selaphiel said. "I thought those weren't real!"

"They're as real as you or I."

Selaphiel glanced down nervously, even though they were a considerable height above it.

"Dragon hunters," Daemos said.

"Just when I thought we had enough to deal with," Selaphiel said. "Is it following us?"

"Yes, but it should stop when we get over the mountains. Or let's hope it does. They are not fond of the cold, but there have not been any dragons in a long time for it to hunt."

Selaphiel growled. "Should? That thing was twice my size!"

"It should stop. And that one is actually smaller than most."

He focused ahead but let his vision drift downward every so often. He felt very vulnerable knowing what was underneath him.

"Small my foot …" Selaphiel's heart pounded as he had a new thought.

"They can't fly, can they?" he asked nervously.

"No. But they were used to hunt dragons by Dothros in the War of Stones. I would rather fight a dragon than one of those. They are incredibly strong and are wilder than the wilderness they reside in."

Selaphiel shivered.

"I am going to fly higher for the time being, until we pass the mountains."

"That would be a good idea," Daemos said, gripping his talons tightly.

———————※———————

Alanias paced in his chambers. Guards stood at attention, awaiting his command. He could hear the fighting outside. He could feel the youthful urge to go and fight as well, but he knew his body could no longer do what was needed. His bones ached. Mothers, children, and the elderly had been evacuated so they would be out of immediate danger. He knew he could have gone with them.

"A king never leaves his people," he whispered.

The horns sounded outside. His stomach clenched as if someone had grabbed his insides and twisted. That horn tone meant the enemy had reinforcements. The guards shuffled nervously, knowing what that horn meant, too.

The room shook, bits of dust floating into the air.

"We are not staying here anymore," he said, sternly pointing to them. "We are better served on the battlefield."

"Or dead," came the voice of someone in the back.

He turned, bewildered.

"Who said that?" Alanias said.

A guard with a hood on stood silently.

"How dare you say such a thing to your king," a burly guard said to the hooded man.

With a quick motion, the blade of a dagger sliced across the burly guard's throat, leaving him wide-eyed and grasping at the outpouring of his own blood. The other guards jumped into action, rushing the man. "Assasin!" they yelled as they leapt to defend their king.

The man struck with his dagger in a ripping motion. Alanias drew his short sword, his hands shaking at how heavy the blade felt to him now.

Another guard yelled before the stranger's blade silenced him. The guard fell as if in slow motion. A pool of blood edged its way outward from his body.

"Alanias."

The king was filled with horror at how quickly his men had been torn down. He dared not call out to anyone outside for fear they would meet the same fate.

"Whoever you are, you cannot undo this. There will be payment for what has been done here!" Alanias said, his beard stained with the spray of his men's blood.

"It was necessary," the man growled.

"No, it wasn't," Alanias said sharply. "I won't let someone like you get away with this."

"You're so certain?" He held up the jagged edge of the dagger. "You couldn't stop the fall of your men."

"Who are you to say such things?" Alanias challenged.

The man wiped his dagger of blood.

"You should remember me, since you murdered my father."

The man removed his hood. He was around mid-life, his eyes shadowy yellow orbs set below brown hair and above a closely-trimmed beard. His lips were thin, and he looked malnourished, with dark circles under his eyes.

"Elim," Alanias said, stepping back.

"Yes. Dothros' heir. Though still recovering from what that prison did to me,"

Elim said, looking down at his shaking hand.

"Dothros was a …"

"… Monster? Traitor?" Elim spat out. "Maybe. Dothros was a lunatic, certainly, but he was my father and I am not him."

He advanced on Alanias.

"You are a murderer," Alanias growled, struggling to keep his sword raised.

"Yes," Elim said. "I have ended a few lives for the good of Yadir, so as to make all pay who worked to kill my father."

"So Archkyris' murderer stands before me," Alanias said, blinking through tears.

"Tsal did that. Your death will end the killing. I am just here to finish off the only other who spilled my father's blood."

Elim pointed.

Alanias looked stricken.

"Your father killed thousands, hundreds of thousands, of innocents," Alanias said.

Elim was expressionless as he replied.

"Yes, he did. Remember there are none who are innocent. He did a lot that you or I cannot account for, but still I would rather not breathe while you still breathe the same air. We are not here to discuss my father's sins, but your own."

Alanias leapt forward to strike at Elim, but instead he felt a cold sharpness enter his chest. He looked down and saw an obsidian shard embedded in his right side. The shard didn't hurt until Alanias tried to pry it from his chest. Waves of pain shot through him.

He gritted his teeth and yanked.

Despite his efforts, the glass shard did not budge.

"Father taught me a great deal of magic." Elim flexed his hand. "He was able to corrupt it, make it his own, along with that," he said, pointing at the shard.

"What is this?" Alanias said with a scowl.

"Father had no name for it. Neither do I, but know this: it holds your body together until I choose to release the magic and it kills you. It is truly cruel sorcery. Father knew magic, I'll give him that."

"Graaaaaagh," Alanias groaned as he tried again to remove the shard, but he was unable to get a good grip on it. His fingers slipped uselessly around it.

"Think of it as a seal on a wineskin. If I remove this magic from you, you will die."

Elim cracked his knuckles and rolled his wrists.

"Father killed many in this way. It often persuaded men to follow him. Much as we serve death until we embrace it fully at the end of our lives. I decide when you meet your end." His eyes flashed.

"You …" Alanias said in pain. "What do you intend to do?" Sweat dripped from his forehead.

"Avenge my father with your dying breath. Create a Yadir that truly is free. I'm not here to enslave them, but to set them free from the bonds of kings and cryptic rule. Father had the right idea, but he was cruel, and a lunatic."

"Y-you wish to be king of all?"

"Yes and no. I will oversee its rule, but ultimately they will reign themselves. Father was shallow. That title might have been more suitable for him."

Elim looked away, saying, "He always wanted to be Archkyris. Who didn't? But I only wish respect to be paid, and for those who would rise up against me silenced. I will offer them protection, the pursuit of their dreams, their hearts' desires at the price of their allegiance. They will never be enslaved as I was in that hopeless prison."

"Archkyris gave them hope," Alanias coughed. "You cannot lead when you cannot serve."

The shard glowed, making him cough blood.

"I have nothing to apologize for. I did nothing of free will in the War of Stones. I was not quite a man when you sealed me away. I didn't wish to kill; I was forced to."

Elim's face lost its composure.

"I have been locked away because of the sins of my father. A debt I had to pay for his sins."

Elim looked at Alanias, emotionless once again.

"You will die in this room," Elim said. "I do not enjoy watching people suffer, despite the fact that I use this method of killing. And believe me, I will give Yadir what is best for them. I do not want the worst for this realm."

Alanias crawled on the ground, sweat and blood drenching his beard.

"M-my sons."

"What about them?"

"They will not let this happen without repayment."

"You will never know what happens to them. There can be no comfort for you."

"You will never succeed," Alanias said through bloodied teeth.

Elim clenched his hand. The sound of shattering glass echoed through the room. Alanias fell flat to the ground, looking at Elim. Elim turned his gaze away from the dying king. The room was quiet. Outside, men yelled and the sound of steel on steel clanged. Elim grabbed Alanias' crown, lying some distance from the king on the floor. He walked calmly through the castle until he reached the window.

"I already have," he said under his breath.

He tossed the crown into the hearth nearby. The once gleaming gold vanished in the flames. He watched it glow as the metal melted.

"Alanias of Lifesveil. A pitiful legacy."

He grabbed the scepter sword in his hands, examining the jewels and weight of the blade.

He did not look at the blood-soaked floor as he stepped over the bodies strewn across his path. He walked away with no additional words, leaving Alanias in the room where none were left alive.

Arius watched as the obsidian dragon flew across the war-torn sky. Its hues of red and black shone in the sun. He turned away. His cloak rippled in the sharp wind.

"Alanias is dead," his deep voice rasped.

Zarx could barely stand, blood blurring his vision. He could barely think.

"No," he whispered.

Elim landed in their midst.

"No," Zarx said again, his eyes wide.

Zarx's armor was dented and his cloak was torn and bloody.

Elim had removed his disguise and now wore ordinary garb of a brown cloak.

"The kingdom is yours," Arius said.

Zarx looked down, defeated.

Elim seemed displeased. He dropped the scepter, and it rolled until it was in front of Zarx, who looked away with a pained expression.

"Why? Why have you done this? Just to rule in his place?" he said bitterly.

Elim shook his head, closing his eyes.

"I do not desire to rule here. Just to make an example. Alanias' actions stacked against him until they collapsed upon the pious king."

Tritus reached into himself for any magic he could possibly muster, but it took all the energy he had just to hold himself steady.

"You will rule Lifesveil," Elim said.

"What?" Zarx said, still reeling from the news of Alanias' death.

"You will rule Lifesveil."

"I would never serve you."

Arius reached for his khopesh.

Elim lifted his hand, stopping Arius' movement.

"You will rule. Or I will kill the remainder of your men. Consider it my mercy. In addition, I could seek out those who were sent away, too. I do not want to do that."

"You …"

"Speak no more. If you do, I will give the order to kill all your men. It would not be a hard task to complete."

Elim narrowed his eyes.

"You will rule, but you will serve me by doing it. Provide me with your resources, gold, wood, stone, and metals. However, there is one thing that must be done. The blood of Alanias no longer has claim to the throne. Alanias' lineage is over."

Zarx lifted his sword in an aggressive gesture.

Elim eyed him dangerously.

"Do not make trouble for yourself. We already hold a blade to your throat. Think of your people. I am; what does it say about you that you do not?"

Zarx closed his eyes.

Elim tilted his head.

"Your answer, General? You may speak now."

Tears poured from Zarx's closed eyes as he bowed his head in defeat.

"I will accept this offer … to save lives." Zarx's eyes snapped open. "But for no other reason."

"I am pleased with your decision," Elim said. "You may even grow to like this, but I must warn you, King Zarx, if any of Alanias' sons show their faces, you are to send them away, banished from Lifesveil. If they return or are found within these walls …"

"Just leave," Zarx said angrily.

Elim narrowed his eyes.

"They will be killed, and if you get the idea to try and fight against me," Elim's eyes glowed as he spoke, "Your captain will not be the only one missing limbs. I will disassemble you piece by piece as if you were a castle made of stone."

Zarx glared.

Elim turned from him and flew into the sky.

"Sons should not have to pay for their father's sins. I am showing you a great kindness. I will return soon. Think hard about your people."

Arius chuckled and called his Taneem to follow him. Zarx's men gathered near him, standing quietly as the winning army left.

The ground was broken, the castle in ruins.

Carrion birds flew overhead.

Men ran toward them, offering aid.

Zarx shoved them off and pointed to the hold of Alanias. He hoped against hope there was something that could be done. His heart broke as they confirmed to him with fists on their chests that Alanias was indeed dead.

Zarx's anger flared inside of him. He held the scepter in his hands, gripping it tightly. Tears of sorrow streamed down his face—the sorrow of a defeated general.

CHAPTER 12
DRAGON'S EXILE

———✦———

Uriaelh flew across the sky, searching relentlessly for any sign of movement. Anger fueled him and sparks sputtered from his nostrils as he breathed. His slender, agile, metallic frame shuddered as adrenaline coursed through him. Shields of scales adorned his body; if light had hit him, he would have looked the color of sacred stones. With a growl he veered downward in a fast movement, dropping to the ground with a flap of his wings. Dust and dirt flew into the darkness as he landed. He looked around in astonishment as he observed the scene.

The temple stood before him, desolate and broken. His eyes flickered red, not from magic but from bewilderment. He climbed the walls quietly, despite his massive size. All attempts at finding Albion had been useless. He was angry with himself for not being successful. He had hoped to return with their dear friend. He hesitated, scanning the courtyard, and landed inside the wall, part of the section giving way under his weight. Uriaelh grimaced and righted himself. Scorched black stains were visible on the temple walls, along with tremorous cracks everywhere. The once-great tower now looked like a mountain of rubble, with but a few floors remaining. Lady Hoakama had told him to be cautious, and he paused to make certain no one had seen him.

Besides, he thought to himself, they were no longer concerned with this place. He shuffled through some rubble, anxious to find the compartment hidden within Elder Derrick's room. At first, he had considered it treasonous for Derrick to have hidden so many fragments, but now he was thankful for his wisdom. The stone symbol in the floor was still intact. With a breath of fire, the symbols lit up, opening a secret mechanism within the fallen pieces of stone. The door lowered, revealing a stone staircase, serpentining down into a void of cold darkness. He changed to his human form with a burst of light and knelt beside the staircase. He peered into the darkness and looked around him to be sure no one had seen his momentary light.

With a blind hand, he touched the sides of the staircase, guiding himself until he was sure he was out of sight of prying eyes. He used magic to light up the remainder of the steps. His footfalls echoed dully as he descended. He reached the bottom and found the ornate box Elder Derrick had described to him. He pulled the box from its shelf and noted all the other objects sitting on shelves around the walls. He froze as the sound of quick footsteps caught his ears. He looked around, still holding the box. The other side of the staircase was dark and blocked off by an arrangement of swords. He quickly moved behind them and saw a polishing cloth, which he threw over the box. Darkness surrounded him as he released his magic.

The steps grew louder until an unknown form entered the room. The breathing was shrill and shallow.

"I was told there were no more of these secret compartments."

"Yes, but on the off-chance they returned, we wished to be ready to ambush them," a second voice said.

"There appear to be no more fragments, but we may have lucked out. Our guest left this."

"Part of Maseeoufin war armor?"

"Yes, a shoulder piece it appears. Elim will not care we didn't catch him. He only cared about this. Etghar was incredibly informative."

"Should we give chase?"

"No. We have what we need. We will be rewarded for this. Besides, there is no telling how many companions are with him."

"I see why Tsal didn't destroy the entire temple."

"Yes, now, grab the magic armor; we leave immediately. Etghar said that there might be one last reservoir."

"What of these swords?"

"Common steel, nothing significant about them. Leave them."

Uriaelh stayed in his hiding spot for what felt like hours. After the footsteps were long gone, he walked slowly up the staircase, struggling under the weight of the stones. He felt shaky and light-headed thinking of the items that had been taken. But not these, he said to himself reassuringly, looking down at the covered box he held in his arms. He emerged slowly, looking around to make sure his visitors were gone for sure.

With a burst of light, he turned into a dragon once more and carried the now small box easily in his claws. He ascended high into the sky, above the cover of the clouds, even though it was dark. He felt the chill of the wind on his wings and, being paranoid, he kept looking behind him as if expecting an enemy to appear. He quickened his pace, half with anticipation and half with fear. He emerged below the clouds, drenched from the moisture in them. He leaned to the left and let his wings slow him as he came closer to the ground. With one final flap he landed softly on the cool grass. With a burst of light, he returned to human form.

"Uriaelh."

He turned quickly, and he felt a shiver go through him.

"Jakobin?" he said, surprised. He recognised him by his appearance. Everything he had heard about him from Derrick made him able to put two and two together.

Jakobin stood next to him, perplexed to have found him.

"What are you doing here?" Uriaelh asked.

Jakobin shrugged. "What's in the box?"

Uriaelh looked at the box in his hands, the colors still hidden by the cloth he'd thrown over it.

"Where have you been? Your brothers have been looking for you," Uriaelh answered question with question.

Jakobin looked impatient.

"Uriaelh, do not ignore my question."

Uriaelh took a step away from him.

"I know those are Ashen fragments. Give them to me."

"Why do you want them?" Uriaelh asked.

"I am an Ashenborn." Jakobin paused. "I only am protecting those I care for. Now, the box," he said again, gesturing toward it.

Uriaelh put the box in his left hand and drew his sword with his right.

Jakobin tilted his head and shook it.

"I don't want to fight you."

Uriaelh let his power flow through him.

Jakobin gritted his teeth, and a look of solemness came upon him.

"Please."

"Stand aside, Jakobin."

Jakobin did not draw his sword.

"I only do this to protect my brothers." He put his hand to his back, touching the two swords sheathed there.

"By giving these to whom?" Uriaelh said, now getting angry. "These stones in the wrong hands would enslave all of Yadir."

Jakobin did not appear to hear him.

"Uriaelh, you wouldn't understand. Elim cannot be stopped; all that I can do is protect you. I don't want to kill anyone."

"Why? Why are you with them? Have they such a hold on you? Did they threaten to kill Selaphiel and Cordoc? Because if so, they are more than willing to take that chance."

Jakobin's eyes misted over.

"It is not as simple as that."

"Jakobin …." Uriaelh paused. "It is never too late."

Uriaelh walked past him, carrying the box at his side. Jakobin quickly drew his swords. His blades touched Uriaelh's back.

Uriaelhh did not move but looked forward, expressionless.
"Explain to my brothers why I am taking this from you."
Uriaelh turned his head.

"I am cursed. I have no choice. I do this for them."

Jakobin's face reddened.

"Now give me the box. Please."

Uriaelh walked forward calmly.

"This is the last warning. I promise you. Leave it," Jakobin said, his eyes drifting off into the darkness. Uriaelh followed his gaze, seeing several eyes looking at them from the underbrush.

It all became clear to him.

Uriaelh stood still.

"Do I have a chance?" he whispered.

Jakobin hesitated. "You would be a fool to refuse."

Uriaelh could feel the blade now pressing harder into his back.

"Lady Hoakama is here. And your brothers are safe."

Jakobin began to shake. Uriaelh noticed the scratches on his body and the dark circles under Jakobin's eyes now. Something had happened to him, much more than could be imagined.

"Alanias would be proud of you, Jakobin."

Jakobin was having trouble holding up his arms.

Several figures landed among them now. Uriaelh was aware that Jakobin had turned to protect him. Uriaelh put the box between them and held out his sword.

"Jakobin, we warned you if you did not negotiate with him peacefully, we would kill both of you."

"That was our agreement, but now … the odds are in my favor," Jakobin said confidently.

"In your favor? You are unable to transform due to the overuse of your fragment! Why do you think we never allowed you to replenish its power?" The voice cackled.

"Besides," the other voice interjected, "Uriaelh, it was stupid to come alone."

"I am not alone," Uriaelh said.

Lady Hoakama's eyes lit up behind them in the darkness. Bright, beautiful green plates glared down upon the group.

"As he said," the dragonic voice of Hoakama spoke. "They are not alone."

Belial's face appeared beneath the hood of his cloak.

"And we are not without our own power," he said, his face expanding and snapping as it enlarged. Jakobin looked at him, astounded.

"What in Yadir?" Uriaelh said, horrorstruck.

The second Taneem began to change as well, demonic wings grotesquely growing from its back. Belial's arms shrank into his body, and his back began to curve and elongate as well. His legs grew large talons, and his eyes began to turn a bright green. Ugly legions of scales bubbled onto them, blotting out anything that could be mistaken for skin. What stood before them were two wyrms, puffing out green flames.

Wyrms that breathe green smoke, Uriaelh thought. *Just what we need.*

Uriaelh transformed quickly and met the wyrms with a spark of metal.

"They are poisonous!" Jakobin yelled as he unleashed a magical flame on Belial.

Hoakama pinned the other wyrm, who roared in protest and slapped Hoakama away with its claws. Hoakama stumbled backward, growling in displeasure.

Uriaelh faced Belial as Jakobin fired magic from behind the trees. Belial was much larger than the other Taneem and looked more like a dragon.

Belial's sharply rimmed mouth hissed. Pale green smoke came from his nostrils. Uriaelh clawed at his face, and Belial snapped at him as he ascended into the air. Uriaelh let loose bright flames that scalded Belial's side, which seemed to have no effect on him.

"Help Hoakama," Uriaelh called down as he chased after Belial.

Jakobin nodded, a new air of energy hitting him. He stood beside Hoakama, who flapped her wings, challenging the small wyrm.

"What makes it poisonous?" Hoakama asked.

Jakobin never took his eyes from the creature.

"Its bite. If it breaks the skin, you will survive but a few minutes."

"Can you change?"

"No, they have made sure that I would not be able to while they held me prisoner."

Jakobin pointed to the jagged black spikes that protruded from his chest.

"Elim's magical curse."

Hoakama roared and scarred the ground as she leapt forward. The horns on her head stabbed into the belly of the monster. The wyrm's breath was knocked from it, and it crumpled to the ground, gasping for air and struggling to regain its balance.

Jakobin charged, his blades held high as he cleaved one of its legs in two, causing it to bellow in pain. Hoakama curled around it like a viper and bared her fangs. Hoakama's jaws clamped down on its neck, and Jakobin ran up her back, using her spikes as stepping stones. With a leap, he drove both blades downward into the wyrm's skull. With a harsh motion, his blades tore through the top of its head. The wyrm's eyes glazed over and Hoakama released her grip, dropping the creature to the ground with a thump.

Uriaelh circled Belial, as each tried to gain an advantage on the other. Wherever he moved, he found Belial upon him move for move. He exploded to the left and lashed out with his tail, but Belial anticipated it and moved out of the way.

Hoakama landed beside Jakobin.

"We must get you to your brothers."

"What about him?" Jakobin yelled, barely making himself heard over the noise of the dragons.

"Uriaelh can handle himself. You have been affected by a powerful magic, something that will take great care to fix."

She lowered her gaze to his level. Jakobin picked up the box and held it close to him. A trumpet of a roar sounded in the distance.

Hoakama's head jerked in that direction.

"Stay here!" she yelled as she ascended to help Uriaelh in the struggle above. Uriaelh saw her coming as he worked to hold off Belial.

"No! Take Jakobin and go!" Uriaelh growled, clasping Belial's wings.

Hoakama ignored him.

"We need all we have in the battles we face," Hoakama said. "That includes you!"

Jakobin looked up from the ground and tried to rouse his fragment. He punched the tree as the fragment did not respond.

Hoakama knocked Belial from the sky with a cruel crunch. Belial fell hard onto the ground a good distance from Jakobin. Jakobin moved to fight him but Uriaelh landed in front of him, fangs bared.

"Let's go," Uriaelh said as Belial began to get up from the fall with effort.

Hoakama was beside them now. She scooped Jakobin into her claws and shot into the air like a freshly released arrow, Uriaelh not far behind.

"Stay low," Hoakama whispered as they flew under the canopy of trees, leaving Belial behind.

The trees shook from a strong wind above them. The hair on Jakobin's neck stood on end.

"Fly slower," Hoakama said to Uriaelh.

Uriaelh slowed to a glide, only flapping his wings when necessary.

Belial's roar echoed from far behind them.

"What about Belial?" Uriaelh whispered.

Hoakama shifted to avoid a group of trees.

"He is wounded. He will not pursue us. I made sure of that."

Uriaelh nodded. Jakobin felt the spikes of magic in his chest burn. He gripped his side and began to shake.

"Are you all right?" Hoakama asked, worried.

"Yes," Jakobin said. "I'm feeling weak, though."

Two more dragon roars sounded high above them.

"Tsal," Uriaelh said.

"And Malakh by the sound of it," Hoakama said, her face concerned.

"What do we do now?" Uriaelh asked.

Hoakama looked around them as trees blurred by.

"Jakobin. Hold on tight; we are about to emerge from the tree line."

Uriaelh looked at her with fear in his eyes.

"With those two up there?"

She grinned.

"We are faster than them; besides, they don't know where we are," Hoakama said.

Her head turned to Jakobin.

"Hold on."

She arched her back and emerged from below the trees like water, along with Uriaelh. Jakobin felt an unpleasant feeling in his stomach as he was propelled forward with her. He adjusted his grip on the box.

Nothing was around them but darkness.

The roars faded behind them.

Jakobin lost consciousness, but his grip on the box only loosened slightly.

"Jakobin?" Hoakama said, noticing he was limp.

"What's wrong with him?" Uriaelh asked.

"Elim's shards; they drain him of his magic."

Jakobin awoke with black, soul-less eyes.

"Jakobin?" Hoakama coaxed.

Jakobin's blade ripped into her chest and she yelled as a spray of blood exited her wound. Jakobin pushed away from her and fell into the darkness below.

Uriaelh yelled and glided under Hoakama as she breathed harshly.

"Jakobin!" he growled.

They landed in a clearing. Jakobin was nowhere in sight.

Hoakama's wound was directly in the center of her chest.

"I will heal you," Uriaelh said, reverting to human form.

"Jakobin …" she said softly.

"He will pay for this," Uriaelh said angrily as he summoned wisps of fire into her wound. She calmed her breathing as her wound glowed. The sinews of flesh stitched together until a fresh layer of scales covered her injury.

She lay with her head down, breathing softly.

"Are you okay?" Uriaelh asked.

"Yes," she said, moving normally after a few moments.

Uriaelh kicked the ground. He looked at his fragment and nearly cursed.

"Healing me has depleted your fragment," Hoakama said as she reverted to human form.

"Yes," Uriaelh said.

Hoakama stood up and sat back down, nearly falling. Uriaelh put his hands under her arms in time.

"I did not will it to be human again. My magic is used up, too," Hoakama said, her voice softer than before. She looked pale and barely held her eyes open.

Uriaelh sighed.

"Are you all right?"

"Yes, for now. At the least we have escaped those who follow us," Hoakama said.

"Where is that traitor?" Uriaelh said, looking around them.

"He is not a traitor. Elim's magic did that to him; I was foolish not to see it," Hoakama said.

"The fall itself may have killed him," Uriaelh said, "whether he is a traitor or not." He picked up the box, which had fallen near him.

"We must find him," Hoakama said.

He looked around them.

"In this dark?" Uriaelh remarked. "With no magic?"

"Even still," she replied.

He paced back and forth anxiously, considering what to do.

"Grab two fragments," she said, pointing weakly at the box.

He opened the box carefully, a glow of lights cascading out of it. He grabbed two blue gems and walked back over to her.

"Should I use the glow to find Jakobin?"

She laughed softly.

"That will not be enough to see in the dark."

She took a breath.

"Strike them together after gathering kindling. They will produce flame, a most old form of making fire."

Uriaelh looked at her, dumbfounded.

"Use sacred stones?" he said, looking at the gems.

She let a small smile play around her lips.

"Even something so sacred must be able to do everyday tasks; otherwise they are not so extraordinary as we make them out to be."

Uriaelh acknowledged her wisdom.

"Then we can renew our own fragments," he said, realizing what she planned.

She nodded and closed her eyes.

"Are you going to be okay?" he asked, concerned.

"I need to rest is all. Hurry and make the fire. We can better proceed from there. Make it small so as not to attract dragons," she said casually.

Uriaelh thought that statement would be funnier in different circumstances, considering the two of them were dragons.

He stumbled around in the brush and found small twigs and debris that he tied into a bundle with some long grass nearby. He turned to check every so often just to make sure Hoakama was still breathing.

He put all the materials together and ground the fragments against one another. Red sparks fell into the wood underneath. After several tries, smoke twisted out of the debris. He blew gently into it, and within a moment, blue flames licked around the rotten log.

He exhaled when the logs caught into a small fire.

He placed his hand in the flames and walked over a makeshift bundle to Hoakama so she could put her hand in the flames, too. The gems under their skin began to gleam and return to their normal colors. Hoakama opened her eyes when she felt warmth on her face.

"Pleasant?" he asked.

"Yes," she said.

He sat down beside her. His eyes remained on the fire in case it became large enough to be seen by anyone from the sky. The trees around them did a good job of hiding them.

Bugs chirped in the dark all around them. He knew he was grateful the forest wasn't silent. The flames popped and sizzled, signifying the gems were fully restored.

After their power was replenished, he smothered the fire and stamped on the ashes.

Uriaelh summoned starlight, its glow illuminating the woods before them.

"We must be quick; these are not like the fire. They are bright."

Haokama stood up, a vision of strength.

"Amazing what a little fire will do," Hoakama said.

Uriaelh chuckled.

"Where did Jakobin fall?" she asked him.

He pointed toward the north.

He walked ahead, forging a path through the undergrowth. Hoakama followed, carrying the box.

They moved as quickly as they could, knowing time was short.

"There he is!" Uriaelh motioned and ran over to the fallen body. Above it, he could see broken branches and tree limbs.

Hoakama put her fingers to the pulse on Jakobin's neck.

"He's alive, but barely."

"He survived the fall?" Uriaelh asked.

"Yes. Derrick said he was Ashenborn as well. There is much that we can survive. You should know that."

Uriaelh shrugged. "I knew, but not to what extent." He eyed the magic spike protruding from Jakobin's side.

"What's to be done about that?"

"He will be healed when we are back. Besides, the magic used to preserve him would more than likely keep him unconscious for awhile."

Uriaelh doused his magic.

Hoakama looked at him, confused. The trees moved under the wind that had begun to pick up. They realized a monsterous wyrm was the source of the movement.

"Belial …" he mouthed. He picked up Jakobin as he and Hoakama moved quickly and quietly behind some covering.

---------※---------

Derrick watched as Elim flew away from the castle, followed by the army of Taneems on the ground. The dragon was massive, but he could not make out any details. It was large, larger than any dragon he had ever seen. Larger than himself. He shook his head. Tears formed in his eyes. He could see Zarx, kneeling on the ground. The scepter of Alanias lay in front of him. The guards clutched their chests. This was an undeniable proof of the king's fate.

"No," he mouthed as he looked away.

He watched as Elim's form circled above them. Another dragon flew from the west. Derrick clenched his fists, aware that it was probably another one of his former friends. He could not tell at first, but as the dragon got closer, he realized there was something familiar about him. The dragon was sapphire blue and had streaks of lighter blue on its scales. Derrick squinted through his tears. Ashenborn had the ability to recognize one another, even in dragon form.

"Cordoc!" he said, waving his hand so that Elim couldn't see but the blue dragon could. Pity and joy crept into him as he saw the prince. He hoped Cordoc had not been spotted by Taneems or Elim.

The blue dragon angled down, landing quietly beside him.

"Elder Derrick," Cordoc said, changing into human form and crouching behind the broken sentry post with Derrick. His face was full of torment.

"Our home," Cordoc said, his face pale.

Derrick didn't know what to say, so he remained silent as they took in the scene. Nothing in his mind sounded appropriate.

"Is Father okay?" Cordoc said, searching his face, desperation in his eyes.

Derrick closed his eyes and then looked at Cordoc with as much love as he could muster, opening his mouth to deliver the news. He felt his eyes moisten and no sound came out.

Cordoc stopped him by holding up his hand. Tears streamed down his face as he fell to his knees. He already knew the answer. Derrick knelt with him, tears coming from his eyes, too, despite his attempt to stop them.

Cordoc looked up at him.

"They will not get away with this," he declared through sobs. "They will not." He looked up at the other dragon flying away from the carnage.

"Did he do it?" Cordoc asked, his face filled with pain. He had known so much pain in such a short amount of time, Derrick thought.

They watched as Elim flew away, disappearing into the distance. Luckily, he had not seen them.

"Cordoc, I am going to follow Elim to find out where he is going. He killed your father. If you wish to stay here with your father, no one will blame you, but I must leave now in order to make sure your father's death is avenged."

Cordoc wiped his face, his eyes red from tears.

"I am coming with you. I will grieve my father once his killer has met his end."

He stood, shaky and unbalanced. Derrick nodded, saddened that they would not have time to grieve Alanias' death.

"Fly high beside me," Derrick commanded as they both changed to dragon form and took off into the air, following the direction Elim had taken.

They flew above the clouds, Elim some distance in front of them. They took care not to be seen.

Derrick wondered where Selaphiel was, but he remained silent because they had the current task at hand. When they had flown some distance, he looked over and saw silent tears coursing down Cordoc's face.

"Where are your brothers? Are Malfait's forces coming?"

"Malfait has fallen; all of them are dead. Selaphiel and Daemos are behind us some distance. They will be fine."

"Dead?"

"All of them. The journey was useless," Cordoc said as he shook his head in disbelief.

The black dragon flew out over the southern ocean, away from the mainland.

"When you can, we have much to discuss," Derrick said as they left the realm of Yadir.

"Does Selaphiel still have the windowspeak?"

"He holds a small piece of it, but it broke when he was captured."

"Captured?" Derrick turned to him, alarmed.

"It's a long story, and it's my fault for letting it happen."

Derrick searched Cordoc's expression, his own that of understanding and curiosity.

"I will try and make contact with your brother when we reach a safer place, but don't worry about it right now."

Derrick turned back toward the black dragon they were following.

For now, he thought, it might be best to fly in silence and reverence. It would take time for this new revelation to sink in. He hated not being able to honor his king. He hated the fact he had been unable to save him. The best course of action now was to avenge him. The Taneemian had killed too many already. It was time that they found a way to kill them for good.

CHAPTER 13
EMBRACE OF THE COLD

———✦———

Z arx looked at Selaphiel with sad eyes. "Believe me, I understand your pain. But this is how it must be from now on. I didn't choose this."

Selaphiel could feel anger bubbling inside of him as his face reddened.

"You betrayed my father, your king."

Zarx shook his head. "I merely followed Alanias' orders at his request."

Selaphiel clenched his fists.

"The king foresaw these events and knew that the enemy had no interest in destroying Lifesveil, just its king. Elim only asks that we do not interfere with him. Lifesveil will be spared."

Zarx stepped toward him, his arms held out.

"Elim simply wanted revenge for his father. He started with the High King, the Ashenborn, and finally your father. As horrible as that may be, Elim is sated, he has no more desire to kill. That does not mean we will not prepare to fight him, but for now we must lay low."

"You are more of a fool than I realized," Selaphiel spat.

Zarx looked at him squarely.

"A general who chooses to stay out of a fight, just to sit on the sidelines, after so much talk …" Selaphiel trailed off. "Elim will not stop with just a temporary revenge."

Tears of anger and sadness formed in Selaphiel's eyes.

"Elim wishes to make all of Yadir pay. There are more than just a few who fought Dothros. Wulvsbaen, for example, and all the other kingdoms."

"I will excuse your insults, considering your loss, but I cannot tolerate you any longer. This kingdom needs a new ruler," Zarx growled. "If it must be me, so be it. I would rather anyone else."

"This kingdom falls to Cordoc," Selaphiel said.

Zarx gritted his teeth.

"Elim has decreed that none of the blood of Alanias can rule, a request that is dependant upon him not destroying the entire kingdom."

Selaphiel looked at him, shaking his head.

Magic surrounded him, and the room shook.

"You mean to rule," Selaphiel whispered.

Zarx stood calmly. Dozens of Silver Talons surrounded Selaphiel.

"You would use our own men against us?" Selaphiel said, shaking.

"They are loyal to their kingdom," Zarx said.

"No," Selaphiel said. "You spit in the face of all that you ever have said or done."

Zarx waved away his men.

"I can handle him; do not interfere."

Zarx turned back to Selaphiel.

"Selaphiel. Your father knew this to be the case before the enemy fell upon us. Alanias ordered me to do this. He wanted to save you and your brothers. And by me ruling, you three will live."

Zarx breathed in deeply. "Even if that means turning you away. I have not accepted Elim's rule. I merely must temporarily follow it."

Zarx placed his hands on Selaphiel's shoulders.

"I followed the words of your father, and I will honor his death, but your father died so that no one else had to, and believe me, we all would have died."

Selaphiel pushed him away roughly.

"How do you know that? Do not tell me of my father's honor as if you had a part in it."

"I did not. I wanted to fight until I drew no breath," Zarx said. "But your father believed in what he was doing, and he was king."

Selaphiel stumbled back, tears streaming down his face.

"Cordoc was right. Father sent us on a pointless journey. Did you know Malfait was destroyed?"

Zarx clenched his jaw.

"Yes."

Selaphiel shook and grabbed his temples. His vision itself was shaking.

"I honored your father's wishes. I cannot apologize for that. He wanted to save all of you. I cared enough to keep the promises I made him."

Selaphiel started to breathe quickly.

"We must find men to fight him. For now, we must plan in secret. I cannot risk Elim finding you or Cordoc within these walls. Yes, your father lied, but he wanted to protect you, as I am doing now. You know I would not do this unless I had to. Think of your people. Our people," Zarx said.

Selaphiel clenched his teeth, fighting tears of anguish.

"I am sorry, Selaphiel. I will serve the people of Lifesveil the best I can. You must go and find your place in this world now. I cannot guide you. Your father did not want you to get involved in a war, but there can be no doubt there will be one."

Selaphiel did not seem to know what to do as he stumbled backward, the weight of everything he'd experienced bearing down on him.

"I will leave." The words coming out of Selaphiel's mouth felt foreign. "But I want to know one thing before I go."

Zarx looked stricken as he motioned for him to tell him.

"Why didn't you stay with him?" Selaphiel said, and for the first time in his life he had daggers behind his words.

Turning away, Zarx closed his eyes.

"A general should never outlive his king," Selaphiel whispered.

Selaphiel left quietly, not waiting for a reply. Zarx blinked his eyes to stop tears of guilt spilling from them. Zarx already blamed himself for the king's death. He knew Selaphiel's words would haunt him until the day he died.

"I wish I had," he whispered.

"Your father's body is in his chambers," Zarx called after Selaphiel.

Daemos stood outside the doorway as Selaphiel emerged.

"There is nothing here for me. What we do now is up to you," Selaphiel said, stalking down the stairs.

Daemos followed him.

"I will go wherever you go. I am loyal to you and your brothers."

Daemos glared at Zarx as the door shut behind him.

Selaphiel nodded appreciatively at his words.

"I want to see Father one last time before I leave for good. After that …" he said as words left him.

"We will figure that out when the time comes."

Selaphiel felt a mixture of emotions. He knew he should not have put so much blame on Zarx, but half of him didn't care. His father was gone, and he couldn't return home.

"I may have spoken unjustly," Selaphiel said.

Daemos nodded.

"You have no reason to apologize to anyone right now. We all grieve."

———— ✶ ————

"You are too weak to fight him alone," Hoakama said.

"There were swords before there were Ashenborn," Uriaelh replied.

Belial unfurled his wings like a bat's, poison dripping from his teeth.

"Stay here," Uriaelh said as he put her behind a tree.

"I can fight," she said, closing her eyes and leaning her head back from fatigue.

"Thank you," he said softly. "But I will fight him alone."

She murmured as he walked from behind the tree.

"Where are the stones?" Belial roared, his wound dripping. He hopped awkwardly.

Uriaelh saw no sign of the other two dragons. He lowered his sword, the blade pointed toward Belial.

"What stones?" Uriaelh said.

Belial flapped closer.

Uriaelh struck at his good leg and like a viper, the wyrm sprang backward.

"Having trouble getting used to it?" Uriaelh said in a mocking voice.

Belial growled and hissed in pain.

Uriaelh realized that even though his magic was spent, he would have the advantage. Belial appeared to be near the end of his transformation. His wounds were draining both Belial's strength and his reservoirs of magic. Belial breathed laboriously and spread his wings to hold his one good leg in place. He flapped, attempting to keep his balance. Uriaelh walked toward him slowly, not taking his gaze off him.

"Tsal and Malakh will find us soon," the wyvern said, baring his teeth. "I could still rip you in two."

Uriaelh dove forward under the wyrm's belly in an agile maneuver and cut the creature's soft underside before Belial could react.

"Graaaaagh!" Belial gurgled.

Uriaelh backed up, fresh blood on his sword.

Belial's one good leg collapsed, his wings the only thing still holding him up. His belly touched the ground. His snout pressed into the dirt, blood sputtering from his mouth.

"You use what you do not understand," Uriaelh said.

Belial breathed in raspily.

"Even so, I will learn with my many lives," Belial ground out.

Uriaelh circled him, aware that Belial was a wounded animal that could strike at any moment.

"That makes you sloppy and blunted," Uriaelh said with no emotion.

Belial laughed.

Uriaelh struck out again, catching Belial on the shoulder. A clean stab, dead into Belial. The wyrm collapsed. Its wings folded like pieces of crumpled paper.

"Blasted flesh," Belial sputtered.

Uriaelh stood over him, sword raised.

"Death is not permanent for me. But I will remember you, Uriaelh of Edywin," Belial said as dirt and blood fell from his mouth. "You will surely die."

"All men die," Uriaelh said as his blade cleaved Belial's head from his neck. The sound of the head hitting the ground was eerily quiet. The wyrm did not move as the final blow fell. Its body burst into flames and liquified. Only charred bones remained. After the flames died out, the bones crumbled into dust.

"Too bad you're not going to remain dead," he said, wiping his sword clean in the grass. He knelt beside his sword, huffing. After he had caught his breath, he turned and picked up Hoakama in his arms. She lay still, her eyes closed. She appeared to be in deep sleep. The leaves crunched underneath his feet. He was tired, but despite the fact he couldn't feel his arms, he kept walking. He watched the skies where he could see through the trees. His thoughts went to Jakobin as he walked.

"What happened to you?" he whispered.

He could no longer hear the pursuing dragons. His fight with Belial could have potentially alerted them to their position. If they could find Jakobin and the fragments, they could renew their strength and fly out of there. If Jakobin was even alive.

Hoakama stirred as he leaned her on a tree.

"I thought the fragment rejuvenated you?" he asked.

She smiled with her eyes closed.

"Perhaps there was more internal damage that your magic did not heal immediately," she said.

He nodded, adding, "That would make sense."

She groaned.

"Sore?" he asked, worried.

"Yes," she said quickly.

"I bet you wish you had taken my advice about taking additional men with us."

She scoffed. "We will not risk more lives than necessary."

He spread out his legs and leaned more firmly on the tree.

"You killed Belial?" she asked.

"Sort of," he said, knowing she knew what he meant.

"And Jakobin?"

"I have not found him yet. Is he worth finding?"

"All are worth finding. Besides, he is merely cursed against his will. He stabbed me, and I still want him found," Hoakama said.

Uriaelh couldn't help but laugh at her sarcasm.

"For you, my lady, we shall continue."

Hoakama smiled.

———————✳———————

The ice held firm under his footsteps. He watched as behind him, the ship sailed off into the horizon. The ripping cold wind tore into him, but he was used to it, and it did not bother him. The shining white snow and ice was home to him, the wind a cold embrace. There was not much before him but pearlescent wasteland, an expanse of space littered with frozen boulders of enormous size. He breathed a sigh of satisfaction. A cloud of steam appeared from the warmth of his breath.

"Home," he said out loud.

The wind howled as if responding to his greeting, a greeting he knew was more of a warning than a welcoming. The wasteland was cold and unforgiving; only those who grew up here could hope to survive the cruelty of its cold grip. He adjusted his furred cloak so that his mouth and nose were shielded from the winds. This place made people hard and strong; it had no use for anyone else. Strength and resolve were required in order to survive. It would take him half a day to make it from the ice to solid ground. Half a day for most men would mean a death sentence. He hated to think how many times the guards had found the frozen remains of an unfortunate victim of the wilderness.

He could not help but wish he had a horse, and he thought fondly of Wulvsbaen's trek as a young child. Wulvsbaen's tradition was for a child to trek the great expanse alone when of age. The child would fight hunger, weather, and animals to make it back to the kingdom's walls, where he would be given the right to be called a man or woman of Wulvsbaen. He reminisced about his own journey, remembering how cold and alone he had felt. He knew everyone needed to know how to survive out here if they were going to live there and call it home.

"A horse would be nice, though." He laughed under his breath.

He held his breath as the waters behind him churned.

"Surely not," he said, turning around and eyeing the sea skeptically. Years of seeing the water move like that had made him alert. The waters rose, cold salt spray splashing near him. Drops of salt and cold misted and fell onto the ground. He ran quickly, slipping behind a large pillar of frozen rock and peering from behind it at the water. He had seen it too many times to not know what was going to happen next.

The waves thrashed about until they gave way to the familiar blue scales and fins. The ice serpent blinked its lidless eyes, shaking its head to rid it of water. The great monster hissed and slithered onto the snow, dragging a mixture of slush and water with it. Thornbeorn ducked behind the rock and grasped his icicle sword in his hand in preparation. The serpent sniffed the air; its slits of pupils dialating at the smell of human flesh. It slithered noisily from side to side. Thornbeorn punched the side of the rock. He was aware of how bleak of a situation this was; if he could speak without being discovered he knew he would not have anything good to say. Often serpents were taken down by groups of four or five, but he was one person against a particularly large one. He peered around the rock again and saw it was heading toward him. It was larger than he had ever seen.

"Great," he muttered silently.

He wanted nothing to do with this creature. He knew he couldn't outrun it. Despite it dwelling in water more than land, it could easily outpace him. He considered moving from rock to rock, but not all were substantial enough to provide cover, and the creature would eventually find him at the end of his scent trail. He called on the magic of his fragment and stilled himself as he heard the noise of scales on snow.

The serpent hissed, its tongue tasting the air hungrily.

A serpent had never been killed by one man alone. The serpent was fully on the ice now. He guessed it was fifty feet long, its head ten feet long. Its icy fangs gleamed with saliva. Its fangs were cold sabers that would instantly freeze whatever it bit into; the ice on its fangs were a result of magic enchantment that had been passed on to others of its kind.

He slowly crept around the rock as the serpent's nostrils appeared. The large white eyes searched, looking for the source of the scent. Thornbeorn snuck toward the middle of the great snake, watching as it used both its muscles and fins to move along the ground. He wished he had learned to fire a magical orb of energy to distract it, but he saw a rock on the ground that would do the same. He threw the rock. It clanged on one of the boulders. The serpent turned quickly toward the noise.

He watched it move away and raised up his sword and came down with all his might onto what appeared to be a soft fold of skin between its fins. The skin split deep from the force, but it was only enough to make a large gash. The serpent roared in pain and smacked him with a harsh bulge of muscle. He rolled to the side slightly dazed, his body spinning from the blow. He knew he was lucky the blow hadn't killed him. He felt a throbbing in the back of his head but didn't feel any blood.

The great snake turned around, searching for the source of the blow. Red stained the once-white snow. He crouched behind another coil of scales, avoiding the snake's gaze. It benefited him that the snake was so large, and he could hide in the folds of its body. He made his way back to the wound, the snake hissing angrily as it tasted the air with its tongue.

He repeated himself by throwing another rock. Thornbeorn found the wound and drew back to strike the wound again. With as much force as he could put into the slice, he drew more blood from deeper into the wound. He dove to the side as the gaping mouth of the snake crashed into the ground, biting and tearing at the ice. The snake had not been fooled this time. The snake shook his mouth free of dirt and snow.

"You are too smart for that," Thornbeorn said with clenched teeth.

He struck the side of its face, but his sword bounced off, making him nearly drop it. His hands shook at the hardness of the scales.

The serpent lowered its head and slowly moved its coils around him. He dodged what would have been an iron grip around his waist. The snake's large frame made him retreat, moving closer and closer to the ocean. The serpent struck like a spear in its quickness. He dove under the grip of the coil and jumped into the icy water. He gasped as the frigid water engulfed him. He clung desperately to the side of the ice, his numbing hands struggling to maintain their grip. He hadn't intentionally jumped into the water but had just responded on instinct, an instinct he wished he had considered a little more fully before following it. The snake hissed and as it turned, its tail smacked him across his face, heaving him off of the ice and into the water with a splash.

He felt himself sinking. He tried to fight against it, but the weight of his armor carried him further downward. He began to panic as he clawed at his armor in an attempt to take it off. He felt his lungs clench up, and he knew he desperately needed air. He watched as the light slowly disappeared above him and he sank lower and lower. He yelled bubbles as he reached out for a protruding rock. His hands slipped off the slick rock. His legs kicked to try to get some momentum behind him, but he could not stop the speed of his decent. His ears popped dangerously.

He closed his eyes as the icy water wrapped him in its frigid embrace.

Jakobin stumbled through the darkness, leaning on trees here and there as he could. He had survived the fall; despite everything, the curse he carried had actually saved him from what would be to any other a sure death.

He clutched the box in his hands and peered at the items inside. He willed himself to draw from their magical aura. He felt a familiar ancient power course through his veins— power he had not felt in some time because of the corrupting magic of the shard in his side. He looked angrily at the black shard that stuck out of his chest. The fragment glowed like an ember beneath his skin, causing the skin to itch. He grasped the black shard with both hands and pulled. He felt shockwaves of pain run through him, making him fall to his knees as if someone had stuck a knife into his side. This pain was familiar. Tears of anger and pain brimmed his eyes but he wiped them away. Taking a deep breath, he called on what strength he could and pulled again. Hot blood flowed from the wound. His teeth gnashed together roughly as he continued pulling, his vision blinking black.

He let out a growl of pain, and with all he had, he pulled the shard free. The curse shattered like glass as the shard left his body, falling into the leaves and turning into fingers of smoke. With a loud thump he fell to the ground, the taste of metal in his mouth. He was bleeding dangerously now, and he placed his hands on the wound. Magical fire poured into the gaping hole and began to mend tissue and muscle. Sweat poured from him as he fought to remain conscious. The veins in his neck protruded, and he wanted nothing more than to cry out like an animal. He realized a man carrying a woman was standing beside him. He turned to see Uriaelh, who had an alarmed look on his face. He put Hoakama down gently against a tree.

"You pulled it out?" Uriaelh said, astonished. "That could have killed you!"

Jakobin nodded in response, his face losing color.

Uriaelh shook his head in disbelief.

"I'm not sure what I can do, but ..." Uriaelh lifted his arm, a wave of golden fire joining the red, "I will try."

Jakobin could feel the mixture of flames like a warm river coursing over him.

"Th-thank you. I-I'm sorry," was all he could muster.

"It was not you who did this," Uriaelh said understandingly, his face focused.

Jakobin's eyes rolled into the back of his head as he passed out.

Uriaelh put his hand down and absorbed energy from the fragments in the box. With a tornado of light, he transformed and scooped both humans up in his front talons, along with the fragments.

He rose slowly into the darkness, his keen eyes searching for and finding no other dragons. The cool air hit him as he carried both his unconscious passengers higher and higher.

He glided more than he flew, as the added weight made it hard to maneuver in the skies. He watched as the sun began to rise, the beginning of morning already sending warmth from the coming sun. He headed north, where the sun's warmth would be a stranger. Hoakama would need all the help she could get in defending the throne of Archkyris, and her kingdom, the Kingdom of Edywin. Her people needed to be ready for what was coming. He shuddered at the thought of what was making its way toward all the people of Yadir. He looked grim as he passed over the landscape, not noticing another dragon not far behind him.

———————❈———————

Selaphiel looked over the kingdom. He noticed how unlike home it felt, and his emotions twisted within him like a viper. His stomach clenched, tears dripping down his cheeks. He breathed in deeply. Daemos stood a little behind him, a concerned look on his face. Selaphiel's chest rose up and down rapidly, and he closed his eyes. Clear, hot tears burned his eyes. He cried silently, even though he wanted to sob like a child. He felt his body go rigid as he slumped over.

"He did not have to love me," he muttered.

He gritted his teeth, his breath getting shallower and faster.

"Selaphiel …" Daemos said, putting a hand on his shoulder, concern in his voice.

He felt the ground around him shake. He did not turn as he continued to face the shell of a once-great kingdom.

"He accepted me as one of his own, and they killed him. I was a son to him," Selaphiel sobbed.

Daemos looked at him somberly.

"You are still his son. They can never take that away from you. His death will go down as an end to an era."

The ground around him vibrated and Daemos hesitated, the hand he had meant to place on Selaphiel's shoulder held in the air.

"I need a moment," Selaphiel said, searching for words. "I need to say my good-byes."

Daemos bowed dutifully.

"I will be here when you are ready," he replied and continued down the hill.

Selaphiel knelt in silence. He picked up sticks in his hands, feeling the need to grasp at something to weigh himself down so he would not float away. He looked at the lifeless body of his father, wrapped in a white cloth. The smell of fresh herbs and perfumes were pleasant but not comforting.

He sobbed uncontrollably, his demeanor that of a broken man.

"I hope I made you proud. I was proud to have you to as my father."

The ground shook around him, and small flames flared from his fragment. Tiny fires flickered on the ground around him. His eyes illuminated with golden tears. He dropped the twigs in his hands and knelt with his hands open. A new emotion raced through him, one that made new tears.

He thought back to every part of his childhood he could remember. Love had guided Alanias to treat them all equally. He smiled through it when he thought about how his father had not become upset when he made mistakes, or when he was in the wrong. Alanias had been a wise, merciful, and kind king. He had been an amazing father. If anyone deserved the least love, it was him, as he was not blood like his brothers were. But Alanias had not treated him any differently. Alanias had been more than just a king to him.

"I will spend my life honorably because of you."

He shuddered as he saw his father's still face. His eyes were closed. Selaphiel did not want to remember him in that way, but the way that he had been. He shook and closed his eyes, squeezing out more tears. He wanted to reach out to hug him even though he knew their embrace would feel empty. He put the cloth back over Alanias' face, and he rested his hand on Alanias' shoulder. He slowly turned away, each step heavier than the last. The chamber echoed emptily as he exited it. He turned around, wishing that he could will his father back to life. How amazing it would be to be able to turn back time, but it could never be that way. Lifesveil had lost a vital part of itself. The kingdom had been peaceful and prosperous under Alanias' rule. Lifesveil would see change. Lifesveil would have to change. It was no longer under the protection of a great and mightly ruler.

"We have lost our father."

Selaphiel could not help but think back to what his father had said to him some time ago when he doubted who he was: "I cannot make you believe who you are. You have to believe it yourself, but if it is lack of belief that guides you, let my belief inspire you. You are my son and I will act no differently.

If anyone says otherwise, I will silence them with the truth. You are not my blood, but you are blood of my heart. My love is lavished upon you."

Selaphiel smiled through his tears. He knew there was purpose in them.

He had made his way halfway down the hill before he paused to take in the the kingdom one last time. He knew it would be some time before he returned. With the image in his heart, he walked down the hill to where Daemos waited for him.

"My life will reflect who you were to me," he told his father silently. "I will spend what remains of my days fighting for you."

CPSIA information can be obtained
at www.ICGtesting.com
Printed in the USA
FSHW021017230619
59337FS